Emma Burstall writes for national newspapers and magazines including the *Guardian, Independent on Sunday, Woman & Home* and *Woman*. She studied English at Cambridge University and lives in London with her husband, Kevin Maguire, and their three children.

Emma Burstall

Gym and Slimline

preface
publishing

Published by Preface 2008

10 9 8 7 6 5 4 3

First published in Great Britain in 2008 by Preface
1 Queen Anne's Gate
London SW1H 9BT

An imprint of The Random House Group

www.randomhouse.co.uk
www.prefacepublishing.co.uk

Addresses for companies within The Random House Group Limited
can be found at www.randomhouse.co.uk

The Random House Group Limited Reg. No. 954009

A CIP catalogue record for this book is available from the British Library

ISBN 9781848090453

The Random House Group Limited supports The Forest Stewardship Council
(FSC), the leading international forest certification organisation. All our titles
that are printed on Greenpeace-approved FSC-certified paper carry
the FSC logo. Our paper procurement policy can be found at
www.randomhouse.co.uk/environment

Author photograph © Hugh Dickens

Typeset in Palatino by Palimpsest Book Production Ltd,
Grange-over-Sands, Cumbria

Printed and bound in Great Britain by CPI Mackays, Chatham, Chippenham, Wiltshire

FT
Pbk

For Kevin, Georgia, Harry and Freddie
with all my love

The Warm-Up

❦

'Get in there!' the poster said. 'Three out of four members still stay with us because they see results.'

Well, Percy didn't need much persuading.

She'd watched them building the new Gym and Slimline above the supermarket on the High Street. It was part of a well-known chain, and it was just a short drive from her South London home.

Actually, she could even walk to it – but there again, you could take this exercise lark *too* far.

At last, Gym and Slimline had finally opened, and the timing really couldn't have been better. Percy had gained nearly three stone when she was pregnant with Rowan, and lost only two since he was born.

Unfortunately, most of the remaining 14 pounds seemed to have settled round her middle. The term 'apple-shaped' might have been invented for her, she decided. She was an apple on legs. A fact of which she was constantly reminded by her three-year-old, Ben, who delighted in grabbing mounds of her flesh in his chubby little hands and shrieking 'Wibbly wobbly jelly!'

Now, Rowan was six weeks old, and the doctor said it would be OK to start gentle exercise again. Membership was expensive, but what the hell. It was bad enough to be knocking forty; she didn't intend to be fat and farty as well.

There was even a spanking new, fully Ofsted-inspected crèche for the baby. She could hardly wait to begin her new exercise programme.

1

'What you need is plenty of cardiovascular work, as well as some resistance training,' the instructor said. 'If you come three times a week, you'll soon shift that stone and see a big difference in your fitness levels and general muscle tone.'

Hurrah! Percy thought. Watch out yummy mummies everywhere!

Suzanne had lower, some might say more realistic, expectations. She loathed exercise and adored food, especially anything cooked by her delicious house-husband Justin.

She was thus resigned to remaining round all over. Indeed, Justin insisted he lurved every curve, and she believed him. Sort of.

However, after three children (the fourth was yet to come) and a surfeit of Krispy Kremes, Suzanne felt if she didn't do something, the situation could deteriorate. Round was one thing, rhinoesque quite another. Plus, with Justin being so much younger, she felt she must at least make some effort not to show him up at parties and things.

She knew she'd never make it to Gym and Slimline three times a week. She had a demanding career as well as her burgeoning family. But once a week was possible. Maybe. And she could always stick to nice, gentle classes, like Pilates and Hatha yoga (wasn't that the easy one?) So she signed on the dotted line, too.

Patrice didn't have any bulges to lose. Indeed, less charitable (female) members of the club whispered that she could do with gaining a few pounds, but of course they were just jealous. After all, you can't be tall, blonde, skinny and rich without making some enemies.

But Patrice had a lot of hours in the day to fill before her top lawyer husband, Jonty, returned from work, requiring gourmet food and fussing over. She thought she might as well fill those hours productively, by keeping fit.

Besides, her son, Seamus, would benefit from meeting other children in the crèche. Patrice worried that it was going to be increasingly lonely for him as he got older, rattling round in a big house with no one to play with.

It wasn't as though there were going to be any more where he came from, either.

As for Carmen, well, exercise was a way of life. She was all too aware that she couldn't expect to maintain her supple dancer's body without putting in the work. And my! Simon did appreciate that body.

Carmen intended to use Gym and Slimline at least three times a week, if not more, to get her money's worth. And if she met some interesting people, made a few friends along the way, all the better. She might even be able to add them to her client list.

She was a little concerned that the club might be too child-friendly. She didn't mind kids, but she didn't want them rushing round the place, spoiling the serenity of her stretching.

However, being an interior designer herself, she approved of the bang-up-to-the-minute decor (shame they wouldn't allow joss sticks) and was prepared to give it a go. And after all, private gyms were springing up all over the place. They were the new in-thing. She could always leave and find somewhere else if she didn't like it.

That was nearly four years ago . . .

PART I

Body Attack

A group exercise class which ignites your energy systems and pushes your training to the next level. Simply the ultimate cardiovascular challenge.

Chapter One

꧁꧂

It wasn't exactly dignified, Percy thought, with her nose practically scraping the ground like that and her bum in the air. She didn't like to think what it must look like from behind.

It hurt like hell, too, widening her legs and stretching down between them until her hamstrings felt they were about to ping, like a piece of knackered elastic.

It was satisfying, though, to find that she was getting just a little more flexible, week by week. And there was another very good reason why the suffering was worthwhile: a really good stretch took her mind off things, transported her a million miles from home.

Home. A tight lump appeared from nowhere in her throat. *Don't think about him. It'll be all right. Focus on the stretch.* She breathed deeply and the lump started to dissolve.

'Good, stay there, guys. Now I'm going to give you all a push.' Debbie the teacher laughed. Several people groaned.

Being at the front of the class, Percy knew she'd be one of the first victims. She could sense Debbie coming up behind, then her hands were on Percy's back, pushing her down, gently but firmly. Now that really hurt.

Reluctantly, the sinews started to lengthen, the spaces between the vertebrae to expand. To her surprise, Percy went down lower than she thought possible. So low, in fact, that her elbows and forearms were resting on the ground. She hoped nothing would crack.

She opened one eye, then the other, wiggled her knees, her toes. Thank goodness, everything was still in one piece.

And what's more, from down there she could get a remarkably good view of the others through her legs. She breathed again, as deeply as she could.

There was Suzanne behind, trying her best, bless her. But she couldn't get her red curly head much below her pale freckled knees.

Tall, thin Patrice, beside her, wasn't much better – maybe her legs were too long?

Tiny, black-haired Carmen was like a blooming circus contortionist. But horrible Millicent, the be-atch, was truly hopeless. No bend in her at all. Ha! Silicon boobs probably got in the way.

'Percy-fone, yoo hoo! Wake up!' Debbie the teacher's high-pitched voice made Percy jump. She hadn't noticed the others starting slowly to unbend, bone by bone, as instructed. Percy's back twinged. Jesus! She was turning into an old crone.

'Er, Persephone, actually, pronounced Pers-*ef*-fon-ee,' she muttered, but the music was too loud for Debbie to hear.

'Right, guys, you know what's coming next – Superman!' Debbie trilled.

At that moment, Percy truly hated the instructor. She looked so damn jolly, as if she actually enjoyed leaping from one side of the room to the other, with arms and legs outstretched like a demented jack-in-the-box.

Debbie was wearing a black vest top and irritatingly teeny white shorts that showed off her perfectly toned legs. Percy was fascinated by her back view when she turned around. Where Percy's thighs flattened at the top and billowed sideways into squidgy marshmallow, Debbie had these firm mounds of beautifully honed hamstring.

Sweat was trickling down Percy's tummy, which made her itchy. Her legs and arms felt as if they were stuffed with turnips. The room smelled musty and she wished there was a window to open.

Most of all, she wished she could stop.

She glanced at the clock. Big mistake. Half an hour still to go. No wonder the class was called Body Attack. It was brutal. No, masochistic. She was gasping for breath.

'Right, you lot, into skater,' Debbie shouted, sergeant major-like.

About bloody time! Percy thought. She bent forward and did a gentle sort of skating movement. She could feel her thumping heart start to slow. For a moment she imagined she was wowing the crowds in a cute little feather tutu and tiara in *Cinderella on Ice*.

She smiled at her audience in the mirror in front – and crashed into Danny, the only boy in the class this morning. He wobbled, mid-skate, but managed to save himself from falling – just.

'Are you two drunk?' Debbie called out.

'Stupid question,' Percy muttered. 'I'm so sorry,' she said to Danny. She could feel her face burning. Fortunately, Danny didn't seem to mind. He flashed her a charming, not-to-worry grin.

'No problem,' he said, showing off his white teeth.

For a second, Percy felt insanely happy. She sucked in her tummy muscles, straightened her back. Then she remembered: shame she had a bright red face and her hair was scraped back in a sweaty ponytail. Not exactly alluring. Anyway, she probably reminded him of his mum or aunty or something. How depressing.

At last it was over. She flopped on her back and stretched out her aching muscles. No more Body Attack for a whole week. Bliss.

'Well done, class,' Debbie smiled. 'Why don't you stay for Body Pump now!'

'Not on your life,' Percy grimaced, grabbing her towel and water bottle from the edge of the room and heading for the door pronto. 'Thanks very much, Debbie,' she called back, somewhat hypocritically. Once safely outside, she waited for her three friends.

Will he sleep in the spare room again *tonight? Stop fretting. It'll blow over.*

'Hey, how are you doing?' she beamed, as Carmen, Suzanne and Patrice joined her. They strolled together towards the changing room.

Chapter Two

'It doesn't seem to get any easier,' Suzanne groaned, taking a swig of water from a plastic bottle.

'How come you're not at work?' Percy asked her, wiping the back of her neck with her towel and slurping from her own bottle. She could feel the sweat pricking under her breasts and couldn't wait to strip off her sports bra.

'We've got tickets to see *Macbeth* tonight,' Suzanne replied. 'I decided I might as well take the day off. Justin and I are going for a meal before the show.'

'How lovely,' Percy said enviously. 'Mark and I haven't been to the theatre for ages.' She pushed open the wooden door of the women's changing room and the four women walked in to the familiar smell of furniture polish and chlorine, hairspray and shampoo. Percy loved it.

Like the rest of the club, it was tastefully decorated, with off-white walls, pale wood lockers and cream floor tiles. The four friends opened their lockers and started to undress round the slatted benches in the middle of the room.

Several other members were there already, in varying states of undress, and more in another room off the main one.

Percy found it strangely comforting to see women of all shapes and sizes, ages and races, chatting away in the nude – though it could be a tad disconcerting to find yourself standing beside your child's class teacher, or the woman from the newsagent's up the road, completely starkers.

What was the correct form in a situation like that? Should you engage in conversation, or merely smile politely? And if you did chat, where exactly should you focus your eyes? It was a bit of a minefield, actually.

'How are you?' Patrice asked Percy, stripping off her soggy vest top and tracksuit bottoms.

'So-so,' Percy sighed. 'A bit hassled. But hey, I mustn't go on about me. What about you?'

'Good,' Patrice said gently. 'But you're not going on about you. I asked, remember. Why are you hassled, then? I'd like to know.'

Patrice and Percy were naked now. Percy noticed Suzanne, on the other side of the room, giving her a funny look.

'Why are you staring at me like that?' Percy asked, grateful for the distraction.

'What's this?' Suzanne squealed, pointing across the room to the line of pale brown hair between Percy's thighs. 'You've got a landing strip! Don't tell me you've had a Brazilian? I'm shocked. I thought you were far too much of a feminist.'

'Oh,' said Percy nonchalantly. 'You never know, I might get a hot date with George Clooney. It pays to be prepared.'

They all sniggered. Percy loosened her ponytail and tugged the tie out. 'It was bloody agonising and I screamed,' she went on. 'But yes, in case you're wondering, it does feel, erm, nicer.'

'What do you mean?' Carmen shrieked. 'My God, you'll be having a clit ring next. Mark's a lucky man. What's he done to deserve it?'

'I didn't do it for him, I did it for me,' Percy replied primly.

'Perhaps we'd all better go and have them, girls,' Suzanne said, covering up quickly with a towel. 'Right now I'm more Amazon rainforest than Brazilian.'

Percy was still laughing as she went in the shower. The water wooshed down in a delicious rush. She just stood there for a few moments, feeling her tense, tired body relax. Finally, she squeezed some shampoo into her hand. It smelled strangely comforting, of almonds, she thought.

She massaged the shampoo into her scalp. There was a lot of lather. A streak dribbled down her forehead into her left eye. She was surprised by how much it stung. She realised she could very easily cry.

Pull yourself together, you big baby. How old do you think you are?

Patrice joined Percy by the changing-room mirror after their showers. Percy was busy drying her hair. She didn't really know why she bothered. Her hair was shoulder length and mousy, unless she'd just had vastly expensive highlights that she couldn't really afford. It always seemed to look worse after a blow dry: sort of bouffant in all the wrong places.

Patrice took a tortoiseshell comb out of a white, plastic pouch and started combing her own long, sleek, naturally blonde hair. She seemed to have no bouffant issues whatsoever.

'How's Mark?' Patrice asked once Percy switched off the drier.

Percy hesitated for a moment as she got out her make-up bag. 'Oh, same thing. Working hard as usual.' She scrubbed her cheek with the palm of her hand. She'd put on far too much blusher. She always did that. 'How about Jonty?' she asked quickly.

Patrice made a funny noise at the back of her throat. Surprised, Percy put down her mascara wand and looked at her friend.

'Can I tell you something?' Patrice said.

'Of course.'

'Guess when we last had sex?'

Percy was taken aback. This was unlike Patrice. She was usually so reserved. 'I've no idea – a week ago? Last night?' Percy guessed.

Patrice shook her head. 'Over four years ago, the night Seamus was conceived.'

'No.' Percy tried not to sound shocked.

'Are you surprised?' Patrice asked anxiously. 'It's not normal, is it?'

Percy scanned the room. There was no one in the immediate vicinity. Good. 'It's not normal, no,' she agreed. 'But what's the problem, do you think?'

'It's not me, it's him,' Patrice replied. Her face looked all crumpled. 'He's always had a low sex drive, but since Seamus was conceived he's gone off it altogether.'

Percy hesitated. She so didn't want to make things worse, but she had to ask. She took a deep breath and straightened up. 'Do you think he's having an affair?'

Patrice shook her head again. The question didn't seem to have made her angry or more upset. That was something, anyway.

'I've thought about that, obviously,' she said. 'But I really don't think so.'

'What about a health problem?' Percy suggested.

'No, Jonty recently had a health check for work and he's fine.'

'Pats, you've got to do something about this,' Percy urged. 'Talk to Jonty. Sex is an incredibly important part of a relationship.'

Patrice sighed. 'I know. The thing is, he won't discuss it. He just gets angry and changes the subject. But I'd really like to talk about this with you properly sometime.'

Percy nodded and put her make-up bag away. 'Anything I can do, anything at all . . .'

Patrice sounded grateful. 'Thanks, I knew you'd be a good listener. But don't tell Suzanne – or Carmen. It's embarrassing. Just between you and me, OK?'

Percy joined the others in the dimly lit café area. The walls were painted maroon and dark green, which made it feel snug and intimate. Lush green plants in big terracotta pots were dotted around, but there were no windows. It could be pouring with rain or bright sunshine outside. You'd never know.

Carmen and Suzanne were curled up on one of the squishy black leather sofas, mugs of green tea and coffee on the smoked-glass table in front of them. Steam was rising off them.

Percy pulled up a chair. She was so surprised by what Patrice had just told her that she found herself going over and over the conversation in her mind.

'Simon gets home from Eastern Europe tomorrow,' Carmen said, taking a sip of green tea from a glass mug. 'It's been nearly four months. I can't wait.'

Percy was only half listening. She watched, mesmerised, as Carmen put down her tea, twirled her long, black hair round her fingers and fastened it deftly at the back with a silver clip.

Patrice dragged a chair over now, too. Percy noticed that her hair was wet. She hadn't bothered to dry it. She had no make-up on either, but, although pale, she still looked gorgeous and interesting, the lucky cow.

Patrice slipped off her trainers and pulled up her long legs. She put her feet on the cushions and rested her chin on her knees. 'I don't know how you cope with Simon being away so much,' she said, picking up the threads of Carmen's conversation. 'I hate it when Jonty's away, even for a night. I suppose I ought to be used to it by now, though.'

She gave Percy a quick glance. Percy glanced back sympathetically. Fortunately, the others didn't notice or they'd have probed.

Yes, Percy found herself thinking, Carmen's semi-detached set-up with Simon is pretty weird. But how on earth does Patrice cope with no sex – ever? And what does it say about her relationship? What does it *mean*? Now that was really hard to get your head around.

Carmen looked thoughtful. 'I do miss Simon like mad,'

15

she said, nodding in Patrice's direction. 'But the good thing is, I always know he's coming back.'

Percy shuddered, remembering her own situation. She pulled her cardigan more tightly round her.

Maybe Mark won't come back tonight? Oh God. I hadn't thought of that.

She glanced at her watch. 'Blimey, we're late,' she said. 'We have to get Rowan and Seamus. They'll charge us for an extra hour if we don't hurry.'

She and Patrice grabbed their kit bags and made for the swing doors leading to the children's crèche.

'I've got to do a mammoth shop now,' Patrice sighed. 'Seamus'll be appalled, but the fridge is practically empty.'

'Bad luck,' Percy replied.

'Bye, darlings,' she called over her shoulder to the others. 'Sorry to rush. See you on Saturday.'

'Don't forget dinner at mine in the evening,' she heard Carmen cry after them.

Chapter Three

'Don't want this pasta, horrid pasta.' Rowan spat a large mouthful on to his plate.

Percy nearly heaved. 'Don't do that, it's nice,' she said, wiping the globs of food from round his mouth with a damp flannel.

'It's got ham. Don't like ham.'

'Just cheese,' Percy lied. 'You like cheese.'

'Ham.'

She sighed. 'OK, I'll make plain pasta with pesto. But it'll take a few minutes.'

She opened the cupboard and reached for some penne. There was a packet of chocolate digestives on the shelf above. Her tummy grumbled. She was ravenous, but Rowan came first.

She hesitated, remembering Body Attack earlier, and ate four biscuits in rapid succession. How many calories was that? She checked the packet. Eighty-four each. Three hundred and thirty-six in total. Damn. That would have ruined all the hard work she'd put in at Gym and Slimline. No wonder that post-baby bulge still hadn't shifted. She had no self-control.

She wiped the crumbs from her mouth and gave Rowan some paper and crayons while the pasta boiled. What should she do for supper?

Something with chicken, maybe, or did they have that yesterday? Chicken fricassee? Ben liked that. Percy opened the freezer. A packet of chicken nuggets winked at her. Well, it wouldn't kill them to have crappy food occasionally.

'Here you are, sweetheart.' She plonked Rowan's pasta on the kitchen table. 'What's the magic word?'

'Sank you. Can I watch TV after?'

'If you eat your lunch.'

Full up, Rowan settled happily on the sofa to watch CBeebies. Marvellous channel, Percy thought. Open University for toddlers.

He laughed out loud and Percy smiled. It was such an infectious sound. He glanced up at her. 'Love you, Mummy.'

'Love you, sweetheart.'

Her eyes swept round the sitting room. There was no denying, it was a tip. Magazines and newspapers on the floor; bits of Lego and puzzle waiting to trip her over. One of seven-year-old Ben's stinky trainers on the coffee table (where was the other?), plus a half-empty mug with greenish blobs in it. And an apple core beside the wastepaper basket.

Did Ben – because Ben was definitely the culprit – imagine there were squirrels in the house? Or think the apple core would somehow rot down and fertilise the carpet?

It hadn't always been like this, of course. She'd been positively house-proud once, in another life. She'd kept the Dyson downstairs, for easy access. She'd even been interested in storage solutions, for heaven's sake. Now, half the Dyson attachments were missing. She never seemed to have time to vacuum anyway. And she couldn't care less about storage solutions. She had other things on her mind.

She shivered. She wanted to leave the room and close the door behind her. Instead, she got some boxes and shoved in the toys. Magazines went on the piano stool, old newspapers and the apple core in the bin outside. She couldn't face dusting so she squirted a generous spray of lavender polish round the room. Lovely. Smelled so fresh. It made her feel strangely liberated.

She remembered the table lamp she'd bought last week and fished it out of a bag in the understairs cupboard. It had a twisted glass base, with a spotty purple and pink silk shade. It didn't really go with anything, but it was curious, whimsical. It was dead cheap in the sale, too. It might cheer the place up.

She put it on the side table and plugged it in. She stood back for a moment to admire it. Rowan looked up. 'That's beautiful, Mummy.'

Percy smiled, flopping into an armchair. It was all so pointless.

She closed her eyes, remembering Mark's expression last night. It made her shudder. She hugged her arms around her.

He'd looked so cold – hard and angry. She could hardly believe he was the same funny, gentle, sexy man she'd married fifteen years before. Where had it all gone: the shared jokes, cosy chats, lovemaking; that sense that they each knew what the other was thinking without even having to ask?

He'd come in from work, plonked his bag on the floor and started going through the pile of letters on the hall table.

She was sitting in the half light in the kitchen extension at the back of the house, busy on the computer. She didn't get up.

She loved that kitchen. It was her favourite room. All gleaming white cupboards and black, granite worktops. Mark hated it, though. He hadn't wanted to get it done, said they couldn't afford it.

She heard him ripping open letters and held her breath, waiting until he got to the bank statement. It was addressed to them both, but she'd just left it there.

'Fuck.'

Her stomach turned over.

'The overdraft's gone up.'

He stormed into the kitchen. She swivelled round now in her chair to look at him. His eyes rested on the granite worktops.

'It's those bloody worktops,' he growled. 'I said they were too expensive.'

She'd heard it all before, of course. She was the one who'd driven the kitchen project through, saying they needed the extra space. Plus it would be a good investment. Theirs was an up-and-coming area, it could only increase the value of the property.

She knew the repayments would be a struggle. They'd have to tighten their belts. But Mark earned good money, and it would be worth it in the long run. She couldn't understand why he was still so angry.

Sometimes, in fact, she wondered if this was really about money at all.

She felt something snap. 'Oh be quiet.' She was surprised by the venom in her voice. 'You're like a record player that's got stuck.'

He stared straight at her, his eyes full of contempt. She wished she had a snail's shell to shrink into.

He threw the statement down and the papers scattered all over the floor. 'I've had enough,' he muttered.

'What?'

'I said I've had enough.'

A shaft of cold shot through her body. She regretted her bad temper, wished she could take the words back.

'Please, let's talk . . .'

But he'd already left the room.

Later, upstairs, she found their king-sized bed empty. She tiptoed into the spare room. The light was off, but she could make out Mark's bulky form under the duvet.

There was a painful knot in her chest. He'd only ever gone in the spare room once before, early in their marriage, when he'd accused her of flirting with another man at a party. It was just a silly lovers' tiff but she'd hardly slept all night, thinking it was the end of the world.

She stood in the doorway for a few minutes, listening to Mark's slow, heavy breathing, in and out, in and out.

What did he mean, that he'd had enough? It sounded as

if he wanted out of the marriage. She longed to clamber in beside him, cuddle up close, wrap her arms and legs around and insist they make love, make up, just as they always used to. But she didn't dare.

Rowan giggled again at something on the TV and nudged her back to the present. She grabbed the *Guardian* and started reading the front page quickly.

The lead story was about Brussels and the Euro. 'Economic tests,' 'changeover plan', 'sustained and durable convergence'. Her eyelids started to droop. She was so tired. More tired than she'd have believed possible.

The words wouldn't make sense. They were deliberately trying to confuse her. This wouldn't happen if she was reading about Kate Moss or something. God, she was shallow.

Her head fell back on the armchair. She was on a long, golden beach, lying under a palm tree, naked save for a pink leopard-print thong. She hadn't a care in the world and, curiously, no cellulite either. She was pleased about that.

Leaning over her was a handsome, bronzed stranger. He smelled strangely intoxicating – was it lavender? He bent down, nibbled her earlobe and whispered how beautiful she was. She planted kisses on his full, soft mouth.

He started to move down her body, nuzzling her neck, her breasts, her tummy button. He looked up for a moment and smiled, a beautiful, white, reassuring smile.

Ohmigod! It was Danny from Body Attack!

Percy tried to shake herself awake. But it was no good. Before she could say 'Superman', they were climaxing explosively, 'Yes, yes . . .'

'What's the matter, Mummy?'

Her eyes sprang open. Rowan was still sitting, cross-legged, on the sofa, staring at her.

'Nothing, darling.' She jumped up. 'Mummy was just having a dream.'

'Were there any monsters?' Rowan looked interested.

'No, just people.'

'That's boring.' He went back to his programme.

She dashed into the kitchen and put on the floral pinny Ben had given her for Mother's Day. For a moment, her eyes rested on the computer in the corner. It was black, sleek, with a flat screen. She couldn't wait till tonight.

She pulled the potato peeler out of a drawer and plunged her hands in cold water. She'd make the special oven chips that the boys loved. And piles of broccoli. Maybe if she could stuff enough down them it would neutralise the chicken nuggets.

She jabbed at a large potato. A peeling flew out of her hands on to the floor and she bent down to pick it up. Was it normal to have naughty dreams, she wondered? She'd have to consult Suzanne, Patrice and Carmen. She'd bet they'd had some saucy ones in their time. Hmm, maybe not Patrice. She must give her a ring later, check she was all right.

Well, at least that dream proved she hadn't gone into total hibernation down there, Percy thought.

Be nice to Mark when he gets in. Act as if nothing's happened. He's probably forgotten about it already.

Chapter Four

Patrice signalled right and swung into her drive. 'Home, honeypot,' she said to Seamus, flicking a switch on her car keys. The iron security gates swung open.

She glanced in the mirror. Seamus was nodding off in his car seat. She'd bought him a sandwich at the supermarket and he'd managed to get crumbs all over himself and the back of the Mercedes. Jonty would be horrified. She must remember to clean it up. She turned round and tickled Seamus in the ribs. 'Don't go to sleep now, we have to unload the shopping.'

'Don't want to.' Seamus sounded really grumpy, but Patrice ignored him. It would be easy enough to cheer him up. He wasn't a difficult child.

Patrice loved walking into her house. She felt her heart lift immediately. It was ultra-modern, all concrete and glass, and it gave her a huge sense of achievement. Jonty had bought the land five years ago, before Seamus was born. It was exactly as they wanted: wide, airy rooms, pale cream walls and wooden floors throughout. The sweet smell of lilies in a vase on the hall table filled her nostrils.

She staggered in, carrying Seamus on her hip, her gym bag in the other hand. He was getting so heavy now. She plonked her bag on the floor and the phone started ringing.

'Hi, Pats.' Jonty's familiar voice brought a warm feeling to the pit of her stomach even after all these years.

'This is nice,' she said. 'I thought you were in meetings all day.'

'Yeah, and we won't be through till late,' Jonty replied. ''Fraid I'm going to have to stay in Manchester tonight. Sorry. Should be back tomorrow lunchtime.'

Patrice tried to hide her disappointment. 'Can't be helped,' she said. 'I'll miss you.'

'Me too,' she heard Jonty say. There was a pause. 'Where have you been?'

'Huge supermarket shop,' she explained. 'I've literally just walked through the door.

'Right.' Jonty sounded pleased. 'Give Seamus a big kiss for me. And make sure he's in bed by seven. He needs his sleep.'

'I know.'

'And don't forget to iron my shirts.'

'I won't.'

'Pats?'

She put Seamus down. 'Yes?'

'You won't go out tonight, will you? I don't want you coming home in the dark on your own.'

'Don't worry, I'm not going anywhere,' she reassured her husband.

'Good.'

Patrice replaced the phone and sighed. It was lovely that Jonty was so protective, but she sometimes felt as if she couldn't breathe without his permission.

It wasn't just that he hated her going out without him. He seemed to want to control every other aspect of her life, too. He chose nearly all her clothes for her, for instance. He came with her to the shops, held her coat and bag while she rummaged, waited while she paraded in front of him.

He was very definite about what suited her, and he was always right. But she did think it would be fun, occasion-ally, to shop on her own, or with girlfriends. She'd love just for once to buy something really wild and out of character.

She couldn't buy anything for the house, either, not so

much as a cushion, without him seeing it first. He was very particular about how he wanted their home to look, and he insisted everything should be immaculate.

They had a cleaner twice a week, and a gardener, too. But still, when he came home at night, the first thing he did after taking off his coat was to straighten the books on the coffee table and put the last of Seamus's toys away.

But she was so lucky, really, she knew. She shouldn't complain. Carmen's Simon was away such a lot. Justin was a pearl, but Mark was a bit of a nightmare, always working. Luckily Percy didn't seem to mind, though.

Percy. She'd been so kind this morning. It would be great to get her advice. She was so good at listening to other people's problems.

Patrice hadn't intended to bare her soul in that way in the changing room. It had just kind of slipped out. It had unsettled her, but she didn't think she regretted it. She trusted Percy implicitly. It's just that Patrice wasn't used to talking much about her emotions or leaving herself so exposed.

She felt suddenly rebellious. Jonty wasn't her father. Why shouldn't she go out tonight with her friend? He'd never know.

She took a deep breath, picked up the phone. Percy didn't sound keen. 'I should really stay in tonight. I've got lots—'

Patrice was persistent. 'You'll be back by eleven thirty. I really need to see you, Percy – please?'

There was a pause. 'I can probably get Maisie down the road to sit for me,' Percy said at last. 'What time shall we meet?

Patrice felt a tickle of excitement. A night out – on her own! The day suddenly looked completely different. Full of possibilities

Seamus was trundling his toy cars up and down in the playroom, making vrooming noises.

'C'mon, monkey, let's unpack the shopping, then we can go to the park,' Patrice suggested.

'The park? Yessss!' The small boy's body trembled with excitement.

Patrice sat on the park bench opposite the big slide, while Seamus went up and down in different positions: on his back, arms in the air, head first, on his tummy. It was a warm afternoon in early May and she raised her face to the sun, enjoying feeling the rays on her pale skin.

She could stay all afternoon if she wanted. No three-course meal to cook for Jonty. They could have beans on toast if they fancied. It felt like pure luxury.

A woman sat beside her with a baby in a big, old-fashioned pram.

Patrice smiled. 'Where did you get that pram? It's magnificent!'

'It was my mother's,' the woman replied. 'She put me and my brother and sisters in it. It was expensive to have repaired, but it's much nicer than some of those pokey, modern things.'

'How old is she?' Patrice asked, peering down at the cute pink infant dozing under the canopy. 'She's gorgeous.'

'Ella?' said the woman. 'Six months. She's terribly good. My other one, Martha, is three. She was much harder work. Second children usually are easier, aren't they?'

Patrice picked a piece of fluff off her camel coat. 'I've just got one, Seamus,' she replied, nodding in her son's direction. 'He's on the slide.'

'About time for another one then?' The woman grinned.

'Oh, I couldn't manage more than one,' Patrice said. She was shocked at how easily the lie slipped out. Without a hint of hesitation.

The woman opened her mouth to speak again, but Martha came bowling over and interrupted.

'I'm going on the seesaw,' the little girl shouted, excited.

Patrice was relieved when the woman got up and followed her daughter, pushing the pram to another side of the park. Seamus trotted over for a cuddle.

'Like a drink?' Patrice ruffled his blond hair. He looked just like her, everyone said so. But there was no guarantee another would. It might even be dark, like Jonty's father.

She pushed a straw into the carton of orange and held it while Seamus sipped. The park started to fill up rapidly as the older children came out of school and Seamus ran off to join a group of boys on the roundabout, but they were going too fast for him. He raced back to his mother.

'I want lace-up shoes like that boy,' he said, breathless, pointing.

Patrice smiled, lifting him on her lap. 'When you go to big school.'

School. She didn't want to think about it. At the moment he just went to nursery, three mornings a week, and the Gym and Slimline crèche on the other days. That was perfect. She loved having the afternoons with him, but he'd start full-time school before long. What on earth would she do all day without him?

She got up quickly. 'D'you want a push on the swings?'

'Will you push me really, really high?' Seamus begged.

He darted off towards his favourite blue swing in the far corner of the playground. Patrice found she had to run to keep up.

Patrice pulled on some skinny black trousers, a sparkly T-shirt, a black jacket and a pair of killer heels. Over the top for the cinema, but she didn't care. She didn't get to wear her glam clothes much.

She riffled through her drawer for her make-up bag. Some of the stuff had been sitting there for years. She applied foundation, eye-shadow, mascara, brown lipstick, blusher . . . She'd almost forgotten how to do it.

27

She stepped back from the mirror and took a long, hard look. She scarcely recognised herself. She must be nearly six feet tall in heels and her long blonde hair looked sleek and shiny when it wasn't scrunched up in a ponytail.

As she got out of her black Mercedes, a man driving by in a van lowered his window and wolf-whistled. She felt curiously elated. Percy was on the pavement outside the cinema, peering in her bag for something. She looked up and waved at Patrice as she crossed the road.

The town centre looked surprisingly enticing, Patrice thought. By day, it was just one big, heaving mass of shoppers. But now, with the lights on in restaurants and a few, brave people sitting outside, it felt positively continental.

She could see Percy had made a big effort, too. No jeans and trainers tonight. She was wearing a black pencil skirt and way-out purple suede platform boots. She looked fun and quirky. Patrice liked her style.

Percy started to walk towards her. Patrice's mobile went. Damn that stupid ringing tone. She'd have to remember to change it. She was alarmed when Jonty's name flashed up.

'Hi, I wasn't expecting to hear you,' Patrice said.

'Where are you?' He sounded angry. 'I rang home and that girl from over the road answered. You said you were staying in tonight.'

Patrice felt suddenly hot and sweaty. She wanted to take off her jacket. The phone was sticky in her hand. 'Percy rang and asked if I'd like to go to the cinema,' she stuttered, lying. 'She thought I might be lonely on my own.'

'You shouldn't leave Seamus with that girl. She's far too young.' Jonty's words came out in an angry rush, knocking Patrice off balance. 'How would she cope if there was a fire, for instance? Have you thought about that? And I said before, I don't want you coming home late at night on your own. It's irresponsible.'

Patrice steadied herself, pulled back her shoulders. 'That

girl – Katya – is sixteen,' she said. 'She babysat for us before, remember? And she coped fine. And I won't be late, I'm only going to a film.' Why was she having to bite back tears?

Percy was beside her now. 'Are you OK?' she asked, solicitous. Patrice shook her head, put the phone down, away from her, so he wouldn't hear. 'Jonty's not happy about our babysitter,' she explained.

Percy frowned. 'Why not? You've used her before, haven't you?'

Patrice nodded, started to speak to Jonty again. 'I wouldn't ask Katya if I wasn't—'

He interrupted. 'I'm coming home.'

Patrice felt her breath arriving in short bursts. 'Don't do that,' she pleaded. 'I'll miss the film. There's no need for you to drive all that way . . .'

His voice softened. 'You know it's the right thing.'

She turned to Percy, sighing. 'I'm going to have to go home. I'm really sorry.'

Percy touched her friend lightly on the arm. 'Are you sure?'

Patrice nodded. She was almost weeping.

'Don't worry,' Percy replied. 'We can do it another time. I've got quite a lot to do, anyway.'

Patrice attempted a smile, kissed her friend on both cheeks. 'You're a sweetheart. By the way, love the new boots.'

Patrice hurried off, clip-clopping in her high heels towards her car, and drove home. The phone was ringing as she walked through the door.

'You're back?' said a familiar voice.

'Hello, Jonty.'

'Good,' he went on. 'I needed to check. I don't want you leaving Seamus like that again, OK?'

'OK.' Patrice put the phone down carefully.

'Are you all right, Mrs Byrne?' Katya emerged from the sitting room, a worried expression on her face. 'Only I didn't think you'd be back so early.'

'Fine, thanks. Just a bit of a headache.' Patrice opened her purse and thrust a twenty-pound note in Katya's hand.

The girl looked confused. 'You don't need to give me that much, I've not even been here an hour.'

'Take it. Please,' Patrice urged.

'Well, thank you very much, Mrs Byrne.' Katya tucked the note in her jeans pocket. 'I'm going clubbing on Saturday, so it'll come in handy.'

Patrice watched as Katya walked down the floodlit drive. There was a spring in her step, a jauntiness. Clubbing? Patrice hadn't done that in years. Jonty hated dancing and he'd never let her go with friends. He'd say she was far too old for that sort of thing.

She turned out the lights and headed upstairs. She was rich, attractive, she had a loving husband and beautiful son. She couldn't be envious of studenty, spotty, slightly over-weight Katya, could she? That would be stupid.

She drew the curtains. Turned on the TV in her bedroom to drown out the noise in her head. Closed her eyes. What were those lines in *A Midsummer Night's Dream*? She loved that play.

Ah yes.

> And sleep, that sometimes shuts up sorrow's eye,
> Steal me awhile from mine own company.

That's what she craved: sleep. Escape from herself. Oblivion.

She woke some hours later to find the TV still chuntering on.

Percy heard the key in the lock and the thud of Mark's unsteady footsteps coming down the hall. She glanced at the clock on the computer. God he was late, even later than usual – 1.15 a.m. Her stomach fluttered. She clicked sit-out, minimised the image on her screen and quickly pulled up an email.

Mark came into the kitchen. 'Shit.' He must have tripped on the purple suede boots she'd kicked off earlier. Finally, he spotted her darkened form hunched in the corner.

'What are you doing?' He was slurring, but at least he was speaking to her.

Percy rubbed her eyes. 'Catching up on emails,' she said brightly. 'Did you get my text about the cinema?'

She took his grunt as a yes.

'Pats and I didn't go in the end,' she rattled on. 'Jonty called and she had to go home. How come you're so late?'

'Got waylaid by Dave,' Mark replied. 'Wanted to talk about girlfriend problems.' He laughed. 'Told him he'd be better off without one.'

He walked over to the sink, ran the tap and filled a glass with water. He drank it quickly. Then she heard him chucking his keys on the hall table and switching the light on next door.

There was a pause. 'What's that?' He sounded angry.

Percy got up slowly. Her neck and shoulders were stiff from being in the same position for so long. She opened the sitting-room door and blinked. Mark was staring at the purple and pink spotty lamp.

'It's hideous,' he said. 'I can't believe you've been spending again.'

'It was only cheap, in the sale,' she replied, wounded. She swallowed. 'I thought you weren't coming home.'

'Sorry to disappoint you.'

She felt shaky. He swayed. She saw his red eyes before he looked away.

'You're exhausted,' she said gently. 'You should go to bed.'

She reached out to touch his arm. Her fingers lightly brushed the sleeve of his jacket. He pulled away.

She waited until she heard their bedroom door click shut

31

upstairs. So he wasn't going in the spare room again. That was something.

She scurried back to the computer.

Percy could hardly remember, now, how it had all begun. She seemed to have been playing poker virtually all her life. It was her father, David, who'd taught her. Playing cards with him was one of her happiest childhood memories.

Her dad, a country solicitor, was dead now, but he'd been no match for Percy's mother, Antonia. A quiet, self-contained man, it seemed to Percy that he was only really happy when he was betting on his beloved horses or playing cards.

They played at weekends, and more often during the holidays: blackjack, pontoon, rummy, seven-card stud. He taught Percy and her younger brother Zeus everything they knew. But the game she grew to love most was poker.

She adored the seductive vocabulary: wild cards, royal flushes, the river and the big blind. She quickly learned what to discard and what to pick up. She was an excellent bluffer, her father said, and she became really good at reading her opponents, watching for every little telltale sign.

They played for pennies, matchsticks, anything they could lay their hands on. Sometimes her uncle Tom would join them, too. Before long she was beating him and even her father, despite all his efforts to fool her. It made him laugh out loud. 'That girl's a natural,' he'd say to Antonia, who'd shoot him a withering look.

Antonia hated cards and anything to do with gambling. But Percy didn't care. She basked in her father's praise. She received precious little from anyone else.

Once in a while he would hold poker evenings at the house and allow Percy to stay up and watch for an hour or so before bed.

Even now, she found the smell of whisky and cigars strangely enticing. It would take her right back to her childhood home, that front room with the deep red curtains where the men – it was always men – gathered. She was fascinated by how differently they played. Some were cautious, some risk-takers. Some became chatty and animated when they were bluffing; others went quiet. She imbibed it all, processed the information, stored it away for future use.

At university, where she met Mark, she organised once-a-week poker tournaments with groups of other students. They didn't play for much money – just enough to make the game exciting, enough for it to hurt if you lost and make it worth your while if you won.

She gained quite a reputation. The extra cash came in handy, supplementing her meagre student income, but she never allowed it to get out of hand. Her father had warned her about plunging into debt. The thought really frightened her.

Mark played occasionally, but didn't really approve. He was too cautious, said gambling could land you in all sorts of trouble. Secretly, though, she suspected that he was rather proud of his girlfriend's poker prowess. She'd hear him talking about her wins in the college bar.

It was quite by chance that she got into Internet poker. She hadn't played at all for several years, not since before their eldest, Ben, was born.

She'd started chatting to a woman in a queue at the Post Office who'd been admiring baby Rowan in his pram. 'What a lovely little boy,' the woman had said, 'just like my grandson. He's seven now. I took him on holiday to Spain last summer.' Then she winked. 'Used my poker winnings to pay for it.'

Percy was interested. 'Poker?' she said. 'I used to play that.'

The woman nodded. 'On the Internet. My husband normally falls asleep in front of the telly, so I sneak off and have a few games.' She laughed conspiratorially.

That evening, once she'd put the boys to bed, Percy checked out a few websites and was amazed to see how many games were going on at any one time – beginners and free ones, as well as the big cash variety and multi-table tournaments. They mostly seemed to play Texas Hold'em, a variation of the poker she'd played as a child.

She signed up – it was incredibly easy, all you needed was a credit card – and sat back and watched, mesmerised, for hours, dipping in and out of different games, observing what went on.

She could see that online poker was very different from the face-to-face 'bricks and mortar' kind that she was used to.

In the real world, your senses were assailed by everything going on around you: the flicker of a TV, maybe, the sounds of poker chips clacking together, people laughing, music, the smell of wine, beer, cigarettes, crisps.

Online, however, there was just a virtual card table, and although you could hear cards shuffling, chips banging together and checking and folding noises, the sounds were purely artificial. With just your computer screen for company, it was an altogether more intense experience.

Internet poker was much faster, too. You could play more than double the number of hands per hour, meaning you stood to win – or lose – twice as much. Percy could imagine how easy it would be to forget that you were playing with real money and get carried away.

And it was weird not being able to see your opponent. You couldn't take for granted knowing certain things about them, such as their age and sex. You couldn't even tell what time zone they were in. It might be the middle of the day for them, or the middle of the night. A tired player was always easier to beat than an alert one.

But Percy soon gathered that there were other ways of reading players, such as the size of their bets and the amount of time they took to make them.

There was also a box in the corner of the screen, where players chatted using a host of abbreviations such as 'TY', for 'thank you', and 'NH' for 'nice hand'. It was a whole new vocabulary.

She noticed that certain players became verbally aggressive when they had bad hands, while others went stumm. You could get to know a great deal about them through that chat facility.

Watching game after game made Percy's heart thump faster. She'd forgotten the buzz of anticipation, the excitement of playing, the total thrill of a win. It was like a massive hit, magnificent, better than drugs, better even than falling in love. There was no feeling like it in the world.

She realised the potential was there to make a lot of money, too, and it occurred to her that this could be a great way of bringing in some much-needed extra cash. She wouldn't even need to leave the house!

She decided not to tell Mark. He'd go mad. But it would be good to be able to buy a few clothes, household items, without feeling guilty. Better still, if she made enough, she might even be able to reduce the overdraft. He wouldn't complain about that.

Percy's online alter ego was Boadicea, the fearsome Queen of the Iceni, who led a rebellion against the Romans in AD 60. Percy had always rather liked the sound of Boadicea. She was a feisty lass. It was true that she'd been defeated in the end, but she'd put up a bloody good fight.

Soon, Percy was playing every Tuesday and Thursday, after she'd put the boys to bed. At first, she was very careful, putting only small sums down – $2 here, $6 there – they always played in dollars. Before long, she'd built up a little nest egg of £500, which she ferreted away in a secret bank account.

Gradually, as she gained confidence, she started betting bigger sums. She rarely lost. She was too good at reading weak players. Winning was such a thrill. And she loved having something to do that didn't involve pulling pasta out of Rowan's hair, that made her use her brain.

She found she really enjoyed the camaraderie online, too. Often, she'd come across the same people and find out little personal things about their lives – how many children they had, what they did for a living, that sort of thing. She built up a mental picture.

A few players became nasty and aggressive, particularly when the stakes were high, but others were really sociable. Talking to them made the evenings less lonely somehow. It was almost like being in a room of friends.

She had a special 'lucky' outfit that she always wore: a black cardigan, black high-heeled court shoes. And she tied her hair up in a chignon with the same tortoiseshell clip. It made her feel more businesslike, more Boadicea and less mumsy, klutzy Percy Redpath.

The £500 grew to £1,000, the £1,000 to £2,000. Percy had got her old touch back. She felt invincible.

A red message flashed up. She'd been daydreaming. She stared at the screen. 'Whitewitch wins $600 with one pair, kings.'

'NH', someone typed. 'Nice hand'. 'TY' – 'Thank you' – Whitewitch replied.

Percy cleared her throat. Took a sip of water. Rejoined the game. She knew she had to focus.

She was dealt a strong hand and decided to muddle her opponents by varying her pace of play. She liked doing that, keeping them guessing, disguising what she had and trying to be wrongly predictable.

She won and won again. Took another sip of water. Her mouth was dry.

'G1', Whitewitch wrote – 'Good one'. She was a favourite of Percy – always civilised, even when she was losing. Percy knew she had an ailing son at home. She played a lot of poker. It must be a relief to get away from the sickroom.

Percy heard Rowan cry out in his sleep. He often did that. She held her breath, crossed her fingers that he wouldn't wake.

The hours raced. Time always seemed to whiz in poker. She could hardly believe it was 3 a.m. already. She wasn't tired, though. She was feeling great, really confident. Her goal was to get her winnings up to £5,000 and wipe out the overdraft. How marvellous would that be!

She was dealt a pair of aces. Her heart beat faster. One of the players, Johnnypwe, raised $300. She'd come across him before, too. She knew he was American and divorced. And she didn't like him. She reckoned he was a woman-hater. He tended to get ugly when she beat him, which was most of the time.

She'd kept notes on him – she did that on all her opponents. He was a loose player, could be a bit of a maniac, so, with her strong hand, she decided to reraise him $1000. He reraised all-in – bet everything he had – and she called.

You could almost feel the other players' excitement, even through cyberspace. They were probably holding their breath. 'GL', Whitewitch typed in the corner – 'Good luck'.

The pot totalled $4150. They showed their hands and Johnnypwe turned over a pair of tens.

Percy's spirits soared. She knew he'd been playing loose. But the flop – the round when three cards are dealt face up – came 10, jack, queen, giving him trip 10s: three of a kind.

For one wild moment she thought she'd lost it. Then a king came on the turn, the fourth card. She jiggled up and down in her seat. She'd made a straight – five cards in a row in more than one suit. It was the sixth highest poker hand. The game was hers – surely?

She was mentally adding the win to her nest egg and deducting it from the overdraft. She just prayed that the river, the fifth board card, wouldn't be a 10, giving him a full house: three of a kind and a pair. But how unlikely was that? It would be incredible.

She sucked in her breath. The river came a 10.

She stared, disbelieving. There must be some mistake. She felt sick. Half her precious savings – $2,000 – down the drain. In one night. He'd just got lucky. It was a bad beat.

A message flashed up in the chat box. It was Johnnypwe. 'ROFL', he typed – 'Rolling on the floor laughing'. She could imagine him crowing, flexing his macho muscles at her.

She wanted to punch him, but most of all, she wanted to punch herself.

'NH' – 'Nice hand' – she forced herself to reply. She wasn't going to stoop to his level. 'VUL Boadicea', Whitewitch sympathised. Too right, Percy thought. Very, very unlucky.

She rose from her seat slowly. Turned the lights off and walked upstairs. She couldn't bear to imagine what Mark would say if he knew. He'd think her a total fool.

She took off her clothes as quietly as she could and hung them on the banisters. Mark stirred slightly in his sleep as she slipped in beside him. She wished he'd roll over and give her a cuddle, but he didn't.

What would her father's response be if he were alive? He'd had no time for whining self-pity or bad beat stories.

'You're a good player,' he'd have reassured her. 'And good players know they can always get back to even the next day.'

Well, she was bloody well going to prove him right. She'd just have to pick herself up and win it all back – and more – next time.

Chapter Five

❧❦❧

'Bacon?'

'Smells lovely. But I can't, I'll be late.'

Justin was standing by the grill in a black T-shirt and baggy pyjama bottoms. You could see an inch or two of back in between. He had bare feet and his brown hair was sticking up. Suzanne thought he looked about twelve. She gave his cute little bum a pinch.

He turned and grinned. 'Don't touch what you're not going to buy.'

'I'll see you later,' she winked.

'Blow Mummy a kiss,' Justin said.

Felix bounced up and down in his high chair. He was wearing a blue penguin bib, his chubby hand clutching a crust. 'Dadadada,' he crowed, grinning and showing off two perfect bottom teeth.

'No, Mama,' Suzanne said, kissing the top of her son's head. It seemed to be the only place that wasn't sticky. She put her face up close to his. 'Mamamamama,' she mouthed.

'Dadadadada,' he repeated.

Ruby, beside her brother at the kitchen table, looked disapproving. 'Are you going out again, Mummy? You really should see more of your children.'

Suzanne laughed. 'You sound like *my* mother.' She gave her daughter a peck on the cheek. 'I'm just going to Pilates. I won't be long.'

'We can go to the river and feed the ducks,' Justin said, putting a bacon sandwich in front of Ruby. 'We'll take your bike if you want.'

The almost-new silver MPV was parked in the front drive. Suzanne jumped in and picked out a CD. The whole glorious weekend lay ahead. She didn't have much work to do, for once. And Justin had made leek and potato soup for lunch. She could practically smell it.

She turned on the ignition, then turned it off again and ran inside. 'Don't forget Ollie's got piano at eleven, then he has to go straight to Jamie's. He's spending the night, remember? Oh, and see if you can persuade Lara to get her arse out of bed and do some revision, will you?'

'Don't say arse, it's rude,' said Ruby.

Justin kissed his wife gently on the lips. She lingered a moment, unable to tear herself away.

'Stop worrying, gorgeous,' he told her. 'Everything's under control.'

'Tace the mirror, find neutral, tummies in, shoulders pulled down into your back pockets, eyes closed and breathe slowly and deeply. Sloooowly and deeeeply.'

Suzanne felt sleepy. Wouldn't do to drop off now.

'When you're ready,' the instructor went on, 'go up on one foot, then the other, and start pedalling.'

Now that was impossible, surely, to balance when you couldn't see? Suzanne wobbled like mad. If she didn't open her eyes she'd fall over. So how come Percy, Carmen and Patrice could do it?

Every muscle in Suzanne's body was still aching from Body Attack. At least with Pilates she wouldn't break into a sweat. Now that was her kind of exercise.

'Shoulders, shoulders, Purse-phone,' the instructor scolded.

'Pers-ef-fon-ee,' Percy muttered, lowering her shoulders. Suzanne wondered why Percy's parents had given her such a silly name. It was pretty, but no one could ever pronounce it.

'Now I want you to lie on your backs, raise your legs into table-top position, then slowly straighten and lower them to the floor.'

Oh no, abdominals. Suzanne could never do these. She suspected she didn't have tummy muscles. She glanced at Carmen, who seemed able to do all the exercises without any effort. She had a washboard stomach, that girl.

Percy was grimacing, though. And Patrice. It must be hard on the back, when your legs were so long. Unfortunately, Suzanne didn't have that excuse.

The woman on the right had her eyes closed in concentration. She looked almost as if she were meditating. Maybe she was trying hard not to break wind?

Lord! Suzanne hoped not. No one had ever broken wind in the class before, but they did get into some very odd positions.

What was the etiquette in a situation like that? Should you pretend you hadn't heard, or say something sisterly, like, 'Better out than in?' She'd have to ask Percy, Carmen and Patrice about it later.

Unfortunately, Millicent was lying in wait by the door at the end of the class. She was wearing full make-up, the silly mare, and her hair was blonder than ever.

'How's the diet going?' Her voice sounded all sugary.

Suzanne had once let slip she wouldn't mind shifting a few pounds. Big mistake. 'Not great, to be honest,' she said, flinging her towel over her shoulder. She couldn't lie.

'I've lost ten pounds on this amazing detox,' Millicent smirked. She put her hand in front of Suzanne, like a barrier, to stop her walking past. 'Look how baggy my bottoms are.'

She pulled out the waistband of her trousers, revealing a gap of several inches and a flat, brown stomach underneath. She was always tanned, all year round. Fake, of course, Suzanne thought.

Suzanne attempted a smile. 'Well done,' she said, fearing her face might split. God, that woman was irritating.

Patrice, Percy and Carmen were waiting for Suzanne by the water fountain. Suzanne could see her reflection in the glass behind. Her tight red curls were sticking up wildly. She tried to smooth them down but they boinged up again.

'That woman, Millicent, might have the pertest boobs and bum in South London, but her breath stinks,' she hissed. She hated how Millicent brought out this malicious streak.

'Does it?' Percy was interested. 'I suppose that's what happens if you live on a lettuce leaf. It's the ketones or something.'

Suzanne looked at Percy. She was paler than usual, and slightly red round the nose and eyes. 'Are you OK?'

'Fine.' Percy brushed the question off and took a swig of water. 'Bit of a cold, that's all. Kept me awake last night.'

Suzanne was in and out of the shower in no time. She didn't want to waste a moment of the day. She smothered herself in moisturiser and pulled on Justin's sweatshirt. It smelled of him: a warm, woody smell.

She dragged a comb through her curls and looked in the mirror. Marginally better, thanks to quantities of conditioner, but no doubt the frizz would be back soon. Who cared? It was Saturday! Woo woo!

'How's work?' Patrice was zipping up her jeans.

'Good,' Suzanne smiled. 'I'm up for promotion – Director of Communications.' Just saying it gave her a little shiver of excitement.

'Wow. Sounds impressive. Do you think you'll get it?'

'I'm in with a good chance,' Suzanne replied. 'It's a bloody excellent job, but it'll be more responsibility – and even longer hours.'

Patrice put her head on one side. 'How does Justin feel about that?'

Suzanne smiled. 'He encouraged me to go for it. No doubt thinks it'll keep me out from under his feet for longer.'

Patrice ignored the joke. 'You are lucky,' she said, with feeling. 'Justin's so supportive. It's just like having a wife.'

Carmen was in the café, a mug of green tea in front of her. She was sitting, eyes closed, in the lotus position, her elbows in the air, one arm stretching down behind her back.

'Hi,' Suzanne said.

Carmen opened her eyes slowly and smiled. 'Oooh, that feels better,' she said, lowering her arms and giving them a shake. 'My shoulders were so stiff.' She shuggled forward in her seat to be closer to the others. 'Simon says he should be back for a good long spell now.' She beamed. 'Two or three months at least.' She straightened up. 'He's going to need a break. His next contract is a biggie. He'll be helping to set up a new computer system for the Czech Republic Police Force's department for corruption and financial investigations.'

'Blimey,' Suzanne marvelled. 'What a mouthful! Sounds impressive.' Carmen looked positively glowing, Suzanne thought. She admired Carmen hugely. She was so graceful and elegant.

Suzanne examined Carmen's position and decided to attempt the lotus herself. Unfortunately, she couldn't get the second leg over the first. Her thighs seemed to be in the way. Or was it her calves? Annoyed, she tugged at the underneath ankle and managed to lever it into place, but it was agony. She grimaced and tried to untangle herself. For some reason the leg wouldn't unknot. 'Help! My leg's about to snap!' she squealed.

Carmen leaned forward and gently sorted her out.

'Thanks.' Suzanne sniffed. It was a stupid move anyway. Why would anyone want to get themselves all contorted like that? It wasn't natural. She patted her hair down, straightened up in her chair and cleared her throat.

'Now Simon's home, Carmen Chang,' she pronounced, looking severely at her friend, 'you make sure you have that chat about babies.' She wagged her finger like a bossy schoolmistress, making her curls bob.

'Whoooa, steady on. Give the poor girl a chance,' Percy chipped in. She was hunting in her bag for something. Keys, notebook, lipsticks, a comb and a couple of crumpled hankies spilled on to the floor. At last she located what she was looking for: lip balm. 'Ta da!' she grinned, putting some on.

Carmen tut-tutted. She couldn't bear untidiness. 'You need to declutter,' she said. 'You always have so much stuff with you.'

'I need a bigger bag,' Percy retorted. 'A Mary Poppins-style carpet bag would do the job. But listen, Suzanne,' she chided, 'Simon's only just got back. He and Carmen are too busy doing all that tantric sex business to have a serious talk about anything.'

Carmen shook her head. 'How many times have I told you lot, I'm not sure I even want babies anyway. And I most certainly don't want four like you, Suzanne.'

'Quite right,' Percy agreed. 'You've got a great lifestyle. Why go and spoil it?'

Suzanne shrugged. 'Just remember you haven't got for ever, though, Carmen. Don't leave it too late.'

Suzanne's phone pinged. It was a text from Justin.

'Problem?' Patrice asked, coming back from the bar with two skinny lattes.

'I don't know,' Suzanne frowned. 'Justin's asked me to go home asap. That's a bit weird. Better dash. See you all tonight.'

There was quite a lot of blood on the sheets.

Lara was sitting up in bed, snivelling. Ruby, beside her, was patting her big sister's head. There was a towel wrapped round Lara's arm, and that was bloody, too.

Justin was by the sink, baby Felix balanced on one hip, and the taps were running.

'What's happened?' Suzanne tried to make sense of the scene. Ruby jumped off the bed and ran over to cling on to her leg. Her eyes were enormous.

'Lara hurt her arm,' Ruby sniffed. 'Daddy's making it better with a towel. He'll have to wash the sheets, though.'

Lara gave a big sob.

'What's happened?' Suzanne repeated.

'Why don't you tell her?' Justin turned to Lara. She shook her head.

'All right, I'll tell your mother then,' he snarled. 'For some reason, Lara thought it would be a good idea to write her boyfriend's name on her arm – with a knife.' He grabbed a kitchen knife from the sink, to show Suzanne. 'As you can see, she's made rather a mess.'

Suzanne felt dizzy. She had to sit down. Ruby climbed on her lap.

'Mummy, will Lara be all right?' Ruby started to cry.

Suzanne swallowed. 'Yes, poppet, don't worry. Mummy just needs to decide what to do. Let me look.'

She watched as Lara slowly unpeeled the towel. There were several lines of deep scratches on her left forearm. You could just about make out the word 'Noah'.

The blood had started to congeal, but it looked as if the cuts might need stitching. Luckily the 'H' was some way from Lara's wrist. She hadn't tried to slit her wrists, anyway. That was something to be grateful for.

Suzanne gently rewrapped the towel and put her arms round Lara. Ruby crawled between them. Lara's shoulders felt very small and thin.

'You silly, silly girl,' Suzanne murmured. 'What on earth were you thinking of?'

'I'm sorry, I really am.' Lara buried her face in her mother's chest. 'I wanted to show him how much I love him. I didn't mean to cut so deep. It really hurts now.' Her voice sounded tiny.

Suzanne hugged her tighter. 'What are we going to do with you?'

Lara sobbed harder.

Ruby got down from the bed and fetched a box of tissues. 'Here you are, Lara,' she said solemnly.

Suzanne glanced up at Justin. 'We'd better take her to casualty,' she said.

He nodded. His face looked grim.

Lara felt limp, pliable even. That made a change.

'What on earth were you thinking of?' Suzanne said again. Now she started to cry, too. She felt suddenly drained. Ruby joined in. The three of them were sitting on the bed, weeping.

'Girls, girls.' Justin's voice was gentle now. He put Felix on the floor, perched on the bed next to Suzanne and put his arm round her. Then he wiped Ruby's very small nose with a hankie.

Suzanne sniffed, and he wiped her nose, too. He took one of her hands, and one of Lara's. His own hand felt warm and reassuring.

'I can't bear to see my girls like this,' he murmured. 'Stop now. It'll be all right. We'll get Lara sorted. Everything's going to be fine.'

Ruby looked up at her mother, her eyes full of hope. Suzanne managed half a smile.

'C'mon, Lolly,' said Justin. It was his pet name for Lara. 'Mum'll help you get some clothes on, then we'll go to hospital.'

Felix was still on the floor, chewing a sock. Justin took it out of his mouth and scooped him up.

Ruby perked up. 'Can we go in an ambulance?'

'No, but you might see some ambulances when we get there,' Justin replied.

Lara leaned on Suzanne as they went downstairs. Suzanne

was struggling to understand. A myriad thoughts were swirling around her head, jostling with each other, making her brain ache.

Why did Lara always have to spoil everything? What was the matter with her? Suzanne had been so looking forward to the weekend. It was all Lara's bloody dad's fault.

Suzanne felt savage. She wished she'd never clapped eyes on the bastard.

She remembered how he'd put on that pathetic, abandoned expression of his when she'd told him it was all over. Even though he was the one who'd cheated on her.

'It doesn't mean anything, Suze,' he'd said, tears of self-pity in his eyes. She could hear his whining voice even now. 'I don't love her like you. I just can't cope with playing second fiddle all the time. I want us to go back to being how we were.'

Well, that was a laugh, when they had two small children to look after and she was working full-time to pay the bills. Not that he did much of the looking after. Rather he stuck them with a childminder and spent his days dossing around with his stupid band, playing his stupid music.

Why on earth had she fallen for Frank? He was one of life's losers. She must have been mad. But she'd been so young – they both had.

Suzanne clambered into the back of the car, next to Lara. It was a good job Ollie was staying over at Jamie's, she thought. Ollie was a sensitive boy. He'd be terribly upset. Justin strapped the little ones in. Lara was snivelling. She loosened her seatbelt, lay down and rested her head on her mother's lap.

Her hair was chestnut brown and beautiful. Suzanne stroked her head. Lara looked like a small animal, lying there. She was the one who'd suffered the most from the divorce, Suzanne thought sadly. Ollie was too young to remember. The trouble was that Lara loved her father, with that blind adoration of a child. In her eyes he could do no wrong.

Ever since he'd left it was as if, no matter how many good things happened, no matter how hard everyone tried, Lara was still waiting for him to walk back through the door. Or at least to remember her birthdays and Christmas. But he never did.

'OK, hop out,' Justin commanded. The journey had only taken a few minutes. Frank's face broke into little pieces and scattered. Lara peeled her head off her mother's lap and sat up. There was a hot, sticky patch where her cheek had been.

Justin had managed to find a slot right outside the casualty department. He opened the back door. 'C'mon, Lolly. Let's get you seen to.'

Lara struggled out, white-faced, still clutching a bloody towel round her arm, and Suzanne followed. She stood, watching, while Justin lifted the pushchair out of the boot, unfolded it and strapped Felix in.

Ruby hopped on the buggy board at the back and Justin started to push. Suzanne and Lara trailed behind, clutching coats and bags. Suzanne felt about ninety-five.

'Hurry up, you two,' Justin called over his shoulder. 'We haven't got all day.'

A couple of paramedics waiting by an ambulance watched them approach. Lara dropped her jacket in a puddle, squealed and bent down to pick it up. Felix sneezed and Justin stopped to wipe his nose. Ruby fell off the buggy board and started crying. Justin picked her up and put her back on.

'We're like the bloody Addams Family,' Justin groaned, pushing the buggy through the swing doors of the hospital. 'Jesus, what a fucking shambles.'

Chapter Six

The flat looked amazing, Carmen thought. She swept her eyes round the sitting room one more time. Simon had helped carry the kitchen table into the centre of the room and she'd covered it with a white cloth. The French windows were open, and there were lanterns on the decking and fairy lights dotted around the little walled garden. The table was laid with white crockery and tall wine glasses and there was a pink orchid in a vase in the middle.

There wasn't an awful lot more to do now. Time for a shower. Carmen was looking forward to trying out her new organic shampoo. She didn't like massaging chemicals into her hair. She strolled into the bedroom.

The blinds were closed. Simon was leaning against the wall, waiting for her in the gloom. She jumped when she saw him. She'd thought he was still in the kitchen.

'Take your top off,' he said, deadpan.

'I'm sorry?' Had she misunderstood?

'Do as you're told and take it off.'

Carmen blinked. 'Simon, I can't,' she protested. 'I've got six people coming to dinner.'

He stood, motionless, his arms folded in front of him. She couldn't make out his expression. He wasn't smiling, though. She slipped off her T-shirt. Why was she doing this?

'Now your jeans,' he ordered.

'Simon, you really are—'

'Take them off.'

She undid her belt, stepped out of her jeans. His eyes never left her. 'Now your bra,' he commanded.

She hesitated. Looked at her watch. 'They'll be here in less than an hour.'

He moved right up close. She could feel his breath on her neck. She moaned as he slipped his hand between her thighs. 'Look, this is really most . . .'

He whispered in her ear. 'I've told you, take off your bra.'

She pulled down the straps, slid the catch round to the front and undid it. Dropped it on the floor. His breathing was low, heavy.

'Get on the bed,' he instructed. She wanted to slap him. This was way out of order. Instead, she lay down obediently while he slipped her knickers down, over her feet and pushed open her thighs. Then he began planting soft kisses, like butterfly wings, up and down the length of her legs.

Carmen shivered. There was nothing else she could do. She didn't like feeling so helpless, but resistance was futile. She hadn't known the meaning of the word lust until she'd met him.

'Sexy minx,' he murmured.

'What about the crème brûlée?' she whispered, desperate.

'Sod the crème brûlée.'

She lay with her head on his chest, one leg twined around his, trying to avoid the sticky patch. She sighed.

'Simon?'

'Mmm?' His eyes were closed.

'Do you realise we've been together four years?'

'Have we? I suppose we have.'

'I just wondered,' she said. 'I mean, I know you like travelling, having your own place but . . . have you ever thought about children?'

She knew straightaway that she'd said the wrong thing.

He sat up, making her roll off his chest, and reached for his dressing gown.

'Children? Not really, no,' he replied 'I thought you didn't want any.'

Carmen snapped her eyes shut. It was easier to say difficult things with your eyes shut. 'I didn't think I did,' she explained. 'I was quite anti them. But I'm not so sure now. And I can't help thinking, I'm forty now. If I did change my mind, if we did want them, we haven't got much time.'

Simon leaned over and ruffled his girlfriend's hair. 'They're a huge commitment, you know.'

'Of course,' she said. 'But together . . .'

He stood up and slipped on his robe. The hairs on her arms prickled. 'You know me,' he laughed. 'I'm never in one place for more than a month or two. I'd be a useless father.'

She lay there, absolutely still, as he left the room. She heard him go into the bathroom. Pee. Flush the loo and turn on the taps.

She breathed deeply a few times. In, one, two, three, out, one two three. That was better. Now, where was her bathrobe?

She checked the clock beside her bed. God, they'd be here soon. She'd have to be quick.

She rose rapidly and picked her clothes off the floor. She pulled her turquoise silk blouse from the cupboard and rootled for her black skirt and strappy silver shoes. She laid them carefully on the chair.

Simon was right, she didn't really want babies. She'd spent years building up her business, her reputation. It hadn't been easy after the accident. But she'd worked hard, and look what she had to show for it: a beautiful flat, nice clothes, sexy boyfriend, foreign holidays.

Children would ruin everything. She'd told herself that for years. They'd be a huge mistake.

Wouldn't they?

Chapter Seven

❦

'Hi, darlings,' Carmen said, reaching up to kiss Percy, then Mark, on both cheeks, before leading them into the garden.

Percy thought Carmen looked fabulous. She was wearing a turquoise silk blouse tied round the middle with a silver sash. Her hair hung sleekly down her back and nearly reached her waist.

She looked more Chinese than usual, Percy thought. Sometimes her Spanish half seemed more obvious, but not tonight.

'Champagne? Or would you prefer a beer, Mark?' Carmen asked.

Percy spotted Simon scurrying out of the bathroom in a white towelling robe, his hair wet from the shower.

'Running a bit late,' he called. 'Be with you in a mo.'

The doorbell rang and Carmen went to answer. Percy wished she hadn't worn the strappy, figure-hugging cobalt-blue dress she'd picked up in the sales last summer. It was far too tight, really – a size ten. Who was she trying to kid?

She'd been so excited that she'd managed to squeeze into it she'd got carried away. Plus the assistants kept telling her how slim it made her look. But they would, wouldn't they? They didn't have to wear it.

The dress *was* flattering when she stood up, Percy knew. But she was slightly worried the seams might split when she sat down. She'd have to be careful not to eat too much at dinner.

What would her mother say if she could see her? Percy

could almost hear Antonia's voice, soaked in honey, dripping acid. 'Darling, what a fabulous dress!' Antonia would smile, clapping her hands. 'But don't you think it would hang better if you lost a few pounds?'

Antonia was always having a go at Percy about her weight. Always had done, for as long as she could remember. Granted, Percy had been a chubby child, but she'd grown out of it. No thanks to her mother, who'd glare at her over the table if she took an extra potato, and insist, when everyone else had pudding, that Percy should have a piece of fruit instead.

Antonia herself was always svelte and immaculate. She spent hours on her appearance. It mattered to her hugely. Percy felt she could never live up to her mother's ideals, fearing she was a terrible disappointment. No wonder she was insecure about her looks even now. She'd sworn never to criticise her own boys like that. It was soul-destroying.

She tried to brush her mother away. 'Doesn't the garden look beautiful?' she said, turning to Mark. He scowled at her.

Jonty, Patrice, Suzanne and Justin joined them. Suzanne looked almost unwell, she was so pale and drawn. She'd obviously been crying.

'I'm so sorry,' Percy said, kissing her friend and squeezing Justin's arm. Suzanne had called Percy from the hospital to tell her all about it. 'How's Lara now?'

'Sleeping,' Suzanne said. 'Fortunately she didn't need stitches, just bandaging up.'

Percy shot her a sympathetic glance. She was glad that Suzanne and Justin had come. They weren't going to, but Carmen had insisted it would do them good. They'd obviously had a terrible shock, though.

Justin turned to Carmen. 'I need a drink.'

Simon stood in front of the French doors. He was so tall he practically had to stoop to get through. His silver hair was slicked back. Carmen passed him a cold beer which he took, silently.

'Obviously the women all know each other,' Carmen said, smiling. 'But, Jonty, have you met Simon, my partner? And this is Justin, Suzanne's husband. And Mark, Percy's other half.'

They shook hands.

'I know Mark,' Jonty said. 'But I haven't met Justin. And Simon only in passing.'

Percy thought Justin looked strained, like an overstretched violin string. He took a long gulp of beer, nearly finishing the bottle. Suzanne drained her glass, too. She laughed nervously. 'We needed this, I can tell you,' she said.

Jonty looked embarrassed. 'Patrice told me you've been having a spot of trouble . . .' he mumbled. Why did men find it so difficult to talk about emotional things?

Justin cleared his throat and fiddled with the belt on his jeans. 'So you're all Gym and Slimline widowers, too?' he said, changing the subject. 'Suzanne wouldn't miss Saturday morning Pilates for anything. It's sacred.'

Jonty's eyes fell on the younger man. 'The girls do seem keen on it,' he agreed 'Do you think it's all a cover?' He took a sip of champagne and raised his eyebrows quizzically.

Justin laughed. 'What? They're really going to a mass orgy or something?'

Jonty smiled, revealing reddish gums. Gingivitis, thought Percy. She was surprised Patrice hadn't packed him off to the hygienist. Percy might be sloppy about lots of things, but she was most particular about oral hygiene.

Jonty and Justin were still talking. 'Perhaps we should start a rival club,' Jonty suggested. 'Nothing too strenuous, mind you.'

Justin took another beer from the ice bucket. 'A down-the-pub club?' he said.

'Superb idea,' Jonty agreed. 'You're on.'

Percy looked at Suzanne. She seemed less uptight than when she arrived. The champagne was taking effect already.

54

Suzanne tutted. 'You boys should come to Pilates, you know,' she said. 'It's terribly good for men too. It strengthens the core muscles.' She pulled herself up as tall as she could, which wasn't saying much. Even in heels she was titchy. Her green eyes looked bigger than usual.

Mark looked down ruefully at his beer belly. 'I don't think I've got any core muscles to strengthen,' he said.

Percy gave his paunch a playful prod. 'You're right,' she smiled. Mark brushed her hand away and moved closer to the men. They formed their own tight little group.

Patrice said something about Seamus, but Percy didn't hear. Mark was all jokey and chatty now that he wasn't with her. He was positively animated.

Her eyes lingered on him. Despite the bald patch, he was still handsome, especially when he smiled. The other men were good-looking, too, she reflected, though Jonty was too stocky for her taste.

The best bit about Jonty was his thick, dark-blond hair. Every now and then the fringe would flop over his face and he'd sweep it back in one smooth motion. He looked immaculate, as usual, in a beautifully pressed pale-blue shirt. He seemed to be holding court, making the others laugh.

Justin was a honey, in his low-slung jeans and Birkenstock sandals. He was leaning against the wall, his left arm behind his head. You could see a sliver of tummy between his waistline and the top of his T-shirt. It wasn't hard to see why Suzanne had fallen for him.

Simon, the tallest by several inches, looked distinguished, even from behind, in chinos and a stripy shirt. Whippet-thin, he knew how attractive he was. It was all in the body language.

Carmen called them in to dinner. She sat at the head of the table, nearest the kitchen, between Jonty and Justin. Percy had Justin on her right, Simon on her left. Percy was relieved the seams of her dress seemed to be holding.

She considered for a moment, then popped a brown roll on her plate.

The room grew noisier and warmer as the wine and conversation flowed.

Percy listened as Carmen leaned over to Justin. 'How do you find being with the children all day?'

Justin took a spoonful of crème brûlée. It wasn't quite as crispy on top as it should be, but he didn't seem to notice. 'I love it. The kids are brilliant – most of the time.'

'But don't you mind being the only man at the school gates?' Carmen found the arrangement puzzling. She could never imagine her father taking on the role of house-husband. He'd find it humiliating.

'Not really,' Justin replied. 'The mums seem to accept me. I'd like to get to know a few more blokes locally, though, for the odd game of squash.'

Carmen clapped her hands. 'Jonty's your man,' she said, clearly pleased she'd thought of it. She turned to the older man. 'You play squash, Jonty, don't you?'

Jonty dabbed his mouth on a napkin and put it back on his lap. 'Sure,' he said. 'Do you fancy a game, Justin?'

Justin nodded. 'Great idea.'

Jonty appeared pleased. 'I'll give you a call next week,' he said, revealing a sliver of red gum again. Percy had to refrain from whipping out the dental floss she kept in her bag for emergencies.

Simon brought out the after-dinner drinks on a tray. Percy watched him pour a large brandy for himself and finish it in a few, quick gulps.

'How long are you home for this time?' Percy asked. She'd hardly spoken to Simon all evening. She'd been listening to Justin, Carmen and Jonty.

'Couple of months, I imagine, unless another contract comes up in the meantime,' Simon replied.

'Do you like working abroad?' said Percy.

'Wouldn't have it any other way. I can't stand being in the same place for too long.'

He ran his hand through his neat silver hair. Percy noticed a gold signet ring on his little finger.

'I've always travelled,' he went on. 'Father was in the army, you see. Went all over the world. It's in my blood.'

Percy caught sight of Carmen leaving the room. Had she heard what Simon said? Percy hoped she wasn't upset. He was wretchedly non-committal.

Soon Carmen reappeared with an ebony box inlaid with what looked like mother-of-pearl. Inside there were cigarette papers, a lighter and a stash of dark brown cannabis resin.

Percy watched, fascinated, as her friend rolled a joint. Her thin fingers were so nimble. Carmen licked the edge of the paper, placed it between her lips and bent forward to light it over a candle. Then she sat back, took a couple of deep, long puffs and closed her eyes.

Satisfied, she smiled at Jonty and passed the joint to him.

'Thanks,' he said, taking a big drag. Within seconds, his face turned red and his eyes started to water. Percy dug her nails into the palm of her hand to stop herself laughing. He clearly hadn't done this for a while.

Nor had she, for that matter. Only once or twice since university. She wasn't shocked, though. She liked the fact that Carmen brought out this wild streak in her. Her dinner parties were never boring. They made Percy feel young and a bit silly again.

When it came to her turn, she took a quick puff and felt woozy immediately. Oh dear. She was out of practice, too. She took a sip of water and glanced at Mark. She hoped he might look back but he either deliberately ignored her or didn't notice.

She turned to Justin on her right, prodded him in the ribs. 'Your go.'

She felt something light brush her left thigh. It stopped, then started moving up, between her legs. She swung round.

Simon's face swam in front of hers. 'You look very lovely tonight, if I may say so,' he whispered.

She could smell the brandy on his breath. Lord! What should she do? She scraped her chair back and got up, steadying herself on the table. 'Time for some music,' she said quickly, walking to the CD player.

She chose some Aretha Franklin and started swaying to the rhythm. She didn't look at Simon. The lech. 'Come on, girls, come and dance,' she called.

Suzanne joined her.

'What about you, Pats?' Percy asked, signalling to Patrice to come over.

Patrice glanced at her husband. Did he shake his head, as if to say no – or was Percy imagining it? 'Too tired,' Patrice called back, smiling. Percy shrugged.

She noticed Simon move to the sofa and she turned away quickly. She felt so confused. Should she tell Carmen or pretend that it hadn't happened? She wondered how she'd want her friends to behave if Mark did the same to them.

A nasty thought crept into her head.

Maybe Mark's having an affair. Maybe that's what this is all about?

She flicked a strand of hair from her eyes and tried to lose herself in the music.

Carmen was pleased the evening was going so well. Jonty was good company and Justin made her laugh. He was very polite. He'd asked a lot about her business so Carmen had got out a basket with some of her fabric swatches to show him. She'd pulled out some storyboards she was working on, too.

He'd said he liked the curtain samples and the Louis XV theme. He seemed genuinely interested in interior design. He was probably just humouring her, but he was a good actor.

Carmen glanced at Simon on the sofa. He looked a little squiffy. Unlike him to drink too much. He was usually more self-controlled. She felt down, despite the great company. She guessed that their chat earlier, in the bedroom, had unsettled Simon more than he'd let on.

He'd poured himself another brandy, she'd noticed. Carmen had heard snatches of a conversation he'd been having with Percy. '. . . can't stand being in the same place for too long,' he'd said.

It wasn't what she'd needed to hear right now. She finished the joint and stubbed it out. Considered rolling another. She was in the mood for getting stoned. She didn't care what anyone thought.

She'd seen Percy look at Mark earlier on, longer than was strictly necessary. What did that mean? Had she been trying to tell him she was ready to go? Mark hadn't noticed, though.

They'd been married so long, that pair. Sweet. They must have all sorts of secret codes. They probably knew what the other was thinking by now. How lovely to be so comfortable and secure with someone. Carmen couldn't imagine it.

Percy was dancing now, though. Great, thought Carmen, she and Mark had decided not to go home yet after all. Carmen wished Patrice would join in the dancing, she was always so uptight. It would do her good to let her hair down for once.

Carmen hadn't seen Percy's sexy blue dress before. It seemed to hug her in all the right places. But was it comfortable? It looked awfully tight.

She got up to join Percy and Suzanne. 'You look great,' Carmen said to Percy. 'Where d'you get the frock?'

She saw Justin and Jonty wander into the garden, followed by Mark and Simon. Why did men never seem to like dancing? She'd bet Justin was a cool dancer, as well as a great dad. Come to think of it, all the men were dads, apart from Simon. That was funny, considering Justin was so much younger.

The conversation she'd had with Simon came back to her again. It had made her both sad and uneasy. What if he changed his mind in a year or two and decided he did want babies after all? It might be too late by then. What if he found another woman to have them with – or if she changed her mind? She might regret it for the rest of her life.

Carmen wondered if Simon would stay in her flat for the entire two or three months, or if he'd want to spend time in his own. She hoped not but she didn't like to ask. She didn't want him to see her face if the answer wasn't what she wished. She didn't do disappointment.

Patrice was sitting alone, watching them dance. 'Come on, Pats!' Percy called. Patrice shook her head again.

Carmen shrugged and swished her hair around like a horse's tail. 'Women do get weary, wearing the same shabby dreee-es,' Aretha crooned.

Carmen closed her eyes and tried to imagine that she was on stage, dancing in front of a rapt audience. 'Oh, oh, oh, try a little tenderness.'

'Do you want to talk?' Percy asked tentatively. She was terrified of what he might say, but she couldn't stand the cold, silent treatment. It was tearing her apart.

Mark stared straight ahead. 'What's there to talk about?'

Percy wrapped her coat around her. The cobalt-blue dress felt tighter than ever. She couldn't wait to strip off. They were late for the babysitter, but they hadn't far to go. She took a deep breath. 'If you remember, you stormed off on Wednesday, told me you'd had enough,' she said anxiously. 'What was that supposed to mean? That you were fed up and wanted a holiday? Or that you don't want to be married to me any more?'

'I don't know,' Mark replied.

Percy shivered. Her shoes hurt and her brain felt fuzzy. She was still shocked about Simon, too.

'I don't understand,' she said. 'It sounds like you're telling me it's all over.'

'Yeah, well, maybe it is.' His voice sounded dull.

'Do you really mean that?' Tears started to well up. Percy hated the way she always cried; it was so childish.

'Of course not.' Mark's words came out more softly now. 'I just get so fed up with it all.'

Percy detected a glimmer of hope. He wouldn't say 'fed up' if he hated her. Maybe he still cared for her a little.

'I'm sorry about the overdraft,' she said in a small voice.

Buoyed by his silence, she went on. 'I – I wish we could see more of each other. We never seem to go out together – just the two of us – like we used to.'

She could sense him stiffening. She'd gone too far, dammit.

'Yeah, well, maybe if you'd stop spending money on stupid things like table lamps we could afford to go out,' he snapped. 'Anyway, now's not the time to talk.'

Percy bit her lip. She wanted to scream.

'But when is the right time, Mark?' she pleaded. 'You're never at home. It's never the right time.'

They were outside the front door. He got the keys out of his pocket and shoved them in the lock. She followed him up the hall into the sitting room. The TV was on too loud.

She stood beside him, smiling. You'd never know anything was wrong. 'Hi, Maisie,' Percy said. 'Everything OK?'

Maisie flicked the TV off and got up. She had a purple streak in her hair and a nose ring. She looked scary but was actually very sweet. Percy liked her. She wasn't entirely comfortable with the fact that Maisie sometimes took the nose ring out and let the boys play with it, but she turned a blind eye.

'I didn't hear a squeak from Rowan,' Maisie said, smiling. 'Ben came down and watched TV with me for a bit but he went back to bed when I told him.'

Mark looked at Percy. His eyes were narrow, black slits.

'You'll have to pay Maisie. I haven't any cash,' he muttered.

Percy rootled in her bag and produced a twenty-pound note and five pounds in coins.

'Thanks,' Maisie smiled again. 'How was your evening?'

'I'll walk you home,' Mark said quickly.

Chapter Eight

'Jonty, look.'

Jonty pushed open the door and tiptoed into the room.

'Look, isn't he beautiful?' Patrice whispered. She was sitting on the edge of the bed, gazing at her sleeping son. She pulled back the duvet slightly so Jonty could see Seamus's face more clearly. The room smelled sweet, of talcum powder and new baby skin. 'Doesn't he look like a little cherub?' Patrice said.

Jonty bent down and gently stroked Seamus's cheek with the back of his hand. 'He does. A little angel.'

Patrice pulled the cover up again, rose and followed Jonty out of the room. 'Did you enjoy the evening?' she asked, squeezing cream on to some cotton wool.

'I did. How about you?'

'Yes. What did you make of Simon?'

Jonty took off his handmade leather slippers and climbed into bed. 'Pleasant enough,' he said, turning to switch off the bedside light.

'And Justin?'

'Nice chap. Seems very fond of Suzanne and the children.'

'He's good-looking, isn't he?' Patrice said. She dropped a ball of cotton wool in the wastepaper basket, then walked over to join her husband.

'I'm not a woman, I don't notice things like that,' Jonty replied.

Patrice laughed. 'Well, you might have an opinion, that's all.'

She switched off her own light and lay with her back to Jonty. He nuzzled up behind her, putting his arm round her waist and his face in her hair.

'Jonty?' she whispered.

'Yes.'

'Seamus is so gorgeous.'

'Mmm.'

'Wouldn't you like another one?'

She could feel her heart thumping. He pulled his arm away. 'We've had this conversation before, Patrice,' he groaned. 'We're too old. You'd be nearly forty by the time it was born, and that's assuming you'd have no trouble conceiving second time round.'

Patrice bit her lip. 'Forty isn't old. Look at Suzanne – and Percy. And maybe I wouldn't have taken ages to conceive Seamus if we made love more than once in a blue moon . . .'

Jonty was silent, but she could feel his anger spreading like a cancer in the dark. She wished she could take the words back, swallow them whole. 'I'm sorry, I didn't mean to—'

'What are you, some kind of bitch on heat?' His words flew out and hit her like shards of glass.

She gasped. 'No.'

'Then stop going on about it.'

'I'm sorry.'

He waited and she sensed the anger subsiding. His body started to relax. He sighed, wrapped himself around her, spoonlike. 'Night, Pats. Love you.'

'Love you too.'

She lay there, listening to his breathing becoming longer and slower. Soon he was fast asleep, snoring lightly. Gently, she lifted his arm off. It felt so heavy. He muttered something and rolled over to face the other way.

She slipped out of bed. Downstairs, she took a tartan blanket from the back of the armchair and lay down on her side on the sofa. Something startled her. She sat up again, quickly. What was that? Just the wind. Relieved, she pulled the blanket over her. It was wool, a bit scratchy, but she didn't mind.

She slid her hand between her legs and began to stroke herself, allowing her mind to roam free. In her fantasies she always gave herself to Jonty gladly, and he gave himself back with gusto. Her whole body felt alive, on fire.

They always came together, because they were made for each other, two halves of the same whole. A perfect fit. She wished she could make the feeling go on for ever.

When it was all over, she realised she was crying. She wiped her eyes with the back of her hand. It had been such a relief. A release.

She could feel the scratchy blanket against her skin again. It reminded her of what she'd just done, of what she didn't have.

She'd given everything to Jonty. She'd die for Jonty. Yet he didn't want that most secret, precious part of her – her sexuality. Her whole body ached to think of it.

She couldn't understand it. Maybe he found her unattractive. Maybe he didn't love her quite as much as he said he did. She brushed the thought away. That was too horrible to contemplate. Don't be stupid, Patrice. Pull yourself together.

She rose quickly and tiptoed back upstairs. Luckily, Jonty didn't wake. He'd have wanted to know what she was doing. She slipped in beside her husband again and fell into a deep, dreamless sleep.

'Are you sure you don't want me to come with you?' Jonty looked up from the *Sunday Times*. He had his small gold-rimmed reading glasses on. Patrice thought they made him look distinguished.

She was trying to put Seamus's denim jacket on. He was protesting, making it as difficult as possible. 'No, honestly,' she said. 'You know what Father's like, and you'll enjoy having a day to yourself.'

Jonty smiled. 'Well, I do have work to do,' he admitted. 'And I'm quite tired after the party.'

There was no hint in his behaviour of what had gone on between them the night before. He seemed totally at ease. Patrice was relieved. Peace had been restored, thank goodness. That was the main thing.

The car seemed to drive itself to her father's house in Epsom as if on autopilot. Seamus went bowling down the garden path in front of her towards the old man. He was standing, motionless, on the red doorstep, his arms hanging stiffly at his sides.

Patrice willed him to smile and hold his arms out, but he didn't. The small boy stopped halfway down the path, looked confused, wheeled round and ran back to his mother.

Patrice picked her son up and gave him a cuddle, instead. 'Hello, Father,' she said.

The old man coughed. 'Come inside,' he grunted.

It was gloomy in the hallway and the air felt dank. There was an overpowering whiff of boiled vegetables.

'Pooh,' Seamus said.

Patrice whispered in his ear. 'Shhh, don't be rude.'

He wriggled out of her arms. 'Can I see Missy?' He went on tiptoes and tried to reach the knob on the closed sitting-room door.

'Not in there,' his grandfather said. 'In the kitchen. You can't do so much damage.'

He shuffled down the corridor. Patrice followed, gritting her teeth. Don't say anything, it's only for a couple of hours. 'How are you, Father?' she asked, perching on a kitchen stool. It wobbled. She got up and looked underneath, to check. One leg was broken so she pushed it aside and fetched another.

Seamus bent down to stroke Missy, the cat.

'Same as usual,' her father replied. 'Old ticker's not so good. I take it you're staying for lunch?'

Missy hissed and darted out of the cat flap. Seamus tried to grab her tail. His grandfather chuckled. 'You won't be able to catch her,' he said. 'She's too quick for you. Go on, go and find her in the garden.' He opened the back door and Seamus bolted out.

'We'd love to stay for lunch,' Patrice said, checking for her son through the kitchen window. 'Anything I can do to help?'

Her father shuffled over to the cooker. A pan was bubbling away on the hob. He poked a knife into something in the water. He was wearing carpet slippers, corduroy trousers and a plum-coloured cardigan. There was a hole in the right elbow.

'It's nearly ready,' he said. 'You can lay the table. We'll eat out here. Less mess.'

They sat in silence, shovelling mushy sprouts and leathery meat into their mouths. Patrice found it hard to swallow. She couldn't think of anything to say.

Seamus pushed his plate away. 'Don't like it,' he said, wrinkling his nose.

'Just do your best,' Patrice told him gently.

Her father tut-tutted and peered at his grandson over grimy spectacles. 'What's the matter? Not good enough for you, young man?' He turned to Patrice. 'You've spoiled him. In my day we had to eat everything on our plate.'

Just ignore him. We can go soon.

'I'm bored,' Seamus whined. He climbed down from the table and started crawling on the floor.

'Don't do that, you'll get dirty,' Patrice scolded. 'Father, do you have any pens, paper, that sort of thing? Seamus loves drawing. He's very good at it.'

The old man got up slowly and took her half-eaten plate from the table. He shook his head. 'There may be some pens in your room,' he muttered. 'You can go and look if you like.'

She pushed open the bedroom door. Her stomach lurched, as it did every time she went in there. There was the same old, tired pink wallpaper, the nasty nylon quilt on the bed. The dusty, faded curtains; musty smell. He'd even left her skating poster above the little blue sink. It was torn and curling up at the corners.

She opened the top drawer in the old-fashioned wooden desk. She could still make out the letters PG – Patrice Gardiner – which she'd scratched with Biro into the wood. She found a felt tip and notepad.

'Father, don't you think you should redecorate? Jonty and I would be glad to pay,' she asked, walking back into the kitchen. He continued washing the dishes.

'Ha!' he said, his back still turned to her. 'That's all you lot think about. Money. Think it's the answer to everything. Well, I'll tell you one thing,' he said, swivelling round now to face her. There was grey stubble on his chin and the whites of his eyes were yellow. 'It won't change what happened, can't make that better now, can it?' He sounded almost triumphant.

Patrice picked up a tea towel and started to dry the plates on the draining board. 'Oh Father,' she said gently. 'That was all so long ago. Can't you move on, try to live in the present?'

He clicked his tongue and went over to the table to collect the glasses. He plunged them in the hot, soapy water. Patrice hoped they wouldn't break. 'I mean, Mother—' she ventured.

'Don't mention that woman's name in this house.' His face was red now, his eyes flashing.

Seamus looked up from his drawing. 'Mummy?'

'Shh, it's all right,' Patrice reassured him. 'What a lovely picture. Can you do a tree, too?'

They drank their coffee and the old man dipped Rich Tea biscuits into his. Brownish sludge collected in the corners of his mouth. Patrice had to look away. She wanted to laugh or cry when it was time to leave, she couldn't decide which. 'Come on, Seamus, get your coat on,' she said.

She could feel her spirits lifting with each mile that she put between herself and her father's house. But that was bad of her, wasn't it? Unnatural. There again, there was nothing natural about the way he treated her – or Seamus.

'I don't like Grandfather,' Seamus said from the back of the car.

'You mustn't say that,' Patrice admonished.

'But he doesn't like me,' Seamus persisted.

'Of course he does. You're his grandson.'

Later, when she'd finally got Seamus to sleep, Jonty put his arm around her on the sofa.

'Father still blames me for what Mother did,' she said. 'He still honestly seems to think it's somehow my fault.'

Jonty stroked her hair with his free hand and looked her in the eyes. 'You're really upset, aren't you? You should stop going. It always makes you sad.'

She rested her head against her husband's chest. He felt so solid, comforting. He was her rock. 'I can't stop going. He's not very well,' she replied. 'He looked awful, actually. And he is my father, after all.'

'Well, he hasn't exactly behaved like a father,' Jonty reminded her.

'I know,' she said. 'But he's the only family I have, remember.'

Jonty patted her knee. 'You've got us, you silly girl,' he said. 'Seamus and me. We're the only family you need.'

Chapter Nine

❦

Percy was fast asleep when Rowan burst into the bedroom.

'Mummy, I've done a wee wee in my bed.' She lay there for a moment, holding her breath. Was she dreaming? She checked the clock: 6 a.m. She'd only been in bed an hour. Then she remembered. She felt sick. She'd lost again. How could that have happened?

'Shit,' she heard Mark mutter. 'He'll have to go back into nappies.'

She opened her eyes. Rowan's dark outline was hovering by the door. Somehow, she managed to pull herself out of bed, shivering. 'Quick, jump in with Daddy,' she whispered, holding out her arms to her small son.

Rowan had stripped off his soggy pyjama bottoms. His bare bum was white in the dark. He hopped in on Percy's side.

'I'll go and change the sheets,' Percy said, pulling on her dressing gown. Mark, who'd been facing the wall, turned and put an arm round Rowan, pulling him close.

'Come here,' he said gruffly, kissing Rowan's soft head. He never cuddled her like that any more.

She stripped the wet bed and padded downstairs to shove the sheets in the washing machine. Then she filled the kettle and made a cup of Earl Grey.

Worry coiled through her. Her insides felt knotted and painful. She was going to have to do something – quick. She'd lost the rest of her winnings – around £1,000 – last night. And in a moment of madness, she'd dipped into the credit card. Lost another £1,000 on that, too. Mark would go crazy if he found out.

It had all started so well. She'd broken even for the first few hours but then she'd started losing. By 2 a.m. she was $1,200 down. Now, in the cold light of day, she could see that she'd panicked, desperate to claw back some funds. She'd lost sight of the odds and stats, played every pot regardless of her cards. She was playing on tilt – spewing out money like a broken fruit machine. Emotion, not logic, had taken over.

Finally, exhausted and hopeless, she'd crashed out at 4 a.m., $4,000 – around £2,000 – lighter. She realised, with a pang, that she'd been every poker player's dream opponent. It hurt her pride as well as her pocket to think she'd played so badly.

She shuddered, then spotted her old trainers by the door. The gym. Thank God for that. She was supposed to be doing a class this morning. It would take her mind off what had happened. She could forget everything when she was having a really good workout. And she was so lucky to have Patrice, Carmen and Suzanne. She didn't know what she'd do without them.

Percy had met them soon after the club opened. They did the same classes and she'd liked the look of them immediately. Funny how you could often pick out the women you found interesting and were most likely to get on with without even talking to them. But you could also get it wrong sometimes, too.

In this case, though, Percy's instincts had been spot on. The four women had soon got chatting and had really hit it off, despite being so different. In fact the differences somehow made their friendship more fun and interesting.

Percy pottered about, watering the herbs on the windowsill and unloading the dishwasher. It was important to keep busy, distracted. She caught sight of the computer in the corner of the room, then looked away quickly. It would be insane to log on now. It would have to wait till tonight. Forget just playing on Tuesdays and Thursdays only. Now, she'd have to grab every opportunity she could.

She went into the sitting room. Her book was lying face down on the coffee table. She picked it up and read a couple of chapters. She must have dozed off because Ben's Spiderman alarm clock nearly made her hit the ceiling. 'Time to get dressed,' she shouted upstairs. She could hear him moving around in the room above.

He thumped into the kitchen in his uniform. 'Can I have toast and jam – no butter? You always put too much on.'

She pretended not to notice his criticism. 'Morning, darling, how did you sleep?' she asked as Ben plonked himself down at the table.

'Orange juice or milk?' she enquired when he didn't respond.

'Apple juice.'

'Please?'

Ben scowled. 'Please.'

Percy looked in the fridge. 'Sorry, apple juice is out.'

Ben groaned. 'Why do you never buy nice things? Matthew's mum buys smoothies. And she makes waffles for breakfast.'

Percy's body started to go hot. The words rattled out like gunfire. 'You rude boy,' she spat. 'You can make your own effing breakfast if you're going to behave like that.'

Ben looked at her, startled. She'd startled herself. She noticed tears springing in the corners of his eyes. God, she was on a short fuse, she thought. Poor Ben. He could be a little tyke sometimes, but he was only seven. And he didn't deserve to be sworn at.

She ruffled his hair. 'I'm sorry,' she said. 'But you can't always have treats for breakfast, you know.'

"S'all right,' Ben replied, forgiving her. He was always forgiving. He perked up. 'Can I have a friend over for tea?'

Percy pondered for a moment. She was so tired, and she needed to be on top form tonight, it was imperative. 'I'm sorry, darling,' she said, shaking her head 'I've got masses to do today. You can have a friend soon, I promise.'

Ben's shoulders drooped. He looked down at his black school shoes. Percy wondered vaguely how long it was since she'd polished them. 'I haven't had a friend round for ages,' he said.

It was true, she thought sadly. He used to have someone for tea practically every day. There was always a houseful.

She pushed the thought away. It was too painful. She'd make it up to him – as soon as she'd recouped her losses.

Mark appeared at the kitchen door. He'd stayed in bed too long and was late. It was his usual morning routine. 'I'm knackered,' he said, slapping a tea bag into a mug and filling it with boiling water. 'You'll have to stop giving Rowan drinks in the evening.'

'He can't help it,' said Percy, spreading jam on Ben's toast. 'I can't not give the poor chap a drink if he's thirsty. And he'd hate to go back into nappies. We'll just have to put up with it till he grows out of it.'

Mark gulped down his tea, grabbed his work bag and stormed out of the house, slamming the door. Percy put his mug in the sink and scrubbed the tea stains off with a cloth.

She put the mug on the draining board. It was the bright pink one with 'Absolutely Fabulous' written round it in black lettering. Suzanne had given it to her one birthday.

Percy started, recalling something. She scurried into the hall and fished her mobile out of her handbag.

'How's Lara?' she texted. She felt bad. She'd been so caught up in her own problems that she hadn't spoken to Suzanne for several days.

A message pinged back almost immediately. 'L much better thanx. Back to normal stroppy self! C u soon. S x'

That was a relief, anyway. One less thing to worry about.

'I'm going up to wake Rowan up now,' she told Ben. 'We have to leave in twenty minutes. Please learn your spellings.'

Rowan was snoozing peacefully in the corner of the bed she'd had to vacate more than two hours earlier. The little devil. He'd be full of beans all day while it felt like lunchtime to Percy already.

But seeing him lying there like that, his fair hair, still baby-soft, spread out around him on the pillow like a fan, she couldn't really be cross. After all, he was her latecomer, her wonder boy, who brought her so much joy.

She threw on an old pair of jeans and a khaki sweatshirt and woke Rowan with kisses all over his sweet, soft face and arms. Then she carried him, still rubbing his eyes, into his bedroom to get dressed.

Spinning was a forty-five-minute session on bikes rooted to the spot. It made Percy horribly sweaty and out of breath. Good for the legs and bum, though, she had to concede. And a great fat-burner

Sally, the instructor, turned down the lights and put the music on loud. Percy lowered her head and started pedalling away furiously.

The woman beside her turned, grinned and puffed theatrically. Percy puffed back. There was good camaraderie, anyway.

'Go on, you can do it,' Sally shouted as they headed up a virtual hill. Percy put her pressure gauge up. It was agony on the legs. She hoped she wouldn't develop sumo thighs.

'Don't give up now. Think of yourselves in those bikinis on the beach,' the instructor hollered.

Percy pushed harder. Usually, she cheated and didn't raise the pressure too much. But she wanted to punish herself today, and it would be good to be able to wear that green and white spotty bikini without feeling self-conscious.

'OK,' Sally shouted. 'You're at the top of the hill. Now it's a race to see who can get to the bottom first.'

The music, which had been slow and heavy, started to beetle along. Percy's legs whizzed round so fast, she thought she might fall off the bike. She imagined herself chasing after Rowan, on the back of someone else's bike, desperately trying to catch up. It wasn't a pleasant thought, but it made her cycle faster than she believed possible.

The music stopped beetling. 'Well done, ladies. Now slow down gradually,' Sally said. 'Let's get your heartbeats back down.'

Percy wiped her forehead with the towel and took a swig of water.

'Now we're going to do the track all over again,' Sally beamed. Percy wanted to kill her.

The abdominals class was next. Percy got a mat and sat down beside Patrice and Carmen. She was surprised to see Danny walk in, place his mat right at the front of the class and turn to face everyone. 'OK, ladies, I'm taking you today. Let's get started,' he ordered.

He was tall, with nice broad shoulders and muscly arms. He was tanned. Mediterranean-looking, Percy thought. Nice black wavy hair, too.

He lay down on his mat, his knees up, and opened his legs. 'Suck in those abs, imagine there's an orange under your chin, one hand supporting the head – but don't pull it or you'll injure your necks. Remember to breathe, guys, breathe,' he went on. 'Up, two, down, two, up, two, down, two. Now pulse, pulse, pulse, pulse, pulse, pulse, pulse.'

Percy was dismayed to find she was lying with Danny's black, Lycra-clad crotch in full view. She practically had her nose in it when she crunched up from prone.

Her mind started to wander. What would he be like in bed? He was so fit that naked, you'd probably be able to see virtually every muscle beneath his skin. And would his hair be soft to the touch, or wiry?

She stopped herself. This was ludicrous. She was a married mother of two, for heaven's sake. She wasn't supposed even to notice other men, let alone . . .

'Right, guys,' Danny continued. 'Legs up in the air, reach one hand to the opposite foot, twisting from the waist not the shoulder. Now reach, reach, reach, reach. And again on the other side . . . reach, reach, reach, reach. Repeat twenty times on each side.'

Percy groaned. Her stomach was burning. She looked at Patrice and Carmen. They were still going strong, unlike some of the others who'd packed in and were lying, flat out, on their mats. Quitters.

'Come on you lot, keep up,' cried Danny. 'Now, I want you all to imagine you're going to hit the ceiling with the soles of your feet. Don't rock backwards, it's only a small, upward movement but it's great for the lower abs. Do it twenty times.'

Percy imagined running her hands along his chest and down to his tummy button – would it have fluff in it? and below, into the warm, furry area above his . . .

Stop it. Get a grip, girl.

'Purse-phone, you can do much better than that.'

She opened her eyes. 'Pers-*ef*-fon-ee, actually.'

Danny was standing right over her, looking down into her face, grinning. His teeth were very white. 'Come on,' he said. 'See if you can hit my hands.'

He placed the palms of his hands, one on top of the other, three or four inches above Percy's flexed feet. She strained her stomach muscles as hard as she could, took a deep breath and with a mighty push, managed to knock his hands up in the air.

He laughed, in a nice way. 'Good work, babe.'

Babe? What was that about?

At the end of the class, Percy hung back. 'Thanks, Danny.' She smiled. 'I didn't realise you were a fitness instructor.'

'Yeah. I like going to some of the classes myself, though, just to see what other instructors do.'

Percy hesitated. 'Can I ask you something?'

'Sure.' He picked up his towel and sweatshirt.

'I've been coming to this class for a year and I do feel my abs are tighter,' she said. 'But I've still got this flabby bulge here.' She squeezed the stubborn roll of podge below her midriff.

He came up close, examined the roll and gave it a pinch. Cheeky.

'It's not too bad,' Danny said, grinning. 'You just need to do more of those lower ab curls. And make sure you push up as high as you can, like I showed you.'

He winked and gave her bulge another, quite unnecessary, squeeze.

Extremely cheeky. Percy had half a mind to pinch him back, but she managed to restrain herself – just.

Chapter Ten

Suzanne was relishing her new role as Director of Communications, Dace UK. She was responsible for managing all the car company's internal and external communications, supervising a large team of public-relations staff, creating communications strategies and serving as the key spokesperson and media contact for the whole organisation.

The hours were punishing. She wouldn't mind, except that she feared Justin was feeling the strain. She was rarely home before 9 p.m. these days, sometimes later, and she usually had to take work home at weekends, too.

She ran through the itinerary on her desk for the umpteenth time. Everything seemed in order. Her staff had done a good job.

The press and their families were to arrive at the hotel at around 4 p.m. on the Friday. There'd be a fleet of cars to collect them from Stroud railway station. After being shown to their rooms, there'd be a quick briefing downstairs, then tea for the children was at 6 p.m.

She thought for a moment, pulled a red pen from behind her ear and put a squiggle on the six. Actually, five thirty would be better. Justin always fed their kids then. He said they got ratty otherwise. The adults would dine at eight.

Suzanne turned over the page and continued to scan down. On the Saturday morning, she and her team would hold a press conference about the new Amélie, seven-seater, hybrid family car. She double-checked the guest list. She was pleased that a number of features editors from women's magazines were coming as well as the usual macho motoring correspondents.

Suzanne was the one who'd insisted the glossies should be invited. After all, research showed it was women who made the final decision about which family car to buy so it made sense to target them as well. She was going for maximum publicity.

After the press conference there'd be a treasure hunt. Each family would be given an Amélie to test drive and the clues would take them round the pretty Cotswold countryside. Then there was a full programme of entertainment lined up for the afternoon and evening, including clowns and face painting for the kids. No expense was to be spared.

Suzanne was determined the weekend would go well. There was a lot resting on the success of the Amélie. It could revive the company's fortunes.

Justin and the children would be there too. Not Lara, of course, she wouldn't come. Suzanne didn't feel she could trust her enough to stay at home on her own, though. Much to Lara's disgust, she'd been told she'd have to go to a friend's.

Suzanne had already warned Justin that she wouldn't see much of him. She'd be too busy working. He'd have to look after the kids, but they'd love the swimming pool, the entertainment and beautiful grounds. Plus it would look good, when the company was promoting a family car, to show that its staff were family friendly too.

Suzanne was secretly rather pleased that one of her suggestions had been included in the final design – special insulated compartments to store frozen food in on the way back from the supermarket. It was only a small thing, of course, but she'd heard Justin complain that the ice cream and frozen peas were invariably melted by the time you got home. It had stuck in her mind and she'd raised it at a meeting with the Board of Directors.

Not that Suzanne really knew much about supermarket shopping, of course. Even in the bad old days, after Frank had gone, she'd left all the shopping to her au pairs. Now Justin took care of it.

The truth was that she preferred it this way. She hadn't slogged her guts out at university and got a first for nothing. She'd always been determined to make something of herself. Wasn't it odd, though, that back then she'd somehow imagined Frank would be a good partner, that they'd complement one another? She shuddered, recalling her mistake, twisting a coil of hair round and round her finger until it tugged painfully at her scalp.

She and Frank had met at secondary school. They'd fancied each other desperately for months but neither had dared make a move until that New Year's Eve party when large quantities of cheap alcohol had washed away the inhibitions. After that, they were inseparable.

Everyone assumed it would fizzle out when they left school, that Suzanne would leave him behind. After all, she'd got three As at A level and a place at university to read Economics. But he'd flunked his exams and was stuck living with his mum and dad, working part-time in a music shop.

He'd said it didn't matter that he'd done so badly, because he was going to be a famous musician. And the stupid thing was, she believed him. Far from splitting up, he'd visited her every weekend in Leeds and lived the student life without actually being one. They'd had a brilliant time. They were in love. They enjoyed the same things: music, dancing, parties, lazing in bed till midday on a Sunday, reading the papers.

After university, Suzanne had got a job with a top PR firm in London and Frank had come, too. They'd rented a tiny flat in Dalston and she'd rapidly climbed the corporate ladder. She'd found her niche in male-dominated fields like mobile phones and, later, cars. Being a woman was a distinct advantage because she stood out. The fact that she was small and pretty was probably a bonus as well. It knocked people off their guard, made them challenge their perceptions of the product she was promoting.

She glanced at the picture on the wall beside her desk. Lara had given it to her one birthday years ago and Suzanne had had it framed. It had 'My Mummy' written across the top in big, childish writing. Underneath was a drawing of Suzanne: two blobs, one for a head, a bigger one for the body. Stick arms with five fingers on each, two stick legs. There was a huge grin on the face, which was topped off with a mass of orange hair. It made Suzanne smile whenever she looked at it.

Her mind slipped back to Frank; she couldn't help it. It was odd that he'd been so desperate for babies, considering he never bothered with them now. But it had seemed to make sense to her, too, at the time. She was ambitious; she thought big. She wanted lots of everything, including children.

They'd had their two very young, in fairly rapid succession. Lara came first, then Ollie. Suzanne tried to blank those years out because they had been such a nightmare.

She chewed the end of her pen and stared out of the window. It was still surprisingly sunny. Her office was on the fourteenth floor, with magnificent views over London. It made her giddy to peer down at all the tiny people below.

She'd come such a long way from those early days, she thought, that dinky Victorian villa in Stoke Newington. She'd been so proud of it: their first house. Paid for by her, of course. But, God, it had been hard. She was the one who'd got the children up, shovelled in their breakfast, dropped them at the childminder on the way to work, before putting in a full day.

Frank had collected the kids and made tea – or opened a few tins, more like. But he'd always waited for Suzanne to get home to bath and put them to bed, even if she wasn't back till 9 p.m.

She remembered it as a time of permanent, crushing exhaustion. And Frank's band had been going nowhere. They'd had huge rows. By the time she was pregnant with Ollie, Suzanne knew the end was in sight. But it had still hurt desperately when Frank told her he was having an affair with the girl from Snappy Snaps up the road.

She'd felt as if he'd kicked her in the stomach. She hadn't suspected: too busy working her arse off to notice.

She picked up the glossy press pack in her in-tray and examined the photograph on the cover. She really should get on. She'd had such a busy day, though. Endless meetings. She was tired.

The photo was of an attractive, conventional-looking family, grinning in a new silver Amélie: Dad at the wheel, Mum beside him, two blond, blue-eyed kids in the back.

She wondered, for a moment, if it was pure coincidence that, in Justin, she'd found another man who was content for her to be in the driving seat?

She supposed not. But the differences between Justin and Frank were immeasurable. Justin loved being at home with the children and was always there to support her. He understood the deal, whereas Frank had just wanted an easy life.

She twisted the wedding ring on her finger round and round. It felt solid. Comforting. Dear, kind, sexy Justin: she was so lucky to have him.

A thought crossed her mind. She checked her watch. Bugger. It was 7 p.m. already. She felt a stab of guilt. She'd promised him she'd be home by eight. It wasn't as if Justin asked her often. In fact she couldn't remember the last time he'd wanted her to get home early to babysit. And he never complained when she failed to make it to some parents' evening or other. Or said she'd be back for dinner only to waltz in at 10 or 11 p.m.

Would it be quicker to get a taxi to the station? Debatable at this time of night. Maybe, if she got her skates on, she'd just make the 19.35 from Waterloo which would only make her fifteen minutes or so late.

She grabbed her briefcase and shoved in a thick wad of papers. She'd have plenty of time to finish what she was doing and polish her presentation speech tonight while Justin was out.

She rose, took her jacket from the back of the chair and quietly closed her door. There were quite a few people about still, bent over computers. The CEO's light was on, too. She scurried past, her head down, hoping he wouldn't notice.

'He's here, Mummy! Daddy's friend!' Ruby raced down the hall into her mother's arms. She was wearing her pink Barbie nightie and slippers.

'Oh, OK.' Suzanne stood at the door, panting. She'd run practically all the way from the station.

She hung up her jacket and kicked off her high heels. She couldn't wait to strip off her hot, sweaty tights as well. A glass of wine wouldn't go amiss, either.

She walked into the kitchen. Jonty rose from a chair. He'd clearly been entertaining Ruby. There were pens and bits of paper all over the table.

'Hi, Jonty, where's Justin?' Suzanne asked, surprised. 'Sorry I'm late,' she added.

Jonty sauntered over, gave her a kiss on both cheeks. He was wearing white shorts, trainers and a white T-shirt. They looked new, they were so bright and clean.

'No problem.' He smiled. He ran his hand through his blond hair and swept it off his face. Suzanne spotted the sandy freckles on his arm and the gold Rolex.

'The court's not booked till nine p.m. so we'll be all right,' Jonty went on. 'I think Justin's upstairs, looking for his squash racquet. Ruby here's been showing me how to draw cats.'

Ruby skipped over to the table and held up a piece of

paper covered in squiggles. 'Look, Mummy, I had to show that man how to do whiskers.'

Suzanne laughed. '*That man* is Jonty, Ruby, Seamus's daddy – remember?'

Ruby shrugged. 'I forgot.'

Suzanne ran the tap and poured herself a glass of water. 'How's Seamus – and Patrice?' she asked. Jonty seemed not to hear. He was absorbed elsewhere. Suzanne turned towards the door. Justin had appeared, wearing his navy shorts and a crumpled, pale blue T-shirt.

'At last,' he said, triumphant, brandishing a racquet. 'Couldn't find it anywhere.' He was slightly out of breath. 'It was in the cupboard under the eaves in Lara's room. Just shows how long it's been since I've played.'

'I'm so sorry I was late,' Suzanne said.

Justin shrugged. 'No problem. Felix is flat out now, anyway.' He walked over to Suzanne, kissed her lightly on the lips and gave her bottom a pat. Then he grinned at Jonty. 'I'm all set.'

Suzanne watched the two men walk down the drive. It was a beautiful, warm evening and the roof on Jonty's silver BMW was down. Justin climbed in the passenger seat beside the older man and Suzanne and Ruby watched the car pull away.

'Bye, Daddy,' Ruby called. 'Have a nice time.'

Justin turned and waved. He looked so happy, Suzanne thought. It would do him good to have a night out with the boys. She'd have to make a big effort to get away early if he wanted to play squash regularly.

Jonty's blond hair flew out in the wind as the car disappeared round the corner. Ruby took Suzanne's hand. 'It's nice Daddy's found a friend to play squash with, isn't it?' the little girl said.

Suzanne undid the waistband on her skirt and sighed with relief. It was just that bit too tight.

'I hope he doesn't hurt hisself,' said Ruby, gravely.

'Himself,' her mother corrected. 'No, darling, he won't hurt himself. It's not that kind of game. It's a fun game. Now, what have you been reading with Daddy? Let's have a chapter before bed, shall we?'

Lara was sitting at her desk, staring at the computer. It was obvious she'd been chatting to her friends, because she shut the page down immediately.

'I thought you were revising?' Suzanne said.

Don't be confrontational. It'll only get her back up. Keep calm. Try again.

She cleared her throat. 'Darling, don't you think it would be a good idea to do a little work?'

Lara scowled at her mother. There was still a bandage on her left arm, where she'd cut it. 'I've been revising. I'm just taking a break now, OK?'

Suzanne picked a mug and an empty chewing gum wrapper off the floor. She tried to ignore the dirty knickers lying crotch up on the bed. It took a lot of willpower. Lara did seem to have a lot of breaks, too.

'OK, but your exams start in, what, three weeks?'

'I know,' Lara barked. 'I don't need fucking reminding.'

Suzanne flinched. She started to leave the room and noticed the pack of cigarettes on the chest of drawers. Her whole body felt hot. 'You've been smoking again,' she said accusingly.

Lara glanced at the cigarettes. 'I haven't. They're Noah's.'

'I told you we'd cut your allowance if you carried on smoking,' Suzanne snapped. 'It's so bad for you.'

'You smoked,' Lara spat.

'I know, and it took me years to give up.'

Lara got up, stood less than a foot from her mother and practically pushed her nose in her face. 'Anyway, it's none of your business if I smoke. Or what I choose to do with my life. What do you care? You're never fucking here anyway.'

Suzanne didn't mean to do it. There was a rush and something burst in her brain. Her hand shot up and she slapped Lara across the cheek. Not hard, but it was definitely a slap. She could see a red mark appear almost immediately.

Lara gasped. She put her hand to her cheek. Tears sprang in her eyes. 'How dare you do that,' she hissed. 'I can't believe it. You assaulted me. I'm calling ChildLine.'

Suzanne backed away. 'I'm sorry. I didn't mean to,' she whispered. 'It's just . . . you made me so angry.'

Lara walked over to her desk, picked up the phone, started punching in the numbers.

'Who are you ringing?' Suzanne asked. Her mind was racing. She realised she was scared.

'None of your business,' Lara shot back.

Suzanne wished Justin hadn't gone out. This wouldn't have happened if he'd been here. Why wasn't he here? For a second, she felt resentful. Bloody Jonty and his squash.

'Guess what, Noah?' There was a smile dancing on Lara's lips as she spoke into the phone. 'Mum's completely lost it,' she went on. 'She just slapped me across the face.'

Suzanne bit back tears. How could this have come about? She was so organised and in control at work. She never lost her temper. Everyone said how calm she was in a crisis. They called her Superwoman. If only they could see her now. Lara was the only one who had this effect on her. Her own daughter. Suzanne felt tight with misery.

'Can you come over now?' Lara went on. She looked at Suzanne. Smirked. 'Great. I need protection – from my own mother.'

Percy put her arms round Suzanne and held her.

'Don't worry,' Percy reassured. 'These things happen. We

86

all lose our tempers sometimes. I once booted Ben on the bottom. He's never let me forget it.'

'Did you?' Suzanne couldn't quite imagine it. Percy never seemed to get het up.

'Yep,' Percy went on. 'Ben was walking down the road in front of me, kicking a Coke can. I asked him not to several times, told him he might scratch one of the parked cars, but he just carried on. Then, sure enough, he whacked the can into a car. A black Mini Cooper, I seem to recall. He didn't mean to, of course, but I was absolutely furious and I kicked him – quite hard – on the bum. He was outraged. Couldn't believe his own mother would do such a thing.'

Suzanne laughed. 'Served him right.'

She poured two large glasses of wine. They took them in the garden. There was a sweet smell of honeysuckle in the air.

'I so hoped things would be better after the knife incident,' Suzanne said sadly, sitting on a wooden bench. 'We talked a lot, Lara and I, and I thought we'd cleared the air. It seems not.'

Ollie came out with some homework to show them. It was maths graphs. And something about probability. Percy made admiring noises. 'That looks very impressive,' she said.

Suzanne examined the graph and picked her son up on a few points. 'Bloody hell, Suze,' Percy gasped, 'don't tell me you actually understand it?' No sooner were the words out than her hand shot up to cover her mouth. 'Whoops, pardon my French,' she apologised.

Suzanne waved her hand dismissively. 'Oh, don't worry, they've heard far worse,' she said, meaning the children.

'Yeah,' Ollie agreed. His voice came out as a squeak, then a growl. At thirteen, it was just starting to break. 'Mum's favourite expression is "bugger my teddy". Isn't that disgusting? I've even heard Felix say it.'

Suzanne pretended to be shocked. 'Nonsense,' she retorted. 'Felix says "fuck" like his daddy.'

Ollie scratched his head. His fair hair was quite long around his ears. A bit greasy. He had a few spots, too. Where had they come from? But his face was still sweet, vulnerable somehow, and he had a beautiful smile that always made Suzanne's heart melt.

'I'm going to do some PlayStation now,' he said. 'Night, Percy. Night, Mum.' He gave Suzanne a clumsy kiss on the cheek. 'Love you.'

'Love you too,' she replied.

'You see,' Percy said, when he'd left. 'He's gorgeous. The others are, too. They adore you. You're doing a great job.'

Suzanne felt better. Percy was right, she was doing her best. After all, no one was perfect.

Percy rose. She seemed keen to leave. 'Maisie's babysitting,' she explained. 'I promised I wouldn't be late.'

'Won't Mark be home now?' Suzanne asked.

'I doubt it. I never really know with him,' Percy replied.

Suzanne followed her friend to the door. 'It must be hard, not having him there in the evenings.'

Percy put on her short cream linen jacket and did up the buttons. 'Not really,' she shrugged. 'I'm used to it.'

Suzanne gave a sympathetic smile. 'I couldn't imagine it. Justin and I always sit down with a glass of wine at the end of the day and chat. It's our ritual. What do you do? Watch telly?'

Percy gave her friend an odd look, then cleared her throat. 'Yeah, I read, watch telly, that sort of thing.'

'I like the jacket,' said Suzanne, changing the subject. 'New?'

Percy nodded. 'Retail therapy. Hey, you look after yourself,' she said. She gave Suzanne a hug. 'And stop worrying. You're a fabulous mum.'

*   *   *

Suzanne tiptoed upstairs and knocked on Lara's door. The room was dark, save for the light coming off the TV screen. There was an amorphous lump on the bed. The air was incredibly hot and close, and there was a strong smell of cheese and onion crisps.

As her eyes got used to the gloom, Suzanne could make out two figures staring at the screen. They appeared to be fully dressed. That was a relief, anyway.

'Lara, I'm so sorry about earlier on,' Suzanne said softly. Silence.

'D'you think it's time for Noah to go now? You've got school tomorrow.'

'He'll go in a bit,' Lara said, without taking her eyes from the screen. 'We're watching the end of the programme.'

Suzanne could have jumped for joy when she heard the key in the lock. She beetled out of the sitting room and bumped into Justin in the hallway. 'How was it, darling?' she said.

His skin was flushed. He'd obviously had a shower and changed. His hair was still damp and he smelled of soap and shampoo.

'Great,' he said, beaming. 'Jonty won, but I gave him a run for his money. It's so long since I played.'

Justin propped his racquet against the wall and hung his jacket on the banister. Suzanne thought he looked particularly gorgeous tonight. In different circumstances, she'd have pounced on him and dragged him off to bed immediately. He tended to have that effect on her.

'How's your evening been?' he asked.

He noticed her little face was tight, took it in both hands and looked into her eyes. Such a dear, kind look, Suzanne thought. She bit her lip.

'What's the matter, gorgeous?' he asked. 'Let me guess – Lara?' Suzanne nodded.

Justin made a clucking noise with his throat. Suzanne

loved that noise. He held her hand and led her into the kitchen.

'Come on, Suzie,' he said. 'I'll get a glass of water, then you can tell me all about it.'

Chapter Eleven

❧

Carmen kept her pills in the drawer beside her bed. She always took them in the morning, with her first cup of green tea.

She opened the drawer, pushed the white pill out of its plastic bubble and looked at it in the palm of her hand. It was so small. It was amazing to think what power it had.

Her stomach fluttered. Did she dare? Go on, she told herself. Nothing might happen, anyway. She walked into the bathroom, dropped the pill in the loo and flushed the chain. She watched it swirl around in the water before disappearing.

Well, that was that. Now it was a question of wait and see.

She picked up her kit bag and checked her watch. It was 9 a.m. She was meeting Percy in fifteen. She'd have to hurry.

Carmen lowered herself into the warm water. She pressed the button and the bubbles started to rumble round her ankles, fizz up to the surface and pop. There was a nice smell: chlorine mixed with eucalyptus. She watched Percy climb into the Jacuzzi beside her.

Percy was in good shape, Carmen thought, considering she'd had two children. She didn't look bad in that pink tankini. She seemed a bit agitated today, though. Sort of jumpy. Carmen wondered if Rowan had woken early.

The two women lay back, resting their heads on the tiles behind. Carmen shuffled a little to one side, so she could get right in front of a jet. The pressure felt wonderful on her back, like a massage.

'How many lengths did you do?' Percy asked.

'Fifty,' Carmen replied, closing her eyes.

Percy whistled. 'I only managed thirty. Will you show me how to do those snazzy tumble turns sometime?'

'Sure,' said Carmen. 'It's not difficult, honest.'

'How is it, having Simon back?' Percy asked after a while.

Carmen smiled. 'Wonderful.'

Percy cleared her throat. 'Um, there's something I ought to tell you about—'

Carmen interrupted. She was desperate to share her news. It was a miracle she'd managed to wait this long. 'Can I let you into a big secret?'

Percy nodded.

Carmen leaned over and murmured in Percy's ear. 'I've stopped taking the pill.'

She watched Percy's face. Percy's eyes were huge. Carmen wanted to laugh.

'What?' Percy said. 'But I thought . . . ? That's wonderful!'

Carmen reached under the water and put her hand on Percy's knee. 'You mustn't tell anyone, though. Simon doesn't even know yet,' she warned.

Percy's expression changed. Her forehead became a mass of wrinkles. 'He doesn't know? But how will he take it?'

Carmen thought for a moment. 'I reckon he'll be shocked at first, but he'll come round to the idea. Men usually do, don't they? But hey,' she said, trying to sound bright, 'most likely nothing will happen anyway.'

'Hi, ladies!'

Carmen glanced up. She was annoyed to see a pair of hairy legs and some red, skimpy swimming trunks. Well-filled, by the looks of it. She hadn't finished talking to Percy.

He lowered himself into the water and spread himself out. Carmen had to move her foot to get out of the way.

'Mmmmm,' he murmured, enjoying the warmth.

'Hi, Danny,' Percy said. 'Haven't seen you for a while.'

Carmen didn't like the way Danny looked at Percy. It was sort of over-familiar.

'I've been out of the club a lot, doing personal training,' he explained. He had a South London accent. He didn't pronounce his 't's at the end of words.

'Where do you do that, then?' Percy sounded interested.

'At people's houses, mostly. Hey, how's the belly?' He winked at Percy and grinned.

She grinned back, rather foolishly, Carmen thought. What on earth did it mean?

'Needs work,' Percy said. Then she did something Carmen had never seen before. She raised herself out of the water, lifted up her tankini top and wiggled her bare tummy. 'Look,' she said proudly.

'Not bad,' Danny said, eyeing her up. 'But I can help you tone up even more if you want. Give you a few personal sessions. We'll have you super shipshape by the summer holidays.'

Carmen couldn't help staring at Percy. The hussy! She looked thrilled, as if she'd just been given a present.

'Could you really?' Percy said.

'Sure. I'll leave my card at reception,' Danny grinned. 'Just gimme a call.'

The women got out of the Jacuzzi. Percy sat on the wall and stood up, but Carmen took the long way, past Danny and up the steps. He didn't even look at her.

That was strange. Men always looked at her. And she was wearing her slinky gold bikini. He was a total meathead, anyway, she thought. What was Percy thinking of?

'Be careful of that Danny,' Carmen said in the changing room. 'I think he fancies you.'

Percy slipped off her tankini. 'Nonsense!' She laughed. 'I'm practically old enough to be his mother.'

93

Carmen tut-tutted. 'I reckon he likes older women. Have you seen the way he chats up the mums? Besides, you're not exactly over the hill.'

Percy wasn't having any of it. 'He's just friendly, that's all.'

Carmen had to rush straight off after her shower. She'd have liked to stay for a drink but she was meeting a client in central London.

Percy followed her to the car park. 'Are you sure you're doing the right thing?' she said anxiously. 'About you know what? I won't tell anyone, of course. But it's a huge decision.'

Carmen put the key in the ignition and wound down the window. She tried to look more confident than she really felt. 'Thanks, Percy, but don't worry,' she said. 'I'm a big girl. I can look after myself.'

Chapter Twelve

◈

Percy couldn't say anything now, could she? For all she knew, Carmen might even be pregnant already. She'd never be able to tell her about the pass Simon had made at the dinner party.

From now on, she'd just have to keep quiet and not breathe a word of what she really thought of him. It wouldn't be right. But, bloody hell, did Carmen know what she was doing? It was a huge gamble. Now Percy had something else to worry about.

She pulled the card from her jeans pocket. It was white, with black lettering. It looked discreet and professional. 'Danny Fusco, Personal Trainer'. There was a mobile number at the bottom, and a website.

It was tempting, certainly. Percy had always fancied having a personal trainer. It would be interesting to see if he could really make a difference. She remembered the red swimming trunks and tanned torso: he was bloody gorgeous, too. But that was irrelevant. The main thing was, could he get rid of her jelly belly before the summer holidays?

She checked herself. Don't be stupid. It would be a shocking extravagance. They absolutely couldn't afford it. It would make Mark even madder than he was already if he found out.

A familiar, niggling feeling wormed through her: so, was Mark having affair? It would certainly explain a lot. But somehow she couldn't quite believe it. He was too tired, always working. And in a curious way, despite the evidence – the late nights, the physical rejection – it didn't ring true.

He'd never been a flirt. In fact, friends always told her that she was lucky, because he was a one-woman man. And it wasn't as if he were suddenly taking more interest in his appearance, for instance. But still, she couldn't be absolutely sure. The way he was behaving, anything was possible.

A thought crossed her mind and her spirits rose. Maybe if she toned up, looked stunning, Mark would come back to her. She'd pay any sum for that. She shoved the card back into her pocket. There was no hurry. She'd check out the website later.

Percy wandered into the sitting room. It was unusual not to have Rowan right behind her, clinging to her legs, demanding something. She picked up a photo from the mantelpiece and wiped away the dust with her sleeve.

It was her and Mark outside the church on their wedding day. She looked so young and fresh, her long fair hair laced with flowers. She was smiling up at her new husband. He appeared very manly, tall and proud. He was looking straight ahead at the camera, his arm protectively round her waist.

She thought back to how they'd met – in the students' union bar at university. She was going out with someone else at the time but Mark had pursued her relentlessly and seen the other bloke off. She hadn't been that keen on him anyway, he'd never stood a chance against tall, dishy Mark.

After about a year she'd had a wobble – told Mark she was too young to be trapped in some intense relationship. In reality, she feared she was getting in too deep. She was scared that before long Mark would turn around and say he'd had enough, that it was time to move on.

A different kind of man might have been put off, she mused, but not Mark. He adored her, everyone said so. He begged her to change her mind and, in the end, she agreed. He said they were soulmates. After that, she had no more doubts. She felt joyful and secure, probably for the first time in her life. Here was someone who really loved her, imperfections and all. He even claimed he liked her pot belly.

Percy examined the photo more closely. There were pink and white roses round the church door. You could almost smell them, they were so lovely. They'd held the reception at a hotel near the family home. Her mother had made out that the whole thing was a frightful ordeal when, in truth, Percy and Mark did most of the organising. But Antonia wore a fabulous frock and hat and behaved all right on the Big Day.

Percy was a teacher by then and Mark had got into photography. They'd managed to buy a tiny flat in an unfashionable part of London. They worked hard and money was tight, but they were happy. They were in no rush for children. They wanted to have time alone together first.

Ben didn't come along until Percy was in her mid-thirties. They agreed she should give up her job and concentrate on motherhood. Mark was doing well, work-wise, and they could just about afford for her not to earn.

Everyone said having babies would put a strain on their relationship, but Percy hadn't found it to be so. In fact, she and Mark seemed closer than ever.

She smiled, recalling how Ben would lie on his playmat in the evenings, gazing at his mobile, while she and Mark ate supper on their knees and she filled him in on their son's every little new development. Then she'd give Ben his final feed, put him down, and they'd race to bed and make love, quickly and passionately.

She was hazy now about when things started to go wrong. Was it before Rowan was born, or after? They'd moved into a new home, their pretty, four-bedroomed Victorian villa between the park and the river Thames, with a big garden for the children.

Mark had warned that he'd have to work longer hours to pay for it. But Percy knew it would only be for a while. Most young couples she knew were mortgaged up to the hilt. And besides, as he became more successful – which he surely would – things would get easier.

She wondered, though, whether after that, they hadn't seemed to stop talking as much as they used to. She minded, of course, but told herself that it was only a phase they were going through. A very long phase, she thought now, miserably.

She felt a rush of sadness. She'd always imagined, in those early days, that Mark was a great communicator, unlike so many men. It was one of the things that had attracted her to him. Now it occurred to her that perhaps she'd done most of the talking while he'd just listened. Well, he certainly didn't listen any more.

She glanced at the photo again. He had lots of brown, wavy hair back then. Beautiful. It was a shame he'd lost most of it. He'd worshipped her. It was a shame he'd lost that, too. She wiped away a tear. Life could be so hard.

The bell rang and Percy opened the door. A waft of cold air whooshed into the hallway and Antonia pushed past her into the kitchen. She smelled of Pond's Cold Cream and dry-cleaning.

'Can you have a word with Zeus, dear?' Antonia said haughtily. 'He's behaving most oddly.'

'Hi, Mum,' Percy sighed.

Antonia plonked her jacket and handbag on the kitchen table and filled the kettle. 'Your brother won't talk to me,' she said, fishing a porcelain teacup and saucer from the back of the cupboard. She wouldn't use mugs. She said they were common. 'I don't know what's come over him.'

Percy hung her mother's jacket and bag on the coat stand and sat down. 'Could it have anything to do with the fact that you called him a useless little toad in front of his wife and children?' she suggested.

Antonia blew out her cheeks and made a puffing sound.

'Well,' she whined. 'The mirror was wonky. And I had asked him not to put it too high.'

Percy sighed again. 'Maybe you did, Mum, but if your son was kind enough to offer to do it for you, you could at least have sounded grateful, even if he didn't get it exactly right. And there's no need to use horrible names.'

Antonia sat down opposite her daughter, plonked a mug of tea in front of her and ran her perfectly manicured nails round the rim of her own cup.

Percy noticed she'd had her hair done. It was looking particularly sleek and toffee-coloured, a whipped caramel-cream bob.

'I know, I know,' Antonia said. 'And I'm sorry. But will you ring him? Tell him I'm terribly upset. Pretty please?' She tipped her head to one side and gave Percy her best little-girl-lost look.

'All right.' Percy sighed. She was always having to resolve her mother's feuds. If it wasn't Zeus, it was one of Antonia's girlfriends. She said the most awful things sometimes and really upset people.

Percy stared into her mug and blew on the tea to cool it down. She remembered how, once, Antonia had told Percy's godmother Pamela that her granddaughter's legs were too chunky for the short skirt she was wearing in a photo. Pamela had been devastated. She'd been on the phone to Percy immediately and Percy had felt obliged to invite Pamela and the granddaughter and Antonia to a performance of *The Phantom of the Opera*, by way of apology.

Pamela and Antonia had sat, frostily, as far apart as possible. Thankfully, after a few gin and tonics in the interval, the ice had started to melt. It had cost Percy a fortune, though, and caused her a heap of aggro.

In fact the Pamela episode just about summed up Percy's role in her mother's life, she thought, taking a sip of tea: peacekeeper, smoother-over of problems, dogsbody, doormat.

Percy couldn't remember a single occasion when Antonia had put her daughter's wellbeing before her own. With Antonia, it was all me-me-me. If Percy felt tired, Antonia was exhausted. If Percy was unwell, Antonia was so ill she had to go to bed and have Percy bring her soothing drinks.

Perhaps it was because Antonia was an only child, the apple of her parents' eyes, and had never learned to empathise, never stopped craving the centre stage. Whatever the reason, she seemed to believe the world revolved around her and threw terrible tantrums when things didn't go her way.

Percy's father had never stood up to his wife. Dazzled, probably, by Antonia's good looks, wit and sparkle in company, he'd pandered to her egotism right up until his death, making her special little meals, bustling around her like an over-zealous waiter.

He seemed not to notice when Antonia neglected the children or was mean to them. He apparently never thought it odd that, from the age of about seven or eight, it was Percy who got up, made breakfast for herself and her younger brother and took her mother tea in bed.

Percy suspected her father was secretly scared of his wife. Percy certainly was. Looking back, she realised that he'd been weak and foolish, but she couldn't find it in her heart to condemn him. She knew he'd loved his children, in his own way. And they'd had their poker.

But age didn't seem to soften that familiar blow of envy and regret that Percy felt when she heard friends speak affectionately of their mothers. In many ways, she was still the little girl wanting a reassuring cuddle from her mum, wishing she was there for her instead of the other way round, wishing she'd love Percy for who she was, not what she wanted her to be.

'Guess what?' Antonia said, pushing her now empty cup and saucer to one side. 'I've booked a week in Crete in September, to see the ruins. With Isobel.'

Percy snapped out of her daydream.

Antonia looked really pleased with herself. Percy's heart sank. Her mother was always so horrid about Isobel. It was bound to end in tears and, once again, Percy would be picking up the pieces.

She wanted to tell her mother what she really thought. Instead, she walked over to the coat stand and handed Antonia her jacket.

'I have to collect Rowan from a friend's,' Percy said firmly. 'Just be careful, Mum. You're always falling out with Isobel. It might be better to go on your own.'

Antonia waved her hand dismissively and picked up her handbag. 'Nonsense, Persephone,' she said. 'Isobel and I get on like a house on fire.'

Antonia peered round the sitting-room door on her way past. 'You really should sack your cleaner,' she tutted.

If I had a cleaner to sack, Percy thought grimly. She hustled her mother out. 'I have to go.'

Antonia stopped by the front door and checked her reflection in the mirror. 'How's the family? That husband of yours?' she enquired, touching up her red lipstick.

Percy hesitated. It would be so lovely to confide in her mum. Maybe, just maybe, for once, Antonia would say something comforting. She might even be able to help Percy out of this mess.

Her stomach flip-flopped as she remembered her situation. She now owed two thousand pounds on the credit card. How had that happened? She kept losing, that's how. Night after night. She couldn't understand it.

It was an enormous sum for her and Mark – practically enough for a family holiday – but two thousand pounds would mean nothing to Antonia. If Percy could only ask her to write a cheque – Mark need never know a thing.

'Um. Well, actually . . .' Percy began.

'Good,' said Antonia briskly. She pecked her daughter on

the cheek and rubbed off the red mark from her lipstick with a finger. 'Tchh.' Then she took a step back and examined Percy critically. Percy dreaded what was coming next.

'You need to get your hair done,' Antonia admonished. 'Roots.' Percy swallowed. 'And I'm going to send you that diet Isobel gave me,' her mother went on. 'She absolutely swears by it. You can eat as much as you want – so long as it's only vegetables.'

'Great,' Percy muttered.

'Now, don't forget to call that brother of yours for me, will you?' Antonia added, clicking down the path in her high heels. 'And let me know how it goes. I need him to cut down the forsythia at the back of the garden.'

Chapter Thirteen

For some reason, Saturday morning Pilates was packed today. There was hardly any space to put your mat. Suzanne was seriously not in the mood, though. She'd rather have stayed in bed.

'Are you sure you all booked?' said the instructor. She read the names out, one by one, to check. Suzanne waited, with bated breath. At last the instructor got to Persephone.

'Persy-fonny?' she enquired. That was a new one!

'Pers-*ef*-fon-ee,' Percy grumbled. Suzanne had to stifle a snigger. It was a good job Percy's mum hadn't gone for a third child. What would that have been called? Odysseus? Clytemnestra? Poor little sod.

Suzanne turned and smiled at Percy, and spotted Patrice and Carmen at the back of the room. Millicent, unfortunately, had plonked herself right beside Suzanne, who couldn't help noticing the nasty cold sore on Millicent's lower lip.

Run down, Suzanne thought, pleased. Obviously not getting enough nourishment. She'd love to stuff a big fat bun down that smug gob. She checked herself. God, she was a bitch. Why did Millicent always have this effect on her?

It felt terribly hot in the class. They tried out a few new, excruciating moves. Suzanne noticed Millicent giving her a sly look during the push-ups routine. The woman had arms and legs of steel and a backside of fibreglass. Maybe she was really a robot?

Carmen, Patrice and Percy were discussing the wife-swapping weatherman story in the tabloids when Suzanne joined them in the café afterwards.

The place was buzzing. Small children were racing round, playing chase. Groups of men and women were sitting in sports gear round low tables and there was a smell of ground coffee in the air.

Percy had had her hair cut, with more layers put in and honey highlights.

'Looks delish,' Suzanne said, momentarily distracted from the wife-swapping.

'My mother ordered me to,' Percy explained. 'She seems to spend her entire life in the hairdresser's.'

Carmen took a sip of green tea. 'I never really believed wife-swapping went on,' she said thoughtfully. 'Imagine if Mr Brown at number twenty-two put his hand on your knee at a dinner party and invited you upstairs. You wouldn't know which way to look.'

Patrice giggled. 'And what if your husband rather fancied Mrs Brown, while Mr Brown was a toad with a face like a smacked bum? Awkward or what?'

Suzanne hooted. She glanced at Percy, who was staring into her mug.

'You're quiet, Pers,' Suzanne said. 'Not like you to deprive us of your opinions on a topic of major importance like this.'

Percy smiled. 'Bit tired, that's all.' She got up. 'I promised Mark I'd race home to take over the boys.'

Danny appeared from a side door and strolled over to join them. He was wearing a white tracksuit and trainers, sipping water from a bottle.

He greeted them all with a wide grin. 'How are you doing?' he said, before focusing on Percy in particular. 'I haven't heard from you.'

Suzanne glanced at Patrice, who raised her pale, perfectly arched eyebrows. They were practically wiping the ceiling.

'I haven't had a chance to call,' said Percy, lowering her gaze. 'I've been so busy.'

'Well, no time like the present,' Danny replied cheerfully. 'Let's get you booked in right now.'

Percy sat down again.

Danny sauntered over to the reception desk, picked up a big black book that was sitting on the top and brought it back. 'Which day is best for you?' he asked, perching on the arm of Percy's chair.

Percy stared into the distance, thinking through her commitments. 'Um, let me see, Tuesday morning, I guess,' she said finally. 'Could you make it early, like nine thirty?'

'No problem.'

She looked suddenly flustered, as if she'd just remembered something. 'Do I need anything in particular – to wear, I mean?'

'Nope, just tracksuit bottoms, trainers and a T-shirt. Oh, and I need your address.'

Danny passed her a pen and she scribbled her address down in his big black book. He got up to leave.

'Mine's the house with the overgrown garden, halfway down the street on the left,' Percy called after him.

He gave her the thumbs up without turning and loped away. Suzanne couldn't help noticing the contours of his tight buttocks through his trackie bottoms. They looked very rude, somehow.

She was speechless. Patrice's jaw was on the floor, too. 'What are you up to, Persephone Redpath?' Suzanne asked.

Percy went pink. 'Look, I'm just going to have a few personal-training sessions, if that's all right with you?'

'So long as he doesn't offer you any extras,' Suzanne warned. 'And you're not allowed to get too lithe and gorgeous and make us all jealous.'

Percy puffed out her cheeks, putting on her fat face. 'No chance of that, sadly,' she said, picking up her bag and heading for the door. 'See ya.'

'How's Lara?' Carmen asked Suzanne. 'You haven't mentioned her for a while.'

Suzanne wrinkled her nose. 'We-eell,' she said, considering. 'She hasn't cut herself again, thank God – as far as we know. But she did have two holes punched in her left ear the other day, on top of the one that was there already. Needless to say she hadn't informed us of what she was planning.

'I think they look ghastly, but I guess that doesn't matter. At least she went to a reputable ear-piercing place. No emergency visits to casualty required this time.' Suzanne gave a wry smile. 'Noah's still around – unfortunately.'

Carmen looked sympathetic. 'It must be so difficult.'

Suzanne turned to Patrice. 'Isn't it great the husbands get on so well?' she said, changing the subject. She'd clearly had enough of talking about Lara. Patrice nodded.

Carmen looked interested. 'Are they playing much squash, then?'

'Every Tuesday night, and most weekends,' Suzanne replied. An idea struck her. 'Patrice, how about we take the kids to Richmond Park this afternoon, while Jonty and Justin play? You're not doing anything, are you?'

Patrice shook her head.

'You can come too, Carmen,' Suzanne said. 'If you can face our screaming children.'

Carmen laughed. 'Er, no thanks. Simon and I are going to friends. Otherwise I'd have loved to.'

Suzanne chuckled. 'Yeah, yeah.'

Carmen looked suddenly serious. She rested a small, slim hand on Suzanne's arm. There were several thick, ornate silver rings on her fingers which made them look even neater and more delicate.

'I don't have children but that doesn't mean I hate them, you know,' Carmen said gently. 'I might even have one of my own one day.'

Suzanne sat up straight. 'Blimey, you've changed your tune.' She was all set to rattle off some questions, but Carmen had already risen.

She smiled enigmatically. 'Have a nice afternoon, ladies,' she said, walking quickly away. Suzanne and Patrice, silenced for once, stared after her.

It was drizzling slightly, but not enough to keep the women indoors. Typical British summer, thought Suzanne. Huge, dark clouds hung high over the damp trees. It was warm, though. And there were patches of pale-blue sky in the distance, waiting to burst through.

Felix was sitting up in his buggy, under the hood, flapping his arms excitedly at Seamus and Ruby. They were in their element, climbing over logs and having swordfights with sticks.

The looked so merry, in brightly coloured raincoats. Every now and again the children would spot some deer, lurking in the bushes, and race back to their mothers for reassurance. But the deer were far too timid to come anywhere near them.

Suzanne had sensed something was wrong the minute Patrice climbed in the car.

'I don't know what's the matter with me,' Patrice said, staring at the muddy ground and kicking some stones. 'I feel miserable, as if something's missing.'

Suzanne was puzzled. Patrice seemed to her to have everything. 'Like what?' she asked.

'Oh, I don't know,' Patrice replied. 'I feel so hemmed in sometimes, as if I can't breathe. Jonty watches everything I do. Maybe I need to get a job,' she said suddenly.

They stopped and observed while Ruby and Seamus dipped sticks in a puddle. Seamus pulled his out, covered in dirty leaves, and waved it in front of Ruby's face. She yelled and backed away.

'Stop it, Seamus,' Patrice chided. 'You wouldn't like it if Ruby did that to you.'

They continued on their way. Suzanne, unsure what to say, stooped to pick up a plastic car that Felix had thrown out of his buggy. He immediately threw it down again and she put it in the basket underneath.

'Has Jonty always been like that – sort of controlling?' she asked at last. It occurred to her that maybe she didn't know Patrice as well as she thought. After all, they'd only met a few years ago. It wasn't as if they'd been friends since school or university.

'I think so,' Patrice replied. 'Though maybe it's got worse. I didn't mind at first, when we met. I quite liked it. I was so timid and insecure, and Jonty made me feel protected. But he doesn't even want me to go out in the evening with girl-friends on my own.'

Suzanne thought for a moment, decided to play safe. 'What would you do, job-wise?' she asked. She'd always assumed her friend was quite happy being at home, and they certainly didn't need the money.

Patrice put her hands in her pockets. 'I guess I'd go into law. I'd need to do some courses. I never practised, remember, because Jonty asked me to pack it all in when we married. But I've got the basic qualifications.'

'What about Seamus?'

Patrice had obviously given this some thought. 'I could wait till he starts school then get some sort of nanny.'

'And how would Jonty feel about that, do you think?'

Patrice stopped. A frown spread across her forehead. 'He'd hate it,' she said. 'He wants me at home. I reckon he'd feel threatened.'

Suzanne stared at her, open-mouthed. 'Threatened? Why?'

'Because he wants me to be dependent on him,' Patrice explained. 'That way, he knows I won't leave him.'

Suzanne laughed. 'You can't be serious?'

Patrice was silent.

'But that's ridiculous,' Suzanne went on. 'You wouldn't leave him anyway.'

'I know,' Patrice said. 'But beneath all the bluster and bravado he's quite insecure himself, believe it or not.'

Suzanne frowned. 'He's the exact opposite of Justin, then. He has no problems with my going out to work. He likes me being the breadwinner.'

She was interrupted by Ruby pulling on the leg of her jeans. 'Where's Seamus, Mummy?' the little girl asked.

The two women looked around. They couldn't see Seamus. Just trees. 'Oh God,' Patrice said, covering her mouth with her hands. 'Oh my God.'

'Where were you playing?' Suzanne asked. She felt guilty for taking her eyes off them. She'd been engrossed in conversation. But it could only have been for a couple of minutes.

'Over there,' Ruby pointed. 'We were doing hide and seek.' She looked tearful. 'But I couldn't find him. I looked everywhere but he wasn't there.'

Suzanne took Ruby's hand. 'He's probably found a very good hiding place and is sitting there, giggling at us and feeling pleased with himself,' she said.

She glanced at Patrice, whose eyes were darting this way and that. 'Where is he? Where is he?' she said, walking round in circles like a caged animal.

Suzanne put on the buggy's brake and started to hunt systematically behind trees and bushes. She called Seamus's name, but there was no reply.

Patrice was down on her haunches now, scrabbling in the undergrowth, moaning. She wasn't much help, Suzanne thought. She felt guilty that it annoyed her. But Patrice was weeping too much to be able to search properly.

An elderly couple in rainhats and green wellies walked by with their golden retriever. They stopped, turned back and offered to join the search. 'What does he look like?' they asked. 'What was he wearing?'

Patrice couldn't answer coherently so Suzanne described Seamus's clothes: blue shorts, a red and yellow raincoat. Only about five minutes could have passed, but it felt much longer. Patrice started to run towards the lake, way off in the distance.

Suzanne shouted after her. 'He couldn't have got all the way there, surely?'

She didn't know who was giving her more cause for concern – Patrice or Seamus. This was turning into a nightmare. Suzanne pulled her mobile out of her pocket and started to dial 999. Before she got to the final 9, Seamus's head popped out from a tree stump a little way off.

'Here I am,' he shouted. 'Tricked you!'

Patrice swung round and raced back towards him, her hair flying behind her. 'Seamus,' she screamed, scooping him into her arms. 'I was so worried.' She cradled him to her, smothering his face and head in kisses. 'You must never, ever do that again.'

'Thank goodness.' Suzanne sighed with relief. She turned to the elderly couple. 'Thanks so much for your help.'

They smiled and went on their way, the dog lolloping joyfully after them.

Suzanne looked back at Patrice. She was still crying, fear etched on her face. Seamus started wailing, frightened by his mother's sobs.

'There, there,' Patrice said, rocking him in her arms. 'Mummy's here. Mummy won't let you come to any harm.'

She turned to Suzanne. Her cheeks were stained with tears. Some seagulls from the lake circled above them, screeching.

'He's my world,' Patrice said. Her voice was anguished. 'My whole world. If something happened to him, I'd kill myself.'

Seamus buried his head in her shoulder. Ruby, confused and frightened, started to weep, too. Suzanne picked her up.

She was shocked. Patrice was seriously over-reacting. It had been scary, but Seamus hadn't actually been in any danger. It was just a naughty, childish prank. Lots of people lost their children and found them again. Every parent had a story to tell.

They'd lost Ruby in Trafalgar Square once. Suzanne remembered she'd been frantic for five minutes, before finding her behind a lion. She wanted to tell Patrice to pull herself together, but gave her a hug instead. Patrice collapsed into her arms.

They half walked, half stumbled back to the car and Suzanne dropped Patrice and Seamus outside their security gates. Suzanne was relieved to be getting away. She was exhausted.

Things must be seriously bugging Patrice for her to behave like that, she thought. Her reactions had been way over the top. Suzanne couldn't help thinking that her friend hadn't given her the full picture. She must be concealing something. But what?

Chapter Fourteen

Percy was lying on her bed listening to Carmen describing her new shoes. The two women often chatted on the phone on Sunday evenings. It had become a bit of a ritual.

'They've got round toes, a strap and a little buckle,' Carmen said.

'What colour?' Percy asked.

'Sort of olive green.'

'Mmm. Unusual. And the heels?'

'Squarish,' Carmen explained. 'Quite high. Oh, and there's a small platform.'

Percy brightened. 'I do like a small platform. But what's the overall message, would you say?'

Carmen thought for a moment. 'Mmm. Difficult. Mary Jane meets Judy Garland?'

Percy was impressed. 'I like that, where d'you get them?'

She didn't hear Mark walk into the room.

'Not more clothes,' he snapped. 'We've no money.'

Percy put her hand over the receiver. 'I'll just be a moment. It's Carmen,' she informed him.

He flung his bag on the bed and started unbuttoning his shirt. 'In case you haven't noticed, I've just got in from work,' he growled. 'And Rowan needs his bottom wiping.'

Percy quickly wound up the conversation and followed Mark downstairs. She heard him put the TV on in the sitting room. That was annoying. It occurred to her that he always put the TV on to avoid having to talk to her. It certainly worked. Rowan would want to watch now, too. It'd be hard to get him to bed.

After seeing to Rowan she went to check on Ben. He was sitting at the kitchen table reading a comic. He was supposed to be doing maths homework. Her skin prickled with irritation. Why couldn't he ever get on with things on his own?

'Have you finished your maths?' she asked, knowing full well what the answer would be.

'I can't do it,' Ben replied, not looking up from his comic.

'Well, at least have a try, then I'll check it for you.'

'I need you to show me.'

She had enough on her plate, she thought, without this. 'You haven't even looked at the questions,' she snapped. 'Unless you knuckle down this minute there'll be no TV all week.'

She bent over and snatched the comic away. Ben jumped up and tried to grab it back, but she held it above his head.

'I hate you,' he said, tears springing in his eyes. He put out his foot to kick her, but she backed off just in time.

'Don't you dare,' she barked. 'Go to your room immediately.'

Ben stomped upstairs, snivelling. Percy sat down on the chair he'd just left and put her head in her hands.

She was shocked. Ben had never said 'I hate you' before. They used to get on so well. What had happened to him recently? What had happened to her?

It crossed her mind that maybe she needed some sort of help, professional help. She seemed to be losing all the time now, a hundred here, two hundred there; she was haemorrhaging money. Her head kept telling her to stop, but somehow she couldn't. Each evening, once the children were in bed, while Mark was out, she was ineluctably drawn to the computer again, convinced that tonight was the night, that a win was just round the corner, that she'd be able to make everything OK.

She'd lost £4,500 now, including her nest egg. She couldn't bear to think about it. But if she tried to get help, people would find out – Mark, her family and friends. She shuddered. They must never know about the poker, none of them. It was disgraceful. She must deal with this on her own.

Later, once the boys were asleep, Percy stood at the kitchen door watching Mark make cheese on toast. He'd been working a lot of Sundays recently, as well as the usual late nights during the week.

He was still in his black leather jacket and she wondered vaguely why he hadn't taken it off.

'I've got jobs on all next weekend,' he said, opening the grill and putting the toast inside.

'I'll miss you,' Percy replied.

Silence.

She moved behind him and put her arms round his waist, her face against his back. His body felt rigid, like hardboard.

He hesitated, still facing the grill. Then for one second his shoulders drooped and he seemed to soften.

'D'you want to meet me after work tomorrow?' He sounded uncertain. 'We could go for a pizza.'

His voice was gentle. Just as she remembered it, before he became so furious with her. Her heart fluttered.

Then she remembered. There was a big tournament tomorrow. She was banking on winning. She shivered, imagining what he'd say.

'I – I can't', she said. 'I mean, Monday's not a good night to go out, is it? Why don't we wait till the weekend?'

She felt him stiffen. 'Forget it,' he said, unwinding her arms and pushing her off. 'We can't afford it anyway.'

'Don't be cross,' she said.

Please, please don't be like this.

The cheese on toast started to burn. The smoke stung Percy's eyes.

'Fuck.' Mark pulled out the grill, slapped the toast on a plate and pushed past her into the sitting room.

She felt her sympathy dissolve. 'Well, that's not very nice,' she shouted after him.

'Well, you're not very nice,' he shouted back.

Tuesday morning. Percy glanced at her watch. Danny was due any minute. Bugger. She hadn't got her exercise gear on or even brushed her hair.

She raced upstairs and pulled a comb through the tangled mess, scrunching it up in a high ponytail.

She glanced in the mirror, catching sight of the bags under her eyes. Last night had been a total disaster – again. She'd been low on chips and decided to go all-in. SiriusC called. She hadn't come across him before, didn't know anything about him, except the little that she'd been able to glean during the course of play. He seemed like a pretty competent player; he certainly didn't give much away.

The flop had come up king of clubs, king of spades and 4 of clubs. Since he was the only one who'd called, they'd flipped their cards over. She had king of diamonds and jack of diamonds. She'd been elated. Then she'd seen his hand – king of hearts and ace of hearts. She'd wanted to weep.

But there was still a chance. She needed the jack for a full house – three of a kind and a pair. The turn came and it was a 4, pairing the board again and negating his ace. She was on the edge of her seat, thinking there was a God after all.

But the river was an ace, giving him a full house. She was done for.

Standing there at the mirror, Percy felt the bile rise again in her throat, making her choke. It burned as she tried to swallow it down.

She'd realised with a sickening clunk the moment she lost that she'd maxed out the credit card – all £5,000 of it.

She couldn't believe it. All these losses in a row, it was terrifying. It was beginning to look like a horrible pattern.

At least the post arrived after Mark left for work. She'd be able to rip the statement up when it arrived before he got his hands on it.

She was going to have to get some more money somehow. Five thousand was so much – and there was the overdraft, too.

She swallowed and told herself again that poker was a game of ups and downs, that bad patches were normal, you just had to hold your nerve. And the truth was, all she needed was a couple of big wins.

The blood rushed to her head, making her feel giddy. She closed her eyes, breathed deeply, tried to relax.

The bell went and there was Danny in the doorway. Percy hadn't realised quite how tall he was. He seemed massive, practically filling the doorframe.

She noticed his tight black Lycra shorts and his skin-tight vest. Calm down, girl, she whispered to herself as he loped into the house.

'I've come to the right place, then?' he confirmed. 'Let's get started.'

Percy led him into the sitting room. While he unpacked his kit, she pushed back the coffee table and rolled up the rug, leaving a clear area in the centre of the room. Clear, that is, except for the crumbs, sweetie wrappers and orange peel. Percy was horrified. It wasn't the sexy, sophisticated image she'd intended to portray at all.

She grabbed a newspaper, folded it up and lifted the curtain at the bottom of the sofa. Then she flicked the whole lot of rubbish underneath in one deft swipe.

Danny made a noise. Percy turned round and caught his eye. He'd seen it!

'Oh gosh,' she said, ashamed. 'I don't normally do that.'

He looked shocked and amused at the same time. 'I'm very glad to hear it.'

Dammit, Percy thought, he'll think I'm a slut. *I am a slut.*

Danny got out a black mat and a couple of weights. They looked scary.

'How are we going to do this?' Percy asked.

He leaned against the wall and folded his arms, businesslike. 'First we'll do a warm-up. Then we'll go outside for a fifteen-minute jog,' he explained. 'We'll build up gradually, fifteen minutes this week, twenty next. Then we'll come back and do some floor exercises.'

Percy made a face.

He laughed. 'Easy! Now I need to take your pulse and ask a few routine questions about your health.'

Madonna. That was it. Percy was going to look like Madonna. She had kids, and thighs of steel. She was in her forties. It could be done. A vision of herself in that conical bra thing swam before her eyes: a corset, toned arms, red lips . . . lumpy cellulite. No, it wouldn't work. She shook the image away.

Madonna or not, though, she was going to work really hard, she decided. It was costing enough. Mark would be appalled.

They ran round the park together. Percy hated running but she didn't want to make a fool of herself in front of Danny.

'You're doing great,' he said, jogging beside her. 'Make sure you get your breathing right. You have to take the air right into the bottom of your lungs to get oxygen to the muscles. That's it. Much better.'

Praise! She hadn't had that in a long time. She'd forgotten what it felt like. For a moment she was all warm and glowing inside.

Back at the house, she went for a drink of water. Danny had his back to her when she returned. He was studying her photos on the mantelpiece. She saw sweat glistening on his broad shoulders and trickling down his neck. His bum looked amazingly tight in those Lycra shorts.

She wiped under her arms and round her neck with a towel. They did some press-ups, arm exercises and stomach crunches. Danny squatted beside her, holding her legs firmly on the floor, to make her stomach muscles work harder.

After an hour and a half, Percy was worn out and aching all over. She must have used every muscle in her body, but she felt good, powerful – euphoric, even. The endorphins, no doubt. 'That was brilliant,' she said truthfully.

Danny started packing up his bag. 'Same time next week?' he asked.

She nodded, realising she didn't want him to leave. 'Would you like tea or coffee, or a cold drink, before you go?'

He looked pleased. 'Yeah, I'll have a cold drink – whatever you've got.'

They perched, slightly awkwardly, on kitchen stools, facing each other, sipping elderflower cordial. He asked a lot of questions.

He seemed very interested in her and Percy felt oddly comfortable with him, as if she'd known him a long time. The way he looked at her with those dark brown eyes, nodded his head and made pertinent comments made her feel as if she were the most engaging woman in the world.

Maybe it was all part of a tried and tested seduction plan, but she didn't care. She was enjoying it.

'So, what does your husband do for a living?' he asked.

Percy sighed, untied her hair and shook it out. 'He's a photographer. He's got his own studio on the other side of town.'

Danny looked impressed. 'Who does he work for?'

'Anyone and everyone, really. Newspapers, magazines. He does commercial stuff, too – food photography for restaurants. But he doesn't like that side of it.'

'Must be a fantastic job,' Danny commented.

Percy sipped her drink. 'Yes and no,' she replied, honestly.

'He's good, but it's very competitive. And it's hard to make money. Not like working in the City, say.'

Danny finished his drink and put his glass in the sink. 'But it's creative, innit?' he persisted. 'Not dealing with numbers and pound signs. That must be really boring.'

He looked in her eyes. His own were huge, chocolate-brown pools. And he had long black lashes, like a cow. Shy, Percy looked away.

'How long you bin married?' he asked.

'Oh, years,' she replied. 'We met at university.'

'But you have a good relationship, right? You're lucky. Cos most women I seem to meet aren't happy in their marriages.'

Percy rubbed her lips together and fiddled with the seam of her trousers. 'We argue a lot,' she said, lowering her voice. Why was she telling him this?

Danny touched her shoulder lightly. It made her shiver. 'He must be very proud, having a beautiful, intelligent wife like you,' he said. 'And you've got two kids, too?'

She nodded. 'He's always angry with me,' she said. She realised that must sound sad, but it was the truth.

Danny frowned. 'Well, you make sure he takes you out for a romantic meal once in a while, babe, cos you deserve it,' he said softly.

She smiled. He was flirting with her! Nothing wrong with that. There again, she might just be imagining it.

She lowered her head and tried to look up at him coquettishly through her eyelashes. Her neck cricked. Ouch! It was a long time since she'd done this seduction lark.

'No chance of that,' she said. 'My husband's not the romantic type at all.'

She felt a stab of guilt, remembering the pizza invitation. But he'd been so cold and horrible since. Danny raised his eyebrows. Had she gone too far? Had she put him off?

He took a deep breath. 'Well, you're with the wrong man,'

he said finally. She was about to reply when he leaned over, put his hand on her thigh and squeezed.

She jumped and he moved his hand away. It had felt nice, though, she thought, firm and gentle at the same time.

'You know what? Maybe I can take you for a meal sometime?' Danny suggested.

Blood rushed to Percy's head. She hadn't expected this. Boy! He was moving fast! Or was he just being kind?

'Maybe – sometime,' she said, attempting to simper. She couldn't remember how to simper. She hoped she didn't look ridiculous. And did she sound too keen, or not keen enough?

Danny looked at her intensely. For one wild moment, Percy thought he was going to lean over and stick his tongue down her throat, right there and then. But he didn't.

She was relieved. She'd have fallen off her chair in shock.

'I must go,' he said, shaking his long, bronzed legs. Was it to loosen those tight Lycra shorts? He grinned. 'See you next week.'

Naughty, Percy thought, heading upstairs to shower. She took the steps two at a time. She was positively springy. Naughty but nice.

She could hardly wait till next week.

Chapter Fifteen

❧

Swan Lake had always been Carmen's favourite ballet. Ever since she was a little girl, she'd imagined herself as Odette, Queen of the Swans, dancing on the stage at Covent Garden, with her parents watching in the stalls, pride written all over their faces.

Instead, here she was in the audience, staring in rapt silence as another woman performed her arabesques, pirouettes and pliés and stole the show. It still hurt.

Carmen glanced at Simon beside her. He was immersed in the ballet and didn't notice. He had such a strong, handsome profile, she thought. Distinguished was the word Percy used. She, Carmen, had much to be thankful for, really.

They sat sipping wine in a bar afterwards.

'The queen was magnificent,' Simon said. He was facing Carmen on a leather bench seat. They had a wooden booth to themselves, a bit like a railway carriage, with a table in the middle. The lights were low.

'She was fab,' Carmen agreed. 'I always imagined myself in that part.'

Simon topped her glass up with red wine. 'Still disappointed?' he asked, taking a handful of nuts.

There was a white candle in the middle of the table. Carmen picked at some gooey wax and moulded it into a ball. 'Sometimes I still can't believe it happened,' she said. 'It was so stupid.'

Simon crunched the nuts and swallowed, putting his hand

on hers. 'But you've made the best of it, haven't you?' he said. His voice was gentle, soothing.

She nodded. 'Yeah. And who knows? I mightn't have been successful anyway.'

Simon smiled. 'I bet you would.'

She nodded and sniffed. It was all in the past now.

His flat was just round the corner. Carmen hardly ever went there. He usually stayed at hers. She was struck with how tidy it was.

'I'm impressed,' she said, casting her eyes round the immaculate sitting room. 'Where do you put all your clutter?'

He handed her a small glass of icy limoncello, her favourite, and placed his whisky on the mahogany side table.

'I don't have much,' he replied. 'Don't spend enough time here to accumulate. Can't stand mess, though, like you. Everything gets chucked out or put away.'

Carmen sat on a leather swivel chair next to the bookcase. She spun herself round a couple of times with the balls of her feet.

'Fancy something to eat?' Simon asked, taking a swig of whisky.

'I wouldn't mind a sandwich,' she agreed.

'I can do smoked salmon on rye?' he suggested.

Carmen smiled. 'Perfect.'

She could hear him clattering in the kitchen. She picked out a biography of Winston Churchill, flicked through the photographs in the middle and put it back. Simon seemed to have lots of biographies, technical computer books and a few well-thumbed thrillers: that was all. There was no Jane Austen or Hardy, indeed there were hardly any novels. His collection was very male.

In fact the whole place felt male and functional. There were chocolate sofas, beige walls and Venetian blinds on the windows. The flat felt expensive, tasteful, but there was nothing pretty or charming. The rooms were well proportioned, with high ceilings and elegant cornices, but there was no warmth.

If she ever got her hands on it, Carmen thought, she'd rip everything out and start again. Give it some soul.

He handed her a plate of food and sat down on an armchair opposite.

'Simon?' she asked, trying to sound casual. She fingered the rye bread without eating it. 'I've been thinking,' she said, tentative.

He got up and put on some music. She waited until he sat down again. He seemed to take for ever.

She took a deep breath. 'Why don't you sell this place,' she suggested, 'and we could maybe buy somewhere together?'

He looked at her intently. 'I like this place,' he said.

Her stomach knotted. She tried to sound practical. 'I know, but if we pooled our resources, we could get something bigger.'

He put his plate on the floor and scratched his head. She thought he'd never speak.

'Look, Carmen,' he said at last, 'when I come back from travelling, I need my own space.' His voice wasn't unkind. 'Much as I love being with you, I've got to be able to get away sometimes.'

He spoke to her as he would a child, she thought. Patient, explaining.

She took a mouthful of smoked salmon and rye bread. It was something to do. It wouldn't seem to go down, though. Her mouth felt so dry that she had to swallow several times.

'Of course,' she said, backtracking. She looked at the floor. 'I just thought I'd ask, that's all.'

He seemed relieved. 'Well,' he said, slapping his thighs. 'I've got something to ask you, now.'

He was talking, but she didn't really hear. She just caught the odd word – 'Venice', 'hotel', 'views'. Everything around her seemed faded, blurred, faraway.

'Carmen, are you listening to me?' he repeated.

She came back slowly. 'Sorry, what did you say?'

He raised his voice a little. 'I said I've booked us a few days in Venice, beginning of next month. A friend recommended a hotel right in the centre, with great views of the city.' He got up, fetched a brochure and handed it to her. 'Look.'

She stared at the glossy pages, but they were just a blob of shapes and colours.

'Well?' he said.

'Lovely,' she replied.

She could see he was hovering, waiting for something, so she smiled a thank you and drained the last of the limoncello from her glass.

'Another one?' Simon asked.

She shook her head.

She saw his eyes fall on her legs. She was still sitting, wearing a thin cotton dress that had risen up above her knees.

'C'mon, sexy,' he murmured. 'Let's get you to bed.'

She followed him to the bedroom and allowed him to remove her clothes, one by one.

'I'd love to see you in a white feather tutu,' he whispered. She could tell he was smiling. 'And nothing else.'

She knew she should stop now and tell him to use a condom. Her life would just meander on as it always had since the accident. But something in her hardened. Stop dithering, Carmen, a voice said. Make a decision one way or the other. No one else is going to do it for you.

She sighed, closed her eyes and leaped into the darkness.

'You're an animal,' Simon whispered after he'd finished with her, pulling up the duvet. She lay quite still, on her back. She wanted to raise her legs – wasn't that supposed to help? But that would really give the game away.

He fell asleep immediately, but she stayed awake for what seemed like hours, her hands resting lightly on her abdomen. Listening to the stillness. Thinking, wondering.

Chapter Sixteen

Carmen remembered the moment so vividly. It was etched into her brain. It was the moment certainty ended and her life veered off on a new, entirely unfamiliar path.

She was standing in the corridor, waiting to go into the studio. They were all in leotards and leggings, their hair scraped back off their faces.

There was a lot of noise and laughter; everyone was excited about the summer holidays. It was the last day of term at the Royal Ballet School.

'Why not come to France for a week or two?' Hannah suggested. 'There's loads of room.'

Carmen stretched, smiling. 'I'd love to. But I've got to help out in the restaurant.'

'Not for the whole holiday, surely?' Hannah sounded shocked.

Carmen thought for a moment. She had to raise her voice above the hubbub. 'I guess if I earn enough I could maybe come right at the end?'

The door of the studio opened and students started to spill out, sweaty, talking loudly. Carmen was in front of Hannah in the queue.

Hannah nudged her in the ribs with her elbow. 'Me first,' she teased.

Carmen nudged her back, harder. 'No, I'm first.'

They started to jostle, hunker down and push with their shoulders.

'You're not getting past,' Carmen panted.

The other students gathered round. 'How old are you?' someone shouted. 'Go for it, Carmen. Don't give way,' another yelled.

The teacher appeared at the door. 'What's all the noise?'

Carmen and Hannah stood up, quickly.

'Hannah was trying to queue jump.' Carmen giggled.

'I wasn't,' Hannah said, wide-eyed. 'Carmen wouldn't let me past.'

The teacher looked unimpressed. 'For goodness' sake, get in here.'

The line started to move. Carmen was still nearest the door. Hannah put her foot out, in front of Carmen's. 'Not so fast,' she whispered in a silly voice.

Carmen felt herself trip. She tried to regain her balance. Everything went into slow motion. She stumbled forwards. Put her arms out to save herself. She crashed into the person in front, who staggered and toppled sideways.

Carmen felt her foot buckle. She was still falling. There was a snap, a searing pain. She cried out. Her voice didn't sound as if it belonged to her. It was a strange cry, as if from a bird wheeling in the sky.

She landed in a huddle on the floor.

'My ankle,' she screamed. Students circled round, processing the scene. Someone shouted, 'Call an ambulance.' She blacked out.

Carmen spent the summer hoping they could fix her ruptured Achilles tendon. But finally they broke the news: she wouldn't be going back to the Royal Ballet School. She'd been considered one of the best in her year. She'd had a glittering career ahead of her. Now she was finished.

Hannah visited a few times, but what could she say? It could have been the other way round. Sorry was so inadequate. It was better when she stopped phoning.

Carmen thought her life had come to an end. She stayed

in Crawley, helping in her parents' restaurant, and spoke only when spoken to.

Then one day her father whispered gently, in his pronounced Chinese accent, 'You have to pull yourself together, Carmen, find something else to do.'

He looked so sad and broken that she did it for him really, not for herself. She went to sixth-form college then art school, and settled on interior design. And as the years passed, she found she got a buzz out of it. It wasn't like dancing, of course. Nothing could ever compare with that. But she worked hard, built up a business and gained a reputation.

And she was glad to see pride in her parents' eyes once more. No longer pity and shame. Something in her had changed, though, she knew it. She wasn't the same person.

She'd learned never to want anything too badly again, never to hope too much. Life could pull her along now; she'd just go with the flow. That way, when things didn't turn out as expected, she couldn't be disappointed, could she? Because she didn't have any expectations.

Simon stirred in his sleep, disturbing her thoughts. Carmen was still lying on her back, her hands resting on her abdomen.

It crossed her mind again that she should raise her legs in the air, while he was asleep, to boost her chances. The thought suddenly made her want to giggle. She was shocked by the inappropriateness.

She wondered what time it was. She had no idea. She turned over, sleepy at last, and put her arm round Simon, snuggling into his back.

She realised she felt strangely calm and peaceful; in control, even, which was odd, considering. She wasn't used to feeling in control at all. She'd left it to fate, or God, or providence, whatever you cared to call it. 'In control' was a good feeling.

Chapter Seventeen

❦

Small spidery handwriting covered both sides of the dusty pink paper. Patrice opened the letter, as she always did, with a sense of dread. 'My dear Patrice,' her mother Caroline began. Patrice grimaced. 'I hope this letter finds you well . . .' As if she really cared one way or the other.

Patrice skimmed through the usual drivel about how short of money her mother was, how awful and soul-destroying she found her job in the gift section of a Sydney department store. How unfortunate she was to have married two such unworthy men. Patrice was on the point of chucking the letter in the bin when something caught her eye. 'I am in despair over your brother Edmund . . .' she read.

Patrice felt herself perk up. What vile crime had poor Edmund committed this time? 'As you know, he gave up his offer of a place at university. Now he's taken a job in a down-market surf shop. He's fraternising with most unsuitable types, drinking beer and smoking illegal substances. I really do fear for his future.'

Good on you, Patrice thought. The more she heard about her half-brother, the more she liked him. At least he didn't seem tainted with their mother's snobby, bitter, cynical outlook, which was a miracle, considering how overbearing she was. By the sounds of things, he liked to live a little.

She'd love to meet him, but not while Caroline was still alive, Patrice thought sadly. She couldn't bear to do anything that might be construed as a conciliatory gesture, some sort of peace offering. She could never forgive her mother, ever.

And she wanted her to suffer from that knowledge till the end of her days.

Patrice finished skimming through the letter, tore it up into little pieces and put it in the bin.

'There now,' she said to Seamus. 'Let's get dressed, shall we? Then we can go to Gym and Slimline.'

Seamus, who had Weetabix all round his mouth, let out a whoop. 'Will Rowan be there?' he asked.

Patrice wiped his mouth with a damp cloth before lifting him down from the table.

'Yes, poppet,' she said, kissing the top of his soft head. 'Who needs family when you've got friends anyway?'

Hand in hand, they climbed the stairs, Seamus counting, 'One, two, three,' as he went. It was hard work, his little legs were so short. At the top, he trotted into his bedroom to find something.

'I'll just go and make Mummy's and Daddy's bed,' Patrice informed him. He liked to know exactly where she was.

She pulled the white duvet over the bed, shook the pillows. Replaced the white, cotton bolsters and picked the rich red and gold Moroccan bedspread and cushions off the chair. They added a wonderful, exotic splash of colour, she thought. She and Jonty had bought them in Marrakech before they married.

Next, she picked Jonty's clothes off the chair. Pants – they were neatly folded, but why didn't he put them in the laundry basket? Socks. The beige, cashmere sweater he had on last night.

She checked down the front. It wasn't dirty, so she refolded it carefully and put it back in the drawer.

He'd hung his brown corduroy trousers over the end of the iron bedstead. She picked them up and gave them a shake. Something fluttered out of the pocket. A card. She looked at it. Oysters wine bar in Richmond. She wondered when he'd been there. He went out a lot in the City where he worked, but she wasn't aware he'd been to many places locally without her.

She popped the card on top of his walnut chest of drawers, where he'd find it. They had matching chests, on either side of the door.

She was about to get some knickers and a bra when something made her stop. She walked back to his chest and opened the top drawer, where he kept his boxers. They were in a neat pile, the navy silk ones he'd bought in Liberty on the top.

She started to riffle through them, even though she had no idea what she was searching for. They were all different colours, red, black, white, yellow, even. He liked colours. And they were spotted, striped, paisley, you name it. But he was very particular about the material. He wouldn't wear anything manmade. Only silk or Egyptian cotton.

Her fingers touched something solid. Her heart fluttered. She reached into the middle of the pile and pulled the object out. She held it in both hands, almost reverentially, testing its weight in her palms.

It was a small box, made of leather, in a distinctive eau-de-Nil colour. It had Tiffany & Co. on the lid in black writing. She felt round the edges, located the catch mechanism at the front, pressed and the lid swung slowly open.

She stared. There was a pair of cufflinks inside. Square, white gold by the looks of them, with a diamond in the middle of each. They were beautiful. She picked one cufflink up, turning it towards the light, so that she could see it better. The diamond glittered, enticingly. She held it against her cheek. It was hard, cool.

She had an overwhelming urge to open the window and fling the cufflink out, across the garden, towards the pool. Fling them both out, as far as she possibly could.

Or, better still, stamp on them.

She was aware of Seamus, by the door. He had a too-small navy T-shirt on back to front. And odd socks.

'Oh, darling,' she said. 'You've been getting yourself dressed. You are clever.'

'Can we go now?' he asked.

Hurriedly she put the cufflinks back in the box, shut the lid and tucked the box back in the middle of the drawer. No one would ever know she'd been in there.

'Of course we can,' she said brightly, pulling off her pyjamas. 'You've been very patient. I'll just get my clothes on and we'll go straight away.'

Jonty rang from his mobile. She could tell he was in the car, because the CD was playing his favourite Mahler in the background.

'What's for dinner?' he asked.

She'd been reading Seamus his bedtime story. 'Lamb tagine,' she replied. 'With apricots and almonds.'

Jonty grunted in approval. 'Don't do me any couscous,' he commanded. 'I'd rather have rice.'

Seamus was pulling on her arm. He was sitting up in bed, annoyed at having his story interrupted. She motioned to him to be quiet. 'Shh, it's Daddy,' she whispered. She breathed deeply. 'Jonty?'

'Mmm-hmm?'

He sounded distracted. She guessed the traffic was on the move.

She cleared her throat. 'I was tidying our bedroom this morning and I found a Tiffany box in with your underwear.' She hesitated. Did he suck in his breath, or was the phone making noises?

'I – I just wondered,' she ventured. Why did she feel nervous? It was ridiculous. 'Who's it for?' she asked brightly.

Jonty paused for several seconds. Had the lights changed? Maybe he was concentrating on a difficult manoeuvre.

'What?' he said at last. Then he laughed. 'Oh, I see what you mean. Sorry, Pats,' he went on jovially. 'Not for you. Bad luck. It's cufflinks for Michael's birthday. He'll be fifty at the weekend, remember? Celia's whisking him off to Istanbul. We're going to have a little presentation in the office on Friday.'

Patrice's hand fluttered up to where her heart was. She felt a giggle bubbling in her throat. Michael? A partner at Jonty's firm. He'd told her Michael was going to be fifty. She smiled. Of course. Becca, Jonty's secretary, must have ordered the cufflinks, online, probably, and given them to him for safekeeping.

She took a deep breath. Seamus punched her upper arm impatiently. It hurt. She'd forgotten about him. 'Read the story, Mummy,' he pleaded.

'Ow,' she said, crooking the phone in her ear and rubbing her arm. 'I have to go.'

'See you soon,' Jonty replied easily. 'I've just passed Cheyne Walk. Should be back in about forty minutes, traffic permitting.'

She kissed Seamus goodnight and tiptoed downstairs to put the rice on. She decided to lay the table in the dining room rather than the kitchen: make everything a bit special.

She heard the wheels of Jonty's car crunching on the gravel. Any minute now he'd walk in, put down his bag, kiss her on the forehead. Then he'd pop up and change and she'd pour him a drink – wine, probably, or maybe a G and T. She'd light the candles, bring the meal in and they'd sit down and discuss what they'd been up to. No doubt they'd laugh about something Seamus had done or said, just as they always did.

She closed the white plantation shutters and locked them. She was almost totally cocooned now, sealed off from the outside world in her clean, cream and green dining room with the beautiful pale oak floor.

She hugged her arms around her. She looked forward to her evenings with Jonty. They were calm, predictable, safe.

So why were her insides hopping and flapping about like a baby bird that's fallen from its warm nest?

It made no sense at all.

Chapter Eighteen

Most of the guests had already arrived by the time Suzanne reached the hotel. Justin and the children were there, too. He'd collected Ollie and Ruby early from school and driven straight to the Cotswolds, hoping to beat the Friday evening traffic.

The hotel was fab, he said. He'd rung while Suzanne was on the train to tell her all about it. He sounded so excited. She realised he didn't stay in hotels that often, whereas she'd been to dozens.

It was 7.30 p.m. by the time the taxi drew up at the imposing entrance. She'd come as soon as she could, but she hadn't bargained on having to deal with a difficult staffing problem before she left London.

Chris, a senior member of Suzanne's department, had unexpectedly resigned, claiming he couldn't work with Suzanne's deputy, Rob. Suzanne thought rather more highly of Chris than she did of Rob, whom she'd inherited from the previous Communications Director. But she couldn't just sack the man, much as she'd like to, because he was a golfing mate of the CEO and godfather to one of his children, worst luck.

Suzanne had ended up having a lengthy conversation with Chris in her office. He told her he'd accepted a job with a rival company, and Suzanne had promised to top the salary they were offering and throw in various other incentives.

She'd managed to persuade him to have a rethink over

the weekend and was fairly confident he'd change his mind. She hoped so. She'd worked bloody hard on him. She couldn't afford to lose a bright spark like that.

She'd come away furious, though, that Rob had caused all this aggravation. She realised that she'd have to do something about him sooner rather than later, if she wasn't to lose more staff. He was a hopeless manager and didn't seem to have any ideas, either. She'd just have to be very clever, very cunning, about 'letting him go'.

She dumped her bag in the foyer and signed in. 'I believe your husband's upstairs with the children.' The receptionist smiled. 'You're in the Galaxy Suite,' she added, handing Suzanne a key. 'The porter will bring your bag.'

Suzanne walked up the impressive flight of stairs and along the thickly carpeted corridor to her room. The hotel must have been built sometime in the nineteenth century, she guessed. The walls were adorned with vast oil paintings, mostly of hunting scenes, and a few rich, red tapestries. There was a lot of dark wood and a strong but not unpleasant smell of furniture polish filled the air.

Suzanne tapped lightly on the heavy wooden door before opening it. A huge bed covered in a green canopy filled a sizeable part of the room, and there was a giant, lead-paned window behind. It was getting dark outside now, but she imagined they'd wake to wonderful views of the countryside tomorrow morning.

Justin had his back to her and was sitting on the bed with Ruby in his arms. Felix was beside him, playing with some plastic toys. There was water running in what Suzanne assumed to be the bathroom next door. Ollie taking a shower? A corridor off the main room ran, Suzanne supposed, to the children's room.

'Hi,' she said. She was surprised Justin hadn't sprung up to greet her.

He shuffled round slowly, with Ruby still on his lap.

Suzanne could see now that she was snivelling. Her face looked very pale.

'She's just been sick – in the loo, thank goodness,' Justin said, stroking Ruby's hair. She made a sad choking noise.

Now that he mentioned it, Suzanne realised there was a faint but unmistakable whiff of puke.

'She said she was feeling ill in the car, but she seemed a bit better when we arrived and ate quite a big supper. That was a mistake,' he added grimly.

'Oh no.' Suzanne threw her handbag down and took off her jacket. 'What bad timing,' she said. 'I hope she's not going to be ill all weekend.'

'Me too,' Justin said, lifting Ruby gently off his lap and laying her down on the bed. 'I don't want to be stuck in this room for two days, magnificent as it is.'

Suzanne felt Ruby's brow. It was very hot. She tutted, then bent down and kissed Felix's head.

He took a red and yellow plastic toy out of his mouth. 'Dadadada' he said merrily before shoving the toy back in.

'No, Mamamama' she scolded. 'Mamamama.' Felix ignored her.

Ollie came out, rubbing his hair with a towel. He'd grown a lot recently. He looked somehow awkward in his body, as if he didn't fit it properly yet. She felt a rush of love.

'Hey, Mum,' he said. 'This place is fantastic. There's an indoor and outdoor pool and trampolines and tennis courts. Can I play tennis tomorrow?'

Suzanne smiled. 'Of course.'

She checked her watch, sucking in her breath. 'I need to find the team and ask how the briefing went earlier. Then I have to meet the journalists for dinner. What shall we do about Ruby?'

Justin shrugged. 'I'll have to try and get her and Felix off to sleep. Then we can use the baby-listening service.'

Suzanne frowned. 'I'm sorry . . .'

'Don't worry,' he replied. 'I'll join you later. Save me some food, will you? I'm starving.'

'Of course,' Suzanne said. 'I'll tell them you'll be down. Ollie? Do you want to find the games room? There should be some other boys your age around.'

Suzanne was seated at a table with six journalists and one of her press officers, Amy. Amy was young, blonde, pretty – and very good at social chit-chat.

The woman next to Suzanne, who was called Liz, was the features editor of *Mary-Beth* magazine and said she had two children. Suzanne took an instant dislike to her husband, a paunchy advertising exec who seemed rather more interested in Amy and the waitresses than he did in his wife. But Liz seemed nice.

Suzanne reckoned they were about the same age and she felt a certain rapport. They traded horror stories about London schools and bonded over house prices and the vexed question of Move v Extend.

Suzanne liked the fact that Liz had lived a little. She'd been through a divorce, too, and could well be heading for another one, Suzanne thought grimly as she watched the husband undress Amy with his eyes. Plus, Liz was pleasantly appreciative of everything that had been laid on, unlike most of the other spoiled hacks Suzanne came in contact with.

It wasn't until much later that Justin finally joined the table.

'How's Ruby?' Suzanne asked, pouring him a glass of wine and passing it to him. 'We've had pudding, but they're keeping your food warm in the kitchen.'

She noticed Liz do a double take.

'Sorry,' Suzanne said, 'this is my husband, Justin.' He smiled, slipped in beside Amy, on the other side of the table.

Liz blushed slightly. It amused Suzanne. She was used to

other women staring at her husband, she didn't really mind. But Liz could scarcely conceal the fact that she clearly fancied the pants off Justin. Not surprising. He looked like a Greek God beside her fat, leery ad man.

Justin polished off a plate of cheese and biscuits – he declined the main course. Suzanne appreciated that he didn't want to hold everyone up.

'A drink at the bar?' he asked. There was a general murmur of assent. He was so good at schmoozing, Suzanne thought gratefully. He was a real help on occasions like this.

They'd just risen when one of the waitresses came over and tapped Suzanne on the shoulder.

'Are you in the Galaxy Suite?' Suzanne nodded. Justin moved over to be beside her.

'One of your children is crying,' the waitress said.

Suzanne hesitated. Justin frowned. 'I hope Ruby hasn't been sick again,' he muttered. Suzanne took a step towards the door. He stopped her. 'I'll go.'

'I'm sorry,' Suzanne called after him. How often had she said that to him recently? It occurred to her that it was becoming a bit of a mantra.

He put a hand up, without turning round. 'Have a nice time. See you later.'

Suzanne refocused on the guests. Liz gave her a sympathetic smile.

'He's amazing,' she said. 'I wish my husband would look after the kids sometimes. He leaves it all to me – even though I work, too.'

She shot the paunchy ad man a vicious look, but he was too busy staring down Amy's cleavage to notice.

'I am lucky,' Suzanne admitted. 'I just hope Ruby hasn't thrown up all over the bed.'

She was tempted to excuse herself and run after Justin. Then she remembered where she was and what she was

138

supposed to be doing. The guests were waiting. She smiled. 'Let's go to the snug. I've heard they do an excellent Irish whiskey.'

It was 1.30 a.m. when Suzanne finally crept into the bedroom to join her family. The journalists had been quite a laugh, drunk as lords but full of entertaining tales. She'd thought several times that she ought to leave, to help Justin. But the motoring correspondents in particular were becoming increasingly indiscreet and she didn't want to miss anything. She'd been careful not to drink too many herself. She'd nursed the same Irish whiskey for hours.

She opened the bedroom door and the lingering smell of sick made her retch. She pinched her nose and breathed through her mouth. She noticed the curtains weren't fully drawn and a window was open. Poor Justin, having to deal with all this while she was downstairs chinking glasses. There was no let-up.

He was asleep on his back, with Ruby beside him. She was snuggled like a mouse into his side. Suzanne walked through the small corridor into the adjoining room, where Ollie was snoring lightly. Felix was in his cot beside him, and there was a spare bed – which should have been Ruby's – freshly made up for Suzanne.

She took off her clothes and hung them on the chair in the corner, before clambering beneath the crisp, cotton duvet. She sighed. She was exhausted; she knew she'd go straight to sleep and she needed a good night. Tomorrow would be a demanding day.

But the thought of Justin next door made her sad. She wished she could join him, wished she could snuggle like Ruby into his delicious body. But she didn't want to disturb them, not now they were peaceful.

She and Justin had talked about coming here for weeks, she mused. Even discussed, guiltily, what a relief it would be to leave Lara behind for a couple of days, not to have to think about her.

'I'm sorry, Justin,' she found herself whispering again in the dark. 'I'll make it up to you, I'm sorry.'

Ruby was a little better in the morning – her temperature seemed to have gone anyway – and they trooped down to breakfast together. Suzanne offered to carry Felix, but he was having none of it.

''Way,' he said crossly, pushing her away with his chubby hands.

'He's a tinker,' Justin said, shaking his head. Suzanne decided she needed to spend more time with Felix. This unfriendly behaviour wasn't on. But she couldn't worry about that now.

'Fancy being thrashed at tennis later?' Justin asked Ollie as they strolled into the breakfast room.

'I'll thrash you, more like.' Ollie grinned back.

The large, airy room looked out over a magnificent garden behind the hotel. A perfectly manicured green lawn sloped down towards a fountain and rose garden, and all you could see were trees in the distance.

Most of the tables were filled, but Suzanne noticed an empty one in the far corner of the room. She was relieved. She wasn't in the mood for making polite conversation now. She needed to psych herself up for her presentation speech at 10 a.m.

They sat down and looked at the menu. Ruby didn't fancy any breakfast. She waited quietly beside Justin while he and Ollie tucked into bacon, egg, sausage and fried bread. Suzanne had coffee and a croissant. Felix enjoyed himself immensely smearing Weetabix over the white linen table-cloth and tipping sugar cubes into the milk jug.

Suzanne noticed Liz walk in with her two girls, while her husband trailed behind. His face looked very white and puffy,

Suzanne thought, sniggering inwardly. Served him right. He must have had three or four brandies last night, on top of all that wine at dinner. He was probably feeling like death. They helped themselves to cereal at the long breakfast bar and sat down at the last empty table near the window.

Suzanne put a dollop of strawberry jam on her plate. Ruby made a funny noise. Suzanne glanced up. Dismayed, she saw Ruby heave. Quick as a flash, Justin jumped up, held a linen napkin under the small girl's chin and waited while Ruby threw up neatly into the material.

'Bowl,' he commanded, looking sharply at Suzanne, who stared, in wonder, as he wrapped the napkin up and popped the whole thing into the empty dish she'd passed him. Then he wiped Ruby's face with another, clean napkin and patted her back. 'Good girl.' There wasn't a trace of vomit to be seen.

'Gross,' Ollie said, wrinkling his nose.

Suzanne shook her head in disbelief. 'You're amazing,' she told Justin. She couldn't have managed it herself, she just knew. She took a quick look round the dining room. She didn't think anyone had even noticed.

Ruby was crying and shivering now. She obviously felt ghastly. Justin helped her up, levered Felix out of his high chair and wiped his mouth, too.

'Bed for you, young lady,' he said grimly.

Suzanne frowned. 'I'm so sorry . . .'

Justin shook his head. 'I'll see you later. Good luck with the speech. Ollie, I'm sure those lads'll give you a game of tennis if you ask them.' He nodded in the direction of a couple of boys in the corner who looked about Ollie's age.

'Yeah,' Ollie agreed. 'We played pool last night.'

Suzanne watched Justin and Ruby hurry to the door, Felix balanced on Justin's hip. She looked down at her feet. Her black briefcase was still there, and what's more there was no scrambled egg or sick on it.

She glanced at her watch: 9.30 a.m. She rose from the table. She'd run through her speech one more time in the library next door, before making her way to the conference suite. She had her toothbrush and toothpaste in a plastic bag in her jacket pocket. She'd give them a quick brush in the ladies' beforehand.

Ruby might be laid low, Justin's weekend might be ruined, but no one could accuse Suzanne of not being prepared for the big Amélie launch, she thought. She'd given it her all. It was going to be a fabulous success, she was determined.

She couldn't have hoped for better weather, she mused as she said goodbye to the last journalist late on Sunday afternoon. He drove off, waving, in a metallic-blue Amélie, with a large hamper stuffed with goodies on the back seat. One of Suzanne's team would collect the car next week.

The sun had shone for two whole days and Suzanne felt everything had gone swimmingly. The journalists' children seemed to have had a lovely time and everyone had enjoyed the treasure hunt. Several of the journos had commented on how nippy the Amélie was, given its size, and Liz had said she'd definitely do a write-up in *Mary-Beth*. Fifty per cent of her readers were parents, she explained, and the Amélie had just the right image. She loved the special frozen food compartments in the back, too.

It was unfortunate that Justin had had to spend most of the weekend in the bedroom, trying to entertain Felix while Ruby slept. Luckily Ollie had chummed up with one of the motoring correspondent's sons and had spent most of his time in one of the pools or playing tennis.

Suzanne had gone up to relieve Justin once, so that he could take Felix for a walk, but generally she'd had to be on duty, talking to journalists, answering questions and keeping an eye on her team, making sure they were doing their stuff.

There were a lot of phone calls from London, too. Chris

had rung on several occasions, checking out the details of his offer. And Rob had been on the blower to update her on the complaints that were pouring in about the new Amélie TV ad.

Apparently people thought it was sexist – towards men. Suzanne was secretly delighted. It had stirred up quite a debate and was generating lots of publicity. It really couldn't have been a worse time for Ruby to fall ill, though. Suzanne hardly had a spare moment. Not that Ruby really wanted her mum anyway. Justin was the one she and Felix needed when they were poorly.

Suzanne had barely seen Justin since yesterday morning. She guessed he'd still be in the bedroom, so she made her way back upstairs. She started when she opened the door. It was a complete tip, with towels and toys all over the floor. Ruby was sitting on the bed, looking sorry for herself. Justin looked as if he were trying to pack up, but every time he put something in the suitcase on the floor, Felix pulled it out again.

'Where's Ollie?' Suzanne asked, not knowing quite what else to say.

'Playing tennis.' Justin didn't look up. 'I told him to be back by six.'

Felix grabbed a pair of Ruby's jeans from the suitcase. Waved them around.

'Don't do that,' Justin snapped, pulling the jeans out of his son's hand. Felix started to cry.

'Go on then,' Justin said, throwing them back at him. 'It's only a stupid pair of trousers.' Felix, oblivious to Justin's annoyance, beamed and stuffed them in his mouth.

'They're mine,' Ruby squealed from the bed. Justin turned and gave her an icy glare. She fell silent.

Suzanne had never seen him quite so on edge. Frazzled was the word. His hair was sticking up all over and it looked as if he'd slept in his shirt. It wasn't surprising, given that he'd spent virtually the whole weekend stuck indoors. Poor Justin. He'd been so looking forward to getting away.

She checked her watch: 5.55 p.m. Ollie should be here any minute.

'Thanks so much for looking after the children,' she said. 'I've had a brilliant weekend – from a work point of view, I mean,' she added quickly.

Justin shoved the last things in the suitcase and zipped it up. 'Good,' he said. 'Because I haven't.'

Suzanne strolled into the bathroom and checked to see if they'd left anything behind. Then she wandered into the children's bedroom. Justin seemed to have done a good job.

When she came back, he was sitting on the bed beside Ruby. He had one arm round her, and one round Felix on his lap.

Suzanne thought he gave her a funny look. She wondered what it meant.

'By the way,' he said, jiggling Felix up and down on his knee, 'Lara rang this morning. She fell over last night on her way back from a party. Tripped on a kerb, she says, and cut her knee.'

Suzanne was silent, waiting for what would come next.

'She didn't realise how bad it was until she woke up and could hardly bend her knee.' Suzanne could feel herself getting agitated. 'But relax,' Justin went on. 'I spoke to her friend's mother who took her to casualty this afternoon. She's had four stitches but she's fine. It's all sorted. I just have to get her to the nurse in a week to have the stitches removed.'

'I can't believe it,' Suzanne said. 'So you've had to deal with all that on top of Ruby's illness?'

Justin nodded.

'You're a saint,' she said. 'I don't know how you do it.'

'Nor do I,' he muttered.

He paused for a moment. Swallowed. She wondered what was coming next. 'You know this is crazy, Suzanne?' he said, shaking his head.

'What?' Had she heard him properly?

'I mean this,' he said, looking her in the eye for the first time since she came in the room. 'You working round the clock, me looking after the kids. Problem after problem, rush, rush, rush. We never have a moment to ourselves any more.'

Suzanne sighed. She sat down on the edge of the bed and took Felix's chubby hand in hers for a moment, fiddling with his fingers, but he pulled away.

'I know this weekend's been a disaster,' she agreed. 'What with Ruby being ill and me being so busy.' She put her hand on Justin's knee. 'Let's book a weekend away soon, somewhere nice, to make up for it.'

Her mobile rang. 'Bother.' She checked the name, sprang up. 'It's Rob,' she explained. 'About the ad. I need to answer this – sorry.'

Chapter Nineteen

It had all been Suzanne's idea. She'd picked up a leaflet about the new class at reception and read it out to them over skinny lattes one morning.

'"A dynamic, yoga-based class which incorporates t'ai chi, yoga and Pilates,"' Suzanne had recounted.' '"Body Balance invigorates and tones, releasing tight, tense muscles and leaves you in a state of energised calm."'

'Well, whaddayou think?' She'd looked round, expectantly. 'Energised calm? We could all do with a bit of that.'

Patrice had protested. 'Sundays aren't good for me. It's the one day of the week when Jonty and I get to lie in. We put the cartoons on for Seamus and nip back to bed.'

'Aw, come on,' Suzanne had cajoled. 'It's normally me trying to get out of classes. I think this sounds good. Let's at least give it a try.'

Percy yawned and glanced at the clock: 9.30 a.m. She couldn't quite believe that she'd managed to get up and out after so little sleep.

'Right, class,' said the instructor. 'Bend your knees, feet pointing outwards, then slowly stretch your right leg out as far as you can, keeping it dead straight. Next, use your right hand to push your left away from your body, then raise your palms up, slowly, slowly. Then down, slowly, slowly. Lovely. Now circle them round, like waves lapping the shore.'

If she was being honest, Percy thought the t'ai chi yoga section was a bit sissy – all this slow-motion waving your arms for no particular purpose.

'Now, stand with your feet together. Fix your eyes on a point behind me. This'll help you balance,' the instructor commanded. 'Lift your right leg up off the floor. Arms out straight to your side. Slowly bend forward, twist to your right and straighten your right leg out. Try to look graceful, ladies.'

Graceful? That was a laugh. Percy wobbled and glanced around. Well, Carmen was managing it, of course, no problem. She looked like the ballet dancer she was. Suzanne, in front, though, put her foot down.

The teacher smiled. 'Cheating.'

Percy imagined Suzanne was probably glowering – inside, anyway. Percy couldn't see Suzanne's face, but she had a cross back. She hated being shown up. Percy hoped her friend wouldn't explode.

As for Patrice, well, she didn't look exactly graceful. She was too long and gawky. But she wasn't doing badly, particularly when you considered she'd normally be tucked up in bed now. Or at least padding round the house in her dressing gown, like any other sane person.

'I'm not sure I'd do that again,' Percy said afterwards, taking a bite of chocolate muffin. Well, it was Sunday. 'I don't feel as if I've had a proper workout.'

'I would have quite liked it, except the teacher kept picking on me.' Suzanne sounded really annoyed. She had a chocolate and a blueberry muffin in front of her. She hadn't been able to choose, so she'd decided to have both.

'Mind if I join you?'

Percy's shoulders drooped. She'd wanted to get the girls on their own.

'Of course,' she smiled. 'Pull up a chair.'

It was Diana, one of the mums from Ben's school. She was heavily into astrology.

'How are you?' Percy asked. She didn't really want to know, but she hated bad manners.

147

Diana shook her head. 'Always rushing round. Never seem to stop. I take too much on, you see. But, of course, I'm a Virgo.'

'You don't really believe in that crap, do you?' Suzanne said.

Diana looked shocked. 'Indeed I do,' she said. 'What sign are you?'

Suzanne shrugged. 'Leo, I think.'

Diana pursed her lips. 'Well, that explains it,' she said.

Percy and Suzanne exchanged glances. Diana was tall and thin, with the longest neck Percy thought she'd ever seen. It was a wonder it could support her head. Percy noticed her shifting on her seat and grimacing slightly, as if something hurt. She looked at Diana. 'Are you OK?' she asked.

'I had colonic irrigation yesterday,' Diana confided. 'Just a bit uncomfortable. I suffer from terrible constipation, you see.'

Ah yes, Percy had forgotten, she was a health bore as well. Suzanne, who'd been stifling yawns on the sofa, perked up. 'Ooh, what's that like?' she asked. 'I've always wanted to know.'

Diana looked strictly at her, as if she didn't trust her motives. Quite right, Percy thought. She shouldn't trust Suzanne's motives.

'Very effective,' Diana said. 'I'd recommend it. It cleanses the gut completely and leaves you feeling wonderfully clean.

'Sometimes,' she said, warming to her theme, 'they find things like sweetcorn that could have been there for years. Sweetcorn doesn't digest very easily, you see,' she added darkly.

Percy was keen to move the conversation on. But Suzanne wanted the full low-down. 'Can you see anything?' she pressed. 'I mean, as it comes out?'

'Yuck, Suzanne,' Carmen protested.

Diana ignored her. 'Oh yes,' she replied seriously. 'You see it floating by in a tube.'

Percy was aghast. Nothing would persuade her to venture there, not even large sums of money. Let sleeping dogs lie, that was her motto.

'Well, that's put me off my lunch,' she said when Diana finally disappeared. 'I'm supposed to be having the full works, too, roast beef and Yorkshire pud, over at my brother's. Big family gathering. My mother'll be there – worst luck.'

Carmen looked sympathetic. 'It'll be good to see your brother, anyway.'

Percy nodded. 'But not his frightful wife. Or my mum.'

Suzanne licked her finger, picking up the last crumbs from her plate and popping them in her mouth.

'Yum,' she said. 'Shame about the wife and your mother, Pers. But roast beef and Yorkshire pud. Scrummy. Justin's doing the full works for us, too. No sweetcorn, though, thankfully.' She grinned. 'I'm not sure I'll be able to face it again after what Diana said.'

Percy tut-tutted. 'Well, it's your fault, for probing. You shouldn't have encouraged her.'

Suzanne grinned again. 'Sorry, but I couldn't resist it. The vision of Diana with a tube shoved up her backside will remain with me for some time. I reckon she needs her head examined, not her arse.'

'The horseradish, Zeus, you've forgotten the horseradish,' Philippa scolded.

Zeus looked apologetic. 'Sorry, darling,' he said, and scuttled off to fetch it.

Percy lifted her nephew John on to her lap and stroked his soft baby hair. He sat playing with a silver napkin ring, turning it round and round in his chubby fingers. He couldn't care less about his birthday, she thought fondly. He was happy just being surrounded by people he knew. Small children were so straightforward in that way. They hadn't learned to be greedy and materialistic.

Philippa gave Percy a conspiratorial wink. Percy noted her sister-in-law's shiny blue eyeshadow. It had gathered in the sweaty folds of her eyelids.

'Men are such dopes, aren't they?' Philippa said.

Percy gave a thin smile and glanced at Mark. He was tucking a napkin into Rowan's T-shirt and didn't notice.

Zeus reappeared with the horseradish in a bowl.

'You've remembered to take it out of the jar, then?' Philippa said, her tone condescending. 'Well done, you're learning.' She put a silver teaspoon in the bowl and gave it a stir. 'Pass it to your mother,' she commanded.

Antonia was at the far end of the table, beside Mark and Rowan. She waved her hand. 'Not for me. Never touch the stuff,' she said.

Philippa looked surprised. 'My family always has horse-radish with beef. We believe it brings out the flavour.'

Zeus coughed. 'Er, would anyone like another parsnip?' There was a shaking of heads. He sat down with a sigh and helped himself to some vegetables.

'Oh, sugar, we need more gravy,' Philippa said, peering into the gravy boat. 'Zeus, go and get some from the pan.'

She always said prissy things like 'sugar' and 'fudge' and 'spend a penny'. It annoyed Percy immensely. She put John on the floor. 'Sit down, Zeus,' she insisted. 'I'll get it. You haven't had a single mouthful yet.' But he was already up and halfway to the kitchen.

'Oh, don't worry about him,' Philippa said, waving her hand dismissively. 'He's been relaxing all morning with the papers while Guess Who's been slaving away over a hot stove.'

Percy sat down again. 'Well, being a journalist, I imagine he needs to keep up with the news.' She tried to sound tactful.

Philippa's eyes swept ceilingwards. 'The number of times

I've heard that excuse. Of course he needs to know what's going on, but he doesn't need to read every single paper, cover to cover, and listen to the radio at the same time. It drives me nuts.'

Antonia leaned across the table. She'd been experimenting, not entirely successfully, Percy thought, with hot curlers. Her normally smooth, neat bob was curiously lumpy.

'How's your work going, Philippa?' Antonia asked, her curls quivering. Her gold necklace winked in the sunlight. She was wearing rather a low-cut top and her generous bosom was very brown and freckled. 'Getting lots of commissions?' she asked.

Philippa shuffled awkwardly in her seat. 'I haven't really been trying since John came along,' she replied. She picked up her knife and sawed into her beef. Percy noticed a look of satisfaction creep across Antonia's tanned face.

'Really?' Antonia raised her eyebrows. 'What a shame. And after all that money Zeus spent on your course, too.'

'Yes, well, I haven't had time to look for business,' Philippa snapped. 'Of course if Zeus earned more I wouldn't need to work at all.'

Percy glanced at Zeus. He seemed to have shrunk into his carver chair. He nibbled on a parsnip. Antonia sat back, took a mouthful, ruminating.

Percy waited with bated breath.

'Of course, in my day,' Antonia said at last, 'women didn't work. But, you see, we were content to raise our children and be homemakers. We didn't expect holidays and expensive clothes and fancy gadgets.'

Percy noticed that Philippa had gone an odd colour. Sort of puce. It contrasted sharply with the white tablecloth. In fact, Percy feared Philippa might explode.

'Holidays? Fancy gadgets? Pah!' she spluttered. 'I wish I knew what they were. Women like me have to work to pay the mortgage.'

151

Antonia looked all innocence. 'Oh dear,' she said, wide-eyed. 'I didn't mean to upset you, Philippa. Are you all right? Would you like a glass of water?'

Philippa's lips seemed to have disappeared. Her mouth was a thin slot.

'Have I said something to upset Philippa?' Antonia persisted, glancing round the table. 'I'm sure I didn't mean to. It's none of my business, of course, what she does when Zeus is out, earning the family crust.'

Percy looked down at her plate and shovelled in a forkful of mangetouts. She dreaded family gatherings and this one was already living up to her worst expectations.

After lunch, Zeus led Percy into the garden.

'D'you think it's safe to leave them?' Percy asked. She felt uncomfortably full. She'd stuffed beef and roast potatoes into her mouth at an alarming speed. And she hadn't dared say no to Philippa's homemade plum crumble although she'd already had to loosen the waistband on her skirt.

Zeus laughed. 'They were a bit scratchy, weren't they?'

The garden was small but beautifully designed. A sandstone path led from the little terrace outside the house down through the lawn to a circular paved area at the bottom. They sat on a wooden bench under a fig tree. The seat had been warmed by the summer sun.

'It's all looking lovely,' Percy said, motioning to the trees and flowers.

Zeus bent down to dead-head a geranium in a terracotta pot. 'Yes, Philippa's terribly clever.' He smiled. 'She's the one with the vision, you know, I just do the unskilled manual labour.'

Percy looked at him. His face was grey, with deep lines running across his forehead and from his nose down to his mouth. He seemed smaller than she remembered, and very tired.

'Is there much call round here for garden designers?' she asked.

'Could be,' he said brightly. 'Philippa's not had any time to build up business recently, though. John keeps her busy. But you know all about that.'

Percy put her arm round her brother and rested her head on his shoulder. He leaned his head against hers.

'Dear bro,' she said. 'It's good to get you on your own for a moment. I never seem to see you.'

He patted her knee. 'Busy lives we all lead, eh?'

Percy saw Ben and Rowan through the glass doors at the back of the house. They were chasing John round the kitchen.

'I can't believe John's two already,' she said. 'It's gone so fast.'

'And Rowan,' said Zeus. 'He'll be four soon.'

Someone a few doors down got out their lawnmower. The smell of mown grass filled the air.

'It's lovely here,' Percy said.

Zeus shrugged. 'I like it, but Philippa wants to move.'

Percy clicked her tongue. 'But why? You've done so much to the house.'

'Philippa hates Hertfordshire. She'd rather live nearer London. And she wants somewhere bigger.'

Percy took her arm away and turned to face Zeus. 'Are you and Philippa OK?' she said.

Zeus smiled. 'You still look out for me, don't you, dear Percy? And in answer to your question, yes, we're fine.'

Percy caught sight of Ben again, picking John up. She hoped Ben wouldn't squeeze too tight. 'Do you remember how I always gave you your tea when you were little?' she said. 'Mum was probably upstairs doing her nails or something.'

Zeus laughed. 'Yes. And if it was something you were particularly fond of, like chocolate mousse, you'd say, "One for you and one for me" until the whole lot had gone. I got half-portions of everything. It's a miracle I survived.'

Percy sniggered. 'Mum always complained that you were such a skinny little thing.'

The back door swung open. 'Speak of the devil,' Percy muttered.

'Yoo hoo! There you are.' Antonia stepped on to the terrace. They watched her teetering down the path in her high Sunday shoes.

She stood, hot and flustered, in front of her children. 'Zeus, my car seems to be making a funny noise,' she said. 'You wouldn't mind having a peek at it, would you? Please, darling?'

Zeus rose immediately. 'Sure.' Then he stopped and looked at his mother sternly. 'So long as you don't call me a useless little toad again.'

Antonia took his arm. 'Of course not, Zeusy. That was a misunderstanding. Come and see what you think.'

Mark helped Rowan on with his shoes. Ben was filthy. He'd been rolling around on the lawn with John. 'You need a bath when we get back, young man,' Mark said.

Percy kissed Zeus and Philippa. 'D'you want me to drive?' she asked Mark.

He shook his head crossly. Looked away.

Zeus raised his eyebrows. He'd obviously noticed. He smiled at Percy kindly. 'It's been wonderful to see you, sis.'

Percy smiled back gratefully.

Mark took the boys to the car and she lingered behind. 'Maybe I should go to the loo.'

Philippa went upstairs with John, to bath him, as Percy followed Zeus back inside.

'Are *you* all right?' Zeus asked. 'You seem a bit on edge. And Mark's awfully grumpy.'

Percy bit her lip. A sudden thought occurred to her. She couldn't. She must. Her heart started hammering. Did she dare? Now seemed as good an opportunity as any.

She took a deep breath. 'Can I talk to you for a moment?' she asked.

'Of course.' Zeus looked puzzled. He ushered her into the dining room. The table was still covered in plates and glasses from lunch. The windows were closed and there was a strong smell of stale cooking. He pushed the door to.

'What's up?' he said, concerned.

'Listen,' Percy said hurriedly. 'I'm in a bit of trouble.' She stared at her feet, shuffling from one to the other. 'I'm so sorry to ask you,' she stumbled on, 'but can you possibly lend me some cash? Just for a week or two, I mean – until I can pay you back?' She couldn't believe she'd said it.

Zeus cleared his throat. 'You know I'd do anything for you, Percy,' he said. 'But what sort of scrape are you in? Does Mark know about this?'

Percy shook her head violently. 'I – I can't talk about it,' she said. Tears sprang to her eyes. 'If Mark knew, he'd throw me out. Definitely. I know what I'm doing – honestly.'

Zeus hesitated. His brow was a mass of wrinkles. 'How much do you need?' he asked. 'You know I'm not exactly flush myself.'

'Five thousand pounds,' Percy said. She heard him suck in his breath. 'But if you can't manage . . .'

Zeus put up his hand, stopped her. 'I've got a bit stashed away. Philippa thinks it's for John's school fees but I've always fancied a round-the-world trip,' he joked.

Percy managed a small laugh. 'I know which I'd go for. But seriously, Zeus, I can't thank you enough. You'll get it back, I promise.'

She hugged him and he wrapped his arms around her. He felt so warm and comforting.

How different their roles had suddenly become, she thought. Up till now, she'd been the one who'd worried about Zeus, her little brother. Now it was the other way round.

'You're the best bro,' she whispered. 'I wouldn't normally ask but—'

Zeus pulled back a little. 'I'll always be here for you,' he interrupted. 'But I think you should tell me what's up. Maybe I can help?'

She was relieved to see Mark's head appear round the door, even though he looked furious. 'What on earth are you doing?' he asked. 'We're waiting for you in the car.'

'Sorry,' Percy replied. 'We were having a sibling moment. I'm coming now.'

She and Zeus walked towards the front door.

'I'll stick a cheque in the post tonight,' Zeus said in a low voice. 'But not a word of this to Philippa.' He raised a forefinger to his lips. 'She'd kill me.'

'Not a word,' Percy promised. 'And thanks again, Zeus. You're an absolute star.'

Chapter Twenty

֍

'It's extremely good of you,' Jonty said, running a hand through his hair and crossing one leg over another.

Suzanne smiled. 'It's a pleasure. You'll have a lovely time with Ruby and Felix, won't you, Seamus?'

Seamus nodded, but he held tight to Patrice's hand. Patrice felt uncomfortable. She didn't really want to leave her son for the weekend, but Suzanne had virtually insisted. She'd said that it would do Patrice and Jonty good to have a night away on their own.

It had crossed Patrice's mind that perhaps she ought really to check with Justin before accepting the invitation, given that he was probably the one who'd be looking after Seamus most of the time anyway.

But Patrice decided it might look odd to go behind Suzanne's back like that. She might take it the wrong way. Besides, Justin would take good care of Seamus. Patrice trusted him totally.

Justin appeared at the sitting-room door. 'Fancy a coffee before you go?' he said with a wide grin.

He'd obviously just come out of the shower. His hair was still wet and his white T-shirt clung to his damp skin. There was the familiar inch of bare tummy above his low-slung jeans.

Patrice shook her head. 'We'd better get on the road,' she answered.

Jonty overruled her. 'A coffee would be lovely.'

Patrice watched Jonty's eyes follow Justin out of the room. She smiled. 'It won't hurt you to miss one day.'

'What?' Jonty replied. 'You mean of squash? Of course not.' He sounded annoyed.

Suzanne sat down on the green sofa next to Patrice and Seamus, who started picking at a hole in the arm. Bits of stuffing came out. Patrice tapped his hand and he stopped. The hole didn't surprise her. Everything in Suzanne's house was a bit tatty and faded. There were so many children. But the place had such a warm, friendly feel. Justin, the home-maker, had a real woman's touch in that way.

'Why don't you go and find Ruby?' Suzanne suggested to Seamus. 'She was in the garden the last time I saw her.'

He looked at his mother who nodded and ruffled his hair. 'I'll call you when we're about to leave,' she promised.

Suzanne's hair was particularly wild this morning, Patrice thought, frizzy and sticking up all over. It looked as if she'd just got out of bed. She probably had. She said Justin always let her have a bit of a lie-in on Saturdays, before Pilates.

Her feet were bare and she was wearing what appeared to be a pair of Justin's old jeans, rolled at the bottom again and again and held up with a belt. And she had no make-up on. Right now, Patrice thought, it was hard to believe that she was this high-powered whiz-kid, running a vast depart-ment with a huge budget. In a suit and heels she was a career woman extraordinaire. Lethal. Today, though, she just looked like any regular mum.

'Justin's devastated to be missing his game of squash with you, Jonty,' Suzanne said. 'He can't go without his fix so he's persuaded Mark to play with him. I think Justin's addicted, actually. Can squash be addictive?' She laughed.

Jonty looked at his nails, pushing back the cuticles. 'No, but you do need to keep it up,' he replied seriously. 'You can lose it very quickly if you don't play.'

Justin reappeared, carrying a tray rattling with mugs. He put it down in the middle of the room, on the stained cream carpet, and got down on his knees. Then he pushed the plunger slowly into the glass cafetière.

Patrice watched, fascinated, as the coffee gathered in a sludgy pile at the bottom of the pot. She noticed Justin's hands. They were nice, clean and strong-looking, but his nails were uneven. He didn't go in for manicures like Jonty, then.

His hands were bigger than Jonty's, too, and Justin didn't have any jewellery. Jonty wore a wedding and a signet ring.

Justin sensed Patrice looking at him. He glanced up and gave her a wide, open smile. 'White or black?' he asked.

Jonty interrupted. 'We should be back in time for a game tomorrow afternoon,' he said quickly. 'Can I leave you to book a court, Justin? For about four, say?'

The hotel was about an hour and a half's drive from London. It was right on the river. There were ducks waddling around on the grass outside the window. They dumped their bags on the wooden four-poster bed and opened the window to let in some fresh air.

Patrice liked the Victorian theme: there was a pretty antique porcelain washing bowl and jug on the chest of drawers and an old oak wardrobe in the corner. The curtains were full-length and swaggy, and the thick carpet was covered in old roses.

Jonty suggested a walk immediately.

'You seem distracted,' Patrice said, as they strolled along the riverbank.

'Do I?' Jonty replied. It was very hot and he had beads of sweat on his forehead. He opened a couple more buttons on his shirt. 'There's a lot going on at work,' he explained.

Patrice took his hand. It felt clammy, but she didn't take her own hand away. 'Try to relax,' she said. 'It's not often we're on our own like this.'

She stopped to knock some small stones out of her sandals. Jonty walked on and she had to jog to catch up with him.

He was in brown suede loafers, so he didn't have the same problem.

They finished dinner early. Jonty had a headache and didn't want pudding. Patrice didn't bother either. She'd never been particularly interested in food, but she'd have eaten something more, just to extend the evening, if he had.

Afterwards, they sat in the lounge with glasses of white wine, watching the other guests coming and going.

'Let's have an early night,' Patrice suggested. 'You're probably tired. You'll feel better in the morning.'

Jonty looked annoyed. 'Stop telling me what to do.'

Patrice felt as if she'd been slapped. She sank into the armchair, wishing she could shrink into the fabric.

Jonty sighed and ran his hand through his thick fair hair. 'Sorry for barking,' he said. 'It's been a bad week. I think I'll have a bath.'

He rose to leave.

'I'll give you a back rub,' Patrice offered. He loved her back rubs. To her surprise, however, he shook his head.

'Might make my headache worse,' he explained.

She followed him upstairs, plonked herself on the sofa and turned on the TV. There was nothing worth watching so she zapped it off again. Then she picked up a glossy magazine from a rack beside the sofa and started to flick through it.

She paused over a headline – 'We hit rock bottom and turned our lives around' – and started to read. It was about three women in their thirties and forties who'd each been through a major trauma and come out the other side stronger and happier than before.

One had been widowed, then started up her own successful business. Another had suffered countless miscarriages before adopting a child from China. The third, a single mum, had got divorced in her twenties. Ten years later, she'd applied to university and trained as an accountant. She was so poor that sometimes, the article said, she'd had to go without supper so her daughter could eat But now she was fully qualified and loving her work.

Amazing woman, Patrice thought. Inspiring. And how stimulating to start on a whole new career like that in later life. But Jonty would hate her to leave Seamus, and he'd loathe her being in an office with other men. He could be incredibly jealous like that.

She looked more closely at the picture of the single mum. She wasn't conventionally beautiful. She had a large nose and thin lips and her clothes were cheap. But there was something very attractive about her. Patrice couldn't quite put her finger on it. Then she realised: it was her smile, full of hope and amusement. It was as if she'd taken her life in both hands, given it a shake and discovered it was full of sweet surprises.

Patrice threw the magazine down. Stupid article. It was probably all made up anyway. She went into the bathroom. Jonty was sitting in foamy water, reading the paper. He had a lot of baths and showers, two a day, usually. It was important to him to be clean.

The air was hot and steamy and the mirror had misted over. He didn't look up. Patrice wandered back to the bedroom, undressed and put her pyjamas on. The sheets were deliciously cool and the pillow felt soft against her cheek.

She heard Jonty groan and rise from the water. He must have pulled the plug out, because the water gurgled noisily down the pipes. She closed her eyes when he came in the room and heard him open his book. Her back was turned to him.

'Jonty?' she said. She felt nervous but pressed on. 'I sometimes feel like you prefer Justin's company to mine.'

He paused, then patted her side, under the sheet. 'Don't be silly,' he said. 'Whatever gave you that idea?'

She thought for a moment, opened her mouth to speak, closed it again. It was safer not to reply. She didn't dare.

But her mind was filled with the image of Justin, smiling his bright, friendly smile, an inch of flat tummy showing between his tight T-shirt and his low-slung jeans.

She tried to brush the picture away, but it kept reappearing, like a computer screensaver that's been wrongly set.

The only way to banish the picture completely, she found, was to think of her father.

Chapter Twenty-One

❧❦❧

Suzanne had noticed it as well, the way Jonty's eyes followed Justin around the room. She laughed. 'I think he hero-worships you.'

Justin was stirring the Bolognese sauce for lunch, Felix perched on his left hip.

'What do you mean?' he asked, swinging Felix away before he could grab the spoon.

'He seems to think you're the bee's knees,' Suzanne explained. 'You've got a new fan.'

Justin put his finger in the sauce, tasted it and smacked his lips. 'Delicious.' Then he looked at Suzanne. 'I hadn't really noticed, to be honest. But I do know he's a bloody good squash player. D'you want to call the children down?'

Suzanne put some forks and glasses on the big pine table by the back door. She pulled the highchair closer to her seat and lifted Felix in.

'Dadadada,' he yelled, holding his arms out.

She shook her finger at her small son. 'No, you can sit next to me for once, young man,' she said firmly, twizzling a few strands of spaghetti on her fork and popping them in his mouth. Red sauce splattered over his face. How did Justin always manage to do it without making a godawful mess?

Lara sauntered in and pulled out a chair. She was wearing an oversized grey lambswool sweater. The three silver earrings in her left ear winked menacingly.

'Hey, that's mine,' Justin said, annoyed, pointing at the sweater.

'Sorry, I couldn't find anything else,' Lara replied.

Suzanne thought Lara didn't look remotely sorry.

'Have you been going through my wardrobe?' Justin sounded accusing. 'Everything that's yours is mine and everything that's mine is mine, eh? Your mum gave me that for my birthday.'

Lara tossed her head. 'I haven't been in your wardrobe, it was on the back of the door,' she declared. 'What've you got to hide anyway?'

Suzanne felt her temper rise. How dare Lara be so rude? 'Don't talk to Justin like that,' she snapped.

Justin shook his head. 'Leave it, Suze. It needed a wash anyway.' He got up and went to fetch Lara some spaghetti.

She raised her hand imperiously. 'I just want salad. I'll get it myself.'

Suzanne marvelled at Justin's sang-froid. He was a saint with Lara, he really was. So much calmer than her. She could have slapped the girl again.

Seamus was sitting quietly next to Ruby, taking it all in.

'Are you OK, sweetheart?' Suzanne asked. The atmosphere was probably getting to him.

'I miss my mummy,' he said, biting his bottom lip.

'I know, but she'll be home tomorrow,' Suzanne replied gently. She wasn't sure what else she could say. She wasn't terribly good with other people's children. Or with her own for that matter, she thought gloomily.

Justin sat down again and put his arm around the small boy, giving him a hug. 'Guess what?' he said cheerily. 'There's ice cream for pudding if you eat up.'

Lara returned from the fridge and jabbed her fork into a plate of salad leaves. There were black circles under her eyes from yesterday's mascara.

Suzanne thought she looked both pale and thinner. 'Are you sure you're eating enough?' she asked.

Lara narrowed her eyes and stared at her mother for a

moment, then looked down at her plate. She stuck her fork in an olive and popped it in her mouth. She seemed to be thinking about something.

'D'you know what JGE means?' she asked at last.

Suzanne shook her head.

'Just Gay Enough.' Lara grinned. 'It's, like, men who are brilliant cooks and dads, in touch with their feminine side. But they can also mend cars, put up fences, do the macho thing, too. Doesn't that describe Justin perfectly?'

Suzanne laughed, deciding she'd play Lara at her own game.

'Just Gay Enough? I like it,' she replied cheerily. 'The perfect male, in fact. Well, I'd certainly say that's Justin. Wouldn't you, honey?' She smiled at her husband, but he was looking down at his food.

Lara shoved another forkful of leaves in. She pulled a face, as if she'd tasted something bitter. Justin didn't reply. He started carrying some of the dirty plates to the sink.

'I fancy a swim this afternoon,' he said. 'At the pool with the wave machine. Anyone coming?'

There was a chorus of yeses from the younger ones. 'Maybe,' Ollie grunted. He pretended he was too grown-up for family jaunts, but he still liked them, really.

Justin looked at Lara. 'Interested?'

She scowled. 'You must be joking.'

'Mind if I pass?' Suzanne asked. 'I've got some work to finish for Monday.'

Justin shook his head. He started loading the dishwasher and Suzanne rose to help. He was bent over, putting plates in the rack. She put a glass in the wrong place. He tutted and looked up. She caught his eye and smiled. His face was bathed in the sunlight coming through the window.

For the first time, Suzanne noticed creases round his eyes and on his forehead – and were those flecks of grey in his hair, at the temples?

She felt a stab of sadness. He was getting old, her beautiful Justin, just like everybody else.

'Love you,' she mouthed.

'Love you too,' he mouthed back.

Lara's mobile beeped and Suzanne twirled round. 'How fabulous, now all your exams are finished,' she said. 'What are you up to this afternoon?'

Lara read her text message. 'I'm out – with Noah,' she said, snapping the cover of her mobile shut.

'Fine,' Justin muttered, banging the dishwasher closed.

Patrice flung her arms round Seamus. 'I've missed you so much, sweetheart.'

Suzanne stood back and smiled at Jonty. He looked extremely dapper, she thought, in his blue blazer and immaculate chinos. It was so different from Justin's laid-back holiday gear. Justin favoured sloppy T-shirts, baggy shorts and Birkenstocks.

Seamus finally pulled away from his mother's embrace. 'I slept in Ruby's room. We made a pirate's den,' he said. His eyes were bright with excitement.

'Did you?' Patrice grinned. 'You lucky boy! What fun!'

Jonty unzipped his bag and pulled out his squash clothes. He'd remembered his racquet, too. He looked at his watch and motioned to Justin impatiently. 'We'd better go.'

Justin nodded and kissed Suzanne on the lips.

'Have fun,' she said.

She and Patrice went into the kitchen. Patrice watched while Suzanne filled the kettle.

'Thanks so much,' Patrice said, sitting down at the pine table. 'I'd love to return the favour and have your kids sometime.'

Suzanne laughed. 'All four? I don't think so. I wouldn't do that to you. But maybe you could have Ruby and Felix for a night, when Felix is a little bigger?'

The back door was open and there was a warm breeze blowing through the kitchen. Suzanne looked at Patrice. She was wearing a black wrap dress with three-quarter-length sleeves and her long, pale, smooth legs were bare. She looked cool and elegant.

'How was it?' Suzanne asked.

Patrice rubbed her eyes. She seemed tired. 'It was a lovely hotel,' she began to say, but she didn't finish. She made a funny, choking sound and looked at her lap. Her blonde hair hung down in a sheet, obscuring her face.

Suzanne was startled. 'Oh, darling, whatever's the matter?' She pulled her chair alongside Patrice's and put an arm round her.

Patrice tugged a tissue from the bag on her lap. She was crying. 'I'm sorry,' she said, blowing her nose. 'It's just we didn't really have a nice time at all.'

Suzanne was confused. She'd suggested having Seamus because she knew Patrice and Jonty needed time alone. They'd booked a lovely hotel. How could it not have been a success? She and Justin would have leaped at the chance. They always had a brilliant time when they were away together, not that it had happened for an age.

Patrice continued, her voice cracking: 'Jonty was in a foul mood. He went to bed at nine with a headache and has hardly spoken to me today. I felt he couldn't wait to get home.'

Suzanne took her arm away and gave Patrice's hand a squeeze. 'I'm sorry,' she said. 'What's his problem, do you think?'

Patrice shrugged. 'I guess he's just really stressed at work.' She looked at Suzanne. Her face was blotchy and wet. 'I'd been so looking forward to it,' she went on. 'We haven't had a night away together since before Seamus was born.'

Suzanne rose, went to the cupboard and fetched two glasses. 'You could do with a drink, I reckon.' She started opening a bottle of white wine. 'Men,' she said, trying to sound comforting. 'These things happen sometimes. They get so wrapped up in their work, they've no idea of the effect it's having on their poor wives.'

She handed a glass to Patrice and took a sip herself. 'I think you need to have a really good talk with Jonty. Make sure you pick a time when he's not too stressed and tell him how unhappy you feel. It's the only way. He probably doesn't even realise how vile he's being.

'Justin's had to do it with me sometimes,' she went on. 'I get really bogged down at work and dump everything else on him. Once or twice he's hauled me up and told me in no uncertain terms that I'm taking him for granted. It's like a warning shot across the bow. Do you think you could do that with Jonty?'

Patrice tucked her hair behind her ears and dabbed her eyes with the tissue. She'd stopped crying now, almost, but it was obvious she could easily start again.

'Jonty seems so distant,' she said, ignoring Suzanne's question. 'Like his mind's elsewhere.'

She looked Suzanne in the eye. Patrice's expression was intense, almost pleading. It made Suzanne flinch.

'Do you ever feel that with Justin?' Patrice asked. 'That he's somewhere else entirely?'

Suzanne shook her head. 'Not really. I'm lucky. We're extremely close. We argue, of course, like everyone, but we really are best friends as well as lovers. But it took me a long time to find him, remember. I had to kiss a complete frog before I found my prince.'

Chapter Twenty-Two

❦

Percy pressed the quick-start button on the cross trainer and a red light flashed: 'Enter weight'.

She was inclined to fib, but decided not to, on the basis that she'd burn fewer calories if she did.

She checked that no one was leaning over her shoulder and tapped her weight on the keyboard: 57 kilos, give or take. Well, slightly more give than take.

'Enter time', the machine said now. She pondered for a minute. How long could she stand? Fifteen minutes? Think of that bikini. Twenty minutes? Think of Danny. Percy tapped in thirty minutes. Brutal.

'Enter programme': Train Reverse. That was a good firmer and toner.

'Enter Resistance': 7. That was more than halfway up the scale. Her finger hovered over the rewind button. Was she being overambitious? Should she switch to 6? She pressed 'Enter'. Level 7 it was. There was no going back.

The red light flashed again: 'Start'. Percy held on to the two handles in front and began to pedal forwards. It felt a bit like running, only her legs and arms went round in a circular sort of motion. It got to her thighs straightaway, as if she were walking up a steep hill. This was going to be a long half-hour.

She fiddled with the knob to her left and adjusted the volume. There were about six huge TV screens in a row above her, so there was plenty of choice. At least she could stare at something mindless while she sweated.

A dodgy-looking couple with tattoos were screaming at each other in the TV studio. The man got up and hollered at the woman: 'Why did you beeping screw my beeping mate, then?'

Charming, Percy thought. She turned the volume down a shade and waited for the presenter to step in. How were they going to resolve this one?

Percy glanced at the young man to her left. He was sitting on a bench, pushing the handles of a huge metal contraption. He was sweating profusely and you could see veins bulging in his neck. He had a massive chest and enormous biceps. He clearly spent hours in the gym, but there was something deeply unattractive about him. Maybe he just looked as if he tried too hard.

She thought of Mark. There was no chance of that with him – of his trying too hard on an exercise machine. He was far too busy.

Zeus worked all hours, too. Hell. He hadn't asked her about the five thousand pounds yet, but it was only a matter of time. He must be wondering why she hadn't mentioned it.

She felt the sweat trickling down her back. She wanted to be sick. She seemed to feel permanently sick these days. She'd misread Gunslinger badly last night. Usually when he became a Happy Harry, chatting away, it meant he was bluffing, but this time, he wasn't.

Whitewitch, who'd long since left the game but stayed on to watch, had warned Percy to be careful – she'd sent her a private email. Percy had shrugged off her cyberfriend's concerns, tried not to show she was panicking. But she guessed Whitewitch knew her better than she realised.

Percy could see now that she'd been reckless, made stupid mistakes and failed to pick up on the signs. She was dumbstruck when Gunslinger produced a straight flush. There was no getting away from it – he'd totally outplayed her.

She tried to focus on something else and caught sight of

herself reflected in the glass window of the studio. She could see the outline of her pot belly, even from here. Her mother was right, she did need to lose a few pounds, but at least she made some effort.

The machine beeped. 'Slow down and prepare to change direction' it said. Percy eased off and took a swig of water. Now it was time to pedal in the other direction.

Her heartbeat was way up and she was puffing like crazy. She looked at the gauge on the front: 'Calories burned: 232'. Excellent. She should have used five hundred at least by the time she'd finished. She'd have to steer clear of the muffins in the café after, though. It would be too easy to undo all the hard work.

Patrice wandered in, a white towel draped round her shoulders. Percy felt her spirits lift. Goody. She hadn't expected to see her friend this morning. Patrice would take her mind off things.

She was wearing a tiny T-shirt, tracksuit bottoms and trainers. She didn't seem to have any boobs or bum at all today.

She walked over to the tricep press, sat down, adjusted the weights and started to pull. She only did about eight pulls, though, then stared out of the window. She's got her head in the clouds, that one, Percy thought fondly.

The shouting on the TV got louder. The best mate had appeared. He had even more tattoos than the other two. Percy found herself wondering if any fathers, mothers, siblings or offspring for that matter – would be similarly adorned.

She was curious to find out, but *Cash in the Attic* had started on the other screen so she flicked channels. This was more like it. She enjoyed *Cash in the Attic*. She really should try to get on that programme, get rid of a few of her hideous old antiques and make some money in the process. She could certainly do with it.

Patrice followed Percy into the café afterwards. Percy always felt pleasantly high after the cross-trainer session. Less anxious, certainly. Must be the endorphins whooshing round her body. They were more effective than drugs.

'When are you going away?' Patrice asked.

Percy dipped her spoon in the frothy chocolate at the top of her skinny latte. She wondered idly if it was silly, having chocolate when she'd expressly asked for skimmed milk. A bit like ordering Diet Coke and a Big Mac. There again, you could argue that the skimmed milk *counteracted* the chocolate.

'The fourth of August,' she said. 'I'm looking forward to it.'

Patrice rootled in her bag and pulled out an envelope. 'I just had another letter from my mother.'

Percy pulled a face. 'Uh-oh. What does she say this time?' She and Patrice had had many conversations about difficult mothers. They were both victims in that way. It gave them a special sort of bond. The difference, though, was that Patrice never saw her mother, whereas Percy saw hers far too much.

Patrice took the letter out and turned it over to show Percy the spidery black writing on both sides.

'It's the same old thing,' Patrice sighed. She was frowning. 'I get one every week. How much she misses me, how she wishes she'd taken me with her. What a miserable life she has. It's upset me, like all the others. But, you know, I can never forgive her. Nothing will ever change that.'

Percy frowned. 'Do you ever write back?'

'Only very occasionally,' Patrice replied. 'Just to tell her about the big things. I wrote briefly when Seamus was born, for example. A few lines, that's all.'

Patrice put the letter down, peered in the envelope and pulled something out. It was a passport photo, slightly crumpled.

'Look,' she said. 'My half-brother, Edmund.'

Percy smiled. 'He looks nice,' she said, examining the photo. 'Much darker than you.'

Patrice nodded. 'I'd like to meet him one day On his own, though, not with my mother. I can't blame him for what happened, it wasn't his fault. I think I'd find it quite difficult, though.'

Percy looked at her friend kindly. 'You should write to him. You might find you get on really well. I bet he'd love to meet you, too.'

Patrice sighed. 'I feel quite sorry for him, actually, stuck in a flat with miserable old Caroline moaning on about her lot. Sounds like he's a bit of a rebel. Gives my mother sleepless nights. Serves her right.'

Patrice tucked the photo carefully in her purse. Then Percy watched as she tore the letter into little pieces and dropped them in her saucer. She took the saucer to a bin in the corner of the room and waited while the pieces fluttered down.

'That's better.' Patrice smiled, settling next to her friend again. 'I feel I can breathe now. It's the only way I can cope.'

Percy needed to call in at the supermarket on her way home to get a few things for supper. It was right below the club, on the High Street. She was probably one of their most frequent customers.

She hated supermarkets almost as much as she hated cooking. It was the drudgery of it all that got to her. Give her a nice little delicatessen and she'd be in ecstasy amongst the olives and ciabatta, but shopping for fish fingers and washing powder week in and week out was something else.

She put Rowan in the trolley and picked up some bread, sausages, salad, yoghurts and a tub of mixed seeds for herself. They were better for her than chocolate muffins, anyway. She was starving.

That was the problem with exercise: it made you ravenous. She remembered her friend, Stella, who'd stopped going to the gym when she was on one of her mad diets because she said she felt too weak.

The conversation had troubled Percy. She couldn't help wondering if Stella had a point. Maybe it would be altogether preferable to eat nothing and lie in bed all day rather than slog away on the treadmill. But that couldn't be healthy, surely? Something else she'd better check with Suzanne, Patrice and Carmen.

Once she'd paid, Percy stood outside the entrance of the supermarket and dug the seeds out of a bag. She tugged at the lid, but it wouldn't come off. It had one of those clever plastic pull things that no one with an IQ below 150 could work out.

She started to tear at it with her teeth. She hoped they wouldn't drop out, but this was an emergency.

All of a sudden, the world went black. She panicked and struggled, before realising it was someone's hand over her eyes. It smelled familiar, of soap and strangely sexy body odour. She pushed the hand away and swivelled round, grinning.

Danny was smiling down at her from a height. 'Hi!' he said. His voice sounded warm and low.

Percy noticed an attractive, late-middle-aged, dark-haired woman behind him. Percy had seen her with Danny in Gym and Slimline a few times. She wondered what they were doing.

Danny continued to grin. Percy cleared her throat and he remembered the woman behind.

'Hey, this is Alicia, one of my clients,' he said. 'Alicia, this is Par-see-fone.'

'Er, Percy,' said Percy, smiling. The woman nodded coolly.

Percy felt suddenly flustered. What was her hair like and did she have any make-up on? She remembered she was wearing her Diesel jeans and French Connection top. Big relief. And of course she'd washed her hair in the gym.

She glanced at Rowan. Luckily he was looking particularly cute in the trolley, munching an apple.

Danny turned to him. 'Hello, young man,' he said, shaking Rowan's hand. Rowan gave him a big beam. He liked Mummy's big friend.

Danny swivelled back to face Percy. 'You look nice,' he said. 'You've done something to yourself. Had your hair cut?' He stood back, admiring her, as you would a painting.

Percy felt embarrassed. 'I've just washed it for once,' she joked, but she was insanely flattered. She couldn't help it. She glanced at Alicia, but the older woman was looking the other way. Percy sensed she was impatient to be off. She didn't blame her. Alicia wouldn't want to stand around listening to a complete stranger.

'What are you up to?' Percy asked Danny, when he showed no signs of leaving.

He opened the carrier bag in his hand and she peered in. There was a pack of sandwiches and a carton of juice. 'Lunch,' he explained.

Percy tugged at the lid of the seeds and it came off, at last. 'Want some?' She pushed the tub in Danny's direction and he took a handful.

'Tasty,' he said, his eyes fixed on her.

She motioned to Alicia to see if she'd like some, too, but Alicia shook her head. She must be getting really bored now, Percy thought, but Danny hadn't finished.

'Hey, I have to take you to that Italian place sometime, if your husband will allow it?' he said, a smile playing on his lips.

Percy felt her face go hot. She didn't want to sound like a silly little girl. She straightened her shoulders.

'Of course he'll allow it,' she said haughtily. 'I don't need to ask his permission. I'm an independent woman, you know.'

Danny whistled. He looked impressed. 'I can see that!' He grinned. 'How are you feeling from the personal sessions?' he went on, changing the subject. 'Are you noticing a difference? Cos I am.'

Now Percy could feel her neck as well as her face on fire. And was he laughing at her or was it just her imagination?

'I have to go now,' she said quickly. She was eager to get away. It was too embarrassing, with Alicia there, watching. 'I'll see you on Tuesday.'

Danny nodded. 'Cool. Take care of yourself.' He turned to Rowan. 'And bye to you, young man,' he said, taking Rowan's small head in two big hands and giving it a gentle squeeze.

Rowan's cheeks squidged together and his mouth puckered. Percy laughed. When Danny stepped back, Rowan held out his arms.

'He wants a hug, I'm afraid,' Percy explained. 'He adores you.'

Danny stooped down again to Rowan's level and gave him a big bear hug. He's so good with children, Percy thought. He was always playing with the kids in Gym and Slimline. It certainly endeared him to the mums. There couldn't be many young single men like that.

She saw Alicia had started walking off and Percy began pushing her trolley towards the car. Something made her stop and turn. Danny was still standing there, watching her. She thought he'd have gone by now.

She waved, and he winked back and grinned again. Saucy. She felt thoroughly self-conscious pushing her trolley now. She feared his eyes were fixed on her bum, examining each rounded cheek for evidence of unwanted undulations that he'd have to work on with her. But the next time she turned, he'd gone. To join Alicia, she supposed.

Chapter Twenty-Three

Percy resolved to send Zeus an email. Easier than phoning. That way she wouldn't have to hear the worry in his voice, or the disappointment.

She decided to use his work address, so there was no chance Philippa would see. Fingers crossed he'd be on a job somewhere and wouldn't get the message till tomorrow. She'd be out of the country by then.

'Hi, bro,' she typed. It was important to sound cheery. 'Just off on hols. Praying for good weather. Boys v excited. Shall get cash to you on return. Hope Philippa and John well. LOL xxxx'

God she was a coward. And a liar, too. There was no way she could get the five thousand to him now – because it had all gone. She swallowed. Wiped the tears away with her sleeve. Self-pity wasn't going to get her anywhere. She clicked 'send'. They were leaving for France first thing. She'd just have to redouble her efforts and win it back on her return.

She left the kitchen and stumbled down the garden to the garage. The large suitcase was on a shelf, above the bikes. She pulled it down and gave it a dust.

Despite everything, she still felt a little tingle of excitement. She adored Provence. She'd fallen in love with it when she and Mark had a holiday there before the children were born. They'd promised each other they'd return. Now, finally, they were going to do it.

She dragged the suitcase up to her bedroom, plonked it on the bed and unzipped it. Then she opened her chest of drawers. Knickers: seven pairs should be enough. After all, there was a washing machine at the villa. Not that she intended to do much washing. A few bras – including the nude strapless one she'd bought for a Christmas party. Could be useful under her new summer frocks.

She wondered about towels – did they provide them? She couldn't remember. She rummaged in another drawer, pulled out some sheets of paper and examined the pictures she'd printed off the Internet. There were several images of their villa and the pool, surrounded by lavender bushes and olive trees.

She closed her eyes and took a deep breath. Sun, swimming, sex. That's how she hoped to spend the two weeks. No poker. The thought made her feel light-headed. She wasn't sure she could do it. But they'd only have Mark's laptop, and she doubted she'd get the chance to slip away to play. Whatever happened, she mustn't make him suspicious.

It would be incredibly hard to blank everything, when all she really wanted was to win back the ten thousand pounds she now owed. Pay off the credit card. Give Zeus what was his. She swallowed. Ten thousand pounds. It didn't seem real. Things like this didn't happen to women like her. She felt like a character in some terrifying film.

She shook her head. She wasn't eating or sleeping properly. She was a wreck. The only time she seemed to be able to forget about it all was when she was at Gym and Slimline, or working out at home with Danny. But she'd have to try her damnedest to act normal, for the sake of the boys, for the very survival of her marriage.

Mark was grumpy and worn out. It would take him a few days to unwind, but they always got on better on holiday. Surely, if she could only escape from poker, two weeks in Provence in August couldn't fail to bring them closer?

She checked the information on one of the sheets of paper. Yes, they provided two towels per person. And someone would come in once a week to clean. Marvellous. And there was a pool man and a gardener. Luxury.

She finished packing and went down to make tea for the boys. There was hardly anything left in the fridge – she'd deliberately run it down. But there were a few eggs, at least. They could have scrambled eggs on toast. Nice and easy.

It took her ages to get Ben and Rowan off to bed – they were on a high. They kept taking things out of their suitcase and trying them on: goggles, snorkels. A pair of Rowan's underpants ended up on his head, his face poking through one of the legs.

'I'm a knight,' he explained, lunging at Ben with a pretend sword. Percy couldn't help laughing, until Ben rugby-tackled Rowan. He fell over, caught his shoulder on the corner of the bookcase and started howling.

There was no sign of Mark. What was he playing at? She felt a pang of regret, remembering how her own father had loved their family holidays in Cornwall when she was a girl. He'd taken her and Zeus crabbing nearly every day, bought slabs of bacon and helped them tie the fatty bits on to the ends of pieces of string.

She and Zeus would hang their legs over the quayside and wait till they could feel that thrilling bite. Then they'd quickly pull the string up, to find, sometimes, three or four crabs hanging on for dear life. Percy would squeal and back away, but Zeus was much braver. Even though he was younger than her, he'd pick the crabs up by their shells, carefully avoiding the pincers, and pop them in a bucket of seawater.

Percy couldn't remember ever getting bored with the game. She could have gone on for ever. When their father finally said it was time to go home, they'd tip the crabs back in the sea. Then they'd return to their cottage and sit by the fire, playing pontoon and poker while Antonia went for drinks with the other couples nearby. There was always quite a community in August. Most families returned year after year to the same place.

Percy finally tucked the boys up and padded downstairs to make herself something to eat. She glimpsed the computer in the corner of the kitchen. At least if Mark was going to be late she'd be able to play. She felt for the new Tesco card in her pocket. She was amazed how easily she'd been able to get hold of it. But she hadn't expected to dip into it again tonight.

For a split second it had crossed her mind that she could use it to repay Zeus. But then she'd still have the other five thousand pounds to explain away to Mark. She'd dismissed the thought instantly. No, she must win the whole lot back, then she'd be able to relax.

She walked over to the fridge and peered in. The boys had polished off the eggs. She'd have to make do with toast and marmite. Good job she wasn't particularly hungry.

She put the bread in the toaster, poured herself a glass of white wine while she waited and took a slurp. Then she felt in her other pocket and found the tortoiseshell hairclip.

She pulled her hair off her face and coiled it up in a neat twist. That felt better. She took the black cardigan from the back of the chair and put it on, did the buttons up, slipped her feet into the black heels that were under the desk. Cleared her throat.

The toast was ready. She took a bite and dusted the crumbs off her cardigan, set the plate down beside the computer and logged on.

She felt immediately different. Focused, mean, a force to be reckoned with. She browsed around a bit and found Johnnypwe. Good. She had a score to settle with him. And how marvellous it would feel to recoup her losses before the holiday!

She felt a shiver of fear and excitement. A message flashed up: 'Welcome to the table.'

'Back for more, Boady?' Johnnypwe taunted. 'You're a glutton for punishment.'

'LMAO – laugh my arse off, loser,' she replied.

'Now, now,' someone else chided.

She sat back and waited for the game to begin.

'I'm not coming.'

'What?' It took Percy a moment or two to unscramble the words. She'd been concentrating so hard. She clicked sit-out and minimised as usual. Pulled up an email. She felt agitated. She needed to get back in before the big blind. She turned. Mark was standing at the kitchen doorway. His body looked huge and bulky in the gloom.

'I said I'm not coming,' he hissed.

She swallowed. Her mouth felt instantly dry. She tried to collect her thoughts. 'What do you mean?' she asked. 'Where have you been?'

He ignored her questions. 'I mean,' he said, 'that I'm not coming on holiday. You'll have to cancel, or go with the boys on your own. What are you doing anyway?' he added, registering where she was.

She stood up shakily. The enormity of his words were sinking in. 'Mark, you can't do this,' she said. 'Please let's talk about it.'

She walked towards him. She was aware of the moments ticking by. She sensed him stiffen in the dark.

'We've already paid for it,' she stammered. 'And the boys—'

'They've offered me two weeks' holiday cover,' he interrupted. 'I can't afford to turn it down.'

Percy put her hands over her eyes. She couldn't believe what she was hearing. A lump appeared in her throat. She'd been pinning so many hopes on this holiday.

'What shall I tell the boys?' she repeated.

Mark thumped the wall, making Percy jump. 'That's your

problem,' he said. 'Don't blame me. You booked it, you deal with it.'

They stood there, facing each other, adversaries, for several seconds. Percy felt giddy. It seemed as if the floor was giving way, the walls likely to fall in on her at any moment.

'What's the matter, Mummy?' A small voice broke through the silence.

She looked up, glancing round Mark's black bulk. Rowan was standing in the hall clutching his teddy. The raised voices must have woken him.

'You should be in bed, darling,' she managed to say. How long was this going to take?

Rowan didn't move. 'You are coming on holiday with us aren't you, Daddy?' he asked. He had his blue Thomas the Tank Engine pyjamas on. His wavy hair was sticking up.

Mark groaned. He was still facing Percy. She waited, holding her breath. Mark swung round, as she knew he would. He paused, squatted right down and held out his arms. Rowan raced into them, making Mark wobble. He steadied himself with one hand on the floor, burying his head in his son's soft hair.

'You are coming, aren't you?' Rowan mumbled again, through his dad's shirt and jacket. He was pressed close to Mark's heart.

'Of course I am,' Mark said gently, rocking backwards and forwards comfortingly. His voice sounded funny, sort of crackly. He squeezed Rowan tighter.

They stayed like that for several seconds. Finally, Rowan pulled away. His face looked hot and sticky. Mark stood up slowly. 'Come on,' he said brightly, 'hop on my back and I'll carry you up. We're leaving in a few hours.'

He bent down again and hoisted his small son up in a piggyback. Rowan squealed with delight. Percy took a deep breath. She was safe. Crisis averted.

She was desperate, now, to get back to the table. She

wouldn't have long to wait. At the corner of the stairs, Mark turned and looked at her. His eyes were hard, cold.

'I will come – for them,' he whispered through gritted teeth.

Rowan dug his feet in Mark's sides, as you would a horse. 'Come on, Daddy, giddyup.'

A nasty, ugly emotion gripped her. She tried to shake it off but it clung on tight. She realised she was jealous – of Rowan, of her own son. *She* wanted to be the one with her arms round Mark, laughing, joking, being loved and loving back. Just as they used to.

Mark bent down, put his hands on the stairs above so he was on all fours. Rowan squealed. Mark started to move. He turned to look at her one more time.

She shrank from his glare.

She was relieved to sit down at the table again, to shut it all out. She didn't have to think about anything else when she was playing poker. She was in another world.

'Hi again,' someone said and typed :) – a smiley face viewed sideways. 'LOL' – 'lots of laughs'.

Not tonight it isn't, Percy thought. Tonight is serious. She'd had some great hands at last, she was on the up. She'd got that winning feeling back, and she liked it.

She decided to act conservative for a while and she folded a lot. She took a sip of wine. Johnnypwe got lucky with a couple of calls but was playing too loosely as he so often did. Jennywren had been weak-tight all evening, clinging in with a couple of lucky hands but too timid to bluff.

Percy was on the button, meaning she was the dealer, and also the last player to receive cards and act on the flop, turn and river. She felt quietly confident when she was dealt two jacks.

The flop turned up a rainbow – king, 2 and jack, all unsuited – giving her the adrenalin rush of trips.

Predictably, Jennywren folded. Johnnypwe bet $200 but took his time.

Percy was convinced that crucial few seconds of delay meant that he was bluffing the kings. She raised him $200 and again, after hesitation, he called. When a harmless-looking 7 came on the turn, her heart skipped a beat. Then the river produced a king.

Percy groaned. Her head told her to fold – it was too risky – but Johnnypwe had been playing so loose and she'd convinced herself a big win was on its way. No one needed it more than she did.

He put in $400, and she raised him $400 immediately.

He reraised $500. She felt the blood drain from her face. Did he have a pair of kings? Surely not. He was just a big, fat liar.

'Worried, sweetheart?' he goaded.

She gulped and called.

She was all set to leap from her chair, punch the air and race around the room like a wild thing.

Two kings flashed up, giving him an incredible four of a kind. She stared at the screen, rubbed her eyes. The bastard had got the third highest poker hand. She was stunned. She'd lost $2,500.

She realised, with a thud, that she'd committed the cardinal sin of falling in love with her hand. Her father had told her about that. Shame she hadn't remembered his warning.

She didn't wait for Johnnypwe's sneering comments. Gripped with terror, she staggered from her seat into the downstairs cloakroom and threw up violently in the loo.

Chapter Twenty-Four

❧

'Mum, is Seamus going to be there?'

Percy opened her eyes. She hadn't been asleep, but it was a relief to shut out the sunlight and the unending road ahead.

Rowan had asked the same question about twenty times.

'No, darling,' she said, again. 'But you'll have Mummy and Daddy and Ben to play with.'

Rowan was silent, thinking about it. They were on the autoroute, just south of Paris. There were hours and hours to go. Mark put on a CD, some Mozart. That should calm the children down.

'Can we have a story?' Ben piped up. He'd been on his PlayStation Portable. Percy had almost forgotten about him, he'd been so quiet.

'In a minute,' Mark replied. He braked suddenly and Percy jumped. There was a huge traffic jam. 'Shit,' he muttered.

Percy bit her tongue. Normally she'd have ticked Mark off about swearing in front of the children and they'd be having a row by now. But she hadn't any energy left. He could say what he liked.

Mozart wafted through her overheated brain, cooling it a little. She laid her head on the rest behind and closed her eyes again.

She longed to doze off, but sleep was impossible. The events of last night were playing over and over in her mind. She felt peculiar, disoriented, as if she'd just flown thousands of miles and stepped off the plane in what should have been the middle of the night into broad daylight.

After her disaster, she'd sat downstairs on the sofa staring into the dark until Mark's alarm went off.

Then they'd roused the children, dressed and carried them, still dozing, into the car. He hadn't asked why her eyes were red, her face all puffy. Probably hadn't even noticed. He wouldn't look at her; he was hardly talking to her.

She tried to imagine the fresh blue pool awaiting them. But her mind was filled with dread. She had no idea for how much longer she'd be able to cover her tracks. She felt everything was closing in on her, as if she were moving relentlessly towards some horrible and inevitable conclusion.

'Get off!' someone screeched. Ben.

Percy craned round to look in the back. Rowan had made a grab for Ben's PSP and she caught Ben thumping Rowan on the arm. Rowan started to cry.

'Stop that, both of you!' Percy said. She repropped the pillow she'd put between them as a barrier. 'Ben, let him have a quick go?' she pleaded.

Rowan looked hopeful but Ben scowled and shook his head. Rowan looked at his mother and sobbed louder.

'Shut up in the back there,' Mark shouted without turning round. His voice was louder than anybody else's. Silence descended.

'I'm waiting for a work call,' Mark continued, more quietly. 'When my mobile goes, you've got to be ABSOLUTELY SILENT.'

Percy exchanged glances with Ben. He sniggered silently, behind his hand. She could see his shoulders shaking. For some insane reason he made her want to giggle, too. She bit her cheek, to stop it. It would annoy Mark so much to see her laughing.

Rowan's eyes had got very big. He spotted the PSP again and made another grab for it over the top of the pillow, but Ben was too quick.

'No, Rowan, it's only for big boys,' Ben said, whipping it

out of his reach. He started waving it in the air above his little brother's head, then in front of his nose, then in the air again, teasing.

'I am a big boy,' Rowan replied.

'I am a big boy,' Ben mimicked.

Percy reached in the back and tried to grab the PSP off Ben to defuse the situation, but it was too late. Rowan started to wail, louder than before.

The phone went and Mark's bellow reverberated around the walls, bouncing off the surfaces. Percy could have sworn that the whole car shook.

'SHUT THE FUCK UP OR I'LL PUT YOU OUT OF THE CAR AND YOU CAN ALL WALK HOME!' Mark shouted. He jabbed the answer button on the phone. 'Hi, Martin?' he said, silkily sweet. 'Great, yeah. We're just beyond Paris.'

Percy almost marvelled at how quickly he'd managed to switch tone. It was quite an art. She wasn't sure she could do it.

They stayed overnight en route in a small hotel and continued their journey the next morning. To her surprise, as the hours went by she sensed a little of the burden lifting slowly from her shoulders.

Despite everything, she realised, it was a relief to get away. Maybe, just maybe, she could fool herself for two weeks that everything was back to normal – that they were an ordinary family enjoying their summer holidays and none of this nightmare had ever happened.

It dawned on her, too, that she was glad to leave everyone back home. Patrice, Carmen, her mother, Zeus. Even Suzanne, who was usually low maintenance, had been calling a lot to talk about the dreaded Lara.

On top of everything else, Lara was now on a stupid diet and was losing weight, even though she didn't need to. That girl seemed to have an in-built self-destruct button.

Friends could be exhausting, Percy thought. She loved

them dearly, but right now she just couldn't give them the time they needed.

They arrived at their villa at around 4 p.m. Percy had a quick look round while Mark unloaded the car. It was everything she'd hoped for. An old farmhouse, it was built in the beautiful, honey-coloured brick of the region, with jade-green shutters and a wide, vine-clad terrace overlooking the pool.

Inside, the floor was covered in cool, pale-green tiles and the walls were simply whitewashed. There was all they needed: dishwasher, washing machine, table tennis, beautiful bed linen and traditional, brightly coloured Provençal bedcovers and cushions. All very jolly. And there were loads of fluffy towels.

The sun was shining, hot, and the cicadas were clacking noisily in the background.

It had cost a lot, in the height of the August holiday season, but Percy had decided it was worth it. For the past few years they'd camped in France or Spain, but Mark always complained about the communal washing areas and lack of privacy. She'd been determined to find somewhere with a bit of luxury this time.

She flung open the shutters in what she quickly decided would be their bedroom and gazed out over the fields beyond the house. Everywhere she looked she could see gnarled old olive trees, and the smell of rosemary and lavender was intoxicating. The Alpilles – the mini Alps, soft and greeny mauve in the late-afternoon sunshine – were rising up in the distance.

'I'm glad you came,' Percy said quietly, turning to Mark, who'd followed her into the bedroom.

'I couldn't let the boys down,' he replied, flinging a bag on the bed. 'I'm knackered after that driving. I'm going to sleep.'

Disappointment spread over her like damp fog. He hadn't even bothered to look at the view. How could he still be angry, even in this place?

She sighed. Mark had taken his shoes off and was lying,

fully clothed, on the bed. His face looked grey and greasy. She wanted to ask him to shower before he climbed beneath the crisp, cotton sheets but she didn't dare.

She tried not to feel angry herself. Of course he was tired. He'd been home so late last night. They'd rowed. He'd just driven hundreds of miles. Leave him be, she thought. She walked out of the room and closed the door quietly behind her.

The boys were sharing a room next door. Rowan had put Bear and Rabbit on his bed. They looked quite jaunty, Percy thought, sitting there on the yellow and green Provençal bedspread. They were well-travelled teds.

Ben was rummaging in his suitcase for swimming trunks and goggles, flinging clothes all over the room. 'I need a swim. I'm so hot,' he said.

'Of course,' said Percy. 'But please stop throwing your clothes round and put them away in drawers. Look, you've got two chests of drawers in here, one for each of you.'

She started to pick his clothes up and fold them. 'Also, you mustn't go in the pool without Dad or me being there,' she went on. 'I'm not so worried about you, it's Rowan.'

Percy knelt down in front of Rowan, to be at his level. Now seemed as good a time as any to have the talk. She'd read a story only a few days ago about a little boy of three drowning in a pool in France on the last day of a family holiday. His parents, busy packing, hadn't noticed that he'd wandered off. She'd had nightmares about it.

She put her hands on Rowan's shoulders and looked him in the eyes. 'Do you understand?' she said. 'You mustn't go in the pool, or even near it, without Mummy or Daddy, OK? Because you might fall in and drown.'

Rowan looked serious. 'OK, Mummy.'

She felt confident the message had sunk in.

Ben was in his trunks now, his goggles on top of his head. He turned to Rowan. 'Coming?' he said. 'We can play catch.'

Rowan's eyes lit up. Percy helped him struggle into his swimming trunks and water wings. He still had a fat little baby tummy, which popped over the top of his trunks. The rest of him was quite slim, though.

He looked very pleased with himself. He liked his new bright-blue trunks with crabs on them. She'd bought similar, slightly more grown-up ones for Ben, too.

'Pinch, pinch crabs,' Rowan said, nipping Ben, then Percy, with pretend claws. Percy laughed and tickled him back.

She tiptoed into her room and delved in the suitcase for her bikini. Her book and sunglasses were in her handbag in the hall. Outside, she settled on a lounger beside the pool while the boys squealed and splashed in the cold water. The unpacking could wait till later, she decided.

She was pleased with the bikini. It was sage green, with dinky cream bows on either side of the bottoms, and the halter-neck top seemed to conjure up an impressive bust from nowhere. She looked down at her tummy. Those personal sessions with Danny had definitely paid dividends. The marshmallow mountain had hardened and flattened; it was more of a hillock, now. Boy, it had been hard work, though, and expensive.

It occurred to her how strange it was, in a way, that she cared about how she looked at all. There was no one here to see, except Mark, and he wasn't exactly interested. But it was a relief to have something else to focus on. Above all, she needed not to think about poker.

She couldn't wait for Mark to come out and join them. It was so beautiful.

'It's lovely, Mummy, come in.'

Rowan was bobbing around in the cold blue water. Ben appeared to be practising his crawl.

'I'm going to read my book for a little,' Percy replied.

There was such a lot to do and see in the area. She wanted to take the boys to the famous Roman aqueduct, the Pont du Gard, and to the ruins at Les Baux. Then there was Arles, Avignon and Nîmes to explore.

But most of all she wanted to spend lots of time by the pool, swimming, sunbathing and eating lovely local produce: big, ripe tomatoes, delicious cheeses and salamis, nectarines, peaches, figs from the local market. They'd all go home healthier and more relaxed. Then, maybe, she'd be in a better position to find a way out of her trouble.

She just hoped Mark's mood would improve, that he'd be nice to her.

Later, after a hot shower, she drove into town to get food. All they had was water and some bread and cheese left over from a picnic at lunchtime. Then she and the boys laid the table and she poured herself a glass of wine.

She sat, with Rowan on her lap, on a wicker chair on the terrace. The sky was a deep orangey-red. It was going to be a lovely day tomorrow.

'Hi!' Mark's voice came from the house behind her. She turned. He was standing in the doorway, rubbing his eyes. He yawned. His clothes were crumpled: he'd obviously just woken. Percy put down the book she'd been reading to Rowan and checked her watch. 7.30 p.m. She smiled tentatively.

'Supper's ready,' she said.

He glanced at the table. 'You went shopping?'

She nodded. 'You were fast asleep.'

There was salad, spit-roasted chicken, baguette. She'd lit the lights round the pool, too. Maybe they'd go skinny-dipping later, she thought. Rowan would love it. He was usually tucked up by 8 p.m. He'd find it hugely exciting.

'Sorry,' Mark said. 'I'd no idea I'd slept so long.' He wouldn't look her in the eye.

She smiled again. 'You must have been exhausted.'

They sat down and Percy prepared a plate of food for Rowan.

'What do you think of the house, boys?' Mark asked.

'Fantastic,' Ben said. 'There's a table-tennis table, and loads of DVDs.'

Rowan tore at a chunk of French bread with his teeth. Being so small, his nose was practically on the same level as the white tablecloth. The bread looked almost as big as he was.

Percy laughed and reached for the camcorder. 'Excuse me,' she said, getting up and moving to the other side of the table. 'I must record this for posterity.'

Mark's eyebrows knitted. 'Where d'you get that?'

She pretended not to notice the anger in his voice. 'John Lewis,' she replied brightly, pointing the lens at Rowan, still chomping on his bread. 'A couple of months ago. It was on special offer.'

Mark threw his knife and fork on the table. Rowan jumped.

'For God's sake, Percy,' Mark said. He hadn't taken a single bite yet. 'There's no money tree at the bottom of the garden, you know.'

She reeled, as if he'd slapped her, and lowered the camcorder. Ben was staring at his plate while Rowan's eyes were enormous. He looked from Percy to Mark to Percy again, uncertain.

'There's no such thing as a money tree, is there, Mummy?' Rowan said seriously. 'Silly Daddy.'

Percy tried to smile and moved over to cuddle Rowan. Bless him. He always took her side. Not that he should ever have to take sides.

She sat down again and picked up her knife and fork, but Mark had spoiled the moment. The food seemed tasteless in her mouth, the white wine bitter. She wanted to cry, but that would be childish. They were both exhausted, that was all. Things would be better in the morning.

But she didn't feel like suggesting a late-night swim under the stars any more.

Later, in bed, she touched his thigh, lightly, with her hand. 'I'm tired,' he said, turning to face the wall.

Percy lay awake for some time, listening to the owl hooting outside. She felt so sad. How could they not be close, put aside their differences, even in this beautiful place?

Is there no hope for us?

But she awoke to glorious sunshine after a long sleep, the longest she'd had in ages. She felt woozy, but pleasantly so. Almost as if she'd been drugged. Home, the computer screen, those endless nights at the poker table, seemed strangely far away, like a distant memory or a dream. She wondered if she'd actually lost any money at all.

She could hear the boys chatting happily next door. She lay on her back for a while, thinking about what she wanted to do: explore the garden or the surrounding area. She started to get out of bed but Mark put his hand on her arm to stop her.

'I'm sorry about last night. Let's try to make this work.'

She was surprised. He looked fresher today, younger. He'd clearly slept well. She took a deep breath and smiled, relieved. Maybe he was going to make a real effort.

She dressed and walked to the local boulangerie on her own to buy chocolate croissants for breakfast. They ate them with orange juice and coffee on the terrace, then Mark took a book down to the pool.

He started reading, but soon got up to fetch his laptop. He was engrossed in something, checking work emails, Percy guessed.

Her stomach reeled. She realised, suddenly, that she desperately wanted to talk to her online friends, particularly Whitewitch, to go over what had happened. Most of all, she wanted to play.

She wondered if Johnnypwe had lost his winnings already. It was only a matter of time, he was such a fool. The thought gave her some satisfaction. She had an overwhelming urge to jump in the car and drive. There must be an Internet café somewhere. Maybe if Mark looked after the boys this afternoon she could slip away.

She shoved the thought from her mind. It would be far too risky. She dived into the water quickly with Rowan and Ben and swam ten lengths of crawl as fast as she could.

Once she'd got her breath back, she spent a good half-hour in the pool, pretending to be a shark and inventing silly ball games. There were a couple of giant inflatable animals which Rowan loved sitting on.

The temperature rose to 35 degrees, and she had to slather both boys in suntan cream and put on hats and T-shirts, which Rowan kept trying to pull off.

After lunch, she felt tired. Mark was still on his laptop, tapping away. She felt more rational now. Of course she could manage two weeks without poker. A break was the best thing. She'd go back to the tables with renewed vigour. Her luck would have returned by the time she got home.

'I feel exhausted,' she told Mark. 'I could really do with a siesta. Would you keep an eye on Rowan and Ben for an hour?'

He didn't look up from the screen. 'Sure,' he replied.

She wandered inside, closed the curtains and lay down under the cool sheets. She could hear doves, cooing, in the garden next door and the faint hum of the children's voices round the swimming pool. The heady smell of rosemary and lavender filled the air.

Percy felt suddenly as if she were in heaven. She wiggled her feet under the sheets, turned on her side and allowed her tired body to relax completely.

There was a piercing screech that seemed to go on and on, boring into her subconscious. She sat up, shocked.

Mark was standing at the door with Rowan in his arms, who was screaming. Rowan seemed to be dripping wet. Ben was standing behind Mark, a worried look on his face.

'What's happened?' Percy said. She jumped out of bed and grabbed Rowan from Mark. The boy's little body was trembling. He stopped screaming and buried his wet face in her chest.

'What happened?' she said again. She felt slightly dizzy. She sat down on the bed, her arms still wrapped round Rowan.

'He fell in the pool,' Mark said. 'Ben was brilliant. He saw him immediately and jumped in and pulled him out.'

'Why wasn't he wearing water wings?' Percy asked through clenched teeth.

'He was playing round the edge, he didn't want to swim. So I hadn't put them on. It was all right, Percy,' Mark insisted. 'We were both right there. He's had a shock, that's all.'

Percy felt as if her head were about to explode. She could hardly speak, then found she couldn't stop. 'I can't believe it,' she said. 'I go inside for half an hour and this happens. Why weren't you watching? He could have drowned.'

Mark took a step back. His face looked black in the shadows, and there were dark rings under his eyes.

'For God's sake, don't be so dramatic. I was there, beside the pool, right? He was trying to reach a ball in the water and just tipped over and fell in. It could have happened to anyone. There's been no terrible accident.'

Percy reached for a towel and wrapped it round Rowan. He was still clinging to her, whimpering, but his little body wasn't shaking quite so much.

The words spilled over like boiled milk. 'You were on your laptop, weren't you?' she hissed. 'Go on, admit it. What were you doing? Talking to your girlfriend?'

Mark took a step back – as if she'd hit him. There was silence for a moment. Percy was vaguely aware of the boys, wide-eyed, looking from one parent to another.

'I can't believe you just said that,' Mark replied at last.

His voice was hollow, expressionless. 'How dare you accuse me of being unfaithful.'

She opened her mouth to respond but, before she'd had the chance to speak, he'd slammed the door behind him.

For the next few days, she kept her distance. She didn't want to risk a row and spoil things for the boys. Mark did the same, skirting round her, acting formally, like a polite stranger.

Several times she caught sight of him, his familiar head bent over book or screen. He didn't look happy, he couldn't be. She didn't want him to be unhappy. But she couldn't reach out to him, either.

He hadn't apologised and didn't seem to feel the weight of what he'd done. She felt bad that she'd questioned his fidelity, but she didn't know what he was up to. How could she when he wouldn't talk to her?

Her nights were haunted by the image of Rowan's little body sinking, sinking, lower and lower into the water. Bubbles rising, arms and legs thrashing. Struggling to reach the surface, and all the time the precious air seeping from his lungs.

She was terrified of drowning. The thought of Rowan drowning was more terrifying, yet Mark had dismissed it as a little accident.

For the boys' sakes, she wore a mask: a happy mummy mask. Mark did his best, too, but they could have been on separate holidays, on different planets. Percy thought her heart might break.

Mark worked on his laptop in the sun or under the shade of an olive tree, avoiding her. He was on his mobile a lot, too. She had no idea to whom he was speaking.

She visited a few places on her own with the boys. Keep busy, she told herself, keep distracted. That way you won't feel so sad, and you won't want to sneak off and play poker.

One afternoon, while walking with Ben and Rowan at the

foot of the Alpilles, where Van Gogh painted 'Starry Night', Percy was gripped with a peculiar sensation.

She'd been fretting about Mark as usual – and the game. She stopped, sensing a sudden association, a connection. It occurred to her that when things were bad between them, she always wanted to play poker. She must have used it in some way to mask the upset, fill the void.

It had worked for a while. But now, the very thing that had been her friend had become her enemy, had got her in its terrifying clutches.

She looked up at the mountains, feeling tears prick in the corners of her eyes. The Alpilles were so beautiful, majestic; they'd been there for millions of years, strong, unchanging.

She made a promise to herself, right there, amongst the parched vegetation and olive trees. Whatever happened between her and Mark, however things turned out, as soon as she'd won the money back, she'd stop playing poker. Never gamble again. She owed it to her wonderful boys – and to herself. She'd be free.

They stayed in the villa to eat most evenings, on the terrace. Mark was always keen to clear away, close the shutters and go inside. He was permanently tired. They chatted with the boys, but not each other. Percy felt stifled beside him, trapped. How could they be so joyless, even here? She couldn't understand it.

On the final evening, they went to a little restaurant in the old part of town. Percy was miserable. Soon, Mark would be back at work and the boys at school. All her problems would come crowding back in. She'd have to speak to Zeus. Try to put him off for a bit longer. Return to poker. Provence would become a distant memory.

She'd enjoyed spending time with Ben and Rowan, but the holiday, really, had been a disaster. It hadn't brought her and Mark closer. In fact, they'd never been further apart.

'You're looking good, Percy,' Mark said suddenly. 'The summer agrees with you.'

She smiled. She didn't think he'd noticed.

They were sitting outside the restaurant under a vine, sipping coffee. The boys were finishing their ice creams. She was wearing the cotton halter-dress she'd bought especially for the holiday. She'd bought a few other new clothes, too, to cheer herself up, but most of them were still sitting in her suitcase. She hadn't even bothered to unpack them. She hadn't felt like dressing up. But she was tanned and healthy-looking at least, she thought.

'Thank you,' she said to Mark. Painfully polite. 'You're looking well, too. I hope you're feeling more relaxed.'

Mark nodded. 'I've managed to read four books. Marvellous.'

But what about me? What about us? Don't you realise we're in big trouble?

That night they lay there, side by side, listening to the owl hooting. Percy's eyes were closed and she could hear Mark's breathing. It was shallow and fast. He was definitely awake.

'Mark?' she said.

Silence.

Should she go on? It would be easier not to. Maybe the wine at supper had given her courage. She spoke again.

'I'm not happy and I know you're not either,' she whispered. 'What are we going to do?'

She could hear him thinking in the velvety darkness.

At last he spoke. 'Would you be happier or unhappier without me?' he asked.

It seemed an odd, negative sort of question. She racked her brains and tried to picture the scene: telling the boys, selling the house, tearing everything apart. There would be so many tears.

'I think I'd be unhappier without you,' she said finally. It was hardly a ringing endorsement, but he seemed satisfied, for the moment, anyway.

'Well then,' he said.

She crept her arm across the bed. There was only a small space between them, but it could have been a chasm. He shifted away from her, out of reach.

Back in London, the phone started ringing almost immediately. There was the unpacking, the obligatory piles of washing and the garden was even more overgrown than usual.

Percy grabbed the letters before Mark could get to them and filtered out the credit-card statements she'd been expecting. She guessed she'd have a couple of days' grace before Zeus called. He'd know she'd only just returned. She needed to get back to the game as soon as she could.

She remembered Danny. He'd be coming on Tuesday. Good. At least there was something to look forward to. She'd decided before she went away to continue the personal sessions for a bit longer. She was enjoying them. They were a welcome distraction.

Now, Danny would be able to admire her tan and, what's more, she hadn't put on an ounce in France. Stress was great for the figure, anyway. There were some compensations. She could hardly wait to see him.

She rang Patrice and asked her to look after Rowan that morning as there was no nursery school. She'd fix Ben up with a friend, too. The day before, she'd put on a face mask and deep-conditioned her hair. It needed it after Provence.

She remembered how she used to do that with girlfriends when she was about fifteen. They'd spend hours getting ready for a party. They even made their own lumpy honey and oatmeal masks and put beer on their hair to make it shine. The beer never seemed to wash out properly and made their hair all sticky. You wouldn't want to run your fingers through it. They'd burn joss sticks, sip Mum's Cinzano Bianco with lemonade and feel terribly grown-up. It was usually a whole lot more fun than the actual party.

Percy had been to a strict all-girls' school and there were rarely enough spotty boys to go around. You lived in fear of failing to 'get off' with anyone, and feeling like a total pariah. It was pretty stressful, really.

Would Tuesday be the same, she wondered? Would the getting ready bit turn out to be the most fun – or the session with Danny itself? She'd soon find out.

PART II

Body Pump

An innovative and exciting 60-minute muscular workout using barbells and weights. It tones and conditions each muscle group and can help you to lose weight and ultimately change your body shape.

Please attend a Body Pump clinic before commencing a Body Pump class for the first time.

Chapter One

❧

Danny turned up on the dot of 9.30 a.m. Percy thought he looked more handsome than ever. He sauntered in as if he owned the place, and his body seemed to be made of elastic, all springy. Each step was a sort of bounce.

'Did you have a good holiday?' he asked.

'Beautiful weather,' she replied. 'The villa was gorgeous – surrounded by lavender and olive trees.'

She stood on one foot, her back to the wall, and tried to look nonchalant. It wasn't easy. She had butterflies in her stomach and her palms were sweating. She wondered if the face mask had made any difference.

'Look at you!' he said, as if reading her mind. He took a step back and stared at her admiringly. He whistled. 'Clearly the French lifestyle suits you.'

She beamed. She knew she was looking good. Thinner. He'd think it was the personal training. He wasn't to know she and Mark had been at daggers drawn. Her eyes were clear, and her hair seemed glossier, too. That was weird, she thought, when she was fundamentally so miserable and wound up. She supposed it was all the extra sleep. She'd gone to bed at around ten or eleven every night in Provence and caught up on all those hours she'd missed playing poker until God knows when.

They went through their usual routine: a run in the park, followed by squats, lunges, push-ups and some stability-ball work.

She felt full of energy and powered through the exercises.

She'd feared she'd be out of condition after a break, but in fact she felt stronger, fresher.

She had no idea how it would happen, she just knew it would. She'd played out the scene, or variations of it, many times in her head. Now it was for real.

She went into the kitchen to get them a drink and Danny followed. She turned on the tap and put her hand out to test the coldness of the water.

She sensed him hovering right behind her, building up confidence, probably. He placed his hands lightly on her waist and whispered softly in her ear. 'Per-seff-own?'

It didn't even matter that he still couldn't pronounce her name. Her whole body tingled and she turned to face him.

At that moment, she knew she could look away, refuse to meet his gaze, take a step towards the other side of the room. It would have been all right, not too embarrassing. He'd have got the message.

Instead, she raised her face towards him and looked him in the eyes. They were big, brown, limpid. For a second she remembered Mark. She felt a hiss of guilt, but it soon evaporated. That bastard, for spoiling their holiday.

Danny's lips met hers. They felt warm and soft. His tongue was wet, hungry. She closed her eyes. What the hell, she thought, she was going to enjoy it.

He slipped one hand between her thighs, prodding through the soft, cotton trousers with his fingers. The other hand slid up her T-shirt and under her bra.

His hands were so big, he could squeeze both breasts together and roll the nipples at the same time.

Percy moaned. 'Quick, let's go upstairs,' she said.

There wasn't a lot of time. He nodded and they stumbled up to her bedroom, grabbing bits of each other as they went.

She pinched his solid little bum – she'd wanted to do that for weeks – and drew the curtains. Mustn't let the neighbours see.

She turned to him and grinned. 'OK, Mr Personal Instructor. Let's see what you're made of!'

He started to pull her top off. It was tight, sweaty, and she raised her arms to help. He bent down to undo her trainers. She kicked them off. Then he pulled down her track-suit bottoms and pants while she ripped his tight little Lycra shorts down. She'd been looking forward to that.

He stood up and she stared at it for a moment. It was enormous, much bigger than Mark's. He grinned, exposing his white teeth.

'Come here, babe,' he urged.

He drew her to him, running his hands down her back, her bottom. She lay on the bed and he stood over her, parted her thighs with his hands and looked down at her appreciatively.

She licked her lips, nervous, closed her eyes and waited. She felt him shove inside. She was taken aback. So soon? What about the warm-up? But he was far too heavy to push off.

He started to move in a long, slow rhythm at first, then faster and faster. The bed squeaked. Hang on a minute, Percy thought, but the brakes were off and there was no stopping him.

He moaned, one almighty groan, and it was over. Percy couldn't believe it. She was outraged. At least Mark was gentleman enough always to let her come first.

Mark, she thought suddenly. Miserably.

What have I done?

Danny pulled himself off and lay beside her on the bed, his hands behind his head. She thought he looked pleased with himself, which was irritating.

'That was great,' he said.

'Was it?'

'What do you mean?'

'Well,' said Percy, 'it was all over rather quickly, I thought.'

He looked at his watch and jumped up. 'Sorry, babe, I couldn't wait, know what I'm saying?' He started picking up his clothes. He wasn't interested in post-mortems, clearly.

'Got to go,' he said, pulling on his shorts. 'I've got another client. See you soon, OK?'

He bent down and pecked Percy on the cheek. Did he think that was the done thing on such occasions?

'You stay. I'll let myself out,' he said, leaving the room. He didn't seem to notice that she hadn't said goodbye.

She heard him spring downstairs, pick up his bag, then the door clicked. She lay there, thinking. She could feel the stickiness between her legs. Her chest felt heavy, painful.

She'd been faithful to Mark all these years. Now, in just a few moments, she'd broken all her promises and it hadn't even been close to the glorious consummation she'd imagined it would be. It was too late now for regrets. She wanted to cry.

Bloody hell. A thought raced through her mind. She hadn't made him wear a condom either. Why ever not? She felt scared. Suppose he'd passed on some horrible sexually transmitted disease? She'd go to the clinic and get herself tested, before she let Mark anywhere near her.

She got up, turned on the shower and tried to scrub Danny off with a loofah. Why on earth had she imagined he'd be a great lover? Weren't young men always selfish? He probably went round shagging most of his female clients, especially Alicia. And now he could add Percy to his list. It was degrading.

She dried herself and put on a clean, pale pink linen frock. She didn't wear it much because she thought it made her look prim. But right now, prim was good.

She brushed her teeth, stripped the bedclothes, shoved them in the washing machine and put fresh sheets on the bed. She felt a bit better after that.

Percy checked the clock. It was nearly time to collect Rowan from Patrice's. Thank goodness. Darling Rowan. He'd take her mind off what had happened.

First, though, she went into the sitting room and picked up the wedding photo from the mantelpiece. Right now, all she wanted to do was hug Mark, hold his dear, familiar, precious face in her hands and kiss him, as lovingly as she knew how.

However cold he'd been with her, however angry and cruel, he was very much the wronged party now. There was no doubt about that. But did she have the power to make amends, to turn things round?

She replaced the photo, picked up the car keys and left the house, locking the front door behind her. There were a few people about and she felt as if they were watching her, casting aspersions.

What were they thinking? Whore? Adulteress? Don't be silly. In this day and age, people didn't think like that any more – thank God. But she was relieved, anyway, to get away from the scene of her crime.

She'd ring Danny tomorrow, tell him she wanted to cancel their personal-training sessions. He might try to dissuade her, but he wouldn't really care. He had plenty of other fish to fry.

Chapter Two

Carmen had picked the heaviest barbells she could find. Lying flat on her back, she heaved them in the air above her head and repeated it ten times. She could feel it most across her chest and shoulders: a heavy pulling and dragging sensation.

By the last two, she thought she might drop the weights. But somehow she found the strength to keep going. Good. That'd keep her toned. Now for another ten. Three sets in all. A tall order.

She was boiling hot, sweating like mad. She dreaded to think what she must smell like. Lucky everyone else was the same. There were groans coming from various corners of the studio. They were all finding it really tough.

She didn't mind the step section next. Up and down, up and down to music, with heavy weights in both hands. Her bottom and thighs were throbbing but she pushed herself to go faster.

Stamp, stamp up and stamp, stamp down the step in front of her. Grapevine to the left, grapevine to the right. Then stamp, stamp on and off the step again. It was a great way of getting rid of nervous tension, and she certainly felt tense today. She should have been doing kickboxing, not Body Pump. Kickboxing was an even better stress-burner.

She, Patrice and Percy were joined in the café by Regina, who often wafted in and out of the club but was rarely seen doing any actual exercise. In fact they wondered if she even possessed a pair of trainers. They secretly referred to her as Vagina.

Regina was dark and pretty, with a lot of unwanted hair. She talked about it a lot, too. She waged a constant battle against it.

She sat down opposite Carmen, her skinny latte on the table in front. She'd been to the beauty clinic next door.

'I tried threading this time,' Regina said, pointing to her upper lip area.

'What's threading?' Carmen asked, taking a sip of green tea. The others stopped talking. They were all agog. They loved hearing Regina's depilatory tips. She'd tried hot wax, lasers and creams, as well as shaving, of course, but threading was a new one.

Regina clearly liked an audience. 'Well,' she said, rubbing her thighs. She had a strong Scottish accent. 'It's an ancient Indian hair-removal technique. They roll taut cotton thread over the skin.'

She said 'rrrrroll' for 'roll'. It was much more descriptive. 'It's supposed to be less painful and more precise than waxing,' she added.

Carmen had a quick look at Regina's upper lip. It was rather red and angry-looking. 'And is it – less painful?' Carmen asked. She had her doubts.

'Och, not really,' Regina replied cheerfully. 'But I'll try anything once. Anyone for another skinny latte?'

Millicent came over to join the group. She was wearing a denim mini-skirt and gold sandals. Her legs were very brown. Definitely fake tan, Carmen reckoned, but there were no streaks. And she looked about sixteen. You'd never guess she'd had three kids.

Millicent didn't sit down. She just wanted to say hello. Or make sure they'd all taken in her itsy-bitsy skirt and perfect pins.

'I've got a doctor's appointment for Jake,' she explained,

tossing her blonde hair. She bent forwards, lowering her voice. 'Can't seem to get rid of his nits.'

Carmen chortled inwardly. She couldn't wait to tell Suzanne. It would make her day.

Everyone seemed to be in the club today. A moment later, Danny appeared. He came out of the men's loo, looking left and right, checking who was around.

He spotted the women huddled round a table, underneath the giant TV screen, and strolled over. 'Hey, ladies,' he said, with a big grin.

Carmen looked at Percy. Her eyes were fixed, firmly, on her coffee. She didn't look up at all.

'What was that about?' Carmen asked, when Danny had sauntered off.

'What do you mean?' Percy was all innocence.

'I mean,' Carmen hissed, 'why didn't you speak to him?'

'Didn't I?' Percy said, surprised. 'Oh, I was thinking about something else. I'm not doing personal training any more, anyway.'

Carmen was suspicious. Something was up. She wanted to know more, but there was no time to tackle Percy right now. It would have to wait till later. She had an important assignment.

Carmen said her goodbyes and scurried downstairs to the supermarket.

Her heart was thumping as she sat on the loo. For a moment she thought she wouldn't be able to pee at all, despite all the water she'd drunk. She was too nervous. But at last it started to flow.

She sat there, staring at her watch. She'd never known a minute last so long. She could hear cars stopping and starting outside. People talking in the street. Dogs barking. A pigeon cooing on the windowsill.

Her flat was on a busy main road. It was weird to think

people were going about their business as normal while here she was, counting the seconds before what could turn out to be the most momentous news she'd ever received.

She looked at her watch again. Just over a minute. More than enough time. She closed her eyes, pulled the white stick from underneath her and took a deep breath. Be brave. She opened her eyes again and stared at the little window in the stick.

Her stomach flipped over and over, doing somersaults. Her head felt light. Best stay sitting for a moment, she thought, or she might collapse. The line was blue. Very definitely blue. Wasn't it?

She held it up to the light and stared at it some more. She couldn't be imagining things, could she? No, blue it was.

For a moment, she wanted to cry. Then she felt like throwing up. But this was silly. It's what she wanted, after all. She could hardly believe it, though. Maybe someone up there was having a big laugh.

A warm feeling started to spread through her body, from her toes, through her legs, right up into her face. Soon she was bathed in warmth.

She was going to have a baby! There was a tiny new person growing inside her. Everything was different now.

Carmen got up, put the stick back in its box and washed her hands. She looked at herself in the mirror. How odd. She half expected to see a stranger staring back at her, but it was the same, familiar reflection. That was comforting, really.

She went and lay down on her bed. She needed to think. She pulled up her T-shirt, opened her jeans and put her hands on her abdomen. She loved her body for not letting her down, for doing what it was supposed to do. It was a miracle.

Already she thought she could detect a slight rounding, the merest hint of a bump, but maybe she was imagining it.

She closed her eyes and tried to visualise what it would look like. Would it be a girl or boy? Would it have her dark-brown oriental eyes, or rounder ones, like Simon?

Simon. Her stomach flipped again. How to tell him? He'd be back tonight. She'd better not delay it. He'll be fine, she told herself. They'd been getting on so well recently. Like two lovebirds.

He couldn't not be thrilled once he knew there was a baby – his baby – growing inside her. But how was she going to break the news?

She decided to prepare supper. She needed to do something, keep busy. Work would have to wait. She strolled into the kitchen and got out a sharp knife and the wok. She'd chop up a load of vegetables and some chicken. All good, nutritious food. And no more alcohol now. After all, there was someone else to think about.

She wasn't on her own any more.

She tied her hair up in a chignon and fastened it with the silver clip. She could feel little wisps coming down around her ears and the back of her neck. She put on a pair of long, dangly diamanté earrings and some black kohl round her eyes. Heaps of red lipstick.

She heard the key in the lock and Simon walked in. He stopped in his tracks when he saw her, standing there in the middle of the room surrounded by candles.

'You look beautiful,' he said.

He kissed her on her neck. She bent her head to one side, to make it easier for him.

'Thank you,' she whispered. He made her glow inside with pleasure. Then she remembered. Her body stiffened.

'Why don't you have a shower? I'll finish supper.'

She'd planned to tell him after he'd eaten, but he looked so relaxed after his shower, all warm and clean and affectionate, that it seemed like as good a moment as any.

She took a deep breath and drew herself up. 'Simon,' she said, 'I've got something to tell you.'

He looked at her and a frown spread across his face. 'What is it?'

She tried to smile, but she knew her face was etched with fear. He could probably smell it. 'You'd better sit down,' she said.

She'd been rehearsing this moment, but it didn't make it any easier. She half pulled, half pushed him to the sofa and sat down. She felt as if her stomach had dropped into her pelvic floor and the contents might spill out over the sisal carpet.

'What is it?' he said again. He sounded irritated. She knew he hated surprises.

'Simon, there's no easy way to tell you this – I'm pregnant.'

Carmen searched her lover's face. She expected to see shock, nerves – panic, even. But she hoped there'd be a glimmer of excitement and wonder, too. But there was none. All she could see was dismay – no, anger – in his cool grey eyes. Or was she just imagining the anger?

'But how?' he stuttered, incredulous. 'You're on the pill.'

'I don't know,' Carmen lied. She couldn't bring herself to admit the truth. 'It's not a hundred per cent foolproof, you know.'

Simon ran his hands through his hair as he absorbed the news. 'How many weeks?' he asked. His voice was dead.

'About six, I reckon,' she replied. She folded her hands in her lap. 'I've just done a pregnancy test.'

They sat, side by side, for what felt like an eternity, staring at the wall. Carmen longed for him to put his arms around her, hug her, congratulate her. She sensed a distance, like a cold chasm, opening between them. She felt very alone.

She waited, silent, for something from him. Some sign of acceptance. At last, he bowed his head, resting it in his hands, and said quietly: 'Carmen, I'm not ready for this.'

She couldn't quite believe what she was hearing. She'd lain in bed earlier, trying to imagine a completely different scenario. She felt sick. But something in her, a small voice, told her that this was just the beginning. He'll come round. Don't worry. He just needs time, that's all.

'Don't worry,' she said. Her voice sounded very far away to her. 'I'll look after it.'

He laughed, without humour.

She ploughed on. 'I didn't think I wanted a baby but now I'm pregnant, I do. Very much. I'm forty and time's running out. I'll have it on my own.'

'Don't be ridiculous,' he replied bitterly, head still bowed. 'Where will you put it? You've only got one bedroom. And who will look after it when you're working? And get up in the night to feed it, and change the nappies and deal with all the puke and shit? Have you thought about that?'

He turned to face her now, his eyes glaring, hostile. She felt suddenly angry – how could he feel so differently from her? How could he not see what a wonderful thing it was, the product of their four years together, their passion and tenderness? She'd even been thinking about names, for God's sake!

She felt her face go hot. 'Well, I'm not going to get rid of it, if that's what you're thinking. No way,' she said. 'This baby is going to have the best start in life, I'll make sure of that. And I'll manage somehow – with or without you.'

Seconds passed. Simon's body un-tensed slightly. He put his arm, stiffly, round her shoulders and pulled her to him. She felt a lump in her throat.

'Look, I wouldn't just leave you, walk out on you, if that's what you're thinking.' His tone was softer than before. 'It's just such a shock. I need time to think, to take it all in.'

'I know, Simon,' she replied, comforted by the warmth of his body. 'I'm sorry to give you such a shock. I wasn't sure when was the best time to tell you, but I didn't want to wait. Apart from anything else, it'll start to show soon.'

He shuddered. 'Fuck, I suppose it will,' he said. 'Well, I guess I'll have to get you a supply of tent dresses. And those huge maternity bras.' He almost managed a smile. 'And support knickers.'

'Support knickers? I don't think so.' Carmen laughed. 'Where did you get that idea from?'

He stared down at his fingernails. 'You're not going to tell anyone yet?' He looked worried.

Carmen was surprised. It seemed unimportant, it was just a detail. 'Not now. But I'll have to soon,' she replied. 'Anyhow, it's difficult keeping a huge thing like this to myself.'

He rose slowly and went into the bedroom. She felt relieved, she realised, though her stomach was still churning. Thank God that was over. And he hadn't taken it that badly, had he? Or at least, he'd seemed to come round, sort of, in the end. At least he hadn't walked out on her, though this wasn't exactly a huge comfort. He was hardly the proud father-to-be but maybe, given time, he'd start to see things her way.

She wondered, for a moment, what it must be like for women who mapped things out, chose themselves husbands, planned their babies, where to raise them. Since the accident, she'd opted out, sat back and waited for things to happen to her. Until a few weeks ago, when she'd made that lonely leap.

Well, it was done now. She went into the kitchen and lit the gas under the wok. She wasn't remotely hungry and nor, she suspected, was Simon, but she must eat. She was going to need all the strength she could get.

Chapter Three

There was a chill in the air and the leaves on the trees round the car park had just started to turn red, brown and gold. Patrice buttoned up her black coat and stamped her feet on the hard ground. The weather had changed so suddenly. It had still felt like summer a few days ago.

She thought of Seamus and hoped he'd be all right with Justin and Felix. She pictured them having lunch together in the big, warm kitchen. Of course he'd be fine, she told herself. Absolutely. They were almost like family to him.

There was a gust of wind. Patrice shivered and hugged her arms around her. Her thoughts turned to Suzanne. They were closer than ever now, since the men had become such good friends. And Seamus was completely at home with Suzanne's children. Ruby and Felix, especially. They had a lovely relationship, almost like siblings. It was good for Seamus, being an only child. Of course it was.

'C'mon, Pats. Time to go.' Jonty proffered an arm. Patrice practically grabbed it and wrapped both her arms around his, leaning on him heavily. She was grateful for the support. She didn't know if she'd be able to do it on her own.

Together they walked through the wooden doors of the modern crematorium. It was faceless, impersonal, but warm inside. That was something, anyway. There was a smell of incense in the air. Patrice could see a small group of people sitting in the front few pews. They looked as if they'd huddled together for comfort.

Percy, Suzanne and Carmen were there, bless them. They'd

probably come in the same car. Patrice loved them for turning up. They hardly knew her father but they'd help to swell the numbers. Mostly, though, she was just so glad to have them near.

She glanced at the pale wooden coffin, surrounded by flowers. It was resting on a platform at the front. There were purple curtains ahead and behind them, she assumed, was the furnace.

Patrice shuddered. She'd wept so many tears in the last week, she thought she had no more left. She was grieving for what she and her father didn't have, for all that they'd missed. She was exhausted with crying. But picturing her father's pale, waxy face, the body moving slowly towards oblivion, made her weep again.

Jonty passed her a clean white hankie from his pocket and ushered her into a pew. She wiped her eyes, studiously avoiding anyone's gaze. She didn't care that people would see her in this state, though. Today of all days, she was allowed to let it all hang out. In that sense, it was her day.

The priest, in his long, white robe, smiled reassuringly at her. His Bible open in his hands, he started to speak. She couldn't really hear what he was saying. It was a formality, anyway, she thought. What could he say about this sad, bitter old man? He'd done the same, boring job for twenty-five years, which he hated. He had few friends and had given nothing beautiful or noteworthy to the world. But he was her father, he'd given her life, at least; and, despite everything, she'd loved him. She didn't know why.

Hot tears continued to trickle down her cheeks while the priest was talking. The hankie was all used up. Luckily she'd come well equipped.

She pulled a wodge of tissues from her pocket. Her nose was really sore, now, from all the blowing, and her lips felt dry and cracked. She glanced up and caught Suzanne's eye.

She gave Patrice such a tender look, it made her feel warm inside.

Jonty had his hand on her knee. He was staring straight ahead. He rose first when it was time for the hymn, and Patrice clung on to his arm again for support.

She mouthed the words, but no sound came out. Just as well. It might have been a squeak, or a wail. Her whole being was preparing for the final moment. She knew she needed all the strength she could muster. She was dreading it, but willing it to come at the same time. Just let it be over.

At last, the curtains started to open, the coffin to move slowly towards its exit. Patrice felt profoundly shocked. She'd never been to a cremation before. She'd been told what to expect and tried to picture it in her head – it was what he'd wanted, after all. But now it was happening for real, she thought it was like some awful, macabre film. A hideous joke.

What if he were really alive in there, hammering on the coffin lid, like Sean Connery in that old James Bond film? What if he were shouting but no one could hear over the music? Don't be silly, Patrice. You saw him in the mortuary. He's dead. Well and truly dead.

She felt her muscles tense. Her fists clenched. She wanted to jump up and run after the coffin, screaming. Lie on it, stop it moving.

Jonty squeezed her knee and took her hand in his. He squeezed that too. He knew what she was thinking. There was an element of restraint in his squeeze. He was right, of course. It would be madness.

They clumped together afterwards in her father's front room, sipping wine and nibbling on smoked-salmon sandwiches. Patrice had arranged for cleaners to come in beforehand to open windows, dust filthy surfaces, scrub sinks and worktops until they shone.

The heating was on and vases of fresh flowers stood all

around, but nothing could erase the desolate feel of the place. It was like stepping back in time. Little had changed in the house since the seventies: the brown and cream wallpaper that might once have been fashionable but now just looked tatty and oppressive; dark brown, nearly empty bookshelves; worn rugs on worn carpets.

Patrice went into the kitchen to fetch some more sandwiches.

Suzanne followed her in and touched her arm. 'Bearing up?' she asked.

Patrice smiled and tried to look brave, but she knew she was doing a very bad job. 'So-so,' she answered truthfully. 'I still can't quite believe it. It was just so sudden. And being here, in this house, brings back so many awful memories.' She pushed her forefingers into the corners of her eyes. Sniffed. She wasn't going to start crying again now.

Suzanne took the plate of sandwiches. 'Here, I'll pass these round,' she said. 'You're doing a great job, Pats.' She touched Patrice's arm lightly again.

Patrice walked down the cramped hall towards the front room. She was half inclined to keep on walking, out of the front door and into the car. Away. But she knew that wasn't an option.

She pushed open the door and made eye contact over the heads with Aunty Margaret. Her heart sank. Margaret immediately left the woman she was talking to, crossed the room and wrapped her arms around Patrice. She smelled of lavender water, hairspray and face powder. A heavy, cloying scent. Patrice had to open her mouth so she could breathe through that rather than her nose.

'Patrice, dear. I'm so sorry,' Margaret said, her arms still clamped around her niece. 'What a terrible thing.'

Patrice waited a moment, then pulled away as soon as she judged she could without causing offence. 'How are you?' she asked, unsmiling. 'And William and James?'

Margaret beamed. Her teeth were small and pointy and there was a blob of red lipstick on one of the front ones. 'Both excellent,' Margaret replied.

She was still standing very close to Patrice. Being much smaller, she had to look up. She had a large, pointed bust, encased in black wool. Patrice could smell butter and smoked salmon on her breath.

'William's busy making his millions in the City,' Margaret said, still beaming. 'James is doing very well in his accountancy firm. Hoping to be made a partner soon, you know.'

Patrice shivered. She hated those boys, or rather men, now, almost as much as she hated Aunty Margaret. She looked around desperately for Suzanne, Carmen and Percy, hoping they'd rescue her. But they were busy trying to be helpful, chatting up the few relatives and acquaintances who'd shown up.

Margaret touched Patrice's arm. She had fat little hands, gold rings, red nails. 'We must get you and the boys together again,' she said. 'You used to have such fun in the school holidays, do you remember? When you came to stay? After your mother, you know . . .' She lowered her eyes.

Patrice felt suddenly hot. She could feel her heart thumping in her chest. Her father was dead, now. There was no need to pussyfoot around any longer. She took a step back, reclaiming her space.

'What?' she said, looking Margaret square in the eye. 'You mean after my mother upped sticks, left me and Father to fend for ourselves and ran off to Australia with the neighbour from number eleven?'

Margaret coughed. 'Well, yes, if you must put it like that.' She shifted uncomfortably on her feet.

She suddenly reminded Patrice of Miss Piggy, with her heavily sprayed, dyed-blonde hair, her oversized frame and small fat feet crammed into too tight shoes.

Patrice felt a rushing in her ears. She was vaguely aware

of Suzanne on her right, putting a friendly arm round her. Patrice opened her mouth to speak, shut it, opened it again. The words came hurtling out. They seemed to have a will of their own.

'Actually, Margaret,' Patrice said. 'I hated coming to your house, and I hated your boys. They were always horrible to me, teasing me and stealing my things behind your back. And you were horrible, too. I was a sad, lonely little girl. I'd lost my mum and missed her desperately. Father was cold and uncaring. He didn't want to look after me himself, so he packed me off to you. He seemed to blame me in some way for what my mother did.

'And you . . .' Patrice drew herself up tall. 'Instead of trying to help me, comfort me, you never so much as gave me a hug.'

Margaret opened her mouth to speak, but Patrice plunged on. 'You made it quite clear I was a huge inconvenience,' she said. 'The only thing you cared about was those nasty, spoiled boys of yours. You didn't even like my father. You had me out of duty, because he couldn't cope. You told me as much.

'I'm sorry, Margaret,' Patrice finished. 'But let's not rewrite history. Let's just stop pretending, shall we?'

Margaret's face had gone bright red and puckered. She stepped back, appearing to shrink in front of Patrice's eyes. 'I . . . I don't know what to say,' she said. 'I'm shocked.' She turned to face the other way. 'I think I need to sit down.'

Suzanne left Patrice's side. She took Margaret by the arm, led her to an old, brown chair in the corner of the room and fetched her some water.

Patrice saw Margaret dab her eyes with a hankie. Then she drew her knees together, put her two hands between them and stared straight ahead. She looked stunned.

Patrice went into the hall. Suzanne found her sitting at the top of the stairs, staring into space, too.

Suzanne grinned. 'You were brilliant.'

Patrice came back to earth.

'Absolutely brilliant,' Suzanne repeated. 'I bet you feel like you've got twenty years' worth of anger off your chest, don't you?'

Patrice looked at her and grinned back. It was the first time Suzanne had seen Patrice smile properly like that for a long time.

'Yes, actually,' Patrice said, getting up and straightening her black dress. 'I feel bloody marvellous. Let's have a drink, shall we? To celebrate.'

Chapter Four

❦

'So what's your secret? How exactly *do* you manage with four children and a high-powered job?'

Suzanne smiled. 'Well, Liz . . .' – Suzanne's media training had taught her to slip the journalist's name in as often as possible, to create a sense of intimacy – 'you know as well as I do working mums like us need lots of support – and I do get it in spades from my husband.'

Liz was the journalist Suzanne had sat next to at dinner during the Amélie launch weekend back in the summer. It had proved a profitable few days in more ways than one. Not only was the Amélie doing well, now Liz wanted to include Suzanne in a feature for *Mary-Beth*, the glossy women's magazine, entitled: 'Real life Wonderwomen – how *do* they do it?' It would be good publicity, Suzanne thought, and the CEO was delighted, especially when she told him *Mary-Beth* sold in the region of four hundred thousand copies a month.

Liz bit the end of her Biro. 'Tell me more about your husband, Justin,' she said, her head cocked on one side. 'He's younger than you, isn't he?'

Suzanne nodded. It hadn't taken long to get round to that one.

Liz was sitting opposite Suzanne, who'd moved out from behind her large, kidney-shaped desk to be closer to the journalist. 'Do you think it helps?' Liz pressed. 'That Justin's so much younger, I mean?'

Suzanne pondered for a moment, instinctively putting her

hand up to her hair to flatten it. She knew she had to be careful. However much she'd warmed to Liz, Suzanne knew her words could easily be twisted and she didn't want to say anything to upset Justin.

'I don't think his age makes any difference,' she replied, not entirely truthfully. The image of Justin's sexy smile, those hunky biceps, the flat stomach, hung tantalisingly for a moment in the air in front of her. Good job Liz wasn't a mind-reader, Suzanne thought. She cleared her throat. 'The main thing is that he's always there for me,' she said crisply. 'And as you've seen, he's absolutely brilliant with the children – including my two from a previous marriage.'

Liz looked disappointed. Suzanne guessed she'd been hoping for something a little juicier. She wondered how many interviews Liz had done that day already, and if her 'Wonderwomen' had all been guardedly boring.

Suzanne crossed her legs and leaned an elbow on her desk, attempting her best, mistress-of-the-universe smile. Except that her elbow missed the desk, catapulting her sideways and nearly off the chair. Before she could stop herself she'd blurted, 'Shitfuckandbuggermyteddy,' through gritted teeth. This hadn't been the plan.

Fortunately Liz, who was scribbling something in her note-book in illegible shorthand, didn't seem to notice. Maybe she swore all the time herself? This possibility raised her several more notches in Suzanne's estimation.

'How do you cope with the sheer numbers of children that you have?' Liz asked seriously. 'All those different sports days and parents' evenings and things? It must be a nightmare.'

Suzanne nearly let slip that she rarely made it to a single one but stopped herself in the nick of time. She remembered how the media-training instructor had said you should try to twist questions to your advantage.

She straightened her back. 'Not really.' She smiled sweetly.

'Now that we have our new Amélie, it's much easier. There's loads of space. We just plonk them all in and off we go. The kids can even choose their own music in the back – there's a separate sound system. And they can watch DVDs too. They don't squabble like they used to. It's marvellous.'

Liz looked distinctly unimpressed. Suzanne hadn't exactly answered the question and, besides, this wasn't an advertorial.

Liz looked as if she were about to speak again. Her mouth opened and shut. But then her eyes widened. Suzanne realised, with a lurch, that Liz's gaze had settled on her chest and seemed to be stuck there.

Suzanne glanced down. The buttons of her shirt had popped undone and her very white breasts were spilling out over the top of her rather too tight beige plunge bra. She wished she'd got round to buying some bigger tops. And a bigger bra, for that matter. They'd definitely shrunk in the wash.

She redid her buttons quickly, looked up and caught Liz's eye. To Suzanne's relief, Liz returned an amused, friendly grin. She had on a flattering black cashmere V-neck. Suzanne bet Liz's boobs never popped out of anything.

'Zara shirt?' Liz asked.

Suzanne nodded. 'How did you know?'

'Recognised the design,' Liz explained. 'It's nice but their stuff is always tiny. It's made for midget Spanish women. You should try Gap. They have some great basics this season.'

Suzanne laughed. 'Thanks for the tip.'

'Talking of which,' Liz ventured, 'what top tip do *you* have for other women juggling jobs and families?'

Suzanne racked her brains. What on earth could she say without sounding trite? She guessed Liz needed something better than: 'Have a massage.' Besides, Suzanne felt she owed Liz one for being so nice about the shirt.

Suzanne frowned, fiddling with her wedding ring. What

would the other interviewees come up with? Banalities, probably. What the hell, Suzanne would give Liz something to write about.

'Um. Masses of sex!' Suzanne said with a flourish. 'It's a fantastic stress-buster and great for the complexion! Forget bubble baths. Sex at least twice a day, morning and night, wins every time. I'd thoroughly recommend it!'

Liz looked thrilled. She was scribbling away frantically. Her CEO might raise an eyebrow, Suzanne thought, but he'd always said the company's image needed spicing up. To be honest, though, it was unlikely anyone she knew would ever read the article anyway.

Liz finally flipped her notebook shut. She seemed really pleased – she'd got everything she needed and more. She promised to send Suzanne a copy of the feature when it appeared. 'It won't be for ages though,' she warned. 'We have a long lead-time. The photographer will be here at midday tomorrow,' she added.

Suzanne got up and smoothed her pencil skirt, which had bunched up round her thighs. Liz's grey pinstriped trousers, on the other hand, looked immaculate. 'You won't, erm, mention the . . .' Suzanne pointed to her now safely covered embonpoint.

'I promise.' Liz tapped the side of her nose.

'And do you know where the article will be in the magazine?' Suzanne ventured. 'You see, I don't particularly want the boss or my friends and family . . .'

Liz looked nonchalant. 'Oh, we'll only be using it small and it'll be tucked away somewhere near the back.'

Suzanne felt relieved.

Liz walked towards the door. Before she got there, she turned and gave Suzanne a big beam. 'By the way, between you and me,' she said, 'you're easily the most wonderful Wonderwoman I've interviewed. I've met quite a few for this piece – all top career women with amazing houses and lifestyles. They may be well dressed but quite frankly they're scary, like robots. They don't look at you, they look *through* you. And they all have these awful, fixed smiles. They don't seem real.'

Suzanne grinned. 'Well, I'm certainly that,' she said.

Anna, Suzanne's assistant, jumped up when Suzanne opened her door and offered to show Liz to the lift. 'Don't forget the CEO at six thirty,' Anna said, glancing over her shoulder.

Suzanne smiled. 'As if.'

She opened her bag and pulled out a mirror. Damn, her mascara was smudged. She licked a paper hankie and tried to wipe the smudge away but it only made it worse. She must remember to redo her make-up before the meeting.

Anna reappeared with a cup of tea. 'I need that,' Suzanne said, taking the mug gratefully. She took a sip. Just how she liked it – not too strong, lots of milk. She reopened the document she'd been working on. *Amélie: The Next Phase. Communications Strategies for 2008 and Beyond.* The car had exceeded all expectations in France, Italy, Switzerland and the UK, but they hadn't made much of a dent in the German market. It clearly needed a rethink.

Suzanne was hoping she could lure Dieter Wolff, from rival company Wagner, on to her team. She'd managed to pay off Rob, the incompetent deputy, and hang on to Chris, her senior manager, who'd been threatening to resign. Now she needed to inject fresh blood into the department. She'd got one of her senior team to take Wolff for lunch and he hadn't exactly encouraged her man, but he hadn't given him the bum's rush either. Wolff was a bit of a whiz-kid and he certainly knew Germany inside out. He'd be expensive, but she was convinced he was what they needed. She'd raise the matter with the CEO shortly.

The phone bleeped. Suzanne pushed the answer button. 'It's Justin,' Anna said. 'Shall I put him through?'

Suzanne checked the time: 6 p.m. This was unusual. He'd normally be finishing the kids' tea now. 'Hi, darling,' she said. 'How's things?'

There was a pause. 'Justin?' Suzanne could hear shouting in the background. Was that Lara?

'Be quiet, will you?' Justin said. The shouting got louder. Suzanne's heart sank.

Finally, Justin came on the line. 'Sorry,' he said. His voice sounded tense. 'Sorry to disturb you at work, but I think you should know something.'

Lara shrieked again. It was definitely her, and it sounded as if she was very close to the phone. Suzanne could just make out the words 'don't' and 'fucking'.

'What's happening?' Suzanne said. She really hadn't time for this, she needed to check her notes for the meeting.

'Lara won't eat,' Justin replied. He sounded angry, exasperated. 'She's been starving herself on and off for weeks. I've made her a delicious meal – poached salmon – and she's been pushing it round her plate. I don't know what to do with her. I warned her I'd call you if it didn't stop. Can you come home?'

Lara was wailing now, in the background. Suzanne felt torn in two. She needed to go home to sort things out, but she couldn't miss the meeting. It would look terrible. Really unprofessional.

'Look, I've got a meeting with the boss in twenty minutes,' she said urgently. 'I have to go, it's really important. I'll come home as soon as I can, OK?'

Justin groaned. 'Suze, I'm at the end of my tether . . .'

'Just hang on, will you?' Suzanne pleaded. 'Tell Lara I'll speak to her later. Please, Justin?'

He sighed. 'I saw her in her pants and bra in the bathroom . . .'

'You freak,' Lara screamed. There was a thud. Was she throwing things around – or hitting Justin? Suzanne shuddered.

Justin ploughed on. 'She's lost loads of weight. She looks like a skeleton. I'm really worried. I can't get through to her.'

Suzanne swallowed. She knew Lara had got thinner; Justin had mentioned several times that she wasn't eating properly. But Suzanne had been so busy, and she hadn't realised it was that bad. She didn't eat with Lara that often herself. She guessed she'd hoped the problem would go away.

'Oh God, Justin,' she whispered. 'We don't need this, do we, on top of everything else?'

She heard sobbing. Was that Lara, or poor Ruby, upset by all the shouting? The younger ones shouldn't be exposed to this – or Ollie, for that matter.

'Listen, we'll have a proper chat later.' Suzanne tried to sound calm and soothing, but what could she really do on the end of a phone? 'It can't go on like this, it's not fair on you – or the others,' she added.

'Too bloody right it's not,' Justin muttered.

It was dark by the time she left the office. Suzanne scuttled along Tottenham Court Road towards the tube, her high heels clack-clacking on the pavement.

Waterloo Station was fairly empty. It was way past rush hour. She wished the boss hadn't invited her for drinks and tapas after their meeting, but she could hardly refuse, could she? He'd been delighted with her input and wanted to show his appreciation. He wouldn't take no for an answer. At least she'd be able to get a seat on the train now. Heavens, she was tired.

She gazed out of the window as the train rattled along. She didn't feel like reading the paper. Lights were blazing in the houses backing on to the railway line and she could see a few figures moving around inside.

Suzanne wondered what they were doing. Were they shouting and crying and banging things, like Lara, or was it just Suzanne's weird, dysfunctional daughter who behaved this way?

She thought of Liz and her article. Despite the beige bra episode, she'd probably gone away with the impression that Suzanne really did have the perfect set-up. Gorgeous husband; lots of sex. If only she knew.

Suzanne felt miserable. Poor Lara. How could you love someone so much yet hate them at the same time? And what a terrible thing to admit – that she hated her own daughter. But it was true. At times, anyway, like now. Well, she didn't hate Lara as a person, she hated her behaviour, the way she plunged the whole family into crisis after traumatic crisis.

If only Lara could open her eyes and recognise how lucky she was – how lucky they all were. Justin had been so good for the family. He treated Lara like his own, yet she gave him nothing but abuse in return.

What if Justin cracked and decided he simply couldn't hack it any more? Was that what Lara wanted? To split them up? But he was so strong, Suzanne reasoned. And he really did love her, she knew that. She still couldn't quite believe that she'd managed to hook him.

She reached for the third finger on her left hand. Felt the ring. It was still there. Safe. Funny how they'd met at a friend's wedding like that, she mused, when she'd sworn she'd never remarry.

It was about a year after she'd split with Frank. She remembered it so vividly. She'd left the children with her parents and driven to Hampshire with Kate from uni. They were spending the night in a little hotel near the reception.

Suzanne recalled feeling quite giddy with excitement. It was so long since she'd been anywhere without the kids.

'You look great,' Kate had said as Suzanne jumped into the passenger seat. 'What have you done to yourself?'

'Just washed my hair.' Suzanne laughed. 'And put on a bit of make-up.'

'Let's have some music, Suze,' Kate suggested. They'd bombed along the motorway, singing 'Sisters Are Doing It For Themselves' at the tops of their voices.

Suzanne had noticed Red Bow-Tie Man almost immediately. He was a couple of rows in front of her and Kate on Hester, the bride's side. She's kept him to herself, Suzanne thought.

Kate was obviously thinking the same. 'Oooh, tasty,' she whispered.

Suzanne winked. 'Might have to check him out at the reception,' she giggled.

Hester started to walk down the aisle, wearing a long ivory silk dress with a big train. Red Bow-Tie Man turned and caught Suzanne's eye. He smiled, a warm, amused, sexy smile, and her heart started beating so loudly in her chest she feared everyone would hear. He's far too young, she told herself. Won't give me a second glance.

She'd looked out for him at the reception, though. He and his friends were on a table at the far end of the room. She clocked him through the rows of faces. She could tell he was tall, because although they were sitting, his head rose higher than the others. He had broad shoulders, and a way of throwing his head back and laughing that was strangely moving.

He looked uncomplicated, as if life's disappointments hadn't struck him yet. But he wasn't cocky. She could tell. If anything he looked slightly shy. She wanted to scoop him up and take him home.

The speeches seemed to go on for ever. At last, the bride and groom moved into the middle of the floor for the first dance. Some guests joined them.

Hester noticed Suzanne sitting on her own and came over to talk. Hester's cheeks were flushed, her eyes shiny.

Suzanne smiled. 'You look stunning.'

'Thanks, Suzie. Would you like me to introduce you to anyone?'

Suzanne shook her head. 'I'm happy where I am, honestly.'

Hester turned to go. Suzanne cleared her throat and tried to sound casual. 'Who are those blokes on the other side of the room? You've kept them quiet.'

'I know.' Hester laughed. 'We met them at salsa. The red bow tie's called Justin. He's a sweetie. Single.' She raised her eyebrows. 'But don't go getting any ideas, he's only young. Mid-twenties. You'd eat him for breakfast.'

Suzanne opened her bag, took out a cigarette and lit it. She'd quit – mostly. When she looked up, Justin was beside her. Her stomach cartwheeled. She remembered that feeling even now.

Drops of rain spattered on the window of the carriage. Suzanne realised she hadn't brought an umbrella but she didn't care. She wanted to get back to Justin.

'Would you like to dance?' he'd asked. He seemed hesitant. 'I'd love to.'

She put out her cigarette, thinking her legs might give way when she rose. Justin took her arm and led her into the middle of the room. His hand burned into her skin.

She felt herself collapse in towards him. He put his arms round to support her and they started to move in time with the music.

'I've been watching you all evening,' he said. His voice was alive with meaning.

'Have you? I mean, I didn't think you'd noticed.' She was much smaller than him. She could smell his aftershave. It was subtle, woody.

He brushed the top of her head with his lips. 'Are you free?' he whispered.

'Separated, yes. But I have two children. I'm much older than you,' she added.

'Are you? It doesn't matter. You're beautiful.'

Later, he'd led her into the garden.

'Do you do this to all the girls?' she asked.

232

'Don't be silly. Don't try to fight it. This is something special, OK?'

'OK.'

She was ten years older than him, with stretchmarks to boot. But she remembered how quickly he'd eased his way into her life, ironing out her worries, smoothing over the moments of doubt.

He worked in computers but didn't like it. So when Suzanne fell pregnant, they agreed it made sense for him to give up his job and look after the children. That way, they wouldn't need nannies. She was earning much more than him and was flying high, career-wise. Besides, she'd never done the full-on mummy bit. She wouldn't know how to. The longest she'd ever spent with the kids was a couple of months during maternity leave. She'd only just got them past the waking-for-a-feed-every-two-hours stage before she was back at work full time. She was quite happy for him to take care of that routine stuff. It suited them both.

After Ruby came Felix. They adored him. Suzanne felt so lucky as she kissed them all goodbye and breezed into the office each morning. What more could she want? A handsome husband, four children and a job she adored. Life was almost perfect.

The only cloud on the horizon was Lara. Poor damaged Lara who was now starving herself. Suzanne pictured Lara's darling fat little baby body. The chubby legs waving in the air; the round bottom waiting to be popped into a fresh nappy. How could she do this to herself? It was horrible.

The train jerked to a halt. Good job she hadn't missed the station. Suzanne stood up quickly and grabbed her briefcase from the overhead rack.

She found herself glancing round, wishing she could see a familiar face – someone to go for a drink with. Anything to avoid the scene at home. But that was stupid, selfish. There was no one about now. It was half past ten at night. And Justin and Lara needed her.

The lights were on but the house was quiet when she got in. She took off her damp jacket and shoes slowly, peeled off her tights and left her bag by the coat stand. She was surprised. She'd expected . . . actually, she didn't know what she'd expected, but not silence. She padded barefoot into the kitchen. The supper things had been tidied away as usual, the chairs pushed back under the table. Everything seemed in order.

She left the kitchen and pushed open the sitting-room door. The two table lamps in the room cast a yellowy, peaceful glow.

Her eyes fell on Justin. He was lying full length on the sofa, his head on a cushion, mouth slightly open, a light frown on his brow. He was fast asleep. He looked so young, Suzanne thought, so sweet. She walked over to him, bent down and gently tried to kiss the frown away.

'Justin?' she whispered tentatively. No response. 'Darling?' She shook him lightly.

He opened one eye, then the other. He started. 'What?' He was disorientated.

'Justin?' she repeated. 'You've been asleep. Where's Lara? Is everything all right?'

He came to and sat up slowly. 'What time is it?'

She didn't answer that, she felt so bad. 'Where's Lara?' she repeated.

'Bed,' he replied. He scratched his head.

'Is everything OK?' she asked again.

Justin looked at Suzanne, as if searching for something. She looked away, ashamed – for not having been there.

'She's fine now,' he said heavily. 'It's been a terrible evening. She was ranting and raving. It was a nightmare. But I finally got the little ones down and reassured Ollie and we had a long talk.'

Suzanne sat beside Justin on the sofa and rested a hand on his knee. 'What did she say?' she asked quietly.

Justin took her hand, felt for the ring, twisted it on her finger. 'Surprisingly,' he replied, 'she really opened up. Says she feels bad about herself – claims all her friends are prettier and cleverer and thinner than her. She seems to have a huge inferiority complex. I said I'd help her with her diet—'

Suzanne opened her mouth, to protest.

'Hang on,' Justin went on. 'You weren't there. I know she mustn't lose any more weight but I wanted to get her on board, convince her we're on the same side.

'I said I'd help her with her diet, but only if she agreed to eat healthily. We looked up some low-calorie recipes on the Internet and she seemed quite keen. I also said we'd pay for her to join a gym. I thought that might spur her to get fit rather than starve herself.'

Suzanne nodded. 'Good idea. Did she like it?'

'She did,' Justin said. 'But she was adamant she didn't want to join Gym and Slimline.'

Suzanne swallowed. Lara never failed to find new ways of hurting her mother, small and large.

Justin went on. 'I promised I'd do some research tomorrow. Find another gym, somewhere local. I don't know if it'll work, but Lara certainly seemed happier at the end of our talk. We even had a laugh about the poached salmon. And she made herself a bit of toast and jam, thank God – no butter, of course.'

Suzanne kissed Justin's cheek. 'You're so clever,' she said, meaning it. She felt muddled, though. Conflicting feelings whirred and collided in her head. On the one hand she was relieved – the problem had gone away, for tonight, at least. But she felt guilty, too, and even envious that it was Justin, not she, who'd spoken to Lara, who'd found a way through. Relief and guilt and envy. It was a confusing cocktail.

'I'm sorry I'm so late,' she said at last. That word 'sorry', again. 'I had to go for a drink after the meeting. The boss wouldn't take no for an answer.'

Justin frowned. 'I was pretty desperate,' he admitted. 'But I think – I hope – Lara's seen sense. At least we're speaking again.'

Suzanne thought he was about to rise. Instead, he pulled his legs up on the sofa and wrapped his arms around his knees. 'Listen, Suze,' he said. He was all bunched up, in a little ball. 'I got through tonight, but I really needed you here.'

She swallowed. She knew he was right.

'I know you've got a big job and we all depend on you,' he went on, 'but I think you need to slow down a bit – for all our sakes. Get your priorities sorted.'

She started to speak, but he interrupted her. 'You see so little of Lara, I'm sure she misses you, though she's got a funny way of showing it. And the others would like to see more of you, too, especially Ruby. It's not as if you've got anything to prove now. You're top of your game. You've made it.'

She sighed, nodding. 'I know. I know you're right,' she said. 'It's just that the job is never-ending, there's always something else to do. Plus it's hard to get away from the office when the others are still there. But I will try to cut back, I promise.'

He rose from the sofa and started moving round the room, turning off lights. She got up, too, and waited for him at the bottom of the stairs.

'Coming to bed?' she asked.

He nodded. 'I'll just get some water.'

But he didn't move. She could see he was thinking. She paused, her foot on the bottom step.

'D'you think the other kids will be as bad as Lara?' he asked. 'Because if they are, I'm leaving home.' He laughed humourlessly.

Suzanne looked at him. A nasty, panicky feeling crept over her. His jaw was clenched, his lips set in a thin line. He looked away, but she willed him to return her gaze. At last he did, and his eyes filled up with kindness.

He took her arm, pulled her off the stair, bent down and kissed her tenderly on the lips. His mouth was soft. His face smelled of soap. She reached up and put her hands behind his head, knitted her fingers together, pulled his face as close to hers as she could, fiercely. She breathed in deeply, like a diver sucking on compressed air.

'Don't be silly, gorgeous,' he murmured through her kisses. 'I was only joking.'

Chapter Five

❧

'I hope there isn't something you haven't told me?' Percy whispered.

Patrice shook her head. 'You'll love it, honestly. It's relaxing.'

'Are any of you new to Abs, Back and Stretch Fusion?' the instructor asked, casting an eye round the room. 'Any injuries that I should know about?'

Percy put up her hand. 'No injuries, but I haven't done this class before,' she said.

'My name's Crystal,' the instructor smiled. 'If you've not done some of these stretches, you might feel a bit achy tomorrow. I'll give you simpler and harder options. Just do your best. It'll get easier, I promise.'

Crystal was taut and wiry. She had short brown hair cut in a pixie style, and looked amazingly fit.

The plink-plink bamboo music started. Patrice had already warned Percy about this. Percy quite liked it, actually; it was soothing. But she imagined it could become annoying if you had to listen to it every week.

She stood in front of her mat and looked in the mirror in front. Regina Vagina was there, behind her, wearing a turquoise top with Sweaty Betty across the front. Not like her to be seen anywhere near a class. Percy wondered how the threading was going. She looked forward to an update.

Carmen hadn't shown up. That was surprising. She'd said she probably would. Too much work, maybe. Percy resolved to drop by later to see how Carmen was doing.

'Now, put your palms together and reach as high as you can,' Crystal said. She had a South African accent. Percy went on tiptoe and reached up to the ceiling.

'Now over to the right, stretching, stretching, all the way down your side,' Crystal went on. She said 'stritch' for 'stretch'.

'That's it. Cool,' she smiled. 'And now to the other side.'

Percy imagined the muscles and sinews beginning to spread out and lengthen. It was a good feeling. They had to do full circles, reaching down with the right hand to the left foot, the side, the ceiling, the left hand to the right foot and the floor.

Percy could feel it in her waist and her back as well as her thighs. She could see why Patrice said this was such a good class. Percy thought she probably would be aching tomorrow, given that she was using bits of her she hadn't used for a long time.

They went on to their fronts. 'Time for the Plank,' Crystal explained. She pronounced it 'plink'. 'Up on to your elbows,' she ordered. 'Knees off the floor. Keep your backs flat, bums down. This is great for the core muscles. You've got a minute.'

Percy glanced at Patrice. Her face was red. Percy was sure her own was even redder. It was extremely hard not to buckle. The only way Percy could stay up was by squeezing her stomach so tight it burned. Otherwise her back hurt.

She'd been fascinated when one of the instructors had explained that the tummy muscles support the back. It made total sense now, in this position. Without strong stomach muscles, she'd have no chance.

At last, the minute was up and she flopped on the floor and sat back on her knees, her arms in front, in a shell stretch.

'Now you've got a minute and a half!' Crystal said cheerfully. 'Go on, up you go again!'

The whole class moaned.

'And while you're up there, raise one leg slowly, hold it up, then lower and raise the other,' Crystal ordered.

You've got to be joking, Percy thought. Now her bum as well as everything else was on fire. Jesus! She'd love to know who invented these exercises. They were obviously going for maximum pain.

They finished off with some more stretching. Crystal told them to sit down on their mats, open their legs as wide as possible and get their bodies as low as possible between them.

Percy watched Crystal, fascinated. She couldn't help it. Her legs opened so wide, she was like a doll. She seemed to have plastic rollers for joints. And she went down so low between her legs that she could rest the whole of her upper body and her face on the floor, without seeming to be in pain. In fact her expression was totally tranquil.

'Well, I was a dancer,' Crystal informed Percy from her contorted position. 'Now get down, you, and I'm going to come round and give you all a push.'

On the way out, Percy and Patrice had to walk past the Chest Press. This looked like an instrument of torture but was in fact designed to tone the upper arms and chest area.

Percy was horrified to see Danny bending over someone. She clocked the black wavy hair, black vest top, bulging arms. By the looks of things, he was explaining how to use the equipment.

She was even more appalled when the person he was helping glanced up and caught her eye. Unfortunately, it was impossible to pretend she hadn't noticed.

Millicent beamed. 'Cooee!'

Percy managed a tight smile.

'Danny's giving me a personal-training session,' Millicent called. 'This one's great for the, you know.' She stuck out her big round silicone boobs and winked.

As if she needed any help in that direction, Percy thought.

Danny looked up and grinned at her. She felt her face redden, but he didn't appear remotely uncomfortable himself, which was annoying.

'Hi there,' he said, still grinning. 'How ya doing?'

Percy fiddled with the towel she was carrying.

'It's a shame you stopped our sessions,' Danny continued. The olive skin on his arms and chest was slightly damp with sweat. Percy had to force herself not to drop her eyes to check out the six-pack and the Lycra shorts. Why was he so damn sexy?

He looked her straight in the eyes. 'If you change your mind, babe, just let me know.'

Percy was flustered. The brazenness of the man! But it was almost tempting to give it another try, to see if it would be any better second time round.

Don't be stupid. Think how guilty you feel already. Think of Mark.

Millicent coughed. 'Er, Danny, could you show me where to put the weights?' she simpered. She was evidently feeling neglected.

Danny refocused his attention on her. 'Here,' he said, bending right over Millicent to reach the black weights on the other side of the equipment.

His chest must have brushed against hers, Percy thought. Deliberate or what? Millicent giggled.

Percy decided to leave them to it. Millicent's welcome to him, she thought, pushing the changing-room door open rather too hard and nearly knocking the woman behind unconscious.

'What the—?' the woman complained.

'Sorry,' Percy muttered.

Patrice looked surprised. 'Are you OK?' she asked, as they stripped off their gear. 'You seem a little, erm, stressed.'

'Not at all,' Percy snapped.

After picking Rowan up from nursery, Percy passed by Carmen's flat to see if she was in. She wanted to check everything was OK.

Carmen answered the door in a big, baggy man's shirt over trackie bottoms. She wasn't wearing a scrap of make-up, but looked as divinely exotic as usual.

The house smelled of sisal and joss sticks. There were no shoes in the hall or toys on the floor. Percy thought the place exuded peace and serenity. So unlike her own tip.

'Hey, Percy. Rowan, my little man,' Carmen said, scooping him up for a cuddle as he tried to push past her through the front door. He was very at home at 'Aunty Carmen's'.

It amused Percy to hear him call her that. She could see it made Carmen slightly uncomfortable. She was the least stereotypical aunty you could imagine. Carmen never had sweeties, or chocolate biscuits, or bags of toys or colouring things. Instead, she'd produce an exotic Spanish fan out of a cupboard for Rowan to play with, or a tin of buttons, or coloured chopsticks. But Percy could see she adored Rowan, and he thought she was fantastic. Somehow, at Carmen's, the chopsticks were just as fun, if not more so, than a plastic Batman figure, and 'Aunty Carmen' had stuck.

Rowan was starving. Carmen said all she had in that was remotely suitable was a loaf of walnut bread and some marmite. Percy didn't believe her. She opened her fridge. There were several smoothie cartons on the door shelf, but not a lot else.

She peered in the vegetable drawer and pulled out some alfalfa, mung beans and raw spinach. 'Walnut bread and marmite it is,' Percy said.

Carmen put on *Fantasia* – the only children's DVD she possessed – and Rowan sat chomping his walnut bread on the sofa while the women chatted at the kitchen table.

'So, what's up?' Carmen asked, passing Percy a cup of Earl Grey. 'I can see something is.'

Percy hadn't realised it was so obvious. She'd thought she was a master at disguising her feelings by now. She wrinkled her nose. Carmen's green tea smelled pretty vile. She drank gallons of the stuff every day. She claimed it was great for detoxing but Percy didn't know how she could get it down.

'Nothing's up,' Percy said. It occurred to her that she must sound defensive. 'Well actually, I am a bit blue,' she admitted. 'Time of the month, I expect.'

Carmen looked at her kindly. Percy took a sip of her tea and glanced at her friend over the rim of her cup. She longed to open her heart and spill out all her worries about Mark, Danny, the gambling, everything. Tell her what a mess she was in.

Surely Carmen would be sympathetic? She wouldn't judge. But how could she understand? It was all so shocking. Dirty somehow. She had enough on her plate, anyway. Percy just couldn't.

Rowan walked in and tried to climb on Percy's lap. She helped him up and gave him a cuddle. 'He's ready for a snooze,' she said, tearing off a piece of the kitchen roll on the table and wiping his sticky fingers. 'Nursery wears him out.'

Percy carried Rowan over to the sofa and laid him down. 'There,' she said. 'You have a nap. You'll feel much better when you wake up. I'll be right here, with Aunty Carmen.'

She kissed the top of his head. He protested for a moment, then closed his eyes. Percy smiled. He must have realised by now that when Mummy was in full flow with Carmen, there was no point trying to compete.

Carmen passed Percy a patchwork blanket and a small Chinese peasant figure and Percy laid the blanket over Rowan. He opened his eyes for a second, reached out for the figure, hugged it close to his chest and closed his eyes again.

'He's so sweet,' Carmen whispered, smiling. 'Listen, Percy, I've got something to tell you.'

'What? Oh gosh.' Percy guessed right away what was coming. She needed to sit down to hear it, though.

They went back into the kitchen. Carmen looked at Percy and grinned. Her eyes were sparkly.

'Yes,' Carmen said. 'I'm having a baby.'

'That's fabulous,' Percy cried, clapping her hands. She'd rehearsed this moment in her head several times. She wasn't going to display one shred of doubt, show anything but joy. She was determined, for Carmen's sake.

She jumped up, nearly knocking over her mug of tea and rushed round the table to give Carmen a hug. 'How many weeks?' Percy asked.

'About fourteen,' Carmen replied.

'When did you find out?' Percy wanted to know.

'Back in July – I did a pregnancy test. But to be honest, I knew almost the moment it happened.'

Percy hugged Carmen again. Percy's face was wreathed in smiles. She'd never acted so hard. She didn't want to ask the next question, but felt she must: 'How has Simon taken it?'

Carmen made a face and Percy's heart sank. Carmen cleared her throat and looked at her hands, her fingernails. 'Not that well,' she admitted. 'It was a big shock.

'As I said, he'll take time to get used to the idea. To be honest, Percy,' she went on, 'I don't know if we'll have this baby together, or if I'll be on my own. But I'll manage either way.'

'I'm sorry,' said Percy. She let out a big sigh. She realised she'd been holding her breath. 'But how can he not be thrilled?' she asked. Somehow she wasn't surprised, though.

Carmen shrugged. 'I don't know, it's just the way he is. He's always shied away from commitment. I reckon this has made him feel hemmed in. He's frightened. He's away again now for a couple of months, but I've told him I'm going ahead with it, whatever, and I'm delighted.'

'And you are, really?' Percy asked. She looked hard at Carmen. She was reassured by what she saw.

'Yes, honestly,' Carmen said. 'I know I always said I wasn't sure I wanted a baby but the truth is, I was just putting the issue off. I've spent my life procrastinating. I finally realised Simon was never going to make any decisions for me, so I'd have to do it myself. I didn't want to wait for ever then find my eggs were no good.

'This baby's going to be so loved, I tell you, Percy,' Carmen said. There was real passion in her voice. 'I'm going to shower it with love. It won't be easy if I have to do it on my own, but I'll manage.'

Percy put her arms around Carmen and rested her head on hers, comforting her, like a baby. 'Of course you will,' she said, stroking her friend's silky hair. 'And I'll help as much as I can. So will Patrice and Suzanne. It's wonderful, Carmen, I'm so happy for you. And a playmate for Rowan – terrific!'

A thought crossed Percy's mind. 'Have you told your parents yet?' she asked.

Carmen shook her head. 'I think I've needed time for it all to sink in. Plus I know they won't be happy about the Simon situation. My mother will be horrified I'm having a baby out of wedlock. You know she's a staunch Catholic. I might wait just a bit longer, until I've had all the tests.'

Percy took her arm away and went back to the other side of the table. 'Have you seen your GP?' she asked.

Carmen nodded. 'I'm having my first scan next week.'

'They may offer you an amniocentesis,' Percy went on, 'given your age.'

'When will that happen?' Carmen wanted to know.

Percy thought for a moment. 'At about four or five months. I seem to remember mine was around that time.'

Carmen's brow wrinkled. 'I'm not sure I want one, because there's a risk of miscarriage, isn't there? If there was something wrong with the baby, I don't think I'd want to get rid of it anyway, so what's the point in taking chances?'

Percy put her elbows on the table and rested her chin in

her hands. 'I wouldn't have terminated either,' she said thoughtfully, 'but I wanted to know, so I could be prepared if anything was wrong. It was scary, but I'm glad I went through with it. I don't like surprises.

'It's quite a decision to have to make, though. I just wish Simon was here to make it with you. But listen, if you want me to come with you when you have it, let me know. I can come to any other appointments with you, too. I'll even hold your hand at the birth, if you'd like me to. I'll be your doula. It'd be a novelty to be at the other end for a change.'

Carmen grinned, then turned serious again. 'You know, I'm scared, Percy. I feel such a mixture of joy, fear and I don't know what. Is that normal, do you think?'

Percy smiled. 'Perfectly normal. I wanted both my boys, desperately, but that didn't stop me having sleepless nights before they were born, wondering what on earth I'd done.'

She'd given it her best shot, Percy thought as she kissed Carmen goodbye. She hoped she'd been convincing. But she still felt riddled with anxiety. She was furious with Simon, but she'd been determined not to badmouth him. And she hadn't. After all, it was quite possible he'd remain a fixture in Carmen's life, even if it was on a part-time basis. Indeed, it would most likely be in the best interests of Carmen and her baby if he did.

And who knows? They might even manage to sort things out, decide to be together, get married, even. Though the memory of that hand sneaking under the tablecloth and up her leg made Percy seriously doubt it.

She was relieved when she finally got the boys to bed. They'd been mucking around, being difficult. Ben especially. She was itching to play but she decided to have a quick bath first. It would help to calm her. She played better when she was calm.

She heard Mark come in. Damn. He was early. She glanced

at her watch on the bathroom shelf: 9 p.m. She might have to wait ages now, until he was asleep.

She felt a twinge of nostalgia. She used to long for Mark to come home, she missed him so much in the evenings.

He went into the kitchen. She knew, because she'd left the bathroom door ajar and she could hear the fridge door open and clunk against the wall. She winced. She was always telling the boys not to bash the fridge door because it was getting dents in it. Now she knew Mark was guilty, too.

'Fuck.' His deep voice carried all the way upstairs. What had he done now?

Percy got out of the bath and dried herself. She pulled on a black skirt, tights, a black cotton T-shirt. She decided to read her book for a bit, wait for Mark to calm down. She was into Kingsley Amis right now. He was bitterly funny. That suited her frame of mind.

There was a smash downstairs. Her ears pricked, then there was another smash.

She jumped up off the bedroom chair. The sound of shattering glass made her flinch.

She raced downstairs, her heart thumping. There was a moment's peace, then another crash. It was coming from the sitting room.

She walked in, fearful of what she'd find. Mark was standing by the mantelpiece. There was only one photo left on it, where there had been five or six. She watched him pick it up. It was the one of Rowan's christening in a large, silver frame.

In it, she was holding baby Rowan in a long, white blanket, while Ben sat on Mark's lap. She always thought they looked so sweet and happy, like an advertisement, picture perfect. She remembered having it taken.

'Stop it,' Percy screamed. She grabbed Mark's arm. Their wedding photo was already lying, broken, at his feet. 'Don't,' she pleaded. But Mark tugged his arm away, up in the air, beyond her reach, and hurled the picture on the floor along with the others. Then he stepped on it, grinding it into the carpet with his shoe.

Percy covered her mouth with her hands. 'What have you done?' she whispered. 'Why?' She sucked in her breath, braced herself for what might come. Did he know? He must have found out about the poker. But she'd been so careful.

'Is this about – our debts?' Her voice was so quiet, it was barely audible. But her heart was pounding in her chest.

He looked at her in an odd way, his face full of contempt. 'No, it's not about our debts.' Then he pushed her aside and she heard him stomp upstairs.

She stood there for several minutes, surveying the devastation. Bits of the children's faces, in torn photos and broken frames, stared up at her. The wedding photo was crumpled and you could see the dirty imprint of Mark's shoe.

She felt hopeless; she didn't understand. If he knew, he'd have told her, surely. If he didn't, then there was no explanation. It made no sense, this terrible rage that seemed to come from nowhere.

At that moment Percy hated Mark, more than she'd ever thought possible. She wanted to grind his face into the remains of her babies' images. He hadn't just smashed her photos, he'd destroyed her dreams, too.

She started picking up shards of glass in her hands and dropped them in the wastepaper basket. She pricked her thumb. A blob of crimson blood appeared. Instinctively, she put it in her mouth and sucked the blood away. It tasted tangy, metallic.

She took her thumb out of her mouth, but the blood welled up again and kept on coming. It was amazing how much blood there was from such a tiny nick, she thought.

Is this the end at last? But why now? Why not last week – or next month? And how do you prise apart a fifteen-year marriage? Where do you start?

She wiped away her tears with her sleeve. She felt so weary, as if she could hardly move one limb in front of the other.

She fetched the dustpan and brush and swept up the remaining debris. The mantelpiece looked so bare now. She'd always used it for family photos – her favourite ones. In a way it had been a solid, tangible symbol of their family life. Now it was empty.

She felt peculiar, cast adrift. She wondered for a moment if it was all an illusion: Mark, Ben, Rowan. She thought she might wake tomorrow and find herself completely alone in the world.

She put the dustpan and brush back under the sink and poured herself a large glass of wine. She was impatient to get back to the tables. To focus on nothing but the game. The tortoiseshell hairclip was still on the desk where she'd last left it. She picked it up quickly, scraped back her hair with her fingers and twisted it up behind her head. That was better.

She sat down, pulled on the black cardigan from the back of the chair, slipped on the black heels and double-clicked on the icon, logged on.

Username: Boadicea
Password: Sunshine59

She was pleasantly surprised to see that there was a big tournament tonight. It was a sizeable entrance fee – $2,200 – but the winner would net around $15,000. The thought made her heady.

She wasn't familiar with most of the players, but she knew Johnnypwe, of course. Her old adversary. She felt a prickle of fear – and excitement. She pulled back her shoulders and paid her fee. Ha! Screw Mark, she thought. Screw everything.

If she was an addict it wasn't surprising, the way he treated her. In fact it was a miracle she hadn't laced his cornflakes with rat poison years ago.

Her eyes felt sore from so much crying earlier on. She rubbed them. The blinds – the forced bets that the first two players must put in the pot – started at 25/50, and most of the players seemed pretty lackadaisical – content to limp into pots, calling on the small bets rather than raising them.

She spent the first few rounds hovering around 5,000 chips – in tournaments you always played with chips – down to 4,000, up to 5,500, but never beyond.

After about half an hour, she was down to about 4,200 chips and she was relieved finally to get some good cards. She wriggled in her seat with pleasure. Now things were looking up! By the end of the fourth level her stack had increased to just under 7,000. She felt quietly confident.

In the fifth level she was dealt pocket 10s – a pair. She noticed that NiceOne456 – she hadn't come across him before – was playing increasingly aggressively. His stack had fluctuated more than anyone else at the table. He raised to three times the big blind: 1,000 chips.

Percy guessed that he didn't really have much of a hand, so she raised to 3,000 chips. He called. About two-thirds of his chips were now in the pot.

The flop – that betting round where the three cards are dealt face up – came down 7-8-ace. NiceOne456 moved all in, adding something like another 1,200 chips to the pot. She had around 4,200 of her 7,000 in there.

Percy was on tenterhooks. She'd have to think quick. She considered the possibility that he had an ace in his hand, but she was convinced even before the flop that he'd go all in no matter what, based on his aggressive play and the relatively small size of his remaining stack.

She bit her lip and called.

The turn was a 3, the river – that fifth board card – a 7. NiceOne456 revealed his hand – an ace – so his ace-ace-7-7-8 beat her 10-10-7-7-8. She'd lost more than half her chips. She groaned.

She could feel the sweat appearing on her upper lip and starting to trickle down her back. Johnnypwe had been uncharacteristically quiet. She glanced at the chat box, then wished she hadn't.

'Tut, tut, Boady,' he smirked. 'Bad play.' She flinched, deciding not to respond. He was playing nasty mental games with her, trying to shake her up.

She didn't have a lot of chips left: 2,800. She desperately needed some good cards. But there was still time to turn things round.

They took a five-minute break. Percy scuttled to the loo. Raced back again. The tournament continued and more and more players started to drop out.

She glanced at the clock. Where had the time gone? It was 3.30 a.m. Things weren't going well. Her stack had dropped to about 1,600. She started to feel really panicky.

Percy decided that with any two decent cards she'd have to go all in and bet the last chips she had. She tried not to think about losing. It wasn't going to happen.

Her spirits soared when she was dealt an ace and a 4 of spades. This, after all, was better than the hand that had beaten her earlier.

She was called by Johnnypwe. Him again. Her heart started to hammer in her chest. They both revealed their cards. He had . . . two 10s. She almost choked. The same hand that she'd played with and lost most of her stack on was now likely to eliminate her from the tournament.

She desperately needed an ace or three more spades. It wasn't impossible. If Lady Luck was on her side. The flop was king-jack-6 with two spades. She breathed a sigh of relief. OK, she wasn't dead yet.

The turn was an 8. Not spades. She held her breath. Please, please God. I'll do anything.

She crossed her fingers, her toes. Squeezed her eyes almost shut, so she could only just see the screen.

The river was an ace and a 3. Not spades.

She was out.

Percy stared in disbelief. The unimaginable had happened. She'd convinced herself that sheer probability meant she couldn't lose again. What a fool.

She'd lost another £1,000. And beaten by Johnnypwe to boot. She'd rather it had been anyone but him. It was sickening. Her total debts must be over £12,000 by now.

She pushed away from the desk and stared out of the window. For once, she felt peculiarly calm. She watched the sky turn slowly from black to murky grey and the dawn chorus started. It sounded ugly, discordant. She'd much prefer silence.

She rose from her chair and went to the sink. Filled the kettle with water. Made a cup of tea that she couldn't drink. She realised that her face and body were wet from sweat. She ought to go and shower before everyone woke, but she didn't think she had the strength.

She remembered last night: Mark smashing the photos, their family photos. In a way, there was a certain, horrible aptness about this disaster. It would be a fitting epitaph to the marriage.

Mark would leave her now, for sure, as soon as he knew the truth. The end couldn't be far away now.

And who could blame him?

Chapter Six

❦

Carmen had told everyone her news, now. She'd had to. After all, it was becoming increasingly obvious. She was getting on for five months gone. She was still slim; there wasn't a big bump yet. She knew it was there, of course, but she could still hide it under a baggy jumper. But her boobs couldn't be disguised. They were huge, swollen and sore. She'd had to get a heavy-duty sports bra because otherwise working out would be too painful.

It was a bit of a revelation to her, having big boobs. She'd had tiny ones before; fried eggs, she'd called them. Now she knew how big-breasted women felt. They certainly got in the way.

She was pleased when the Pilates instructor gave her special exercises to do because she was pregnant. No sit-ups, for one. Carmen had to do wussy leg-raises instead. But she didn't mind.

Over the years, she'd seen so many women at the club getting bigger and bigger until they could scarcely move around their mats. Then one day they'd stop coming, and Carmen would forget all about them.

A few weeks later, they'd reappear without warning, with a wee infant curled over their shoulder like a small, snuffling animal.

Gradually, the women would go back to classes. Resume normal relations with the weights and stability balls. Slowly, the floppy bellies would shrink. Little by little, the majority would regain their figures, or something resembling the figures they'd had before.

A few would remain large and lumpy. Too many cappuccinos and muffins in the café, Carmen guessed. But it didn't seem to matter. It was as if they'd entered a new domain, where girlie chats about nappies and breastfeeding replaced obsessing over looks and husbands or boyfriends. For the time being, at least.

Carmen had watched it all quietly. Taken note of the women's round, sparkling faces and their big, fecund bellies when they got to the blooming stage. She'd peeped at the tiny, wrinkled hands and perfect fingernails of their newborns when they'd come to show them off. Observed the mothers' quiet pride, and the way their eyes followed their babies, hungrily, if another woman asked for a hold. They could hardly bear to give them up, even for a moment. It must be something instinctive. Primeval.

Carmen would never risk asking for a hold, though she'd held Percy's and Suzanne's babies, of course. And Seamus. But she'd have felt embarrassed, uncomfortable, with women she didn't know well. Would they be able to spot immediately that she was childless? She wondered if there were special signals you gave off once you'd given birth that indicated to other mothers that you were one of them, that you'd joined the club.

There was no denying she'd been curious, though. She'd tried to imagine what it would feel like. Now it was her turn. She was going to experience it all: the boobs, the blooming, the baby hunger, everything.

It was scary, but she felt special, too. As if she'd been handed this big, unexpected present, all wrapped up. She was surprised, really, by how happy and excited she was. If she'd known it would be this good, she might have done it years earlier.

'Time for the one hundred,' said the instructor.

Carmen snapped out of her daydream. Still on her back, she raised her head and shoulders off the floor. Some had their legs in table-top position, the more advanced straightened them in the air in front of them. Because of her condition, Carmen stayed in table-top.

She straightened her arms and started to flap them up and down, as if trying to take off. She counted at the same time, rhythmically: breathe in, one, two, three, four, five, breath out, one, two, three, four, five. Five flaps each time.

She made a sucking-in noise with the first five counts, a blowing-out sound with the second. It was tiring, particularly on the neck and shoulders, but everywhere, really. She was relieved when she got to a hundred.

She lay back, stretched her aching arms and legs out and looked around the room. Patrice was still counting, her legs in table-top, too. She couldn't straighten them, said it hurt her back. She looked longer and thinner than ever, Carmen thought. Almost scrawny. She'd been terribly upset by her father's death but she seemed to be coping better now.

Suzanne, beside Patrice, was huffing and puffing like a steam train, white, freckly legs in full view, hair all over the place. It was nice she and Pats were seeing so much of each other. Good for Pats, and Seamus too, being an only child. It wasn't as if she, Carmen, had a little mate for him to play with.

A little mate. She felt a tickle of excitement. There was a whole new world waiting to open up.

Percy had finished her hundred now. She was spread-eagled on her mat, drawing breath. Now, she'd definitely lost weight, Carmen thought. Percy would be pleased, no doubt, but she didn't seem herself, somehow. Maybe it was just Carmen's imagination.

Percy was so good, always popping round to see her or telephoning. And she was the one who fixed up girls' nights out. She was a wonderful organiser, along with everything else. She kept them on their toes. Carmen didn't know how she'd cope without her.

It was Percy's turn to get in the skinny lattes and green tea for Carmen. She also bought a plate of hot mince pies. Wicked. She didn't seem particularly interested in them herself, though. She just nibbled on a bit of pastry.

They sat beside the Christmas tree in the corner of the café. The lights were on and there were piped carols in the background.

It was only the first week of December, a little early, but it felt warm and festive. There was a smell of cinnamon from the cinnamon sticks in dried-flower decorations on the counter.

Patrice adopted her usual position, legs pulled up, feet on the sofa cushions, chin on her knees. She had some gossip.

She looked quickly round the room, to check no one was listening. 'I overheard someone say Millicent has split up from her husband,' she whispered.

'No!' Suzanne hollered.

Some people sitting at other tables turned round, surprised. Suzanne coughed, ashamed of her outburst. She bent forwards conspiratorially. 'You see,' she said quietly, spreading her arms in front of her and narrowly avoiding knocking over her coffee, 'it just confirms my theory – you *can* be too thin and gorgeous. Boys don't like it. They prefer imperfection.' She slapped her thighs to demonstrate.

Patrice tut-tutted. 'Now, now.'

'God, you're right,' Suzanne agreed. 'I sound like a complete bitch.' She ran her hands through her hair, making it stick up even more. 'What I should say, of course, is how sad. And three children, too? That's terrible.'

Carmen raised her eyebrows and looked at Percy. 'Isn't Millicent having personal training with Danny?' she enquired.

Percy examined a piece of fluff on her lilac mohair sweater. 'I believe so,' she said.

Carmen thought for a moment, putting a dainty finger in

her mouth. 'Hmmm, I wonder if the two are by any chance linked? Millicent's marriage break-up and Danny's personal training.' Something struck her. 'Hey,' Carmen went on, 'you never did tell me why you stopped your sessions, Pers? Go on, spill the beans.'

Percy shook her head. 'It was just too expensive, that's all,' she said. 'Mark went mad. Anyone for another mince pie?'

Carmen could tell Percy was uncomfortable. She looked so strained, too. Carmen was curious, but decided not to press now. She turned to Suzanne and Patrice.

'I'm sure it's harder to stay with someone for a long time than it is to divorce, don't you think?' Carmen said.

Suzanne looked surprised. 'What makes you say that?'

Carmen shrugged. 'I don't know, I've never been married. It just strikes me that it must be easier to go running to a solicitor when you encounter big problems than to try to compromise, negotiate, whatever it takes to find a way through.'

Suzanne huffed. 'Well,' she said, 'having been through a divorce myself, I wouldn't say there's anything easy about it. In fact it's hell.

'But actually,' she said, tipping her head on one side, 'I suppose if Frank and I were still together, we'd be having frightful rows, rushing to Relate every five minutes.' She shuddered. 'Maybe you're right. Divorce in those circumstances, if you hate each other, must be easier. I'll tell you one thing, though. I'd never want to go through it again.'

Carmen smiled. 'Lucky you won't have to.'

Patrice got a hair tie out of her bag and pulled her blonde hair up into a high ponytail. 'Someone should write a diary. Sell it to a newspaper. A sort of inverse Bridget Jones: "Diary of a Long-Term Married".' She laughed. 'It could be a bit tedious, mind you. "And then we had another row. And then he threw a wet sponge at me."'

Suzanne snorted. 'A new career beckons, Pats. You should get in touch with the *Richmond and Twickenham Times!*'

Percy had been very quiet. She was obviously thinking. 'I suppose one of the problems is that marriages go on so long,' she mused. 'In the old days loads of women would have died in childbirth. It would have been quite usual for men to have two or three wives. And even the men didn't live long. It was unlikely you'd ever reach your twenty-fifth wedding anniversary.' She smiled suddenly, seeming to cheer up. 'Someone should write a handbook to accompany the diary – how to keep the fire burning, perhaps. Top tips, tried and tested. Could be a bestseller.

'On reflection, though,' she went on, 'maybe it would be rather lacking in substance. There are only so many massages you can give each other to restoke the embers.'

Suzanne shook her head. 'God, you lot are miserable old marrieds,' she exclaimed. 'Can't you pay a visit to Ann Summers or something? Isn't that what you're supposed to do to put the va-va-voom back in a tired relationship?'

'Oh, Mark and I tried Ann Summers years ago,' Percy sniggered. 'But the Rampant Rabbit was dicky and wouldn't turn off. It made such a noise it frightened the cat and nearly woke Ben – he was just a baby then. Mark had to shove it in the loo to get it to shut up. And that was the end of that.'

'Serves you right for being such a hussy,' Carmen chipped in. 'Personally, I don't need anything as vulgar as a vibrator.'

'Yeah, yeah,' Percy shot back. 'I bet you've a drawer full of crotchless panties and peekaboo bras.'

Carmen made a face.

'Well, I love my Rampant Rabbit,' Suzanne said.

Everyone stared.

'Really?' said Percy.

Carmen bent forward to hear better. It was extraordinary that they'd never discussed vibrators before. A major oversight.

'But doesn't Justin feel left out?' Percy went on. 'That was always Mark's objection, though he succumbed in the end and bought me one for my birthday.' She looked almost wistful. 'I reckon he was secretly quite relieved, though, when it bit the dust.'

Suzanne shook her head. 'Not at all. Justin likes to sit back and watch the show.'

'Ooh, too much information,' Patrice squealed.

'Please, girls,' said Carmen, raising a hand in mock horror. She patted her tummy. 'Not in front of the baby.'

Percy grinned. 'Sorry, baby.'

Simon turned up around 7 p.m. He'd rung Carmen to say he was getting an earlier flight from Prague. She heard the key in the lock and her heart gave a little fillip. It always did that when he arrived home. She scooted out to greet him.

He looked more handsome than ever, she thought, in his smart navy-blue mac, the top button of his pale-blue shirt undone. He was wearing the purple and blue Paul Smith tie she'd given him for his birthday and his Adam's apple was quite prominent. She'd always liked it. There was something very manly and interesting about it.

She smiled. 'Welcome home.'

He'd had several months to get used to the idea of the baby now. Surely that was long enough? She felt excited and nervous at the same time. She raised her face for him to kiss her, as she always did.

He put his bags down. He had to bend to reach her, he was so much taller. His lips brushed hers, just for a second.

'Long journey?' she asked.

'I had to wait ages for a taxi,' he replied.

She helped him off with his coat and hung it up while he went to the bedroom to change. She wanted to follow him in, rip his clothes off, pounce on him and show him her glorious, swelling belly, but something stopped her. She could sense the distance. He needed space, time to acclimatise. He wasn't in Carmen-mode yet, that was all. His head was still at work.

She went into the kitchen to prepare supper. She'd been to the fishmonger, bought fresh king prawns, clams, squid, some mussels. Her mother had taught her how to make the best paella, with lots of garlic and saffron. He'd always said it was his favourite. She'd just have a piece of salmon, though. She didn't want to take any risks with shellfish.

Afterwards, they sat down to watch a movie. She waited for him to put his arm round her, but he didn't. She nudged him with her elbow and he obliged. Tired, she thought.

'I could feel it kicking last night.' She smiled, stroking her abdomen. She'd been doing that a lot lately. 'It felt a bit like butterflies in my stomach – or wind.'

Simon made no response. He seemed totally absorbed in the film.

She tried again. 'I've been thinking about names,' she said. 'I quite fancy Verity for a girl, and maybe Theo for a boy?'

He cleared his throat. She waited for him to speak, but nothing came.

'What names do you like?' she persisted. 'I'd like to choose something you're happy with, too.'

Simon's eyes remained fixed on the TV screen.

'Simon?' Carmen said quietly. 'Don't you care what your son or daughter is called? Have you no interest at all?'

He took his arm away and turned to face her. She didn't like the look in his eyes. Her heart fluttered.

'I'm seeing someone else, Carmen,' he said. Just like that, dead pan.

'What?' She wasn't hearing properly.

'I'm seeing someone else,' he repeated. 'I'm sorry.'

Carmen's brain felt fuzzy. There was a rushing in her ears. She wasn't sure if she was going to faint, or throw up.

'How long has this been going on?' she whispered.

'About a year.'

'Why didn't you tell me?'

'I was going to,' he answered, 'but then you got pregnant. I didn't want to upset you.'

His face looked hard, suddenly, sort of hollowed out. The skin across his cheekbones was pulled tight. His lips looked thin and dry. He licked them nervously. His eyes seemed to have shrunk into the back of his head, as if trying to escape.

Carmen felt panicky. She wanted to get out of the room and call Percy. 'So why are you telling me now?' she managed to say.

He ran his hands through his silver hair. 'I'm sorry, Carmen, I just can't keep living this lie. It's been hard for me, too, you know – and for her.'

Carmen swallowed. She rubbed her tummy to comfort the baby. Or was it to comfort herself? 'She knows about me, then?' she asked.

Simon nodded. 'I've told her, yes.'

'What about the fact we still make love? Does she know about that?'

Simon was silent.

'I want to be with you at the birth,' he said at last. 'And I'll make sure you're all right, financially, I mean.'

Carmen felt as if she'd been kicked. 'Is she The One, then? Are you going for marriage, the works?' She couldn't control the bitterness in her voice.

'Not yet, no. We thought we'd get this out of the way first.'

He flinched, obviously realising, too late, how that must sound, but he couldn't take it back now. Carmen gasped. She was so shocked, she didn't even cry. 'Out of the way?' she choked. 'This is our baby you're talking about.'

He hung his head. 'I'm sorry.'

At that moment, Carmen sensed something falling into place like a pebble dropping into a well. You waited, on tenterhooks, until you could hear that deep, satisfying plop and knew it had arrived.

She was suddenly curiously calm. 'Actually, you know, Simon,' she said, rising, 'I don't want you to see our baby being born and I don't want your money either. You can get out of our lives right now – I want nothing more from you.'

He rose, too, and looked at her with what seemed very much like pity. Carmen couldn't bear it.

'Don't be like that,' he said gently. He put a hand on her arm, which made her flinch. 'You're very emotional. It's a difficult time for you.'

But she was adamant. She'd rather have his anger than his pity. She stood, ramrod straight, at the bedroom door and watched him gather up his things. It didn't take long; he was only ever really a visitor in her house.

'I'll call you tomorrow,' he said as she opened the front door for him. 'We can talk about this in a more rational manner.'

'Don't,' she said firmly.

'I want to know what happens – about the baby, I mean.' He sounded anxious.

'You can check the birth announcements in *The Times*,' she said.

'I do have rights, you know,' he reminded her.

She laughed in his face and slammed the door.

She went slowly into the kitchen, made herself a cup of green tea and sat down on a stool. She thought she ought to cry, but the tears didn't come. That was odd. All those months, years, of waiting. Waiting for some sign from him, something to show he loved her as much as she loved him. Something to show this wasn't just a casual, passing relationship, this was for real. Confirmation that they had a future together. Marriage, babies, everything.

There, she'd said it now. She'd never allowed herself to

hope for it, but it was what she'd wanted all along, really, wasn't it? What a waste.

She felt scared. How would she manage as a single mum, with a sizeable mortgage and not that much money coming in? She'd known from the beginning that this was a possibility but the reality was still frightening.

She stared into her mug, swirling the liquid round as if searching for answers there. Surprisingly, she found some. She was strong. Hadn't she learned to live without ballet, something she'd never have believed possible before the accident? She'd picked herself up, made a new life, a new career – and learned to love it. And she had her friends – and her mum and dad. They were elderly now, but they'd do what they could.

Percy, Suzanne and Patrice would rally round, especially Percy. And she had this baby now, her baby. No one could take that away from her.

Carmen stroked her tummy again and thought she could feel a little kick. She smiled. 'We're going to be all right, baby,' she crooned. 'You and me, we're going to have a good life, so much fun.'

The phone rang several times, then her mobile. Again and again, like a wasp buzzing in her ear. She knew it was Simon, checking up on her. Doing his duty.

She switched both phones off. She didn't want to talk to anyone now, not even Percy. She'd call her tomorrow, tell her everything.

But right now, Carmen and her baby needed to be alone.

Chapter Seven

'What we all need is a night away.' Suzanne was adamant. She'd been working all hours recently, there was no let-up, despite her resolve to cut back. And although Lara was eating again, thank God, she was still being a real pain, constantly picking fights with her siblings, criticising Justin, and Suzanne when she was at home, over every little thing. It was exhausting.

Suzanne felt she deserved a breather, and Percy and Patrice looked as if they could use one, too. Plus, it would be good for Carmen. She felt a bit guilty leaving Justin but he hadn't complained. He was so generous like that. 'I'll be OK,' he'd said. 'You and I can have a weekend away together some other time.'

'I've found this place in Berkshire,' Suzanne went on. 'It's a dilapidated stately home, run as some sort of collective. They do yoga retreats.

'It's surrounded by beautiful countryside and they serve wonderful-sounding, fresh, organic food. It'll do us good, especially Carmen. She needs it more than anyone.'

Patrice wasn't sure. She didn't want to go away without Jonty. She'd noticed that he'd been staying in Manchester a lot less recently, which pleased her. She didn't want to be the one leaving him now. It made her uneasy.

Percy resisted as well. That was odd, Suzanne thought. She was usually up for anything. She had a very lame excuse, too. Claimed she had too much to do at home.

But Suzanne wouldn't take no for an answer. 'January's

264

such a grim month,' she said. 'It won't be the same without you. And, Pats, it'll do Seamus good to have some quality time with his dad. Father-son bonding. Very important. And Carmen needs our support. Come on now, it's only for one night. It'll be fun.'

So they skipped Saturday morning Pilates and set off together, in the slashing rain, in Percy's ancient, khaki Land Rover. The men had agreed to look after the children.

'It feels like we're bunking off school,' Percy smiled, turning Amy Winehouse up on the CD.

'Hope the place is OK,' Patrice shouted from the back. She had to shout, because the canvas sides were flapping noisily. The wind was whistling around. It wasn't exactly cosy in there, even with the heating up full blast.

'It'll be OK,' Suzanne yelled back. 'Basic, I guess, but lots of good food and clean living. We're going to get really healthy.'

'What, in one night?' Carmen said doubtfully.

She was sitting beside Percy in the passenger seat. They'd all agreed she needed the extra space. The bump was coming along nicely.

'Yup,' said Suzanne. 'We're going to have a booze-free, wholesome forty-eight hours. Treat our bodies as our temples, relax and meditate on life, the universe and everything. Marvellous.'

Percy asked Patrice to look in an orange plastic bag in the back. Patrice rootled around, tutted, fished something out and pushed it through the gap in the seats in front, waved it around. 'Vodka! Really, Percy,' she laughed. 'And it said quite specifically on the brochure that there was to be no alcohol.'

'And doors locked at eleven p.m.,' Suzanne reminded them.

'I thought we might need it after a day of downward dogs and sun salutations,' Percy said innocently.

Carmen groaned. 'Blimey! Why aren't we going to a gorgeous hotel somewhere instead? It sounds like bootcamp.'

'Now, now, girls,' Suzanne admonished. 'This'll be better for the soul.'

The house was just as they'd all imagined: large and rambling, covered in ivy and surrounded by fields. They ran inside to get out of the rain, and were shown to their shared room.

It was in a converted barn, just outside the main building. Four single beds were lined up in a row, with scratchy-looking blankets on them.

'Not exactly luxury,' Suzanne sniffed, taking in the bare floor, thin curtains and ancient-looking sink. She turned on the light, to make it less gloomy. 'But never mind. It's clean, and we're here together.'

She smiled at Patrice. 'Nice to think of Jonty, Mark and Justin with the children, isn't it? It was a great idea of Jonty's to take them to the Natural History Museum.'

Patrice nodded, but she felt miserable. She wanted to talk her worries through with Suzanne and the others, but they might think she'd flipped. Maybe she had. Suzanne might be really angry.

'C'mon,' said Percy. She seemed to have brightened up a bit. 'We'd better change and get downstairs for the first class.'

They walked into what must once have been the grand dining room. Huge, arched windows with wooden shutters looked out over fields of sheep. The rain had started to ease off, and watery sunlight was peeping through the clouds. The sky looked staggeringly beautiful; ethereal, Patrice thought. It almost made her want to cry.

She noticed the window frames inside had been repainted recently. There was still a slight smell of paint hanging in the air. But the old chairs round the edges of the room were tatty and in need of reupholstering. They looked grubby; you wouldn't want to put your bottom on them.

The place didn't feel neglected, exactly. It was too warm and tidy for that, but there was clearly a major lack of cash. Hence the yoga retreats, she supposed. They must be one way for the people who lived here in some sort of commune to make money.

The yoga teacher was a small, brown, wiry-looking man with shoulder-length, stringy grey hair tucked behind his ears. He had a long, beaky nose with a bump in the middle and close-set eyes. He looked intelligent, though owlish.

He said his name was Reggie; Patrice thought it ought to be Amir or something, although he wasn't Indian. Reggie was just too, well, ordinary.

There were about ten other people in the room, a mixture of men and women. Reggie started to read out a list of names, in alphabetical order. Being a 'B', Patrice was one of the first. She waited for the others.

'Pear-sea-fonny.'

'Pers-*ef*-fon-ee,' muttered Percy, jutting her chin out. 'But just call me Percy, will you?'

Patrice could swear Suzanne, beside her, made a strange, snorting noise. Patrice looked around, but Suzanne's face appeared perfectly normal, maybe just a little pinker than usual. And was she sucking in her cheeks, or was Patrice imagining it?

She glanced at Carmen now, standing there with her bump. It was all in front, as they say. The rest of her body was as slender as ever. Her long black hair was hanging down her back in one plait.

She was so beautiful, Patrice thought. And so brave. She, Percy and Suzanne had made a pact they'd be there for her as much as possible. After all, that's what friends were for. They'd been very careful not to show how concerned they were, though. Carmen was fiercely independent and would hate to think she was the focus of so much discussion. They had to pretend they were behaving perfectly normally, when, in reality, they were calling on her much more often than usual, inviting her to things and buying bits and pieces for the baby which she couldn't refuse or take back, because they'd 'lost' the receipts.

Patrice was finding it hard, though, to watch Carmen's tummy swelling, to hear her talk excitedly about the baby. Carmen's relationship had folded, Simon, the bastard, had gone, yet Patrice was still envious. She hated herself for it.

It was sweet torture to wander round baby shops, buying soft white sleepsuits, little vests, blankets. Sometimes her own breasts seemed bigger, more tender, her abdomen rounder, though she knew she was just imagining it.

She wanted to take the sleepsuits and blankets out of their bags, touch them, spread them out in Seamus's room, but she wouldn't allow herself. It was too dangerous.

Beside Carmen, Percy's eyes were closed. She was rocking gently back and forth on the balls of her feet. She must be getting herself in the mood. She was always worrying about her weight, that girl, Patrice thought, but she didn't need to.

Percy was wearing a pale-pink wrap-over top, grey yoga bottoms and thick, bright pink socks with purple spots. She was always well dressed – in a slightly batty way. She did look pale, though. Strained. And she seemed awfully distracted sometimes. Very up and down.

They started with some slow warm-up exercises before launching into a sequence of basic moves. They were doing Ashtanga yoga, which was much tougher than the Hatha yoga Patrice had tried before, and she was aware she was worse than most of the others.

She kept thinking about Jonty and Seamus, wondering what she was doing here. She needed to be with them. It was ridiculous. But at the same time, she wanted to show support for Carmen.

She wished she could just relax and enjoy herself, but her

mind was restless. Like a child in a strange house, she was constantly picking things up, turning them over, poking and peering, behind and underneath. Looking for something, she didn't know what.

She knew Reggie must be looking at her, despairing. She was scarcely listening to his instructions.

They ate lunch round a long wooden table in the old kitchen. Like the rest of the building, the room was sparsely furnished and decorated, with bare white brick walls and a grey stone floor. The food was fabulous, though.

It was served by the people who lived there. It seemed to Patrice that the men all had long, shaggy hair and beards and wore sandals, and the women pale, un-made-up faces and hordes of children. All very alternative. Trust Suzanne to pick somewhere like this instead of a nice conventional spa hotel or something.

They tucked into big green salads sprinkled with nuts and seeds, strong cheeses and homemade brown bread still warm from the oven. After lunch, there was a break from yoga to learn how to give a shiatsu massage.

Reggie told them to stand in a big circle. They had no idea what to expect next. Slowly, he walked round the group, tapping every other person on the shoulder.

'Now turn to your left,' he instructed those he'd picked. 'This is your partner.'

Patrice was relieved that her partner was the pleasant-looking young Irishman in jeans and a T-shirt whom she'd spoken to over lunch. He'd told her he was an actor; his name was Colm. It sounded as if he were far more often out of work than in, but he seemed funny and easy-going.

She glanced across at Percy. She'd definitely got the raw deal. Her partner was the squat, dark, hairy-looking man who'd informed them all early on that he was a very successful banker with a very large house in Guildford.

'Bully for him,' Percy had whispered to Patrice when he'd

taken time out from bragging to swallow a few mouthfuls. 'Sorry about the language, but what an arsehole!'

'To be able to do this properly, you need to get to know each other a little first,' Reggie instructed. 'So I'd like you to sit down and give each other a slow back massage.'

Patrice was appalled. She wasn't remotely touchy-feely. She glanced at Carmen and Suzanne, who were partnering each other, lucky things. They didn't have anything to worry about. Percy was staring intently at the floor.

Nothing for it, Patrice thought. She'd just have to follow instructions. She didn't want Colm to think she had anything against him. It wasn't his fault they were being forced together in this embarrassing way.

Patrice sat, cross-legged, on the floor.

'Will I go first?' Colm asked kindly. She was relieved he'd taken the initiative. 'Do you want to take off your sweater?' he suggested.

She supposed it did look a bit silly, having a massage in a huge, hairy jumper. She took it off. At least the room was warm.

'Not to worry,' Colm whispered in a reassuring voice. 'Just try to relax.'

She closed her eyes while his hands kneaded into her shoulders, her neck, moved down her spine, pressing with his knuckles into each vertebra. His touch was strong, confident, calming, not sexual at all. It didn't make her feel any more uncomfortable than she was already.

She thought of Jonty. What would he say if he saw her now? He'd be aghast. She imagined his angry face and sandy, wrinkled brows. She felt panicked for a moment, before remembering he was miles away, in London with Seamus. He'd never know. She sighed and tried to empty her mind.

When it came to her turn to massage Colm, Patrice felt strangely calm. She hadn't touched another man since she'd met Jonty, eighteen years before. That was a weird thought. But Colm made it seem friendly and natural.

His body underneath his T-shirt felt nice and firm. He was slimmer than Jonty. Less squidgy. She wanted to make things as unawkward for him as possible, just as he'd done with her. It wasn't easy, though. It was hardly a normal situation, to be massaging a complete stranger like this.

She tried to forget who he was and focus on pushing into the muscles, working the knotty bits, easing the tension. She hardly knew anything about him, or the stresses he was under, but she could sense his body relaxing beneath her fingers, enjoying the attention. He was practically purring.

It was strangely pleasurable to be giving pleasure to someone in that way. She could understand now why masseuses claimed to enjoy their jobs.

She remembered Percy. Poor Percy with the odious hairy man. That was a different matter. Patrice glanced in her direction. The hairy man was hunched right over, eyes closed, and Percy was pummelling into his lower back with the sides of her hands.

Patrice could see a thick line of black hairs sprouting from the top of his white T-shirt and running up his neck. The backs of his arms were hairy, too. Percy's back was arched, away from him, arms outstretched in front of her. She looked in some discomfort, as if she'd eaten a raw lemon or a piece of chilli.

Then she spread her hands out and started massaging his ample love handles. Patrice caught her eye. She saw Percy bite her cheek and heard her make a sort of choking noise.

Patrice felt ripples of laughter bubbling up, threatening to explode. She looked away quickly but it was too late. She let out a terrible honk, which turned into bray, then a snort. Everyone turned round to see what the commotion was.

She put her hand up to her mouth and coughed. 'Sorry,' she said, staring down at her feet. 'Bit of a sore throat.'

Concentrate on Colm's back, she told herself. For God's sake, girl, just think of his back.

She was relieved after supper when Percy looked at her, Carmen and Suzanne pointedly and said she was ready for bed.

'I think I'll join you – yoga's exhausting,' Patrice replied.

Carmen rose, too, patting her stomach. 'Me too. I've got no staying power at the moment.'

Suzanne was deep in conversation with Reggie. She looked up when Carmen spoke and Patrice stared meaningfully at her. 'What? Oh, yes, I'm exhausted,' Suzanne said, yawning quickly.

The squat, hairy man pushed back his chair. 'It's very dark out there. Would you ladies like me to walk you over?'

'Nooooo,' they chorused, rather too quickly.

He sat back down, bit into his apple and the juice went flying. The woman next to him wiped her eye with a napkin.

The four friends stumbled, giggling, up the rickety wooden steps to their room in the barn. It was lucky Suzanne had brought a torch as the only light came from outside.

'Bloody hell,' Percy said. 'I wouldn't want to be sleeping here on my own. It's creepy.'

'I reckon Hirsute Man would have happily kept you company,' Suzanne chortled.

'Euuuw, don't,' Percy replied. 'He makes me feel sick. Did you hear him going on about his Porsche and his yacht at supper?'

'Yeah, well, he is only about five feet two,' Carmen tittered. 'The poor man's got to boost his self-esteem somehow.'

Percy had packed little plastic tumblers, tonic, and orange juice for Carmen. 'Sorry there's no ice,' she said.

'The service is rubbish round here,' Carmen joked.

They sat cross-legged on Carmen's and Percy's beds. Carmen had a thick, grey blanket round her shoulders. She switched on her bedside light and got up to turn off the overhead one. 'Much nicer,' she said smiling and sitting down again.

The women's shadows on the wall made them look like an enormous creature with four heads.

'Cheers,' Suzanne said, raising her plastic cup. 'To friendship – and Carmen's sprog.'

'Friendship,' they echoed. 'And the Sprog.'

'I can't wait to meet him or her.' Suzanne smiled, taking a sip of vodka.'I definitely think if it's a girl you should call her Suzanne.'

Carmen laughed.

'No, Patrice,' Patrice chipped in. 'A noble name, don't you think?'

'Well, she's not going to call it Persephone, that's for sure,' Percy said. 'Over my dead body.'

Suzanne looked serious. 'How are you feeling, though, Carmen. About Simon?'

Carmen drew her legs up and hugged her knees into her chest underneath the blanket. 'Miserable, angry, upset, resigned. Confused really,' she replied truthfully. 'All I do know is, I don't want him to have anything to do with the baby. And I definitely don't want any money from him.' Her lips set in a thin, hard line.

Suzanne ran her hands through her red hair, which made a section at the front point up at right angles to her head. It looked like a soldier, standing to attention.

Patrice smiled, but Suzanne's brow was a mass of wrinkles. 'How will you cope financially?' Suzanne asked. 'Will you carry on with your business?'

Carmen nodded and took a sip of orange juice. 'At least I can work from home. I thought I'd put the baby down for a nursery three or four days a week, and my parents have offered to help out with the fees. We'll be OK.'

'Shouldn't you make Simon pay for something at least?' Suzanne persisted. The soldier on her head bobbed up and down fretfully. 'After all, he is the father, and he's got money, hasn't he?'

Carmen made a face. 'I can't bear the thought of him having any say over my child. I feel so betrayed, it makes my flesh crawl just to think of him. And the thought of giving him access makes me sick. I just want him to go off into the sunset with his new loved one, never to be seen or heard of again.'

'Is that really what you want?' Patrice asked doubtfully.

Carmen lowered her eyes. 'Yes. No. Oh, I don't know. I guess so. It's terribly sad to think this baby will never have a father. But it's not like Simon's ever shown any interest. I think it'll be less painful all round if he gets out of our lives altogether.'

Patrice shook her head. Strands of hair fell over her face. She tucked them behind her ears. 'Fancy having an affair behind your partner's back like that,' she said. 'I don't know how he can live with himself.'

Percy recrossed her legs, fiddling with the big buttons on her chunky cardigan. Patrice hadn't seen that one before. It was baby pink, hand-knitted by the looks of things. Darling.

'It happens all the time though,' Percy said seriously.

Patrice was surprised. 'That doesn't make it all right though, does it?' she added. She shivered.

Suzanne rose. 'My jeans are digging into my stomach after that huge supper,' she said, pulling up her sweater to reveal a mound of doughy white flesh tumbling over her waistband.

The others sniggered. She didn't care that they saw, that's what was so wonderful about her, Patrice thought. Millicent would sooner die than reveal so much as an inch of surplus flesh to anyone.

'I think I'll start buying trousers with a nice elasticated waist.' Suzanne grinned and went to her suitcase. 'I'm just going to slip into something more comfortable,' she explained in a silly, American accent.

She rootled around and fished out what looked like a baggy T-shirt that must once have been white and was now grey, and some checked pyjama bottoms. She threw them on the bed.

She stripped off and flung the rest of her clothes in a heap on the wooden chair in the corner.

The room had warmed up nicely now, with all the bodies in it. Patrice took off her cardigan and had another sip of vodka. She didn't much like the taste, but she didn't want to be a party-pooper.

Suzanne walked back to the bed. She looked a mess. The checky PJ bottoms were crumpled and the T-shirt was way too big for her. Justin's probably, Patrice thought.

Then she noticed the writing on the front. It was big and red. 'The Great North Run, 1992', it said. And there was a large picture of the Angel of the North underneath.

Patrice's chest felt suddenly tight, her mouth dry. The saliva seemed to have drained away. 'Where did you get that?' she asked. Stop being a fool, Patrice, she told herself.

Suzanne looked down at her chest and pulled the T-shirt out so she could read the writing. 'What? This old thing?' she said. 'I found it in the laundry basket. I was in such a rush this morning, I just grabbed the first thing I could lay my hands on.'

Patrice felt light-headed. She lay down on her side, propping herself up on a pillow with her elbow, and spoke again, trying to sound normal. 'That's funny,' she said. 'Jonty's got one exactly the same. Did Justin do the Great North Run in 1992, then?'

Suzanne raised her eyebrows. 'Not to my knowledge.' She thought for a minute. 'Justin probably picked it up by mistake when he and Jonty played squash. There seems to be no sign of their enthusiasm waning, does there?'

Patrice didn't say anything. She'd never known Jonty wear that T-shirt for sport. He was so proud of himself for completing the half-marathon, he'd always kept it in a drawer, neatly folded, as a keepsake. But she was being stupid. Paranoid.

'It's great for Jonty, playing all this squash,' she said, as casually as she could. 'It's keeping his latent Michelin man at bay. He and Justin seem to have a riotous time at the pub afterwards, too.'

Percy chipped in. 'I wish Mark would get into it. He doesn't do any sport now.'

Suzanne groaned. 'It's a bit of a mixed blessing, to be honest. You know they're talking about golf next? I just hope they don't get obsessed. I don't want to be a golf widow, too.'

'Jonty loves golf,' Patrice said. Her voice sounded a long way off. 'He used to play with his father.' Why was she telling them this? 'His three brothers played a bit, too,' she went on, 'but Jonty never wanted them to. He said it was the one thing he and his father could do together.'

Suzanne looked interested. 'Didn't he get on with his brothers then?'

Patrice sighed. Her whole body felt heavy, somehow. 'I think he was jealous, because he felt his father preferred them,' she explained. 'They were all very macho, you see. Rugger buggers. Into sport in a big way. Whereas Jonty's mother always says he was different, more gentle. He didn't much like sport as a boy. He preferred reading and helping his mother cook. He loved cooking, still does.'

The words were spilling out now. She couldn't have stopped even if she wanted to. 'His father used to bully him,' she said. 'Tried to make him like the others.'

'How horrible.' Percy shuddered. 'I hate bullies. In what way?'

'Oh,' Patrice sighed, 'he'd take him out and make him play rugby and football in all weathers, or go on runs with the others, who were older. If Jonty fell over or got hurt, his father would roar at him to get up, carry on playing. Jonty

276

says he became furious if he cried. Crying wasn't allowed. I've always thought that's why Jonty's so driven at work. He's forever trying to prove to his father that he's as good as his brothers. Playing golf was the only time he ever felt close to his dad.'

Suzanne looked at Patrice strangely. A frown crossed her brow, then disappeared. She cleared her throat. 'Oh well, we'll just have to go for lunch and hit the shops while they're on the golf course,' she said cheerfully. 'Leave all the kids with Pers, here.' She grinned. 'Only joking.'

Percy smiled. 'I might be out for a long lunch myself, but you can always ask.'

Carmen felt her bump and made a face. 'Ooh, a huge kick there,' she said. 'I reckon he's doing Body Attack.' She shifted to one side, repositioning herself. 'That's better. She turned to Percy. 'What about Mark?' she asked. 'How's he? I haven't heard much about him recently. Are you two OK?'

Percy looked at her lap. 'Yeah, fine,' she said brightly. 'We have our highs and lows, you know. But who doesn't? Top-up, anyone?' Percy refilled the glasses.

Patrice noticed Carmen looking at Percy intently. Her big brown eyes narrowed. 'What's up?' Carmen asked.

Percy's face froze, as if she'd seen something horrible. Patrice was taken aback. Percy was always so reliable, her life comfortingly plain-sailing. She was the glue which held them all together. It was true she'd looked a little over-wrought recently, but surely nothing was really the matter with solid, trustworthy Percy?

Patrice expected her to grin, shrug her shoulders and say, 'Joking.' But she didn't.

Instead, Percy took a deep breath and rubbed her hands together. 'To tell you the truth . . .' she said. It sounded as if she were having to squeeze the words out, like toothpaste from a clogged-up tube. 'Mark and I have been having a few problems,' she blurted out.

Carmen cocked her head to one side. 'What sort of problems?' she asked.

Percy sighed. 'Mark's been behaving oddly for quite some time – incredibly angry and nasty. He shouts and rants and upsets us all. I never told you but a few months ago he smashed all our family photos on the mantelpiece one evening. He wouldn't say why. Christmas was terrible. He was hardly speaking to me – he still isn't. He didn't even give me a Christmas present. The atmosphere at home is ghastly. It's a nightmare.'

She was sniffling now. Patrice got a hankie out of her bag and Percy blew her nose. 'I'm sorry,' she said, 'I didn't mean to—'

Carmen raised her hand. 'For goodness' sake, Percy, you do so much for the rest of us. You're always listening to our problems. A trouble shared is a trouble halved and all that.'

Percy looked grateful. 'I know,' she said. 'It's been getting me down a lot. Sometimes I wonder if he wants out of the marriage. I don't know what's happened to the man I married. I don't think he loves me any more. He can't, not the way he treats me.' She hung her head.

Carmen put her arm round her and gave her a squeeze.

'Do you think it's exhaustion?' Suzanne asked. 'He does work terrible hours.'

Percy nodded. 'I'm sure that's got a lot to do with it. He's worn out most of the time. But I've asked him to cut back and he just ignores me.' She sounded anguished now. 'I know we need the money, but I tell him it's less important than our relationship. That just sets him off again, though! I can't seem to get through to him.'

Carmen gave her another squeeze. 'I'm so sorry, darling,' she said. 'Why didn't you tell us this before?'

Percy gave a sad smile. 'It's a relief to get it off my chest,' she said, 'but it just seems so trivial in comparison with what you've been through.'

Carmen shook her head. 'It's not trivial at all. It's your marriage. Would he consider counselling, do you think? Sounds like he needs it.'

Percy made a face. 'I wish. He's absolutely refused. Says he hasn't got time and doesn't want to go talking to some stranger, anyway.' She looked up. 'I've honestly thought sometimes that we'd be better off splitting up. Even the children say it's nicer in the house when he's not there.'

Carmen shook her head. 'Don't do anything rash,' she pleaded. 'I'm sure you can work this out. As you yourself said, all marriages have their highs and lows.'

Percy looked unsure. 'I know,' she said. 'But something's desperately wrong with ours, and I'm beginning to think we mightn't pull through.'

Patrice felt wide awake when they finally turned out the light. She was so shocked by what Percy had told them, it had temporarily blocked out her own worries. She'd had no idea that Percy and Mark were anything other than happily married. They seemed made for each other; Percy and Mark, Mark and Percy, it was unthinkable for them to be any other way. It was unthinkable for her and Jonty, too.

Damn, she was back to him again. She pictured Jonty in the T-shirt. Then Justin. She definitely wouldn't be able to sleep now, even after that vodka. She wished she'd brought her sleeping tablets. They'd knock her out.

Carmen rolled over and groaned in the darkness. 'Why does pregnancy have to be so uncomfortable?' she asked. 'Whichever way I turn, I can feel a foot or something digging into my ribs.'

'Poor you,' Suzanne mumbled. She sounded half asleep. 'But you know what they say? No gain without pain.'

'That's helpful,' Carmen muttered. She yelped. 'Ow, that practically winded me.'

'For God's sake, go to sleep,' Suzanne grumbled. 'We've got to be up in a few hours for more bloody yoga.'

There was silence for a few moments, followed by a rustle and a thump. 'My bum!' Percy screeched.

Patrice turned on the light. Percy was on the floor, rubbing her backside.

'Whatever's the matter?' Patrice asked, worried.

'I was getting up for a pee but I caught myself in the sodding blanket,' Percy apologised. She looked about eleven, Patrice thought.

There was a long, slow rumbling noise and Suzanne rose from her bed like a monster from the depths. 'WHY DIDN'T YOU HAVE A PEE BEFORE YOU WENT TO BED?' she boomed.

She looked fearsome, her face white, her red hair snaking round her like Medusa's serpents. Patrice felt quite nervous. She was suddenly very glad she wasn't one of Suzanne's minions at work.

'I'm s-sorry,' Percy stuttered and scurried off to the loo.

Suzanne sighed and lay back on her elbows. They heard the chain flush and Percy returned.

'Anyone else need anything before I turn out the lights for the FINAL TIME?' Suzanne said.

'Miss, can I have a drink of water?' Patrice asked in a small voice.

Chapter Eight

As soon as she crossed the threshold, Percy knew something was wrong. She could feel it in the air. It was almost tangible.

Mark was sitting at the kitchen table, waiting for her. She could hear Ben and Rowan next door, watching TV.

She glanced around. Dishes were piled up in the sink. A pan with what looked like the remains of Sunday lunch was on the cooker.

Her eyes fell on Mark again. Dishevelled was the word. His face looked grey, with at least two days' worth of stubble on his chin. He was wearing the same navy sweatshirt as yesterday. What little hair he had left was messy round his ears, uncombed, and there were shadows under his eyes.

He looked at his wife and held something up. A credit card? Percy's stomach lurched. The card looked horribly familiar, well used, slightly tattered at the edges.

'I found it on the desk, by the computer,' Mark said quietly.

Percy didn't move. How could she have been so careless?

'I borrowed it to go food shopping,' Mark went on. 'There was no money on it. Have you any idea how much we're in debt?'

Percy shook her head. 'Mark, I've just come back from—'

He interrupted her. 'Ten thousand,' he said, shaking the card. 'With this and the overdraft we owe ten thousand pounds.' He put his head in his hands. 'I don't know how we're going to pay it back.'

Percy slumped down, opposite Mark. The TV was still chuntering in the background. She hadn't even said hello to the boys. She couldn't think straight. 'I – I'm sorry,' she said. She put out her hand to touch his, but he pulled it away, staring at her. His eyes were tiny pinpricks of light.

'For God's sake, don't say sorry,' he hissed. 'You don't care or you wouldn't have done it.'

Percy flinched.

'I've told you time and again to stop spending, but you won't listen,' he went on. 'Now we're really screwed.'

She felt a lump in her throat and tried to swallow back the tears.

'I don't know what the fuck you spend it on,' he said, shaking his head. 'It doesn't make sense. I know you're always buying clothes and stuff, but I don't understand how they add up to this much.' He shifted in his chair. 'Have you got mink coats or something hidden round the house? Percy?' His voice was softer now.

She made a small noise.

'I'm not kidding, you know,' he said, 'we're in big trouble. Seriously, we may even have to sell up, move house. I work every hour God sends as it is. I can't make us any more money.'

Percy hung her head. A moment ago she'd been feeling buoyant, happy. They'd had such a jolly night. And before going away, things had even been looking up very slightly on the poker front, too.

She hadn't played for days after the tournament back in September, had slept a lot instead. She'd thought she was going mad. But rest had helped.

After a week or so, she'd returned to the tables but avoided the big cash games. She'd played very safe, hoping to get some confidence back, and she'd started winning again – albeit in a very small way. She'd only recouped around five hundred pounds over the entire period, but it had made her feel more optimistic. She was convinced her losing streak was coming to an end.

She hadn't wanted to go with the girls this weekend, she'd felt she couldn't spare the time, but Suzanne had been so persistent. And in the end Percy had persuaded herself that a breather would do her good. It might clear her mind. Plus, it would be enjoyable for Carmen, for them all.

Her face was burning hot. Her heart was beating so fast in her chest she thought Mark would hear it.

Fight or flight. She wished she could fly, out of the house and up the road and on and on, without stopping.

'Are there others?' he asked suddenly, brandishing the card in her face. She hesitated.

'Oh God,' he groaned, recognising the pause for what it was. His shoulders drooped. 'I had no idea.'

She nodded, ashamed.

'Tell me,' he ordered. 'There's no point lying now.'

'I've got a Tesco one as well.' She hung her head. He breathed in and out heavily.

'How much?'

She licked her lips. Her mouth felt dry. She wanted to be a long way away, somewhere dark, hidden. 'Around two thousand.' She squeezed her eyes shut. 'And . . . and I borrowed five thousand from Zeus. That's gone, too.'

He was silent, stunned, totting it up in his head. 'You owe twelve thousand pounds – on top of our overdraft? What have you spent it on?' he said finally. 'What have you done with it?'

Percy swallowed. She opened her eyes and looked at her husband, really looked this time. He seemed smaller, somehow. Shadowy. So different from the fiery, bad-tempered, photo-smashing man she'd described to her friends. He could have been a hundred years old.

Guilt swept over her. 'I'm so sorry, Mark,' she said again. What other words were there?

His hands moved slightly on the table. She flinched. Was he going to hit her? She deserved it. But he wasn't that sort of man. Instead, he placed his hands, gently, over hers. They were cold. He looked in her eyes. He seemed so tired. She returned his gaze.

She realised it was the first time he'd allowed her to do that in ages.

'What do you spend it on, Pers?' he said again, simply.

Percy looked away and shivered. 'Poker.'

She felt him start. He pulled his hands off hers. So he really hadn't had a clue. She'd hidden it well, then.

'Poker?' he said, disbelieving. 'What, gambling?'

She nodded. 'I do it at night, online.' She was whispering. It sounded less shocking, somehow. 'It started out as just a bit of fun, really. I used to play a lot with my father when I was a child – remember? And at university.' Mark was silent.

'It was exciting, a form of escapism, I suppose. I liked having to use my brain and – and I was good at it. It gave me a buzz. I enjoyed the chat, the banter, too,' she went on. 'It's like being in a room of friends.

'I was winning at first, then I started losing. Small amounts to begin with, but they got bigger. I kept thinking I'd win it back the next night and you'd never find out.'

'But why?' he asked. He sounded genuinely mystified. 'You know gambling's a fool's game?'

She sniffed. 'I wanted to be able to buy a few things, like clothes and stuff for the house. I thought if I made enough I might even be able to pay off the overdraft, too, or at least put something towards it. And I suppose for years you've worked so hard, hardly ever been home—'

He interrupted: 'Don't you dare blame me!'

She pushed her hair off her face. It felt sweaty on her forehead. 'Let me finish,' she said.

He growled, but fell silent.

'And when you are home you're tired and grumpy,' she went on. 'We've been getting on so badly. I – I even thought you might be having an affair. Deep down I didn't really believe it, but there didn't seem to be any other explanation. I couldn't understand why you were behaving that way.'

He seemed about to say something, but changed his mind. He shook his head.

Percy ploughed on. 'I once lost two thousand in one night.' She saw him wince. 'It just got out of control.'

Mark's eyes were hollow. 'But what about the debts?' he asked. 'The mortgage, the kitchen loan, the overdraft? Didn't that stop you? And hasn't it occurred to you that I have to work so hard to pay the bills? Why else would I do it? How else would we be in this house, go on nice holidays, have nice clothes? It was all for you, Pers – and the boys.'

Percy felt so stupid. Ashamed, too. 'I know you have to work long hours to pay for everything,' she said, 'and I know I'm extravagant, quite apart from the poker, and buy too many clothes and things and make our money problems worse. It's no excuse, but I think I spend partly because I'm lonely, to cheer myself up.

'I wouldn't mind so much if you weren't so angry and distant. But we can't even enjoy the times when we're together. As for the debt, I hate it, but when I'm playing I somehow manage to shove it out of my mind. I can't explain how. I'm convinced next time I'm going to win that golden pot of money.'

Mark thumped his hand on the table. She cringed. 'I can't believe you've done this to me – to Ben and Rowan. How could anyone be so selfish?' He sounded desperate.

She put her head in her hands. Tears were trickling down her cheeks. She wiped them away with her sleeve. 'I feel so bad, I wake up every single day with this sick feeling in my stomach,' she said quietly. 'I swear to myself I won't do it again, I'll tell you everything. Then the evening comes and I guess I can't resist the temptation of a big win – or even a small one.'

Mark made a face. 'Like some sad old git of a gambling addict?' he said. 'Really, Percy. I thought you were more intelligent.' He was silent for a moment. 'What are you going to do?'

'I'll get us out of this,' she said. 'I don't know how, but I'll do it somehow. I promise.'

He didn't move. What was he thinking? 'You can't,' he replied finally. His voice was deep and unambiguous. 'As I said, we're stuffed.'

They sat there for a few more minutes, saying nothing. Percy removed her hand from his shoulder. It felt awkward, out of place.

She thought of the boys – their beautiful boys – and she knew she didn't deserve them. She didn't deserve anything. She'd dragged them all down, deep into the murk and slime. What would become of them?

The phone rang. It sounded harsh, intrusive. Mark still didn't move. Percy thought she'd leave it to ring, but she couldn't stand the noise. She had to make it stop.

She rose, wearily. 'Hi, it's Stefan, from *Optimum* magazine,' a voice said. 'Is Mark around?'

Percy turned to check. Mark shook his head without looking up.

'I'm sorry, he's working,' she lied. She wished she hadn't picked up.

Stefan sounded disappointed. 'Is he on his mobile?'

Percy thought quickly. 'It's lost,' she stammered. 'I don't know when he'll be back. Maybe tomorrow.' She realised that must sound weird.

Stefan hesitated. 'I was hoping he could do a quick job for us.' He was puzzled, clearly. Normally Mark was so accommodating. He'd shift jobs round to make sure he could do just about everything. 'But no probs,' Stefan went on. 'I'll get someone else. Tell him I called, will you?'

Mark pushed back his chair and rose. Percy wondered if this was it, if he was going to give up. Throw in the towel. She waited, frightened, to see what he'd do next.

'I've got nothing left to give, Percy,' he muttered, shaking his head.

She wanted to tell him it would be all right. But she didn't dare.

He turned and shuffled towards the door.

'Where are you going?' she asked. Her voice sounded high and panicky. She followed him down the hall.

'The pub,' he replied, putting on his shoes and coat. It seemed to require a supreme effort. 'I may be some time.'

Chapter Nine

❧

'Go on, knock,' Suzanne said. Ruby knocked on Lara's bedroom door, turned and smiled at her mother, excited. Her face was all bright and shiny. She was wearing her favourite rosebud dress. It had puff sleeves and a belt which tied with a bow at the back.

Suzanne stood behind, holding the tray. She was relieved when Lara answered. The tray was so heavy.

'Come in,' Lara called.

Ruby gave a little skip and pushed open the door.

Suzanne whispered, 'One, two, three . . .'

They walked in singing 'Happy Birthday To You'. There was a cup cake on the tray, with one candle. It blew out when the door opened, but it didn't matter. Lara sat up in bed and smiled. She was so pretty when she smiled, Suzanne thought.

She put the tray on Lara's bed. 'Sweet sixteen,' Suzanne said. 'Congratulations, darling.'

Ruby sat on the bed beside her big sister, being careful not to knock the tray. 'Look,' Ruby said. 'We've made you orange juice and toast. And there are presents. Shall I open them for you?'

Suzanne laughed. 'That's very nice of you, Ruby, but it's Lara's birthday. Lara has to open them.'

Ruby looked disappointed. Lara put her arm round her little sister. 'You can help,' she said kindly. Ruby beamed.

Suzanne wished she could capture that image and bottle it: the two sisters loving each other for a moment. It made her feel warm inside.

Lara took a sip of orange juice and a nibble of toast. Suzanne glowed inside. She musn't show it, though. That could be a disaster. Lara was definitely eating more. She'd put on a bit of weight. But she could easily go the other way again if they weren't careful.

Lara started to open her cards, reading out the messages inside to Ruby and pointing at the pictures.

Lara let Ruby pick at the sticky tape on some of the presents, but she took the gift out herself. There were some books, knickers, make-up: little things. She was saving the biggest till last.

Finally she picked up the present from Suzanne and Justin. Suzanne felt nervous. She never knew what to get Lara. Depending on whether she was pleased or not, she could be pleasant all day, or sulk and make the whole family miserable. Were they in for storms – or sunshine? Who could tell until the gift was unwrapped and it was too late to rush back and change it?

The iPod fell out of the silver wrapping paper on to the bed and Lara beamed. 'Wow!'

Suzanne sighed with relief. Result!

'You can play music on it,' Ruby said, delighted. She jumped up and the orange juice went flying over Lara's purple duvet.

Suzanne held her breath. Lara picked up the glass, put it on her side table and wiped the duvet with a napkin from the tray. 'Oh, Rubeee,' she said, tickling her sister. 'Trust you, you naughty thing.'

Ruby giggled.

Suzanne picked up the tray and swung it out of the way quickly. The girls were rolling on the bed, having a tickle fight. Ruby was squealing with pleasure. Suzanne was astonished. Lara rarely showed any interest in any of her siblings. The day boded well.

The game stopped. Both girls were panting, red and

dishevelled. A shadow passed over Lara's face. 'Nothing from Dad?' she asked.

Ruby looked at her mother, enquiring. Who was this other dad Lara sometimes spoke of?

Suzanne shook her head. 'Sorry, sweetheart.'

Lara shrugged. 'I wasn't expecting it anyway.'

Noah tipped up around 11 a.m. 'How's college?' Justin asked him.

Felix was squatting at Justin's feet on the kitchen floor. He was on his coloured playmat, building a brick tower. After three bricks, it fell down. He hadn't worked out how to pile them up properly yet.

'I've left,' Noah said. His beanie was pulled down so low, Suzanne wondered if he could see properly. The silver stud on his lower lip bobbed when he spoke. It still made her wince. It looked so dirty, somehow.

Lara fetched him a glass of orange juice from the American-style stainless-steel fridge. They needed a massive one, with all those children. 'Noah didn't like the subjects he was doing,' she explained. 'He's going to reapply next year.'

Suzanne caught Justin's eye and he raised his eyebrows. 'Ah,' he said.

Noah drank the juice quickly. His hands were covered in silver rings and there were tattoos on his knuckles. They looked dirty, too.

Lara walked over to Suzanne and gave her a hug. 'Mum, everyone's parents go out,' she said. Her voice was wheedling. 'Honestly. It'll be fine. If there's any trouble – which there won't be – I'll call you.'

Suzanne wrinkled her brow. She wanted desperately to be closer to Lara. Maybe if they were better friends Lara wouldn't have gone on that stupid diet; they could have talked about things, ironed out some of her problems. But was a party too risky? 'I'm not sure,' Suzanne said.

'It's just a few friends,' Lara went on. 'Nothing big. And we'll clear up afterwards. Won't we, Noah?' Noah grunted. Suzanne looked at Justin. He shrugged and held out his hands, palms up. 'It's your call.'

Lara beamed. 'Thanks, Mum, love you.' She gave Suzanne another big hug, knocking her off balance.

'C'mon, Noah,' Lara said, grabbing her boyfriend's arm and disappearing upstairs. Suzanne had scarcely had time to reply, but she could feel the warmth of the hug still. When was the last time Lara had given her one of those?

She, Justin and the other children trooped round to Percy's house at about 5 p.m. 'It's really good of you, Percy,' Suzanne said. 'I just hope I'm doing the right thing, letting Lara have this party.'

'I'm sure you are,' Percy smiled. 'You're only sixteen once. Lovely to see you.'

Justin put up the travel cot in Rowan's room and Ruby and Rowan, Ben and Ollie vanished into different parts of the house. Ollie liked Ben, despite the age gap. They played computer games together. It was funny how Ollie was still a little boy in many ways, despite the deepening voice, Suzanne thought. So different from Lara. You could hear shouts of laughter and the odd crash coming from upstairs, but Percy didn't seem to mind.

She and Mark, Justin and Suzanne sat in the kitchen, sipping wine and nibbling crisps, while the shepherd's pie cooked. It smelled delicious. Felix was happy on Justin's knee, chomping a breadstick and trying to reach the crisps.

The house felt cold, but comfortingly messy, just like their own, Suzanne thought. 'Are you still thinking of getting new sofas?' she asked Percy. They'd been through some catalogues together and looked in a few shop windows.

'I've changed my mind,' Percy replied airily. 'We don't need them.'

Suzanne was surprised. Percy had seemed so keen on new

sofas. Suzanne glanced at her friend. She looked pale and lined, she thought. Quite unwell, in fact. Suzanne hoped Percy and Mark had managed to resolve the problems she'd talked about on the yoga retreat. She'd certainly not referred to them again. But she was acting rather oddly.

Mark cleared his throat but said nothing. Suzanne smiled at him. He always made that noise when he was embarrassed. She noticed his bald head had gone pinkish, too. She'd better try to get Percy on her own later, she decided. Find out what was going on.

Suzanne liked Mark. He was funny and warm and he loved his kids, and Percy. You could just tell. He looked so tired the whole time, though. Worn out. Percy said he was always working.

'What do you make of Carmen's news?' Suzanne asked him.

He seemed surprised. 'What news?'

'You know, the baby,' Suzanne replied. 'Don't tell me you didn't know?'

Percy stopped talking to Justin. 'I haven't told Mark yet,' she said quickly.

Suzanne was amazed. You'd think they'd have discussed something big like that to do with one of Percy's best friends.

Mark sighed. 'No, I didn't know. That's a bit of a bolt from the blue, isn't it?'

Suzanne glanced at Percy. Her mouth was set in a thin, tense line.

'Is everything OK?' Suzanne whispered later as they went upstairs after supper to bathe the little ones. 'With you and Mark, I mean.'

Percy smiled. 'Fine, thanks.'

Suzanne looked at the time: it was 10 p.m. Should she call Lara to make sure everything was all right? Best not.

'D'you think it's OK that I bought some wine and a few beers for them?' Suzanne asked Percy. 'I know they're under-age, but they all drink. And if I'd just got lemonade, I'm sure they'd have nipped to the off-licence. Some of them look at least eighteen.'

Percy was curled up on the sofa at the other end from Mark. There was a huge thump overhead. She scarcely blinked. Suzanne hoped the children wouldn't wake Felix.

'I guess so,' Percy said, sipping her wine. 'I mean, you know best. I've got all this to come, remember.'

Justin put his arm round Suzanne on the other sofa. She snuggled up close, breathing in his comforting, woody smell. 'Relax, darling, it'll be OK,' he reassured her.

'I wish I could be so sure,' she replied. 'D'you think we should go home now?'

'No, Lara would never forgive us,' Justin replied firmly. 'We'll leave at eleven thirty, as we said. She'll call if she needs us.'

He scratched his head. Suzanne looked up at him. His thick, brown hair stuck up where he'd disturbed it and she stroked it down with her hand. She felt a rush of love. He was so gorgeous in profile, with his small, strong nose and the faint trace of stubble on his chin. She could gobble him up.

'Percy?' Justin said suddenly. Suzanne had no idea what was coming. 'Good job you didn't get new sofas, you know. These are fine.'

Suzanne glanced at Percy. She smiled, but her eyes were sad. For a second, Suzanne wondered if she was about to burst into tears. Justin must have noticed it, too, because he changed the subject quickly.

'Hey, Suzie, we'd best be getting back,' he said, rising quickly. 'It's been a great night. Thanks so much, you two.'

Mark took longer than usual to get up. Normally he'd be there in a flash, helping people on with coats, offering to carry children home and so on. There was definitely a weird atmosphere in the house, Suzanne thought as she went upstairs to fetch Felix. Mark and Percy must have had an almighty row or something, but if Percy didn't want to talk about it, what could she do?

Suzanne and Justin walked, shivering, up the garden path. It was a chilly night and Justin had wrapped blankets around Ruby and Felix and transferred them, still asleep, into the double buggy. Ollie trailed behind.

Lights were blazing in every room. Suzanne was surprised. She'd expected the house to be in darkness, with teenagers snogging behind sofas and bushes, needing to be flushed out. The cold weather didn't usually stop them.

Justin carried the sleeping children upstairs to bed while Suzanne went into the sitting room to investigate. The place smelled like a brewery, but otherwise everything seemed OK. There was no obvious damage.

She walked into the kitchen and found Lara's best friends, Jade and Emily, with black bin bags in their hands. They were chucking beer bottles in and putting glasses in the sink. Very busy.

They looked up. 'Hello, Suzanne.' Jade beamed. 'Did you have a nice evening?'

Suzanne felt uneasy. 'Where is everyone?' she asked.

She saw Jade glance at Emily. 'They've all left,' Jade said brightly.

Suzanne scanned the room, then looked out of the kitchen window. All she could see was blackness. 'How did it go?' she asked, opening cupboards. She didn't know what she was looking for.

'Really well.' Emily's voice sounded sugar-sweet. 'Thanks for the wine and crisps and everything, Suzanne.'

Suzanne half expected Emily to curtsey, she was being so polite. 'Glad you enjoyed it,' Suzanne said. 'But where's Lara?'

It was Jade's turn to speak again. She cleared her throat.

'She was feeling a bit tired,' she explained, fiddling with an earring. 'She's gone upstairs for a rest.'

'We said we'd tidy up for her,' Emily chirped.

Suzanne didn't like the sound of that. Deeply dodgy. 'Thanks, that's very good of you,' she said, looking closely at the girls. They looked away. 'But Lara should be helping. I'll go and get her.'

She walked slowly up the two flights of stairs to the attic and opened Lara's door. She didn't know what to expect, but she guessed it wouldn't be good. What if Lara was having sex with Noah? How would she cope with that? Suzanne had no idea.

It took her a moment or two to get used to the darkness. Once her eyes had adjusted, she could see Lara lying face down on her bed, in what appeared to be just a pair of knickers. She did look thin, Suzanne thought. She realised she hadn't seen Lara without clothes on for ages. But she wasn't skeletal. And she was alone. Well, that was something.

Suzanne called across the room. 'Lara, what are you doing? Your friends are downstairs tidying up.'

Lara didn't stir.

Suzanne walked over to the bed and snapped the light on. She could feel her heart start to thump. 'Are you OK?' she said.

She bent down and gave Lara a gentle shake. No response. Carefully, she moved Lara's head to one side, then she put her hand in front of Lara's nose and mouth. She could feel her warm breath. Thank God.

Suzanne sat down beside Lara and tried to roll her over on to her back, but she was heavy and kept rolling back. Now Suzanne started patting the cheek that was visible, softly at first, then harder.

Lara's face was hot and sweaty, covered in smudged mascara. Her eye half opened. The other one was hidden against the bed. She was barely conscious. Or was she having a joke?

'Speak to me, you're scaring me,' Suzanne said.

Lara's eye fluttered, then closed again.

Justin came into the room, followed by Jade and Emily.

'I can't wake her,' Suzanne said, frightened. Her heart was racing now. 'We'd better call an ambulance, quick.'

Lara spoke. 'No, no, I'm a'right.' Her voice was slurred. She still didn't move. Then, suddenly, she sat bolt upright and opened both eyes wide.

Suzanne jumped.

'Breast, arm, breast, arm,' Lara said, waving her arms around as if launching into some bizarre exercise routine. Jade and Emily tittered nervously.

'Oh, Christ, what's the matter with her? Has she taken something? Drugs?' Suzanne was frantic.

Jade and Emily looked uncomfortable. 'I think she just had a bit too much to drink,' Jade said in a small voice. 'Some of the boys brought vodka. People kept topping her up.'

Suzanne didn't know whether to believe them or not. 'What should we do?' she asked Justin.

He slumped down beside her and put his arm round her shoulders. 'I think she's pissed,' he said. His tone was measured. He was weighing everything up. 'I don't know about drugs.'

Suzanne started to cry. 'Look at her, she's a mess. Should we get her to hospital?'

Justin frowned, then shook his head. 'I don't think that's necessary.' He thought for a few moments more. 'Jade, Emily?' he said finally, turning to the girls. 'Are you planning to sleep up here tonight?'

They nodded.

'OK. I'm going to put Lara in the recovery position, with a bowl beside her,' he went on. 'She's obviously very drunk. If you weren't going to be up here with her, I'd take her to hospital. But as you are, I want you to listen out and if you're at all worried, if you hear any choking noises or anything, come downstairs and wake us immediately, OK?'

The girls nodded.

Suzanne was happy to let him take over. She felt worn out by yet another crisis. They tucked Lara in, leaving the light on outside, and trailed downstairs. Suzanne climbed into bed while Justin made cups of tea and checked on Lara again. Finally, he climbed into bed beside his wife.

'She needs to sleep it off, that's all,' he said reassuringly. 'I did the same thing when I was fifteen or sixteen. Got pissed as a fart at a party and crashed out in the back of my parents' car when they came to collect me. They had to carry me inside.'

Suzanne thought about it. She supposed he was right. This wasn't the end of the world. They'd get through this just as they'd get through everything else Lara threw at them.

Justin laughed. 'She'll have a terrible head in the morning.'

'Serves her right,' Suzanne replied fiercely. 'I hope she has the worst headache of her life.'

He was on his back, Suzanne resting her head on his bare chest. There was some hair on it, but not too much. His skin felt warm and soft. He never wore anything in bed.

'Did you go to lots of parties when you were a teenager?' Suzanne asked.

He was stroking her back, round and round with his fore-finger, in a circle. It was comforting.

'Only in the holidays,' he replied. 'I was at boarding school, remember?'

She thought for a moment. 'It must have been weird, being cloistered away like that. Not seeing any girls from one month to the next. It was so different for me, at a mixed school. It's amazing you turned out so normal.'

Justin stopped stroking her. His body tensed. Suzanne wondered why.

'Yeah, well. I didn't know any different,' he said.

She kissed his chest, then put her finger in his furry tummy button. She was looking for fluff. There was usually some there. 'What on earth did you do with all that testosterone?' she asked, teasing. 'I bet you were all wanking away like mad under the covers, after lights out.'

Justin took her hand away from his navel. 'That tickles,' he said. 'A bit of that went on, sure,' he agreed. 'But I think they wore us out on the sports field. Our fathers were all in the services. It was quite military in a way. We weren't given much time to ourselves.'

He stopped for a moment. Suzanne thought he was going to say something more, but clearly he thought better of it.

'Thank you for being so brilliant this evening,' she said, changing the subject. She felt so much calmer now. After all, it was a rite of passage, wasn't it, to get rat-arsed at a party? You had to do it at least once as a teenager. Lara would be fine. 'What would I do without you?' Suzanne asked.

Justin made a funny choking noise. She looked up at his face, startled. 'What's the matter?' she said, taken aback. His eyes were filled with tears.

'I love you so much, Suze,' he said. 'And the children. I couldn't bear to lose you.'

She sat up, kissed his cheek and brushed away the tears with her lips. 'What's prompted this, you big softie?' she cooed. 'I love you so much, too. You're not going to lose me. No way. We were put on this earth to be together.'

He pulled her to him, burying his nose in her mop of red curly hair. 'You've got beautiful hair,' he whispered. 'I think that's what made me first fall in love with you.'

'Don't you think I'm too fat?' she asked. It did bother her sometimes.

'No. You're just perfect,' he replied. 'Clever and funny and perfect.'

They lay there quietly for a few minutes, her head on his

chest again. It was her favourite position. He pulled her even closer, slid his hand down her side, resting it on the curve of her bottom.

When he spoke again, his voice was steadier. The tears had gone. 'Suze?'

'Mmmm.'

'I did brilliantly, didn't I, getting Ruby and Felix to bed like that without waking them?' he murmured.

'You certainly did,' she replied. She waited to see what was coming next.

'And I settled Ollie – and I was a genius with Lara?'

'You were.'

'Don't you think I deserve a treat?' he asked.

Suzanne glanced up. He had that naughty expression on his face that she adored.

She hesitated. To be honest, she wasn't remotely in the mood. In a way, it surprised her that he was. But then Justin wasn't Lara's father, was he? There must be a difference. He did a great job, but she supposed he'd never feel quite as intimately connected as Suzanne was. Perhaps that's why he was so good at handling Lara's crises. He was able to be just that bit more objective.

It seemed important, now, Suzanne thought, to say thank you, to show her appreciation for all that he'd done. She'd been desperate, earlier on, up in Lara's bedroom. He'd stepped in, taken over, stopped her freaking out.

She smiled. 'You did brilliantly, darling,' she agreed. 'You are brilliant. With Ruby, Felix, Lara *and* Ollie. I think you deserve a great, big, enormous treat.'

Justin grinned, revealing his small, white teeth. She dived down under the covers, and he settled back with a contented sigh.

Later, Suzanne knew she wouldn't be able to sleep. She crept out of bed. Justin was completely gone, lying on his tummy, his face to one side, cuddling the pillow like a baby.

He's taken on so much with us, Suzanne thought, not for the first time. She covered him gently with the duvet. He could be living the bachelor life now. Sowing his wild oats. Most of his friends from university were still single.

She sighed. It was so hard, trying to make sure she gave enough of herself to the children, especially needy Lara, without neglecting Justin. Not that he ever really demanded more of her time. He hardly ever complained. He understood the children had to come first. He was so selfless.

She tiptoed upstairs to check on Lara and the other girls asleep in her room. They were all fast asleep. Lara was on her side, the plastic bowl beside her, just in case. Suzanne checked her watch. 1.30 a.m. She'd come up again in half an hour or so.

It was probably unnecessary, but she wasn't going to take any chances. She hadn't told Justin, though. He'd probably have insisted on doing it for her. But she felt strongly that, for once, this was her responsibility.

She decided to go downstairs and read. There was a stack of magazines in the sitting room that she hadn't got round to. Mostly interiors magazines that Carmen had lent her. Suzanne always imagined, one day, that she'd do something amazing with the house. But there always seemed to be more pressing issues, better ways to spend her time off.

Her eyes were tired, but her brain was wide awake, spinning. At least Justin was getting some rest. He needed it.

This was going to be a long night.

'I'm sorry,' Lara said. She was standing at the kitchen door in her pink pyjamas. She looked like a little girl, her hair pulled up in a ponytail on the top of her head. Suzanne almost expected her to be clutching a teddy.

Her heart melted. She wanted to give her firstborn a hug, be her mummy again. But she was angry, too. Upset and angry. And tired.

She'd trusted Lara enough to let her have a party, but Lara had scared the wits out of her – yet again. Suzanne guessed Lara would push her off if she tried to hug her, anyway, so she carried on cutting up Ruby's sausages for lunch.

'People just kept refilling my glass,' Lara explained. She was very pale, almost yellow, with dark circles under her eyes. 'I know it was stupid, but I was worried about the party and I guess I just got carried away.'

Suzanne tried to pop a piece of sausage in Ruby's mouth. 'I can do it myself,' Ruby said crossly, brushing her mother's hand off.

'What you did was very dangerous,' Suzanne replied, quietly. She wanted to keep calm. This was important. 'You realise you could have died of alcohol poisoning, or choked on your own vomit?'

Lara shrugged casually. Suzanne was annoyed. She knew her voice was rising but she couldn't help it. Apart from anything else, she was worn out.

'Don't dismiss what I'm saying,' Suzanne said. 'Think of that poor boy in the newspaper who died on a school trip after a night's boozing with his mates. It happens, you know.'

Lara was still in the doorway, her arms crossed tightly over her chest.

'And where was Noah when you needed him?' Suzanne went on. She had to get it out of her system. She hated that boy. She saw him as the root of most of Lara's problems. 'I suppose he was off his face in some corner,' she ventured, 'completely oblivious to how you were? Or was he the one who gave you the vodka or whatever it was?'

Lara's face was small and tight. 'Look, I've said I'm sorry. Stop fricking going on, will you? You've made your point; I don't need a lecture. And don't bring Noah into it, he's got nothing to do with it.'

Suzanne narrowed her eyes. As far as she was concerned, he had everything to do with it. She felt dangerous now.

'Orange juice, Lol?' Justin intervened, scraping back his chair. 'You'll be really dehydrated. Bet you wish you'd stuck to Diet Coke.'

Lara smiled, distracted. 'Yeah,' she said. 'Never again, I tell you. I feel disgusting. Thumping head. Any chance of a bacon sarnie?'

Suzanne felt her heart slow. A bacon sarnie? That was a good sign. At least she'd be having a decent breakfast. It wasn't all bad. Suzanne glanced at Felix in his highchair. He had sausage and mash all over him. He made a silly face and she made one back. She took a deep breath. That was better. There was no point having a scene, it would be counter-productive.

Justin turned on the grill and fetched bacon from the fridge. Jade and Emily appeared and sat down with Lara.

They were in their pyjamas, too, their hair up and wearing no make-up. They looked so young, so different from the glammed-up women of last night.

'Miranda was all over Tom like a rash,' Emily giggled, sipping from a bottle of water she'd brought down with her. Like Lara, she seemed to carry it everywhere. It was a fashion accessory.

Ollie was at the other end of the table, leafing through the *Observer* sports section. He was pretending not to be listening, but Suzanne imagined his ears were pricked.

'Yes, until she noticed his shoes. Oh my God,' Jade replied.

Lara looked perplexed. 'What exactly have his shoes got to do with it?'

Jade sniggered. 'Didn't you see them? They were just awful, these big black things with silver chains on. Like the chavvy ones all the boys used to wear in Year Eight.' She shuddered. 'Miranda spotted them and told me he'd have to go. Finished before it even started.'

Justin, standing by the grill, roared with laughter. 'The poor boy. You mean he's history, just because of his shoes? That's terrible.'

'Of course.' Lara sounded surprised. 'You can't go out with someone if his shoes are minging.'

Suzanne giggled. She didn't feel angry any more. She loved listening to Lara and her friends – on the rare occasions they let her.

Felix started to cry. Justin put three bacon sandwiches on the table, lifted Felix out of his high chair and wrinkled his nose. 'Pooh. Someone needs a new nappy.' He carried his small son upstairs.

Suzanne had a slurp of tea. Ruby had finished her sausages and was colouring in beside her. 'That's lovely,' Suzanne said. Ollie was still on the same page of the sports section, she noted with amusement. He probably hadn't read a single word.

Ruby held her picture up and examined it critically, her head on one side. 'I think it needs more pink,' she decided.

'Hey, Mum?' Lara asked. 'Guess what?' She opened her sandwich and squeezed a dollop of ketchup inside.

Suzanne raised her eyebrows.

'The boys think you're a milf,' Lara said.

Ollie suddenly scraped back his chair. He rose from the table, a look of horror on his face. 'Oh my God,' he said. 'That's gross.' He stalked out.

Suzanne ignored him. 'What's a milf?' she asked. She had no idea what Lara was talking about.

Lara took a bite of sandwich and gave a knowing smile. 'Work it out,' she said, her mouth full. 'The first word is "Mum".'

Suzanne was baffled. Mum what? Ollie's reaction, plus the look on the girls' faces, meant it had to be rude. 'Mum in lace frillies?' she guessed. 'Mum in lemon frock?' The penny dropped. She was shocked. 'Goodness, it must mean "Mum I'd like to f—?"' Suzanne spluttered.

Lara nodded.

'That's disgusting,' Suzanne said. Poor Ollie, no wonder he'd disappeared so fast.

Ruby had been paying attention, unfortunately. 'Mum I'd like to what, Mummy?' she asked innocently.

Suzanne winced. 'Mum I'd like to . . . fling you up in the air and catch you, darling,' she said.

The girls snorted. 'Well,' said Lara, 'you should see it as a compliment. They don't say it about all the mums, you know.'

Suzanne got up. 'That's quite enough of that,' she huffed. She was secretly rather flattered, though. Was that terrible? She'd have to ask the girls next time she saw them.

Later, she and Justin took the younger children to the leisure centre. Ollie came too, with a friend. There were slides and a wave machine. Ruby loved bobbing around in her rubber ring.

Felix sat on the very edge, next to Justin, and waggled his feet in the water. He was such a contented child, Suzanne thought. Fat and round and smiley, just as babies should be. It was hard to believe he might one day turn into a horror like Lara.

Suzanne did a few lengths, then joined Ollie and his friend. They did a handstand competition, and races, until Ollie decided it was uncool to be seen with his mum and he and his friend pushed off to the diving boards. Ollie was a good swimmer and diver.

For supper, Justin cooked scrambled eggs, then Suzanne bathed Ruby and Felix and plopped them into bed after a story.

Now, she couldn't put it off any longer. She'd have to have a talk with Lara about last night. It was what any responsible mother would do.

Lara was lying in bed, watching TV. She looked absolutely shattered, with dark circles round her eyes. Suzanne sat down on the edge of her bed. The room smelled sweaty and she wondered when Lara had last changed her sheets. She dreaded to think.

'You know, darling,' Suzanne ventured, 'I was only cross earlier because I was so worried about you. You were in a real state last night.'

Lara said nothing.

Suzanne pressed on. She felt as if she were slithering in flip-flops across wet stepping stones. 'It mustn't happen again,' she said.

She hesitated. Still no response from Lara.

'I've decided that you're not to see Noah or go out with friends for two weeks,' Suzanne announced. 'I want you to stay at home and be with the family. Do some reading and reflecting and catch up on sleep.'

She watched Lara's face harden. It went from soft and pretty, if exhausted, to tight and fixed with fury in seconds. You could almost count back on your hands: ten, nine, eight, seven, six . . .

'You mean I'm grounded?' Lara's voice was low and menacing.

Suzanne sighed. 'You know I don't like that expression but if you must, then yes. I nearly had to call an ambulance, I was so worried.'

Lara launched off. 'For God's sake, Mum. You're such a fucking drama queen,' she spat.

Suzanne closed her eyes. It was easier to cope that way.

'You always exaggerate,' Lara went on, 'but if that's the way you want to play it, fine. Just don't expect me to speak to you again.'

Suzanne bit her lip.

'You just want to keep me away from my friends and stop me having any fun.' Lara's voice was shrill, grating. 'My friends are the only people I can talk to, and now you're trying to separate us.'

Suzanne squeezed her hands together.

'But you won't succeed, however much you want to,' Lara promised.

Suzanne took a deep breath. Keep calm, she thought, for the second time that day. You've got to be bigger than her. Behave better. Don't have a scene.

'Of course I don't want to separate you and your friends,' Suzanne said quietly. 'I just can't have you getting drunk like that. Are you positive it really was just drink?'

Lara was silent, stony-faced again. Why did people say babies and toddlers were hard work? They were a cinch in comparison with this. Or was it just her? Suzanne felt such a failure. She could hardly wait to get back to work.

She walked towards the door and put her hand on the knob. There was no point trying to discuss anything more tonight.

'Mum?' There was a new note in Lara's voice. Suzanne didn't like it. It sounded mean. She waited, silent, her hand still on the knob. 'Do you ever wonder what Justin gets up to when you're at work?' Lara asked.

Suzanne's stomach fluttered. She turned slowly and stared at her daughter. Lara looked different, somehow. Unfamiliar. Not like her daughter at all.

'What do you mean by that?' Suzanne asked. She was surprised how sharp her voice sounded.

Lara shrugged, smiling. 'I just mean he does seem to be whispering on the phone a lot,' she said. 'And he does seem to play an awful lot of squash.'

Suzanne swung round, away from Lara, and opened the door. 'Sometimes,' she said, almost under her breath, 'I wonder what I've given birth to.'

Lara's laugh rang in her ears as Suzanne slammed the door behind her. She scuttled away, as fast as she could. Tripped on a pile of washing on the stairs, nearly fell. She had to find Justin. She needed to see his kind face. Right now. Smell his lovely smell. Wrap herself in his arms, forget Lara had even spoken.

She was just a nasty, stupid teenager. She didn't know what she was talking about. She was just trying to cause trouble.

Wasn't she?

Chapter Ten

It was years since she'd updated her CV and Percy was pleasantly surprised. Seeing all the information there in black and white, her career didn't look nearly as bad as she'd feared: she'd taught English in two quite different secondary schools, one tough comprehensive, one grammar; she'd been staff rep on the governing body for two years and deputy head, at different points, of Years Eight and Nine.

Granted, she hadn't actually worked since Ben was born. But she could certainly put that she'd helped out at his primary school with reading and so on, and say she'd always planned to return to teaching when Rowan was older.

It wasn't exactly true, of course. In fact, she'd never felt happier than on her last day at Fir Tree Girls' when she'd waddled, hugely pregnant, off the premises to shouts of 'Good luck, Miss!' and 'I hope it's a baby,' followed by gales of laughter. She'd sworn then that she'd never set foot in a classroom again. But things changed.

She fiddled around with the text on her screen, cutting and pasting, deciding what to add where. Then she emailed her CV, along with a covering letter, to five different education-recruitment agencies.

It was a satisfying feeling. At last she'd done something positive. She doubted she'd find a staff job immediately, but she was fairly confident she'd get work as a supply teacher.

The woman at Prospero Agency said there was a shortage of English teachers in London and didn't seem to think it mattered that Percy hadn't worked for so long. 'You'll soon forget you were ever away,' she'd chuckled, rather meanly, Percy thought.

Supply teaching wasn't too badly paid, and Patrice would look after Rowan after school, Percy was sure of it. Both he and Seamus were full-time now. Luckily, though, Seamus's day finished before Rowan's, so Patrice would have just enough time to drive over and pick Rowan up. That way, Percy wouldn't have to fork out on childcare.

She'd hate not being able to collect him herself, but there was really no choice. And even if she worked just two or three days a week, it would make a huge difference. She'd done her sums. If she cut right back, she calculated, she could put all her earnings towards their debts. It would take years to pay off the entire seventeen thousand pounds that they owed, but it was possible.

How wonderful that felt! To see a way out. If only she'd thought of it months ago, before she'd landed them in so much trouble.

She shivered, turned off the computer quickly and unplugged it at the wall. Then she threw a sheet over it. She'd downloaded a piece of software that was supposed to block access to gambling sites, but she was worried she could be tempted to try to get round it. The sheet might compel her to think twice.

It was a counsellor at Gamcare, which offered help and advice to gamblers, who'd told her about the software.

Percy had googled the organisation and spoken at some length to a woman on their helpline. She'd found it incredibly difficult to open up at first but the woman had listened patiently while Percy had cried and talked and cried some more. In the end, she found, it had been such a relief to know that she wasn't alone, that other women got into difficulties with gambling, too.

The woman had asked Percy quite a bit about her background and childhood, and told Percy to stop blaming herself.

She'd explained that gambling was an addiction, like alcohol or drugs, and women gamblers often used it as a way of shutting out difficult, sad feelings, perhaps stemming from childhood or relationships. It could make you feel successful, good about yourself – until it spiralled out of control and started to cause more problems.

Percy had listened in amazement as the woman built up a picture of someone just like Percy herself. It was spooky. And she'd gratefully accepted the offer of one-to-one counselling.

She'd had such a shock when Mark had confronted her. It had dawned on her properly for the first time that she really did risk losing everything – her husband, home, even her boys – unless she could kick the habit. It had been her wake-up call. It was time to get real.

The temptation to gamble was still there – it wouldn't just vanish, she knew that. But Mark was coming home more now. She didn't know if it was to check up on her, or just because he hadn't the stomach to work all hours. Either way, she wasn't on her own so much in the evenings so there was less opportunity to sneak off and play.

Mark. She looked at her watch. It was 8 p.m. If the last few nights were anything to go by, he'd be home any time now.

They'd hardly spoken for over two weeks, since that ghastly Sunday. She'd told him several times that she'd stopped playing, stopped spending, but he'd seemed uninterested.

'You do what you want,' he'd muttered through gritted teeth. 'You always do.'

Practically the only time that he'd directed more than a sentence at her was when he'd told her he'd taken out another loan and paid Zeus back. Zeus had tried to speak to Percy several times, but she'd avoided his calls. She wasn't ready. She was too ashamed.

The atmosphere between her and Mark when they passed each other on the stairs or landing was like ice. On several occasions she'd expected to come home and find that he'd packed his bags and gone. So far at least, however, that hadn't happened.

He was still playing with the boys at weekends and trying to make things normal for them. And he'd hung around when Suzanne and Justin came for supper with their brood.

Percy left the kitchen quickly; she didn't want him to find her there and become suspicious. She tiptoed upstairs to Rowan's room and breathed in that warm, sweet, talcum-powdery smell. He was lying on his back, Rabbit tucked in beside him. She kissed the tip of his small nose, making him stir slightly.

It was Ben's turn next. He was sitting up in bed, reading a *Time Warp Trio* book. There were Action Man posters round his walls.

'Time for lights out, sweetie,' Percy said, picking Ben's pants and socks off the floor and throwing them in the corner, ready to take downstairs.

'Five more minutes,' Ben begged.

Normally, she'd have barked at him, desperate to leave, to race down and begin the night's play. It was good not to experience that sickening pull any more, not to feel as if her insides were being squeezed.

'Would you like me to tell you a story like I used to?' she asked. She'd always made up stories for him when he was younger but she'd got out of the habit. She'd stopped doing things with him after school, too, like the puzzles and games he used to love. She could see that now. No wonder he'd been playing up. She shuddered at her selfishness.

Ben's eyes were wide. He gave a shy smile. 'Can you do a Sir Ben and his Naughty Knights?' He couldn't believe his luck.

Percy kissed his cheek. He pushed her away. 'Euuww! I'm

too big for kisses.' But he moved over to make room for her beside him in the bed.

'Once upon a time . . .' she began, pulling the duvet over them both and turning out the light. She was fully clothed, but she kicked off her sheepskin slippers and dropped them on the floor.

'Can we have a dragon – and a black knight?' Ben asked.

'And a hideous, poisonous troll?' Percy smiled. 'One whiff of his breath and you're dead?'

Ben sighed, contented. He was sleepy now, Percy knew, though he'd never admit it.

'And a nest of vipers?' he begged.

'Of course.'

'Wicked,' he said, closing his eyes.

Percy put her arm round her son and kissed his neck. This time, he didn't protest. 'Now shhh,' she said, racking her brains for a plotline, 'and listen to the story.

'Once upon a time,' she began again, 'there was a brave and handsome knight who was named Sir Ben.'

She felt Ben's feet wiggle, contentedly, under the duvet.

'He lived in a big, tall castle in the middle of the forest with his mother and father, his brother Sir Rowan, twelve naughty knights and their pet dragon, Archibald . . .'

By the time she got to the hideous poisonous troll, Ben was asleep.

Percy hadn't told Mark what she was up to, but he found out soon enough. Just a week after contacting the education-recruitment agencies, she got a call.

'We have a job for you, Mrs Redpath,' the Prospero woman said.

Percy gasped. She wanted to shout 'Yes!' and punch the air, but she knew it wouldn't sound cool. 'When?' she managed to squeak.

The agency woman could hear her excitement. 'We do our

best, here at Prospero,' she said, milking the moment. 'The job starts tomorrow morning. One of the English teachers at the school has pleurisy. She could be off for some time.'

Percy's mind was racing. 'Tomorrow'? 'Some time'? That might mean several weeks' work. She'd have to get on to Patrice immediately. A thought crossed her mind. 'Which school?' she asked.

'Ah, well, that's the only thing,' the Prospero lady said. Percy held her breath. 'It's the John Donne.'

Percy gulped. She'd read about that one. Fights in the corridors; staff leaving in droves; dire results.

'It's going through a bit of a difficult time,' the Prospero lady went on, 'what with being in Special Measures and there being no permanent Head and that. But I'm sure you'll be able to cope,' she added swiftly. 'Now, can you take the job or not?'

Percy breathed in deeply. 'Definitely,' she said, sounding more cheerful than she felt.

Bloody hell, she thought after putting down the phone. Talk about a baptism of fire.

Mark was watching *The Godfather* on Sky when she told him. He'd seen that movie so many times but he never seemed to tire of it.

'I've got some news,' she said.

He glanced up. He had a hurt expression on his face. In fact he looked permanently hurt these days, Percy thought sadly.

'What?' he said. There was a sneer in his voice. 'You've blown another ten grand on poker?'

'No,' she replied. 'I've got a job – starting tomorrow. Supply teaching.'

She could see him processing the information. If she could look into his brain, she was sure she'd spot cogs whirring.

'What about Rowan?' he asked, sensing obstacles immediately.

313

'Pats is having him, and Justin's picking Ben up from school.'

Mark frowned. 'A few days won't even make a dent in the debts.'

Percy nodded. 'But the job might turn out to be more than a few days, and when it finishes I'll get another one. Apparently English teachers are in hot demand. And I'll put all my earnings towards what we owe.'

Mark looked at the TV again. 'Good luck,' he said. There was no emotion in his voice. 'You'll be an old woman by the time you clear everything.'

Percy sat down beside him. 'Oh, Mark,' she said, putting her hands in her lap. 'I know we owe a lot and it'll take ages to pay off. But I'll get a permanent job as soon as I can, and in the meantime I'll do supply work. I've cut right back on spending. I'll get us back into the black eventually. I promise.'

Percy watched. She thought she detected a slight change in Mark's expression, a softening. His shoulders relaxed slightly – or was it her imagination?

'It'll help a bit,' he conceded, his eyes still fixed on the screen. 'But only a bit.'

She knew he'd never have suggested that she find a job himself. He'd always said it was her choice whether she worked or not. He was generous like that. But she could tell he was pleased, underneath it all.

'Where's the school?' Mark asked. It was the first glimmer of interest he'd shown in her in weeks.

'Hounslow,' she replied. 'The John Donne.'

He frowned. 'Isn't that the one—'

'With the stabbings,' she interrupted. 'Yes. It'll be an experience, anyway.'

'You'll have to be careful,' he said. He shifted in his seat. They both knew it had slipped out. A chink of light, a glimmer of warmth on a cold day.

Percy felt her heart skip, just for a second. Maybe he still

314

cared for her, just a little, after all. Maybe there was some hope.

'Mum?' It was Ben's voice, calling from upstairs. Damn, she'd thought he was asleep. She hoped he wouldn't disturb Rowan.

She got up.

'Wait.'

Mark suddenly lunged forwards, off the sofa, grabbed her arms and pulled her to him. She toppled, clumsily, on to his lap.

'Come here,' he said softly, folding her in his arms. Her face was squashed against his chest. She could hardly breathe, but she didn't care. She realised at that moment that she'd be willing to suffer almost any pain or discomfort to be allowed to stay there, against his heart, feeling the weight of his arms around her and the warmth of his body beneath.

It was so long since they'd hugged. She'd thought she might never even touch him again. It dawned on her that she was crying: hot, wet tears that soaked his shirt, his chest. He stroked her hair heavily with his hand.

She shifted her head slightly, so she could breathe, and snaked her arms tentatively around his waist. She didn't want to move too much, in case it broke the spell.

They sat there, in silence. A car pulled up outside, a door slammed, but they were noises from another person's life. It felt as if the two of them were completely alone, at the edge of the world. Nothing else mattered. Time stood still.

Mark brushed the top of her head with his lips. She could feel something damp on her hair. She realised he was crying, too.

'I do love you, you know, Pers,' he whispered hoarsely. She squeezed her arms tighter round his waist. He felt so solid, so real. He was her husband, hers. She wondered how she could ever have thought bad things about him, how they could ever have got into this mess.

'I know I've been angry,' he said, 'but I feel as if I've been running around in circles, chasing my tail. Working and working while you've been spending and spending. I just couldn't get through to you.'

He made a choking sound. Wiped his eyes with his sleeve then put his arm round her again. Grasped tighter.

She remained silent. What could she say?

'I'd hate us to split up,' he murmured. 'We're meant for each other, you know – you and me. I've always believed it, ever since I first met you in the students' union.'

She took a deep breath.

If only he knew about Danny. God, could he ever forgive me for that?

'We'll get through this together,' Mark added. 'Somehow. But you've got to stop gambling – you understand? Or we'll lose everything we've worked for, everything we've made.'

She nodded, breathing in his warm body smell. 'I love you too,' she said simply. Her own body felt airy, so light that she thought she might float away.

'No more spending, no more poker,' she promised, her face still buried in his warm chest. 'From now on I'm going to be Mrs Thrifty. Just you wait and see.'

Chapter Eleven

'Darren, will you please sit at the front of the class – now. I don't want you at the back again. And Kyle, pass me your mobile. You know it's not allowed in lessons.'

Kyle, a surly, greasy-haired fifteen-year-old, got up, walked slowly towards Percy and grudgingly handed her his phone. He was much taller than her, but she didn't feel threatened. He was just hard work, and could easily disrupt the whole class if she didn't watch him. She'd been told that he came from a difficult background, but she still felt like murdering him at least once a lesson.

'Is it turned off?' she asked, putting the mobile in the drawer of her desk. Kyle nodded. 'Good,' she said. 'Now sit here, next to Darren, in front of me please. That way I can keep an eye on you both.' She smiled pleasantly.

He certainly had no interest in *Othello*, which she was supposed to be teaching him for GCSE. The only thing that seemed to engage him at all, in fact, was rap music. Percy had found this out after hearing him talking animatedly about Eminem in the playground one afternoon.

She planned to set a piece of homework tonight asking pupils to write their own version of one of Iago's soliloquies in rap. She hoped this might engage Kyle and some of the other disaffected youngsters. It was worth a try, anyway. Of course Kyle would try to get out of it, he always did, but at least this time he couldn't pretend that he didn't understand the assignment.

'Right, open your books please,' Percy said, clearing her

throat. 'Act two scene one. We'll read through first. Zahara, will you start?'

The girl sitting next to Zahara nudged her. She'd been fiddling around, looking for something in her bag. Why was Zahara always fiddling with something? Percy thought, exasperated.

'Pay attention please,' she said. 'And take your chewing gum out.'

Zahara got up theatrically, tore a piece of paper from an exercise book, spat the chewing gum into it, walked to the bin at the front of the class and threw the paper in. The rest of the class tittered.

Percy glanced at the clock and sighed. They'd wasted nearly ten minutes of the lesson already.

Finally, Zahara plonked herself down again and opened her book. '"What from the cape can you discern at sea?"' she read in a silly exaggerated voice.

'Good,' Percy said brightly, 'nice and dramatic.' She ignored Zahara's scowl and the class's guffaw. 'Charlie next, and so on round the room. Try to imagine yourselves in the characters' shoes. The drama's hotting up, remember.'

A loud noise came from somewhere in the middle of the class. Someone had farted. Several of the girls squealed in disgust. The boys roared with laughter.

Kyle seized the opportunity immediately. 'Miss?' he said, raising his hand. 'Someone's done a boff. Can I open a window?'

Sensing impending chaos, Percy thought quickly. 'A boff?' she said. 'That reminds me, has anyone seen *The Comedy of Errors*, another of Shakespeare's plays?'

The room fell silent.

'It's very funny, very earthy,' Percy assured them. 'Lots of references to bodily functions. You should go if you get the chance. Now then, Kyle, let's get on with the play. You read next.'

'Bitch,' Kyle muttered under his breath. She pretended not to hear.

Percy had been at the school five weeks now, and Kyle had done his best to make her life a misery. She was extremely proud of the fact that he hadn't succeeded.

She remembered how intimidated she'd been by Kyle-types when she first went into teaching all those years ago. Even in her second school, a girls' grammar, there had been a few pupils who'd terrified her, though she'd learned to hide it pretty well.

Now, however, having raised two boys of her own and lived a little, she found that she was more confident and better able to keep control. She'd heard on the grapevine that she'd already acquired a reputation among pupils for being terrifying. That gave her enormous satisfaction. Percy reckoned if she started off terrifying, she could ease the reins a little, become more friendly as time went by. But it would be very difficult to go the other way.

The Acting Head seemed pleased with Percy, too. There was even the possibility of a job when the English teacher with pleurisy returned. So many staff had left recently that there were vacancies in almost every department. Percy would have to think hard about that one, though. She reckoned she'd probably be good for the school, but would the school be good for her?

Of course, discipline was only one aspect of being an effective teacher. The other was trying to inspire pupils with a love of your subject, or at the very least to get them through their exams. If only she could spark Kyle's interest in something. He was the most jaded, cynical pupil she'd come across. She felt frustrated and desperately sorry for him at the same time.

The bell went too soon and the pupils started to jostle their way out. Percy had hoped to cover more ground, but at least they'd ended up having an interesting discussion about racism. The class had become quite animated; even Kyle had contributed. It was clearly a subject they could relate to so Percy had let the debate run.

She took a sip of water from the bottle on her desk. Her throat was dry and sore from talking so much: a professional hazard. Thank goodness the school was closing at lunchtime, she thought. It was parents' evening tonight and staff needed time to prepare. Percy had been excused as she hadn't been there long enough.

She checked her schedule. Only one more lesson to go and it was a Year Seven, her favourite – yay! She liked the little ones best, because they tended to be more enthusiastic. You didn't have to concentrate on boring old coursework, either, as they had no exams. You could be a bit more imaginative.

But then a shadow crept over her mood. She was having lunch with her mother. It had temporarily slipped her mind, or rather she'd pushed it out. Damn. She wished she was racing back to see Rowan. Suddenly she felt sad. She missed him so much when she was at work. She shook the feeling away.

Don't be silly. He's fine with Patrice. He loves going there.

The arrangement was perfect, for now. Percy knew she'd need to find a childminder in the longer term, though, especially if she got a permanent job. She couldn't keep relying on friends for ever. It wouldn't be fair.

She packed up her books and left the classroom. To her surprise, Kyle was standing just outside, his back against the wall. He looked embarrassed.

'What are you up to, Kyle?' Percy asked crisply. 'Shouldn't you be going to your next lesson?'

He looked down at his shoes. They were black trainers with an orange stripe, against the regulations, but she let it pass.

'I wanted to tell you I'll do the homework, miss,' he said

sheepishly. He had a strong south London accent. 'I like your lessons. You make fings interesting.'

Percy was taken aback. Was he winding her up? She couldn't be sure. She scanned the corridor, expecting to see his friends lurking somewhere, egging him on. But there was no one.

She realised with a jolt that in his own rough way, Kyle might actually be paying her a compliment. If so, she mustn't rebuff him.

'That's great, Kyle,' she said, feeling a rush of warmth towards this unhappy, difficult boy. She almost wanted to hug him. She'd bet he didn't get many hugs. 'I'll look forward to seeing it.'

Now a little thing like *that*, she thought happily, made all the hard work, the exhaustion, the arguing and exasperation worthwhile. She practically skipped down the corridor and up the stairs into her next lesson.

'Would you like to see the wine menu?' asked the waiter.

Antonia nodded. 'We can have half a bottle between us, can't we, darling?'

Percy looked doubtful. She hated drinking at lunchtime, it made her so sleepy.

'Of course we can,' Antonia went on. 'It's not often we go out together like this, after all.'

Percy looked round the restaurant. She'd never been in it before. It felt cool and classical. The floors were pale stone. There was a huge urn in the corner, filled with flowers. Paintings of ancient Greeks in flowing white robes, adopting noble poses, adorned the walls.

They were sitting right by the window, looking out over the busy street.

'I knew you'd feel at home here, Persephone,' Antonia beamed. 'I brought Zeus once and the waiter was so thrilled. He said his wife was pregnant and they were going to christen the baby Theseus, if it was a boy.'

'Don't you dare tell him what I'm called,' Percy hissed.

Her mother put a perfectly manicured hand on her daughter's nail-bitten one. 'Of course not, darling,' she said loudly. 'Wouldn't dream of it.'

She looked round, to see if anyone was listening. 'BUT PERSEPHONE IS SUCH A LOVELY NAME,' she boomed.

Percy's heart sank. She hated being the centre of attention.

The waiter bustled over. He was small and dark with a strong Greek accent. 'Did I hear you say Persephone? Ah, beautiful name!' he grinned. 'The Queen of the Underworld, no less? Pluto took one look at her and fell in love.' He put his hand on his heart. 'Then he snatched her from a field where she was picking the flowers and took her below to be his wife.' He snatched the napkin off the table to demonstrate.

Antonia fluttered her eyelashes. 'You clearly know your Greek legends,' she twinkled.

He made a little bow and looked at Antonia closely, remembering something. 'Ah, you are the lady who came in few weeks ago, with the son? Zeus?' he said.

Antonia nodded, pleased.

'That is very fine name, too,' the waiter said. 'My wife and I, we have little girl. Tiny baby, few weeks old.' He held his hands just a little way apart, to show the tininess of her, and puffed out his chest. 'We have name her Aphrodite,' he went on with a flourish.

Antonia beamed. 'The goddess of love. How clever of you!'

He winked.

Antonia smiled coyly. 'I studied ancient Greek at school, you know,' she said.

Yeah, for five minutes, Percy thought. You did an O-level and, I seem to remember, got a D. Bet you don't tell him that.

'You are very clever lady,' the waiter said.

Antonia pinked. 'Oh, I wouldn't say that,' she replied, patting her caramel bob into place. 'But I do nurture a love of all things Greek. Homer, Socrates, Plato. The fathers of civilisation,' she said, waving her arm.

The waiter took a step back and clapped. 'Hear, hear,' he said. 'You will have drink on house. No, I insist. Christos, fetch the ladies some ouzo. Quick!'

Antonia popped an olive in her mouth. She was wearing a black polo neck with a purple velvet shawl draped round her shoulders. Percy rather liked it. It reminded her of that poem:

> When I am an old woman I shall wear purple
> With a red hat which doesn't go and doesn't suit me.

Antonia passed Percy the hummus. 'I never see you nowadays,' she sighed. 'You're always so busy. That's why I invited you today. It was the only way to get you on your own.'

Percy dipped some pitta into the hummus on her plate. She was ravenous. 'I am busy,' she admitted, taking a bite. The hummus was deliciously garlicky. She'd stink all afternoon. 'As you know, I'm working three days a week now and on my days off I have to do all the shopping and cleaning and things. Plus, I want to have time with Rowan.'

Antonia frowned. 'As you ask,' Percy continued, looking meaningfully at her mother, 'I'm rather enjoying the teaching, though I do find it very demanding. The money's extremely welcome, too,' she added.

Antonia sipped her wine. 'Yes, well. Money's not everything,' she said, taking another olive. 'What about your poor old mum?' She put the stone in a saucer. 'I still miss your father, you know,' she said, sniffing. 'It's nearly five years since he passed away, but I think about him every single day and I do get lonely.'

She looked at Percy soulfully through eyelashes caked in

mascara. Percy couldn't help thinking her mother was the least lonely person she knew. She was always out gadding with her friends, even if she did fall out with them on a regular basis.

Percy spooned some taramasalata on to her plate. 'I'm sorry, Mum,' she said. 'But it's difficult with a job and a young family.'

Antonia tut-tutted. 'Oh, I know. You and Zeus are the same. There's always some excuse why you can't come and see me.'

Percy felt herself redden. 'That's not fair. We both visit as often as we can, you know we do. And you're always welcome to pop round to us, it's just more difficult for us to get to you.'

The waiter arrived with new plates. 'Having good chinwag, no?' He beamed, wiping the plates with a white napkin. 'Mother and daughter. Very close. That's good. In Greek culture mother is centre of family. Everybody does what mother says.' He wagged a finger. 'If mother speaks, you dare not disobey.'

Antonia straightened her back and looked matriarchal. Percy felt like punching the waiter on the nose.

'How is Zeus?' she said wistfully. Thinking about him made her sad. She still hadn't had the courage to pick up the phone. 'I haven't spoken to him for a while.'

She glanced at Antonia, who was examining the glittering stones on her left hand. She had quite a collection. It was obvious she knew nothing about the money Percy had borrowed. Dear Zeus, she thought. He was so loyal and trust-worthy. She didn't deserve to have him as a brother.

'I think the poor man is completely exhausted by that frightful wife of his,' Antonia pronounced. 'You know she's making him change all the windows in their house now? He says he can't afford to pay someone so he'll have to do it himself, in his spare time.' She laughed, humourlessly.

324

'The only problem is, the poor baby doesn't have any spare time.'

Percy swallowed. How could she have taken his savings from him? She could hardly recognise the grasping, desperate, messed-up woman she had been until just a few, short weeks ago. Tears pricked her eyes.

'But I thought Philippa wanted to move?' she said, trying not to give away her feelings.

For once, she found herself thanking the Lord that her mother was so unobservant. Antonia bit, tentatively, into a piece of kebab. She found something chewy. Grimaced. Put in on the side of her plate. 'Philippa does,' she said, almost spitting her daughter-in-law's name out, 'but the silly woman says the house will fetch more if they have sash windows rather than plastic. Which would be all right if they could afford to get someone in to do it.'

Antonia gulped down a glass of water. She'd turned slightly red. Her eyes were watering. 'Too spicy,' she said, flapping her hand in front of her mouth.

Percy laughed. 'I thought you nurtured a love of all things Greek.'

Antonia glared at her. 'Stop talking and get me another glass of water – quick,' she commanded.

Percy took a sip of water herself. It was a relief, after the spicy meat. She didn't like the sound of Zeus swaying around on ladders, putting windows in. She missed him so much. 'Do you think he loves Philippa?' she asked. It did worry her.

Antonia scoffed. 'Not if he's got any sense.'

Percy looked at her mother. She was less red now. 'Mum, it's a serious question. Do you think he does?'

Antonia put down her glass and thought for a moment. 'I think he probably does, actually. More fool him. He's always had a bit of thing about dominant women.'

Percy raised her eyebrows. 'I wonder why.'

Antonia ignored her. 'I've told Philippa I need Zeus to mend my garage roof,' she said, 'but she's clearly chosen to put her own wishes first. That woman is unbelievably selfish.'

Percy's head felt slightly fuzzy from the wine. Lucky she'd got the train here and not tried to drive through the London traffic.

She noticed a young mother walking by outside, pushing a pram, and she thought of Carmen. She was due any day now. Her parents were being so supportive. Carmen's mother popped over every week with little things for the baby, and treats from the restaurant to make sure she was eating properly. Unlike Antonia, they didn't have much money, but they were generous with what they had.

'Mum?' Percy said. Antonia wiped her mouth on her napkin. 'Can I tell you something?' Percy asked.

Antonia burped quietly. 'Excuse me,' she said, putting her hand over her mouth. 'Delicious food.'

Percy frowned.

'Of course you can tell me anything, darling,' Antonia said. 'Isn't that what mothers are for?'

Percy was tempted to say yes, and this is the way round it's supposed to be. But she didn't.

'I've done something really bad,' she whispered. 'I feel so awful I don't know where to begin.'

She felt scared. Was she doing the right thing? But it was weighing so heavily on her mind, it was driving her mad.

Antonia leaned forward, her eyes wide with curiosity. 'What?' she said. 'What have you done?'

'I've slept with someone else,' Percy confessed. There, she'd said it now. 'My personal trainer.' She couldn't bring herself to mention the gambling as well. That would be too much. Besides, Danny was the more pressing problem right now.

Antonia's eyes widened even more. She didn't move a muscle.

'It was over six months ago and it only happened once,' Percy went on. 'Mark and I had been getting on really badly and I, well, I just let it happen. But now Mark and I are much better and I feel so wretched. Like I've got this big, horrible secret. And I'm frightened Mark might find out, although I don't see how. It's giving me nightmares. What shall I do?' Her voice came out as a sort of wail.

She looked into her mother's eyes. Was Antonia shocked? Disgusted? Her gaze gave nothing away. Percy wished she'd give her a hug. There's nothing quite like a hug from your mother, even when you're grown-up and a mother yourself. But no hug was forthcoming.

Antonia shifted back in her seat, away from Percy, and put her napkin on the table. Cleared her throat. Then she tipped her head back – and roared with laughter.

Percy was so shocked she knocked over her glass of water. She mopped it quickly with the edge of the tablecloth. She didn't want the waiter to charge over.

'Darling,' Antonia said. 'Is that all? I thought you were going to say something terrible. Everyone has at least one affair. It's perfectly normal.

'Good Lord, I had a little flingette with Uncle Ted years ago. Your father never knew. But I reckon he had a bit of slap and tickle with Gretel Pettifer anyway. Affairs are good for a marriage. They keep things fresh. When did this wicked act take place anyway?'

Percy's cheeks were burning. Her father's brother? Uncle Ted? All she could really remember about him was that he let her try on his Panama hat and smoked very smelly cigars. And Gretel Pettifer? From the big house up the road? She'd never liked her. Too much make-up. Big arse, big hair. Never without a glass of wine in her hand.

'I don't know what to say,' Percy mumbled.

'Then don't say anything at all,' Antonia said cheerfully. 'And for goodness' sake don't go bleating to Mark. What he doesn't know can't hurt him. Trust me, I wasn't born yesterday, you know.'

She winked. 'Now, enough of that,' she said, rubbing her hands together. 'Let me tell you about my holiday plans.'

Percy poured a generous dollop of Neal's Yard Seaweed and Arnica Foaming Bath into the tub and swirled it round. She needed to think, and the bath was where she often had her best ideas.

She sank back, breathing in the strange, tangy smell, and closed her eyes. She wished she hadn't told her mother now. She'd been stupid enough to hope for some words of comfort, something soothing, but Antonia had only made her feel worse.

For one, she'd admitted being unfaithful to Percy's father. Dear Dad. The image of his kind old wrinkled face hovered in front of her. He'd have understood that what she needed was a big hug. He'd never stood up for her and Zeus when their mother was mean or neglectful, but he'd always been there with a hug afterwards.

Percy bit back tears. And how could Antonia have suggested he'd had an affair too, with that frightful Gretel woman? Percy couldn't believe it. Wouldn't believe it. Antonia had probably just said it to make herself seem marginally less culpable.

Second, the only advice Antonia had given Percy was to keep stumm, but Percy had been doing that for months now and it was killing her. She longed to relieve herself of the burden of guilt. She longed to come clean with Mark, now that he knew all about the gambling and had so generously forgiven her. But what would happen if she told him about Danny, too?

Maybe he wouldn't be able to forgive her this time? Maybe the fragile peace they'd refound would shatter. Could she – should she – risk it, or was her mother right? Perhaps some things were better left unsaid.

She didn't hear Mark enter the bathroom. She jumped when he spoke. 'You look like Ophelia, lying there with your hair spread out around you.' He smiled. 'Glass of white wine?'

She sat up. 'No thanks. I had lunch with Mum today. She plied me with retsina.'

'How is she?' Mark asked.

'Oh, bossy as ever,' Percy replied.

Mark bent over the bath and splashed his face in the warm water. He grabbed a towel from the heated radiator. 'Any gossip?' he asked, drying his face. 'Has she found herself a toyboy yet?'

Percy laughed. 'Nah. She was shockingly flirty with the waiter, though.'

How I wish I could tell him everything. Husbands and wives shouldn't have secrets, I know that now.

Mark looked at her. Most of her body was underwater, except her breasts, which were poking up out of the bubbles. She felt suddenly self-conscious and sank down lower.

'Boys both in bed?' he asked.

Percy nodded. 'A good hour ago. They were exhausted.'

Mark took off his long-sleeved T-shirt, unbuttoned his jeans and stepped out of his red boxers.

'What are you doing?' Percy asked.

'Go on, budge over,' he ordered.

Before she had time to protest, he'd climbed in at the other end. He slid back into the bubbles.

'Ouch, your heel's in my ribcage,' Percy protested.

'And your knee's digging into my shin,' he retorted.

It was a squeeze, but finally, they both managed to get comfortable. They were spread out, side by side and top to toe, like sardines.

They used to do it a lot when they were first married, Percy remembered. They'd had some great discussions, set the world to rights, in the bath. Sometimes, though, they'd just lain there in companionable silence, enjoying the feel of each others' warm flesh, listening to each other's breathing.

Percy wondered when it had stopped. Not after Ben was born. She recalled several occasions when Mark was late back from work and she'd tucked Ben into his cot, then tiptoed round the flat, lighting candles.

By the time Mark came home, she was ready to explode with excitement. She'd led him, glass of wine in hand, still wearing his jacket, into the bathroom. Stripped him off, there and then, and pulled him into the foamy water beside her. It was a great way to start the evening.

'Reasonable day?' she asked him.

His eyes were closed. 'Not bad. Bit hassly. Overdraft's come down a shade.' He opened his eyes. 'But don't go getting any ideas,' he said sternly. 'There's a very long way to go.'

'I know,' she replied. They settled back into silence.

'Aieeee!' she screeched, drawing her legs up. 'Wandering toe trouble.' She shifted her body to make it more difficult for him. 'Don't do that,' she said crossly.

'Why not?'

'It's rude!' she replied.

'Shall I soap you down?' he asked. 'I'm sure you could do with a good wash.'

She glanced at him. A naughty dimple had appeared in his left cheek. 'You'll have to shut the door properly first,' she warned.

He leaped out of the bath and walked, dripping, across the room to close the door. She admired his bum. It looked remarkably sweet, cheeky even, covered in foam.

He turned back to face her.

'She grinned. 'Ooh, you're standing to attention.'

'On guard!' He laughed, waving a pretend sword in the air.

I will tell him. Not today, but soon. I just have to pick the right moment.

He jumped back in the water.

'Careful,' she squealed. 'You're splashing everywhere.'

He picked up a bar of soap from the edge of the bath. 'Now,' he said in a serious voice. 'Will Madam please stand up.' She did as she was told.

He stood in front of her, turned the soap round slowly in his hands and made a lather. He kissed her neck.

'Where exactly does Madam require washing?' he whispered.

She thought for a moment. 'Um, how about here.' She pointed to her elbow.

'Here?' he asked.

'Yes, here.'

He washed it carefully, then swooshed the soap off with a flannel.

'Er, and here?'

He bent down attentively. This time it was the back of her knee. 'Oh yes, that's grubby.' He sounded shocked. 'Needs a good scrub.'

Then he kissed her tummy, lathering soap all over, up under her breasts.

'My shoulder's dirtier,' she protested.

He peered at it and shook his head. 'No, your shoulder's fine.' He dropped on to his knees and tutted. 'Down here looks absolutely filthy, though,' he murmured, parting her legs gently.

'No, it's OK, honestly,' she squeaked. 'Sparkling.'

'Hmm, I'm not so sure,' he said, running his soapy hands up and down her thighs.

She closed her eyes. 'Mmmm,' she said. The slithery soap felt silky on her skin. She shivered, but it wasn't from the cold. 'Maybe it has been a bit neglected,' she agreed. 'Now pass the soap to me.'

He protested – for five seconds – but she grabbed the soap out of his hands. 'My turn now,' she said firmly.

Chapter Twelve

❦

'Are you sure you ought to be doing Body Attack?' Percy hadn't expected to see Carmen. It was practically her due date.

'I'll be fine,' Carmen said. 'I'll stand at the back and take everything really slowly.'

Percy looked doubtful.

'It's OK,' Carmen insisted. 'Debbie's given me special exercises. Actually, I'd be delighted if it got things moving,' she confided. 'I tell you, I'm sick of being pregnant.'

Percy wasn't surprised. Carmen was enormous now. She seemed to be as wide as she was tall. She'd developed the John Wayne waddle, too. The baby's head must be well and truly descended. Percy half expected to turn round and see it smiling at her, upside down, from between Carmen's legs.

Percy was in no hurry for labour to start, though. In fact she was bloody nervous, having agreed to be there at the birth. She hoped she wouldn't faint.

She smiled at Patrice, who was on tenterhooks, too. They all were. Even career-obsessed Suzanne had agreed to drop everything at a moment's notice to come and help, if needs be.

They all knew Justin and Patrice would cope just fine with Rowan and Ben, for however long it took for the baby to arrive. But they understood Suzanne's desire to feel fully involved.

'Grapevine, grapevine, kick right,' Debbie shouted. 'Grapevine, grapevine, kick left. Now pump, as hard as you can. Harder, faster, give it some welly!'

332

Percy was relieved there was no sign of Danny. She'd had a quick scout outside in the weights area and round the studio when she first arrived, to make sure. She guessed he was out doing personal training.

She was panting, now. There was that familiar, pricking sensation under her breasts from the sweat.

'Form a circle, and run, run as fast as you can. Lengthen your stride!' Debbie yelled. 'Change direction.'

They all ground to a halt, narrowly avoiding a pile-up, and turned the other way. Percy noticed Carmen had left the room. To get some water, or maybe she'd had second thoughts? Really, this was far too high-impact for her. She should be having a gentle swim instead.

'Grab a mat,' Debbie instructed. 'I want to see some juicy press-ups!'

Percy pulled out her hair tie and redid her ponytail. She hated it if her hair got in her eyes when she was trying to concentrate. She squeezed her tummy in and lowered herself down as slowly as she could. She could only get her chest down to the level of her elbows. She was rubbish at press-ups. Some of the others practically had their noses on the floor.

'Now, come up into plank position and raise one leg off the floor,' Debbie said.

Percy grimaced. Not this one. She pulled one leg up straight, then the other, trying to keep her bum down, not arch her back. Her legs were shaking with the effort.

'Now on to your sides.'

It was killing.

'Back on your ankles, shell stretch,' said Debbie.

Thank heavens for that.

Percy and Patrice were surprised not to see Carmen in the changing rooms. She must have showered already.

'How's the job?' Patrice asked, smoothing moisturiser on her legs.

'Good,' Percy replied. 'Exhausting but good. They seem to like me – they keep asking me back, anyway. I've a feeling Carmen's going to go into labour any minute,' she said, changing the subject. 'She looks a bit like a big, ripe tomato, ready to burst.'

Patrice laughed.

Carmen was sitting in the café when they came out. She was in her favourite lotus position on the sofa, eyes closed, breathing deeply. She opened her eyes and looked up only when Percy put a cup of green tea in front of her.

'I think it's starting,' Carmen said. Her eyes were wide open, scared. 'I'm getting these regular twinges, like Braxton Hicks, only worse.'

Percy plonked down on the chair. Now she knew how anxious fathers-to-be must feel. It was almost as bad as being the poor woman. 'Ohmigod,' she said. 'Are you sure? But your waters haven't broken yet.'

Patrice put down her bags, stood behind Carmen and started massaging her back. 'Now keep calm,' she was saying, pummelling Carmen's shoulders.

Carmen winced. 'I am calm,' she said, through clenched teeth. 'But you're doing it too hard. You're hurting.'

Patrice looked sheepish. 'Oops, sorry.'

Percy glugged her coffee down and sprang into action. 'Right,' she said, slapping her thighs. 'I'll take Carmen home. Get her into a hot bath.'

Carmen was about to protest but Percy was having none of it. 'You can't possibly drive, you banana,' she scolded. 'You're in labour, Carmen. Patrice, will you pick Rowan up from nursery and take him home with you? I'll call Justin and ask him to collect Ben.'

Patrice nodded. 'Let me know when you're back at Carmen's,' she said. 'I want regular bulletins.' She bent over and kissed Carmen on the cheek. 'Good luck, darling,' she said. 'I'll be thinking of you.'

Carmen smiled faintly.

Percy walked to the exit with Patrice and gave her the thumbs up. Patrice repeated the gesture. 'Wish me luck,' Percy said, sounding, she feared, every bit as fretful as she felt. 'I'm going to need it.'

It was dark by the time Percy led Carmen, doubled over in pain in the middle of a contraction, up the steps into the maternity unit. Porters quickly produced a wheelchair.

The unit was only a few years old, bright and newly painted. But there was that inevitable hospital smell, and it was boiling hot, too.

Percy took off her jacket and pushed up the sleeves of her sweater. She wished she was in a T-shirt instead. It seemed only yesterday that she'd given birth to Rowan here.

She remembered how Mark had raced her over in the car while Antonia looked after Ben. Actually it was possibly the one and only time she'd looked after Ben.

Mark had been terrified Percy would give birth en route, but in fact it was another twelve hours before Rowan put in an appearance. He was in no hurry to get out; he still liked to take his time.

The porters pushed Carmen into the lift and a couple of midwives were there, waiting for her, when the doors opened. They were all smiles.

Percy was pleased Carmen had a separate room, off the main corridor. You only got one of those, she knew, if the ward wasn't too busy. There was a TV, pictures on the walls and floral curtains. Luxury.

Percy helped Carmen off with her clothes and into a white, man-size T-shirt she'd brought with her. Carmen lay on the bed while one of the midwives examined her cervix.

'Eight centimetres already,' the midwife said. She had a strong Irish accent. 'She's done well to wait this long at home.

My name's Maura by the way. I take it you'll be staying with Carmen today?'

Percy nodded. 'We're best friends,' she explained.

Maura nodded wisely. 'Ah yes, we have quite a few like you.' She smiled knowingly.

Lord! What was that supposed to mean? Percy started to speak. 'Actually—' she said.

Maura interrupted. 'I don't believe in partners just sitting there.' She beamed. 'I expect them to muck in.'

Her smile was pleasant, but there was a hint of steel in her voice. Percy guessed she wouldn't stand any nonsense. 'Now, will you pass me that monitor?' Maura commanded.

Percy passed the equipment obediently and helped strap the monitor round Carmen's swollen tummy. Squiggly lines appeared on the screen beside the bed and blipped comfortingly.

'All fine,' Maura said, peering at them. 'Would you like some gas and air, Carmen?'

Carmen nodded, took a huge gasp and lay back on the bed, peaceful for a moment. Then another massive contraction started to build. Her face contorted. 'Oh God, it hurts so much. I think I'm going to die.'

Percy got a flannel from the sponge bag Carmen had brought and ran it under the cold tap. 'No you're not, darling,' she said, wiping Carmen's brow. You're doing so well. I'm very proud of you.'

Maura moved to the other side of the room and turned the lights down low. She was wearing a tight blue and white uniform, her hair scraped back in a sensible, gingery-white bun. She looked every inch the professional. Well into her fifties, Percy guessed, she must have delivered hundreds of babies in her time.

'That's better,' Maura said of the new, mellow lighting. She bent over to check the squiggles on the monitor again. 'Much more relaxing.'

336

Percy agreed. The glare before had been cold and clinical. Now the room felt quieter, mysterious. She couldn't help thinking how wrong it was that she was here instead of Simon, though. She hated him, the loathsome fool.

Carmen's face and body scrunched up again, shaking with the onslaught of another massive contraction. 'I can't stand it,' she howled. 'I feel like I'm being torn in two.'

Percy's stomach clenched. She felt slightly nauseous. She wished she could stick her head out of the window for some fresh air.

'You're not going to faint on me now, are you?' Maura whispered to Percy. 'You've gone quite green. You can go outside for a while if you want, pace up and down, have a smoke with the other, em, dads.' She laughed in an understanding way.

Percy shook her head. She felt too weak right now to explain. She drew the chair up beside the bed and held Carmen's hand. It felt so small and delicate.

Carmen groaned, digging her fingernails into Percy's palm. Percy yelped. She wished Carmen didn't go in for French manicures. 'You've got good strong nails,' she joked through gritted teeth.

Carmen dug deeper. 'Shame you don't bite them like me,' Percy muttered.

When Carmen dropped off again, Percy loosened her mangled hand and stroked her friend's silky black head. Carmen's eyes looked more oriental than usual today, her face smoother and flatter. Percy wondered what her baby would look like. Would it have black hair, like Carmen, and big almond eyes? Or would it be paler, more western, like Simon? Percy couldn't wait to find out.

Maura made a clucking noise. 'She's beautiful, Carmen, isn't she? How long have you two been—?'

Carmen emitted, a low, frightening noise, like a being from another world.

337

'Another contraction already?' Percy asked anxiously.

Maura nodded. 'They're coming fast now,' she said, looking at her watch.

'There, there,' Percy whispered, brushing strands of wet hair off Carmen's sweaty brow. 'Everything's going to be fine.'

An idea struck her. 'Would you like some music?' she asked, reaching for her bag. She'd brought her iPod and some mini speakers, just in case. But Carmen shook her head. Her face was clammy, her lips dry and cracked. Percy wiped her forehead again.

'Childbirth's horrific isn't it?' she whispered when she was sure Carmen had gone to sleep again.

Maura nodded. 'It is really.'

Percy felt grateful, suddenly, that she had only sons, no daughters. At least they'd never have to go through this.

The minutes ticked by slowly. 'I'm just popping out for a few moments,' Maura said. 'I know I can leave you in charge.'

She winked. Percy opened her mouth. 'Listen, I'd like you to know . . .'

But Maura had already disappeared.

It crossed Percy's mind that maybe she did look a bit mannish, in jeans, Timberland boots and an oversized black sweater. She wished for a second that she was wearing a floral frock, not that she possessed such a thing. That would have shut Maura up.

She suddenly realised how thirsty she was. She poured herself some water from a jug on the windowsill. She got out her book, but the words made no sense. She put it down again.

Carmen was moaning lightly in her sleep. Percy sat down again beside her friend. Watched her features distort as the pain built up once more.

'I can't stand the pain, I need something for the pain,' Carmen screamed suddenly, snapping her eyes open, arching her back, rigid with agony. 'Get me an epidural.'

Percy ran to the door, frightened by her friend's tone. She looked frantically for Maura. 'Help!' she shouted.

Maura appeared round the corner. 'Ach, it's too late for an epidural now, love,' she said, examining Carmen's nether regions. There was no room for dignity in childbirth, Percy thought grimly.

'Good news.' Maura smiled. 'She's ten centimetres dilated now. She should be ready to push before long.'

'So soon?' Percy asked. This was bad enough. She wasn't sure she was ready for the next instalment.

'She was a wee while at home, remember, before you came in,' Maura replied calmly.

She looked at Percy kindly, took her face between her hands and squeezed her cheeks so tightly they hurt. 'Ach, will you stop looking so worried?' She beamed, jiggling Percy's face from side to side. 'You're all the same, you know. Everything's going to be all right.'

Maura had a tight grip. It really hurt. She wasn't going to get at Percy's cheeks again. As soon as she'd stopped jiggling, Percy took a step back, rubbed her sore face and cleared her throat. 'Look, I feel I should tell you, I'm not Carmen's—'

Maura raised a hand. 'It's all right, darlin'. You can trust me.' She sounded more Irish than ever. 'I've seen it all before, to be sure. Nothin' surprises me any more.'

'Can I have some water?' Carmen called, weakly.

Percy had almost forgotten about her. She turned to Maura, who nodded.

'Go on now, stop rabbiting,' Maura tutted, cuffing Percy playfully on the arm. 'Go and see to your poor missus.'

Percy decided there was no point arguing. She strode over to the other side of the room to get some water. She was even beginning to walk like a dad, now. Jesus!

She and Maura stood quietly by the end of the bed while Carmen writhed. It felt a bit like waiting for an exam to start.

Percy's palms were sweaty and she had sick, angry butter-flies in her stomach.

'I've three children of my own, all grown up now,' Maura revealed. She was in a chatty mood. 'And I've the grey hairs to prove it.'

'When did you leave Ireland?' Percy asked, grateful for the distraction.

'In my early twenties,' Maura replied. 'I came over for a year or two and I'm still here more than twenty years on. I still miss my family, you know. I've brothers and sisters over there, see.

'Only thing is, if I'd stayed I'd probably have six babies now, instead of three.' She said 'ting' for 'thing' and 'tree' for 'three'.

'You're not supposed to take contraception, see, in the Republic of Ireland where I come from. Not girls from good Catholic families like mine, anyroad. Not that you need to worry about that, of course.'

Percy was about to correct her when Carmen screamed. Maura bustled over to her side. 'All right now, Carmen, you're ready to push,' she said. There was a new, serious edge in her voice.

Percy felt queasy again and scuttled to Carmen's top end.

'Push as hard as you can,' Maura commanded. 'Good girl, that's lovely. Give me three big pushes. There, you can see the top of the head, look.'

Percy's stomach turned over. She beetled down to the other end, saw tufts of black, sticky baby hair. 'It's coming, it's coming!' she squealed.

Carmen grunted.

'Now I want you to hold off, Carmen, for a couple of minutes,' Maura directed. 'Pant, pant.'

Carmen shook her head. 'I can't, I've got to push.'

'Just a bit longer, love, or you'll tear,' Maura said. 'Good girl. You don't want stitches now, do you?'

Percy could see it was all Carmen could do not to push. But Maura's words had got through. Carmen's face was tense, purple, her whole being focused on holding back

'OK now, Carmen, you can push,' Maura said at last. 'Push. As hard as you can. That's it, and again. Push.'

Carmen groaned, long and loud, an animal noise. Percy could see the head starting to emerge.

'Push now, Carmen, push for all you're worth,' Maura hollered.

Tears sprang in Percy's eyes as Maura eased the head out. It was all wet and slippery, covered in blood and mucus. It looked like a little seal. Percy couldn't decide whether to laugh or cry. She thought she was doing both.

'The head's out now, Carmen,' she blubbed. 'And the shoulders. Darling little teeny weeny shoulders. It's a baby! You're the cleverest woman in the world.'

Carmen heaved a few more times and the rest of her baby slithered out. Percy punched the air. Then she offered up a silent prayer.

Thank you, God, for the safe arrival of this little person. I promise I'll always be here for Carmen's baby.

'Is it a boy or a girl?' Carmen asked faintly.

Percy was too overcome to care.

'A lovely little girl,' Maura said softly.

Quickly, she cleaned the baby's eyes and nose, wrapped her in a blanket and placed her on Carmen's chest.

'I knew it, I knew it would be a girl.' Carmen smiled, looking down at her tiny daughter for the first time. 'Hello, darling, welcome to the world.'

Maura beamed. 'Congratulations to you both,' she said. 'You were a star, Carmen. And no stitches. Actually, you were both stars.'

Percy grinned back. 'Thank you,' she said, putting an arm round Carmen's shoulders and beaming down in a fatherly sort of way at mother and child. 'We were rather good, weren't we?'

For a moment, the baby opened her eyes and gazed up at her mother with a look of infinite wisdom.

'It is a miracle, isn't it,' the midwife said. 'I still think that, even after all these years. What are you calling her, do you know?'

Percy looked at Carmen expectantly.

'Ivy Persephone,' Carmen said firmly.

Percy started to protest. 'You can't—'

Carmen interrupted. 'Ivy because it's beautiful as well as strong and binding. I want her to be strong, and bound tightly to those around her, the people she loves. And Persephone, well, I've always secretly liked the name. Even if no one can pronounce it.'

Percy grinned. 'Well, I've survived it,' she admitted. 'I'm honoured, really. So long as she doesn't go blaming me in years to come.'

Maura had gone, but returned now to cut the umbilical cord. 'Would you like to do it?' she asked Percy.

Percy nodded.

'Ach.' Maura slapped her hand. 'No, no. Like this, see?' Maura showed her where to cut.

Percy half expected Maura to raise her eyes heavenwards and say, 'Men!'

'You have a hold,' Carmen said afterwards. Her voice sounded different. Softer. It was that gentle, crooning sound that all mothers make. Amazing, Percy thought, how instinctive it must be.

Ever so gently, Percy took the newborn infant in her arms. She was perfect, with lots of black hair and surprisingly round pink cheeks. 'Look, she's got elegant little hands, just like her mother.' Percy grinned. 'And a Cupid's bow mouth. She's gorgeous.'

Maura bustled out again, returning with a cup of tea for

Carmen. She put Ivy to her breast where she started sucking immediately.

Had her own babies been that clever, that perfect? Percy wondered. She supposed so. But it all seemed so long ago. She wished at that moment that she could press the rewind button, hold her newborns in her arms again. It all seemed to have gone so fast.

She realised she was absolutely exhausted. She glanced at her watch. It was 1.25 a.m. and she hadn't eaten for hours. She thought of Mark, Ben and Rowan. The boys would be fast asleep, but Mark wouldn't. At least, he wouldn't mind being woken up.

'I'm going to call Mark, tell him everything's OK,' Percy said. 'And shall I call Pats and Suzanne? They'll be desperate to hear the news.'

Carmen nodded without taking her eyes off Ivy. 'Of course, send them my love,' she murmured. 'But listen, you can go now, Pers. Go home, you must be knackered. I'll be fine.'

Percy was doubtful. 'Are you sure?'

'Absolutely. Ivy and I have a lot of bonding to do.'

'Looks like you're thick as thieves already.' Percy smiled. 'But if you're really sure, I could do with some sleep. But I'm only at the end of the phone, remember. And we'll come and collect you tomorrow, when you're ready. Take you home. Is there anything you need?

Carmen shook her head and looked at Percy. 'Hey, Pers. Thanks for everything.'

Percy smiled. 'It's been a privilege.'

She left her friend still suckling her newborn, as if she'd been doing it all her life. Simon didn't deserve to be part of that scene, Percy reflected. He was a fool. It was his loss. She, Suzanne and Patrice would look after Carmen. She didn't need a useless, faithless man.

* * *

343

Although she was exhausted, Percy knew she wouldn't be able to sleep when she got home. She was on a high – euphoric, floating.

She had something to eat, turned on the TV without really watching, flicked through the newspaper. She had butterflies in her stomach. The adrenalin was still pumping. She wondered if midwives ever got any sleep. She supposed they were used to the agonies and ecstasies.

Mark was wide awake when she climbed into bed beside him. She was surprised. 'Why aren't you asleep?' she asked.

'I was waiting for you.'

They chatted for a while about Carmen and the birth. She described Maura and the misunderstanding. They were both laughing. He thought it was hilarious.

He stroked her breast when they'd stopped giggling. 'Will you dress up for me?' he whispered.

'Do you realise what time it is?' she replied.

'I know, but I can't get to sleep now, with all the excitement.'

'I've got no energy left,' she protested. 'I'm done in.'

The landing light was on. He made a little boy face. 'Please?' he said, his head on one side. 'Pretty please?'

The cute dimple on his left cheek reappeared. He had outrageously long, black lashes. They compensated for the bald head.

She couldn't deny him. 'All right then,' she said. 'But you'll have to be quick.'

He laughed. 'You're so romantic.'

She opened the bottom drawer of her chest. Dug out the red basque he'd once bought her for a giggle, the black, over-the-knee boots, the black silk scarf. 'Lie back,' she commanded.

He raised his arms obediently above his head and waited while she tied his hands to the bedstead with the scarf.

She stood up, towering above him.

'Be gentle with me,' he grinned.

Teasingly, she placed a spiky heel – carefully – on his bare chest.

He sighed. 'I love it when you act dirty.'

She giggled. Composed herself. 'Now, you have to do exactly as I say,' she ordered.

'And what might that be?' he asked, pretending to be scared.

'Hmmm,' she said. 'Now let me see . . .'

'Christ, I never knew it could be this good.' He shuddered when she'd finished.

'Neither did I.' She smiled. 'Can I go to sleep now?' She snuggled into his chest.

'Let's go for dinner tomorrow night – just you and me?' he said. 'To celebrate.'

'Lovely, but this isn't like you,' she replied, surprised.

'I just think we should try to go out together more,' he explained. 'It's easier now Rowan's bigger. We could try to make it a regular thing. Once a week, say.'

She felt a glow of pleasure. 'I'd really love that, Mark.'

She waited for him to close his eyes and turn over. But he didn't. The air felt heavy with expectation.

'What's up?' she asked.

He cleared his throat. 'Percy?'

'Yes?'

'I know what went on with that fitness instructor,' he said.

She froze. She'd misheard, surely? 'I don't know what you mean.'

'No lies,' he replied, softly. 'I was there, on that day. I'd forgotten one of my cameras and came home to collect it. I saw you jogging down the road with him, laughing and chatting. You looked so beautiful, animated. I hadn't seen you that happy for ages.

'I parked the car a little way down the street and waited. I watched you go into the house. Later, you drew the curtains.'

345

He swallowed. 'Then I saw him come out, then you, all showered and changed. You had guilt written all over your face.' He gave a humourless laugh. 'I'm glad you washed the sheets afterwards, Pers.'

Percy started crying, softly. Her tears fell on to his chest. Was he going to finish it now? Had that act of love been their swansong? And she'd thought things were so much better between them.

'Don't cry,' he said, still lying on his back, his arm round her, stiffly. 'I know you've done a lot of thinking. I have too. I could have confronted you there and then, asked for a divorce. I thought about it, of course, but then I decided to wait, see what happened. I knew things hadn't been good between us for a long time. I was angry with your spending, fed up with having to work so hard. But I wanted to see if we could turn things round.

'I guess,' he swallowed again. 'I guess the truth is, I didn't want to lose you, Percy.'

She felt a rush of love. 'Why didn't you tell me this before?' she asked, still not quite believing.

'If I'd told you then, just after it happened, we'd have had a huge row,' he explained. 'I felt so angry and hurt – mad with jealousy, too. I tried to bottle it up but I couldn't – remember when I smashed the photos?'

Percy shuddered. How could she forget?

'But now I feel we're getting on much better, aren't we?' he went on. 'It's more like how we were at the beginning?'

'Yes,' said Percy.

'And you haven't seen him again, have you? It was a one-off?' He sounded anxious. She knew this was really important to him.

'No way,' Percy replied. 'I rang him straightaway, told him not to come again. It was a one-off. She sat up in bed, looking him full in the face. 'Mark?' He was like a little boy, uncertain, vulnerable.

'Yes?' he said.

'I'm so sorry,' she said with feeling. 'I so want us to be happy together. I felt desperately sorry the minute I'd been with him. It was all a terrible mistake. We'd had a miserable holiday, remember? I was in a complete mess with the gambling, too, but I know that's no excuse. I'd be mortified if you did the same to me. Will you – can you forgive me?'

He drew her close to him and buried his face in her hair. 'I already have,' he whispered.

It felt, to Percy, at that moment, pretty much like a miracle. She wouldn't have believed that you could breathe new life into a marriage that had gone so sad and stale and wrong. But this felt like a new beginning. A proper one, this time, because now he knew about Danny, too. There were no more secrets.

She kissed his chest. Started to drift off.

'Hey, Percy?' Mark said. 'Let's go for a week's holiday at half-term, with the boys. We'll find somewhere hot. Crete, maybe, or the Canaries. It'll make up for Provence.'

'But the overdraft,' she reminded him. 'The debts. We can't afford it.'

'Don't worry. It's going well at the moment,' he reassured her. 'I've got some big jobs lined up, big payers. So long as you keep teaching, we'll be OK. Trust me, we can manage it.'

They curled up together, spoonlike, satisfied. Percy wasn't religious, but she prayed again, for the second time that day.

Thank you, God, for baby Ivy. And thank you for helping me, Persephone Redpath, to fall in love with my husband all over again.

347

Chapter Thirteen

❦

There were few people around on a Sunday morning and Percy had the pool almost to herself. It was very dark, almost mysterious in there, with no natural light.

The ceiling was dotted with downlighters, and the pool was lit up, too. The walls were painted a dark seaweedy-green colour. The roof was so shiny, you could see yourself in it when you swam on your back.

Percy decided she'd do twenty lengths of front crawl, ten of backstroke and ten of breaststroke. Ten less than Carmen usually managed, but she was building up to it.

The first ten lengths were the hardest. Percy's body was like lead. But after that, she felt less heavy and got into her stride.

Stroke, stroke, breathe on the right, stroke, stroke, breathe on the left. It was monotonous but satisfying, too. And it left her mind free to roam.

She thought about Carmen. Ivy was five months old now, and Simon seemed to have become rather a frequent visitor. After Ivy was born, he'd phoned virtually every day, asking to see her.

Carmen had held him off for six weeks, before reluctantly agreeing. 'He is her father, after all,' she'd explained to Percy and the others. Percy had offered to be there, too, for the visit. But Carmen said she could handle it on her own.

He'd turned up one Sunday with a bundle of clothes from Baby Gap and a big bunch of flowers for Carmen. As soon as he'd left, she'd binned the flowers and shoved the clothes in a bag for Oxfam. It had given her immense satisfaction.

To her surprise, however, she said he'd seemed rather smitten with Ivy. He'd sat for a good half-hour on that first visit with her on his lap, gazing at her little face, letting her wrap her tiny hand round his forefinger.

Carmen said she hadn't offered him a drink or anything. She'd perched on the chair opposite, watching, hawk-like, for any signs of disquiet from Ivy. Rather to her annoyance, though, the baby had seemed quite content, making cute little snuffling noises.

Since then, Simon, who was between contracts, had phoned regularly, asked to see Ivy each week. Carmen claimed she'd made it as difficult as possible, coming up with excuses: she had friends over, Ivy had a cold and so on. But he was persistent, and she'd usually given in.

Percy's goggles were steaming up. She stopped to dip them in the water and put them back on again. That was better. She was in the medium lane. There was a scary man in a swimming cap and goggles in the fast one. He looked as if he'd sooner run you down than stop, even for a second.

Annoyingly, though, an elderly gentleman climbed into her lane in front of her and proceeded to amble, froggy-style, up the lane, blowing lots of bubbles. He reminded her of a very large turtle. She bobbed under the rope that separated the lanes and launched into backstroke in the general swimming area. There were only a few children and parents about. She shouldn't career into anyone.

Where was she? Oh yes, Carmen. Percy continued her train of thought. Earlier in the week, Simon had informed Carmen he'd be going away soon. He needed to see Ivy before he left. She'd agreed he could come this afternoon.

Percy didn't like the way he seemed to be insinuating himself back into Carmen's life at a time when she was particularly vulnerable. What was his game? Carmen claimed

349

she was over him, but Percy wasn't convinced. She'd told Carmen she was going to drop by 'unexpectedly' this afternoon, as a warning to Simon. She wanted him to know that she, Percy, was watching.

Carmen had laughed and said it wasn't necessary, but Percy had insisted. She couldn't pretend she was looking forward to it, though. She hadn't seen Simon for months, hated him, didn't know whether she'd be able to remain polite. She'd have to try, though, for Carmen's sake.

Percy decided to pop in for a quick sauna before getting showered. Mark had taken the boys out for the day, to Legoland, which Percy thought was pretty saintly.

It took a moment for her eyes to adjust to the darkness. The air was so hot and dry, it hurt her lungs when she breathed in. There was a strong smell of pine and eucalyptus.

She closed the door behind her and turned round. A pair of dark, hairy legs were spread out just a few feet in front of her. There was no avoiding the prominent lump, encased in red Lycra, between them, either.

The owner of the legs was sitting on one of the higher benches in the sauna. She had to look up to see his face. Her instinct was to spin round and walk right out again. But a voice said: 'Hey, Pair-say-foon, er, Per-say-foon. How ya doing?'

'Hi, Danny,' she sighed. 'Just call me Percy, will you? I'm fine. You?'

She sat on the lowest bench, near the door, as far away from him as she could. Her back was against the wall. She didn't want to lie down, as she normally would.

To her dismay, Danny hopped down and came and sat beside her. She realised she hadn't seen him for a few weeks. He was covered in sweat. Even his eyebrows were dripping. It was the opposite of sexy.

'You know what, babe?' he said. His voice was soft and low. He put his arm up to scratch his head. Percy was convinced it was to show off his bulging bicep. She pretended not to notice. She dreaded what was coming.

'I've been thinking a lot recently,' he said. 'You know we was good, me and you.' He put a hand on her thigh. It was sticky. 'It's a shame we haven't seen each other for a while. How about we go for a drink sometime?'

She thought of Mark. Lovely, kind Mark, who'd been so forgiving. Who was with the boys now, their boys. Her husband. How could she ever have betrayed him?

'You know what?' she said, removing Danny's hand and plonking it on his own thigh. 'I thought you and me was distinctly disappointing and, frankly, I wouldn't do it again for a million pounds. Now, why don't you be a good boy and run off and join Millicent, who's clearly more impressed with your bedroom performance than I am.'

She felt fifty feet tall as she wandered into the café to meet Suzanne. She'd been using the weights in the gym. Her face was still red.

'You look radiant,' Suzanne smiled. 'Are you in love or something?'

Percy laughed. 'Good workout?'

She didn't hear Suzanne's reply, having been distracted by a small crowd huddling round something in a corner of the room. A couple of people moved and Percy could see through the gap that there was a stall selling ethnic scarves and jewellery. Sometimes there were handmade cards and children's books.

When they'd finished their drinks, Percy and Suzanne wandered over to check out the wares.

'This is divine,' Suzanne said, holding up a chunky silver necklace. 'Look, you can even choose your own charms to go on it.' She pointed to a heart, a book, a key. They were sweet. 'There's even a racquet.' She laughed. 'I'll have to have that. It'll remind me of Justin when he's not here.'

'Still obsessed with squash?' Percy asked, picking out a silver charm bracelet for herself, then putting it back. The new Percy.

'More than ever,' Suzanne said, getting out her money. 'Still, keeps him out of mischief, I suppose.'

Percy glanced round Carmen's sitting room. It looked rather different now from how it was B.I. – Before Ivy. It was a homage to minimalism no longer.

She'd got rid of the sisal flooring – too scratchy for Ivy, apparently – and replaced it with practical, hardwearing carpet in a sensible mottled green that wouldn't show the dirt.

The weeping fig in a cast-iron container in a corner of the room was no more: Carmen said she kept forgetting to water it. In its place was a mound of yellow and red plastic, including a toy cooker from Granny and Grandpa, which Ivy was still far too young for.

Carmen, aghast at the sheer size and hideousness of the thing, explained she'd been tempted to take it back to the shop, but the expression of pure joy on her parents' faces as they held up the garish pots and pans, whisks and spoons for Ivy to see made her change her mind. She couldn't be so cruel.

Wherever you looked now there were books, toys, little piles of clothes, dolls and teddies: Ivy's accoutrements.

'Look who's here to see you, Ivy!' Carmen beamed. 'Aunty Persephone.'

'Ha, time to get your own back!' Percy laughed. She remembered how Carmen had hated Rowan calling her Aunty.

Simon was on the sofa, a few feet from Ivy, who was in her bouncy chair. He was waving a rattle in front of her and attempting to read the Sunday papers at the same time. The rattle tinkled when he shook it and her fat little arms and legs, encased in a cute pink Babygro, waggled with excitement.

Percy was under the impression she'd interrupted something. Simon couldn't hide his annoyance when he saw her.
Charming. He'd changed his tune, then.

He stood up. 'Hi,' he said without enthusiasm.

She'd forgotten how enormously tall he was. He made her
feel dwarfish.

Ivy, perhaps sensing the temperature had dropped several
degrees, started whimpering.

'Right then,' Carmen said, levering her daughter out of
the chair, kissing the top of her head and passing her to
Simon. 'Daddy's going to play with you.'

'Come on, poppet,' Simon said. He looked rather stiff, Percy
thought, but to her dismay the baby went to him happily.
She seemed to snuggle into his chest as if she belonged there.

Percy took off her denim jacket and sat down. It was a
warm September day and Carmen's French doors were open
into the garden. There was a faint smell of jasmine in the air.

'Cold drink?' Carmen asked Percy.

Percy thought she was looking even more gorgeous than
usual. There was black kohl round her eyes and she smelled
of Chanel No 5, her favourite scent. Carmen was wearing
jeans and a loose white cheesecloth shirt with several buttons
undone down the front. Easy access for breastfeeding, Percy
supposed.

She'd shed her babyweight, but there was something
different about her, a softness that was strangely sweet and
appealing. She seemed to have lost that brittle edge she used
to have, the slight defensiveness, the look that said: Go no
further, I'm not answering any more questions.

Simon turned to the door. 'I'll take Ivy for a walk,' he said.

Carmen held up a hand. 'Don't. Percy doesn't mind
listening, do you, Percy?'

Percy shook her head.

'We were just talking about visiting arrangements, weren't
we, Simon?' Carmen explained.

Simon winced. Ha! Let him wriggle out of this one, Percy thought. Let him try bullying Carmen in front of me!

He sat down again, Ivy on his lap. She reached up and gave his earlobe a tug. 'Ouch,' he said. 'That hurts. I was just saying . . .' He looked at Percy. 'I was just saying to Carmen we need to sort out some sort of regular arrangement with Ivy. She's my daughter, after all.'

Carmen laughed. She was still standing, shoulders back, head up. It was a good move, Percy thought. It made her look more in control.

'You weren't exactly interested in her before she was born,' Carmen continued. 'In fact, I seem to remember you were rather keen I should have a termination.'

Simon swallowed. 'Look, this is all very embarrassing,' he said. 'Can't we do this on our own, when Percy's gone?'

Carmen looked fierce. 'I'd like my friend to be here actually, Simon. I don't want to be on my own with you. Please go on.'

He glanced at Percy. Almost pleading, she thought. She shook her head. She wasn't going to help him out. She was enjoying this, the bastard.

'Don't mind me, I'll read the paper,' she said innocently, picking the *Observer* off the floor.

He sighed. 'All right. It's up to you, Carmen. If you don't mind airing our dirty linen in public . . .'

'I beg your pardon?' Carmen replied. Her tone was steely, serrated. 'You make us sound like an old married couple,' she snarled. 'We don't have any dirty linen, Simon. It's long since been washed and put away. Let's get on with the practicalities, shall we?'

Percy felt like cheering. Instead, she pretended to carry on reading the newspaper.

Simon went on quietly. 'I never said I wanted you to have an abortion, I just said I wasn't ready. But now Ivy's here, it's different. I love her. And I want to be a good father to her. You can't keep me out of her life.'

Carmen sat down now, opposite him. Ivy was busy fiddling with a button on Simon's shirt. Percy hoped she'd pull it off. Go girl!

'How's your true love?' Carmen asked, raising her eyebrows. 'Have you set a wedding date yet?'

Simon shifted uncomfortably in his seat. 'What's that got to do with it?' he said. 'But in answer to your question, not yet, no.'

'Why not?' Carmen enquired.

'We just haven't got round to it, that's all,' Simon retorted. He was riled, Percy could tell. Carmen had noticed, too.

'But I thought you were going to get married immediately, once Ivy's birth was "out of the way",' Carmen said. She put a heavy emphasis on the last four words. She was peck-pecking, like a woodpecker on a dead tree.

'We've been busy,' he replied. 'Well, actually . . .' There was a new edge in his voice.

Percy looked up; she couldn't help herself. Simon was staring straight at Carmen, jiggling Ivy up and down at the same time.

'Actually,' he said again. 'It's not going that well. You see I've . . .' He looked all moon-eyed and stupid. 'I think I might have made a mistake,' he whispered, hanging his head. Little boy lost.

Percy was tempted to jump up, grab his collar and hurl him forcibly from the front door. Instead she watched, dismayed, as Carmen leaned forward and smiled gently, sympathetically. Her whole face had changed. She tipped her head to one side.

'I'm sorry, Simon,' she said. All the acid had seeped from her voice. 'I had no idea.'

Ivy was getting bored on Simon's knee now. His button was still intact, unfortunately. She started to fuss. Simon passed her over to Carmen.

'She must be hungry,' Carmen said, unbuttoning her shirt

to reveal a full, round, honey-coloured breast. Percy saw the look of interest on Simon's face. You keep your hands off, she growled under her breath. But she could feel events slipping away from her.

Ivy got stuck in, made happy sucking noises. Carmen stroked her dark, downy head.

'We haven't talked properly about money yet,' Simon said after a pause. 'I want to make sure you and Ivy are all right. I care about you both, you know.'

Using her little finger, Carmen gently unplugged Ivy's mouth from her nipple. It made a popping noise, like a cork. Ivy started to wail, enraged at having her meal interrupted. Carmen quickly switched her over to the other side and plugged her in again.

Percy sensed them all relax.

'It's not easy,' Carmen admitted, still looking down at Ivy. 'I'm rapidly getting through my savings. I'll have to go back to work soon.'

Percy thought she could detect a gleam in Simon's eye. 'You don't have to,' he said. 'I'd like you to stay home and look after Ivy. I'll make sure you're all right – if you'll let me.'

He clearly took her silence as acquiescence. 'That's more like it. Good girl.' He leaned over and patted Carmen's knee. 'Give me your bank details and I'll set up a monthly standing order,' he went on. 'And make sure you get something nice for yourself, a new dress or something.'

Carmen looked up. 'A dress? You must be mad,' she sneered. 'Why would I want a dress from you?'

Simon flinched. He realised he'd overstepped the mark. 'I – I don't mean a dress. Something practical, a jacket or something, for when you take the baby out,' he stammered, trying to backtrack. 'Or if there's anything you need for the house . . .'

'Can't you see what he's up to?' Percy implored, when he'd finally left.

Carmen was putting toys into big baskets, humming as she moved around the room. Ivy had dropped off to sleep in her chair.

'He's trying to get back in your knickers, Carmen,' Percy went on. 'You can see it a mile off. But it'll be the same old story. Him away a lot, not committing. I don't believe he's dumping the other woman, either. He probably likes the idea of having you both on the go.'

Carmen paused, one of Ivy's plastic toys suspended in mid-air. She looked at Percy. 'Don't worry,' she said. 'I know what I'm doing. Honest. I don't trust him an inch, but it's nice to think he'll take an interest in Ivy as she grows up. And if accepting his money means I'll be able to stay home with her for a few more months, not worry about work, then it's worth it—'

Percy interrupted. 'But you said you didn't want his money.'

Carmen nodded. 'I know, but I've changed my mind. He's loaded; I'm not. I just thought, let the bastard do something for me – for us – for once.'

'I agree,' said Percy 'I've always thought he should put his hand in his pocket. I just worry that it'll give him some sort of hold over you. I don't want you to get hurt again, Carmen.'

Carmen dropped the toy in the basket. She picked up one of Ivy's sleepsuits, folded it, put it on the chair. 'I realise that's a risk,' she said seriously. 'But I'm determined to keep him at arm's length. If he thinks he's going to get anywhere near me, he's severely mistaken.'

Percy looked doubtful. 'He just seems to have this effect on you. I don't know. I'm not sure you'll be able to resist.'

Carmen sat down beside her friend and sighed. 'To be honest, Percy,' she said, 'there's another reason why I want him in our lives.'

Percy gulped. She could hear the seriousness in her friend's voice.

'I've had a letter from my GP saying something's shown up on my smear,' Carmen went on. 'They don't think it's cancer – not yet, anyway. But it could turn into cancer if I don't have it seen to. I'll have to have laser treatment.'

Percy groaned, leaned over and gave her friend a big hug. 'You don't need this,' she said, shaking her head. 'On top of everything else. It's just not fair.'

Carmen shrugged. 'No, it's not fair. But life isn't fair, is it? And if something happened to me, I want to know Simon's going to be there for Ivy. I'd be an irresponsible mother if I cut him out. You must understand where I'm coming from now.'

Chapter Fourteen

❦

'On your tummies, please. Abs sucked tight, arms at right angles to your shoulders. Now I want you to raise your whole upper body, without using the muscles in your lower body at all. Your bum should be completely relaxed, wobbly like a jelly.'

'That won't be difficult,' someone joked from the other side of the room.

Patrice could feel it all across her shoulders, as well as in the small of her back. She sucked her tummy in tighter and her back felt less uncomfortable.

'Now I want you to add on the legs,' Romy, the instructor, called. 'Lift them up, then open wide, as wide as you can. Abs in. If you like you can open up your arms, too, to make it harder.'

Patrice decided against it. It was hard enough already.

'Now lower,' Romy commanded. 'Good. Do five more of those, then you can rest.'

It was unusual for Patrice to be in a class without at least one of the girls. But today, Percy was working as well as Suzanne, and Carmen hadn't been able to get Ivy into the crèche. It was always very busy.

Patrice had been expecting to jump straight on the train after Abs, Back and Stretch Fusion as she'd arranged to meet her friend in Covent Garden for lunch.

Since last year, when Seamus started school full time, she had so much more freedom to do things like that. She quite liked it, actually. She'd dreaded having so much time on her hands, but she'd soon adapted and found she even enjoyed it. But her friend had cancelled this morning. Patrice didn't really mind. It was almost a relief, really. She had things she wanted to do at home.

'OK, ladies, now we'll have a good stretch,' said Romy. 'Sit on your bums, legs straight out in front of you and I want you to bend over as far as you can. I'm coming round to give you a little push.'

Patrice managed to curl right over, her elbows on the floor. Her flexibility had definitely improved. She didn't think she could get any lower but Romy pushed her down several more inches.

Patrice's forehead touched her knees for the first time. Result! She had a quick look round to compare notes. She could hardly breathe, but she was quite a bit lower than silly old Millicent. Very satisfying.

She could see Millicent's black roots, too. She was due another trip to the hairdresser. I'm a bitch! Patrice thought, guiltily. Suzanne's influence had rubbed off on her.

Patrice had several messages waiting for her on her mobile when she came out of the changing room. She sat in the spot where she, Percy, Suzanne and Carmen congregated on a Saturday morning to listen to them. She was in no hurry.

'Nice bag,' someone said. Patrice looked up. Millicent was fingering the leather of Patrice's tan Chloé. Patrice loved it. Jonty had bought it for her for Christmas. It was possibly the most expensive present he'd ever given her, apart from her wedding and engagement rings of course.

'Is it real?' Millicent asked.

Patrice kept the phone clamped to her ear, but Millicent sat down anyway.

'I've been seeing an osteopath.' Millicent giggled. She was wearing a low-cut smock dress, very short. Her legs were extremely brown. Patrice had to admit she looked amazing, in a fake, Barbie-doll sort of way.

'And guess what?' Millicent went on. Patrice raised her eyebrows. 'He's absolutely gorgeous – the osteopath,' Millicent informed her.

'Really?' said Patrice, putting down the phone. There was no escape and Millicent was clearly dying for her to ask. 'What do you need an osteopath for?' Patrice said. 'And what do you mean, "seeing"?' She couldn't resist that one.

Millicent ploughed on regardless. She must have rhino skin, Patrice thought wonderingly.

'I've got a sore neck and shoulder,' Millicent explained, moving her head from side to side, wincing slightly. 'My GP recommended this man down the road. He's called Oldfield, Paul Oldfield.

'Well,' she said, leaning forward conspiratorially, 'I was expecting this old geezer, because of the name, you see. So I was amazed when this tall, blond, fit bloke walked into the room and asked me to take off my clothes.'

'What, all of them?' said Patrice. She couldn't help herself.

'No, silly,' Millicent gave a dirty laugh. 'Not my knickers. Just my top half. I mean, I kept my bra on, but it was a plunge one. I hadn't known what to expect.'

'Oh yeah,' Patrice laughed. 'I bet you'd put it on deliberately. Aren't plunge bras meant for the bedroom only, anyway?'

'Are they?' Millicent sounded surprised. 'I never thought about it. But now you mention it, I suppose I do keep popping out of mine. I have to poke myself back in when no one's looking.' She put her hands round her boobs and shuggled them about to demonstrate their waywardness.

'Hi, babe!' Danny came up behind Millicent and sat down on the arm of her chair. Millicent looked as if she'd eaten a lemon.

'Where have you been?' she said waspishly. 'I've left you loads of text messages. Why haven't you got back to me?'

Danny yawned and scratched his crotch. 'Sorry, babe, I've been busy, y'know,' he said languidly. 'I've got a lot of clients, you're not the only one.' He shrugged his shoulders and grinned a big, wide, white grin.

Millicent looked at him, then at her extremely long, red nails. Then at him again. 'Hmmm,' she said.

Patrice was amused. Watch out, Danny, she thought. I wouldn't mess with Millicent if I were you.

Patrice clicked a button on her car keys and the security gates swung open. To her surprise, Jonty's BMW was parked in front of the garage. Damn. She'd been looking forward to having a few hours to herself. Now he'd want feeding and fussing over. She might just as well have gone to Covent Garden on her own, had a mooch around. But it was mean of her not to be pleased to see him, she thought. She'd have to readjust her mind-frame.

She turned the key in the lock and walked inside. She noticed it immediately: the house felt different. Jonty hadn't turned on the hall light, as he usually did. The hall was always quite dark, even in the middle of the day. The only dark area in the house.

She looked at the floor. Jonty's shoes were neatly lined up by the table, which had the usual vase of lilies on it. There was nothing strange there. But there was an unfamiliar pair beside them: big suede Timberlands. Jonty didn't have any Timberlands. There was a strange jacket slung over the banister, too, and a leather holdall at the bottom of the stairs that Patrice didn't recognise.

She walked into the kitchen. There was half a loaf of bread on the work surface, a half-eaten slab of Stilton, an empty bottle of red wine. Two plates in the sink, waiting to be washed up. Two knives with crumbs on them. Jonty had a friend over, that was all, a work colleague. Nothing peculiar about it.

Patrice hesitated. Should she put the dirty dishes in the dishwasher and wipe down the surfaces? She would normally, but today felt different. She went back into the hall. Usually, she'd call out, or whistle a greeting. But something stopped her doing that, too.

Quietly, slowly, she removed her shoes and walked upstairs. It didn't take more than a couple of minutes but it seemed much, much longer. A lifetime.

She wished she could push the rewind button, walk backwards down the stairs, reverse the car, return to Gym and Slimline, begin her workout all over again. But although her heart was thumping, she felt strangely brave.

She counted the seconds in her head. Ten, nine, eight, seven, six . . .

There were clothes strewn across the first-floor landing. Her bedroom door was ajar. She took a deep breath and pushed the door open, just enough to see inside. The curtains were drawn and she could make out two figures lying side by side.

She could hear her heart, now, not just feel it. Boom, boom, in her ears. A banging and swishing noise.

As her eyes adjusted to the half-light, the room became clearer. There was a sheet partially covering the two bodies, a white sheet. She remembered putting it on this morning. And fresh pillow slips. She did it on the same day every week.

The duvet was on the floor at the bottom of the bed and pillows were strewn around. She and Jonty liked lots of pillows so they could prop themselves up and read. She wanted to plump them up now, put them back in their proper place, make everything neat.

The bodies were probably naked under the sheet, she thought. They were naked from the waist up, anyway. They could be dead but she guessed they were asleep. This wasn't a horror movie, after all.

The room smelled stale and sweaty. She would have liked to draw back the curtains and throw open the window, but it would have woken them and she didn't want to do that.

She stepped a little further into the room. Jonty was on the right. He was lying on his back, one arm behind his head.

The other was round his partner who was curled up like a kitten beside him, head nestling on Jonty's bare chest. Sweet. It was the way Patrice liked to go to sleep. It made her feel so safe.

Jonty had a contented look on his face. His blond hair was rumpled and boyish. He had more freckles on his forehead than she remembered and his damp lips were slightly parted.

The other head was dark. Short, dark brown hair, quite different from Jonty's. She could see that. It was breathing long, slow breaths. Relaxed.

'It', she thought. She'd stick with 'it'. She couldn't bring herself to give it a name.

Her eye dropped down the bed and she could see the outline of its arm, beneath the sheets, casually resting on her husband's stomach – or was it his penis? So familiar, comfy. She felt she ought to have her camera with her to record the moment. They were a picture of post-coital bliss.

She scanned up again, and right, noticing Jonty's watch beside the light on the bedside table. The one she'd given him for his birthday. And what must be an empty condom packet. At least he'd used one of those. Their wedding picture in the silver frame was lying face down, so Jonty hadn't had to look at it, she supposed.

For a second she tried to imagine them humping. Did they do it doggy-style, to each other, or was one the humper and one the humpee, so to speak? And if so, which one?

She heaved. Leaned against the wall, to steady herself. She thought of all the times he'd brushed her off, made her feel dirty, even, for wanting to make love with him. As if she was somehow abnormal. And all the time he'd been playing away from home. Except he hadn't, he'd been playing at home, right under her nose, in their bed. The bed Seamus was conceived in.

Patrice cried out, a high, painful cry which seemed to come from somewhere else. She put her hands over her mouth to try to stop it but the peace was already shattered.

Everything seemed so blindingly obvious now: his lack of interest in sex, the late nights after squash, the cufflinks, even the shifty looks. She felt like a stupid, silly little girl.

Her breathing was becoming irregular. She was taking big gulps of air but she felt out of breath. She was dizzy too, and hot, sweating. She thought she might faint or throw up. She couldn't stand any longer, her legs were too weak.

Slowly, slowly she crumpled in on herself until she was a tight little ball on the floor, gasping for oxygen, clutching herself as if she might otherwise break up into little pieces and be swept away.

'Oh my God, Pats, what are you doing?' Jonty was beside her now, his arm over her.

'I can't breathe,' she gasped.

'Sit up and take long, slow breaths,' he ordered. 'Calm down, it'll be all right.'

'Don't come near me,' she said. But she was too feeble to push him off.

Justin was standing there now, too. 'Shall I call an ambulance?' she heard him ask. His voice sounded unreal.

'No,' said Jonty. 'She'll be OK in a minute.'

She found it comforting, somehow, to rock back and forth, tick, tick, tick, rhythmically, like a metronome. To say the same things, over and over.

'I thought you loved me,' she was mumbling. 'All these years I thought you loved me.' Where had the air gone? Her chest felt so tight. 'I thought something was wrong with you,' she continued. Tick, tick, backwards and forwards. 'You weren't into sex. I was actually sorry for you.'

She looked up now and managed a hollow laugh. 'And all the time you were fucking Justin, and now I'll never have another child. It's all gone, everything's gone.'

'No, Pats, it's not like that.' Jonty's voice sounded low, persuasive, comforting.

She took in several gulps of air. That felt good. Her breathing seemed to get slightly easier. The meaning of Jonty's words seeped into her consciousness. She felt angry again. Yes it was like that. Everything was over.

Tick, tick. The rocking got faster. 'No more lies,' she muttered, still not looking at him. 'I can't take any more lies.'

She noticed Justin crouched on the floor beside her, shivering. He had a sheet round him. He pulled it closer. She looked at him and his face was lined, old.

'I'm sorry,' he murmured, not meeting her gaze, staring intently at the floor. 'Don't tell Suzanne. This'll kill her.'

Rage boiled up from Patrice's very core. She stopped rocking and kneeled up in front of him. 'You should have thought of that before you came here, into my bed,' she said. 'Don't imagine I'm going to cover up for you. Poor Suzanne, poor Ruby and Felix. Poor Lara and Ollie. Did you think about them before you sneaked in here with my husband?'

Justin put his face in his hands and started to sob, long, slow sobs. But Patrice didn't care.

'I love them so much,' he was saying. 'You don't understand.'

'No, I don't,' she spat.

Jonty tried to lift Patrice now, to help her off the floor and over to the bed, but she was having none of it. She writhed away from him and managed to stand up. To her surprise she felt suddenly powerful. Made of air, but powerful. She was ten feet tall.

'Don't you dare try to take me anywhere near that bed, our bed, where you've just had sex with a man,' she hissed. 'At least it could have been a woman, Jonty.'

She turned to her husband now and looked him full in the face. He flinched from her gaze. There was fear in his eyes, which she'd never seen before. He'd never seen her like this before either, she supposed.

'You do realise this is the end?' she said. Her voice was quiet now, commanding. She was fully in control. 'I want a divorce, Jonty,' she went on. 'As soon as possible.'

He took a step forward, opening his mouth to speak. She raised her hand. 'Don't come near me,' she ordered. 'You disgust me.'

He stopped in his tracks. She was glad. She couldn't bear him close. His presence made her shudder. She scarcely recognised him. He was someone or something else.

She stood completely still. Straight and rooted to the spot. 'I want you to pack your bags and leave this minute,' she said, pointing to the door. 'I'm going to call a solicitor.'

Jonty made a choking sound. He was naked. Patrice hadn't even registered that before. His balls were dangling there, like stupid maracas. How had she ever thought him manly? There was nothing manly about him.

He sat down on the end of the bed and hung his head. His blond hair flopped over his face. She ignored him. She turned to Justin now, who seemed to have shrunk. His face was white. Why did she ever think he was handsome? He was hideous, snivelling. She had nothing but contempt for him.

'Leave my house,' she told Justin. 'And you'd better think, quick, what you're going to say to Suzanne. I'm going to call her now, in the office, tell her to come home immediately.'

Patrice walked towards the door, leaving the two men in silence. Justin was on the floor, a sheet wrapped round him, Jonty on the bed, naked.

'It's all over, for both of you,' Patrice said without turning round. She was surprised how calm she felt. Maybe she'd always known this would happen one day. Maybe she'd prepared herself in some way. Was that why she was able to do it?

She couldn't think about it now. She thought she might collapse soon, but she'd make it downstairs and do what she had to do first. She'd make the necessary phone calls and arrangements. Percy would come over straightaway. You could rely on her.

'You've lost your wives, homes, families, everything,' Patrice went on. She could hear her voice. It was measured, not panicky.

She was at the top of the stairs now. She pictured their faces in there: anxious, frightened. That gave her some satisfaction.

Finally, she raised her voice to make absolutely sure they could hear. To have maximum impact. 'I just hope it was worth it,' she screamed.

Chapter Fifteen

❦

Suzanne had no idea how she managed to get home. She hopped on and off the train in a daze and half walked, half ran towards the house.

She'd been so shocked by the tone in Patrice's voice. She knew something terrible must have happened but Patrice wouldn't say what, only that the children and Justin were safe and no one had been in an accident or died.

Patrice had insisted, though, that Suzanne needed to know something urgently and she couldn't explain on the phone. At first, Suzanne thought Patrice was joking, then she felt worried, then angry.

Why couldn't Patrice just tell her, for God's sake? Whatever it was, it might not be nearly as bad as she made out. It was the not knowing that was frightening.

Suzanne tried to call Justin but he didn't pick up. He didn't reply to her texts, either. That made her more worried. She'd just have to do as Patrice said.

Suzanne glanced at her watch as she hurried up the street. Justin would be collecting Ruby from school now. She couldn't wait to see him, for this to be over. She could see Patrice on the doorstep, waiting for her as she approached.

Patrice looked odd. Sort of wild. A bit like she had that day they'd lost Seamus in the park. It was early September and Suzanne wondered why Patrice wasn't collecting him from school. Maybe he was going to a friend's for tea.

It crossed Suzanne's mind that Patrice might be having a breakdown. God. How did you deal with something like that? She felt for her mobile in her jacket pocket. It was a hot day, but it seemed easier to wear her jacket than to have to carry it. She was aware she was sweating profusely, though.

Suzanne thought she'd better keep the phone close, in case she needed to call someone quick, for help. She glanced around. There was no one else in the street. It was 3.15 p.m., Wednesday afternoon. All the children would be coming home soon and the road would be busy again. That was a relief.

She wondered whether to call Percy, or Carmen. But something made her stop. She sensed that whatever this was, it was between her and Pats. Her stomach lurched, but she scurried on. Up the garden path, through the front door, Patrice following.

They didn't speak until they were in the hall.

'What's this all—' Suzanne didn't get to finish her question.

They stood, facing each other. Patrice's eyes were darting this way and that, as if looking for something. Her words came out in a sort of rasp. 'They were in bed together. Jonty and Justin. I found them in bed together.'

Suzanne didn't understand. 'What are you talking about?'

Patrice leaned against the banisters. She looked as if she could hardly support herself. 'I went home unexpectedly. They were there, in my bed. They'd had sex.'

Suzanne felt her hand fly up; she had no control over it. She slapped Patrice across the cheek. Just as she'd done with Lara that evening. Only much harder. This time she intended to inflict real pain.

'How dare you,' Suzanne said.

Patrice gasped, scrunched up her face, but she didn't move. 'It's true,' she said urgently. 'They've been having an affair. It's been going on for ages. I've known about it . . .' She looked at Suzanne now, but Suzanne didn't recognise her. Who was this strange, demented woman in her hall saying these dreadful things?

'I've known about it for ages,' Patrice repeated. 'But I didn't want to believe it, so I – I pretended it wasn't happening.' She sank down on the floor, hugged her knees, lowered her head.

Suzanne had a powerful urge to kick her, over and over again, to pull her long, blonde hair. She was shocked by the violence of her feelings. She wasn't a violent person.

Patrice's breathing sounded odd, difficult. She was sort of gasping for air. Suddenly Suzanne was sorry for her. She must have gone properly mad. She'd had no idea Patrice was mentally ill. She needed help.

'Why are you telling me this?' Suzanne said gently. 'It's not true.' She realised she sounded more certain than she really felt. That made her afraid.

Patrice looked up. Her face was deathly white but there was something knowing in her expression. 'It is true, Suzanne,' she said quietly. She sounded horribly sane, not mad at all.

Suzanne staggered back and leaned against the wall for support. She heard Patrice speak, but there were a myriad other voices echoing round her brain, bouncing off tissue and bone, asking questions, jostling for attention. Patrice's was the loudest voice, though. It cut through everything.

'I'm so sorry,' she said. 'It's a nightmare. Seamus, you, me, the children. Jonty's gone. I'm all on my own now. You're all on your own, too. Everything's gone, finished. I'm just so sorry.'

They sat in the garden. Justin was on the wooden bench, his elbows on the table in front, head in his hands. It was early evening and the air was still warm.

Percy had come over immediately, swept up all the children, even Lara, and taken them away, Suzanne had no idea where. The park?

They'd guessed something was up, even the little ones, and hadn't wanted to go. It was amazing how children picked up on things, Suzanne thought. They were far more sensitive than she gave them credit for sometimes.

But, despite their protests, Suzanne had been firm, even fierce. To her relief, Lara had helped. She'd bundled Felix into his pushchair, coaxed Ruby, humoured Ollie and tried to make it sound as if they were going to have fun.

The house felt strangely quiet. In other circumstances, Suzanne thought, she and Justin would be celebrating now, enjoying their unexpected freedom, opening a bottle of chilled white wine and racing up to bed.

She was on a chair opposite him. It didn't seem real, what he was saying. She kept waiting for him to explain everything and make it all right. Or for her to wake up.

'I'm attracted to men as well as women,' she heard him whisper. He kept his head in his hands, didn't look at her. He seemed to be in pain. 'I always have been,' he went on. 'For as long as I can remember, anyway. I can't explain. It's just the way I am. I'm so sorry, Suzanne.'

She was light-headed. She felt a rush of pity. She was so sorry for him. She got up and put her arms round his shoulders. He leaned his head against her and she smoothed his hair with her hand.

He must have been so troubled, in such a terrible, lonely place all these years, she thought. On his own, unable to tell her. Unable to talk to anyone.

She shook her head, struggling to understand. 'We'll get through this somehow,' she said. But it was mechanical, the way she said it. She didn't know how they'd get through it. She didn't know if she really meant it or even wanted to mean it.

Her mind was racing so fast, her brain hurt. She thought any minute the ground might start to rumble, split open and she'd fall through. She thought she was going mad.

Suzanne left Justin's side and sat down again. 'Has it all been a lie, then?' she said softly, staring at the man opposite.

New thoughts were constantly forcing their way in, pushing the old ones out. It was taking a while for the pain to register but it was getting worse. She could feel it getting steadily worse.

She wasn't crying. She'd do her crying later. Still he didn't look at her.

'Has it all been a lie, Justin?' she repeated. 'You, me? Why did you marry me if you knew? It's so cruel.'

He shook his head. 'You don't understand. I love you and the children so much. I knew I wanted you as soon as I met you. I wanted to be with you for ever. I still do.' He sighed. 'I've found it very stressful at home, with Lara mainly. And looking after the other children. You coming home so late, bringing work home at the weekends, too. It was all getting to me, I think. I – I wanted to do it, I wouldn't have had it any other way, but it was such a relief to go out and play squash. I really enjoyed it. It was an escape, a way of working off my frustrations. Then Jonty started coming on to me. He was very persuasive, wouldn't take no for an answer.'

Suzanne butted in, suddenly angry. 'So it's all his fault, is it?' she said. 'Surely you don't expect me to believe that?'

Justin shook his head. 'I'm not saying that. I did fancy him, I'll admit.'

Fancy? It sounded extraordinary. Utterly alien. How could he, her husband, even say it, let alone feel it? He didn't seem to register her shock, just kept staring at the table.

'And in the end I gave in,' he went on. 'But it was a physical thing, not an emotional one. I never felt for him what I feel for you.'

Suzanne closed her eyes. It was a nightmare, surely? Was this really the same man she loved and thought she knew so well? It was slightly more bearable with her eyes closed.

'I tried to break it off several times, Suze,' Justin insisted. 'I felt so terribly guilty. I was terrified of losing you. It was all getting too much, he was always calling, wanting to see me. I think he was obsessed, to be honest.

'I'm not the first one, either. He says he's never been attracted to women, that's why he used to stay away on business such a lot – he'd find men and take them back to his hotel.'

Suzanne shuddered. She wished she had her coat, but she couldn't go and get it, couldn't move from the spot.

'So why did he marry Patrice then?' she whispered. She realised she was clenching her fists and digging her nails into the palms of her hands. But the pain was a relief. It distracted her from the real pain seeping through her.

Justin shrugged. 'Couldn't accept he was gay, I suppose. Didn't want the world to know. Afraid to tell his family, mostly. They're very traditional.'

Suzanne felt sick, as if she was going down with something. Maybe she had a serious illness; maybe she was feverish, hallucinating.

'Poor Patrice,' she said. 'He's just used her.'

Justin shifted in his seat, his head still in his hands. 'I think he does love her,' he said quietly. 'But not in that way, not physically. He started saying stupid stuff to me, like he'd kill himself if I ended it. It frightened me. I didn't know what to do, so I just let it carry on.

'I – I wanted to tell you, but I was too scared. Well,' he said, with a bitter laugh, 'you certainly know now. I suppose you'll want me to move out?'

Suzanne was confused. Her brain was so overloaded she thought it might explode. Justin move out? How could she live without him? It wasn't possible. She loved him.

Justin with Jonty? How could she live with him? Did he mean it when he said there was no emotional attachment? Did that make it any better?

'Have there been others?' she asked, swallowing. Did she really want to know? But she needed to.

He folded his arms across his chest and hunched further forward over the table. 'Only one, when I was at boarding school,' he said simply. 'An older boy. It was just a silly, adolescent thing. There's been no one since then.'

She opened her mouth, but he interrupted her. 'Let me say one more thing,' he pleaded. He stared at her now, with those precious, beautiful eyes. He looked so sad. Broken. She wanted to hit him. She hated him. She wanted to twine her legs, her arms around him and crush his head against her heart.

'I just want to say that I still love you, Suzie,' he said. 'I've been a fool. An utter fool. I've made a terrible mistake and I've cheated on you. I don't deserve your forgiveness. Lots of people have affairs...'

She opened her mouth again but he raised his hand to stop her.

'I'm not saying it's right,' he continued, 'but they do. The difference is mine was with a man, not a woman.'

Suzanne covered her face with her hands. Why did she feel so cold? She'd never been so cold. 'It's a pretty big difference,' she said.

Justin nodded. 'It's a lot to accept, but I'm not gay, Suze. I suppose I'm bisexual, but more heterosexual than gay. That's only a small part of me, though, the bisexuality. I want us to stay together. I want to keep the family together. If you can forgive me? If I promise, faithfully, it won't happen again? Will you think about it, at least? Please?'

She took a deep breath. She didn't know what to do. Something occurred to her. 'What about AIDS?' she hissed. 'You might have given me AIDS. You bastard.'

He swallowed. 'No, Suze, honestly. We wore condoms. It was quite safe.'

Suzanne was quiet for a moment. There was so much to consider. 'What'll we tell the children?' she blurted. 'What'll we say to them?' She could feel anger bubbling up inside.

'Did you think about how they'd feel, the effect on them, before you decided to shag another man?'

She pictured Jonty's white, freckled arms, the gold Rolex, the thick, sandy hair on his legs. Tried to push the image from her mind. 'It's disgusting,' she spat. Now, for the first time, tears sprang into her eyes.

Justin was silent, hunched over the table still, fetal. There was nothing he could say to comfort her.

She wanted someone to take control, to tell her what to do, but there was no one. Instinctively, she twisted the white gold wedding ring off her finger. It came off easily because her hands were icy. She stood up and threw it straight at him, with all her force.

She saw him flinch as it hit him on the shoulder. She hoped it hurt, or stung at least. It bounced off and landed some-where – on the grass maybe. There was no noise.

Justin left the table and got down on his hands and knees to look for it. She could hear he was crying.

'I need to think,' she said. She'd concentrate on the prac-ticalities. 'I'd like you to sleep in the spare room. For the children's sake, I don't want you to move out yet. I'll tell them you snore and I'm exhausted, I need sleep.'

He nodded, on all fours still, searching.

'In front of them, we'll be civil, friendly,' Suzanne went on. 'I don't want the younger ones to get a whiff of anything, you understand? I don't want to upset them any more than necessary.'

He nodded again. Let out a sob.

'But you mustn't see Jonty,' she said. She could hardly bring herself to utter his name. 'Not all the while we're under the same roof.'

Justin found the ring. He seemed relieved. He held it tight in his fist, stood up, looked at her. 'I don't want to see him, Suze,' he said. His eyes were pleading. 'You've got to believe me, it's over. And I'm glad. Like I said, I wanted it to be over a long time ago, I just couldn't seem to get out. I don't want anyone but you.'

She didn't know if she believed him. It was irrelevant really, anyway. He'd slept with another man. That was what mattered.

She rose slowly. Her body felt so heavy. She swayed slightly, steadying herself on the table. She'd never felt so tired. How was she supposed to function at work tomorrow? Maybe she wouldn't go. But she wanted to keep things as calm, as normal as possible – for the children. She couldn't make any decisions now.

'I need to go to bed,' she told Justin. 'I don't feel well. You'll have to call Percy and settle the kids down when they come back.'

She wished her mother lived close by, but at least there was Percy, and Carmen. She wondered for a second about Patrice but she pushed her from her mind. She couldn't think about her. She didn't know what she thought about her. She, Suzanne, had enough problems.

'I might go away for a few days,' she said. 'We'll talk about it tomorrow.'

Justin followed her indoors.

Later, she heard the children return. She wondered what Justin said to Percy at the door. In any case, Percy didn't come in.

'Where's Mummy?' she heard Ruby ask.

'She's not feeling well,' Justin replied.

Ruby started to protest.

'Come on, Ruby, let's go for a bath,' Ollie said in his squeaky, growly voice.

Bless him, Suzanne thought. He's trying to help. He must be so confused and worried.

Suzanne lay in bed, in their cool, white bed, and closed her eyes. For a moment she imagined Justin climbing in beside her, smiling that mischievous smile, stroking her hair, putting his soft, warm lips on hers.

Then she saw Jonty's face, his big, white body, imagined him with Justin, her Justin. It was too much to bear.

A vision of her ex, Frank, swam in front of her now, and collided with the other images. They fragmented. She remembered how Frank had cheated on her. She'd imagined she'd never hurt like that again, but this was worse, much worse. Justin was her soulmate. Frank had never been that.

She buried her head in her pillow and stuffed the white cotton into her mouth so no one would hear. Tore at the sheets with her fingers. Sobbed until her throat hurt, her eyes stung, her cheeks ached. Until she could sob no more.

Hours later, Suzanne heard the bedroom door open. She wasn't asleep. She jumped. He wouldn't dare.

'Who's that?' she said, frightened.

'Only me.' Lara clambered in beside her mother and wrapped her arms around her. She smelled of shampoo and soap and young, sweet skin.

Suzanne put her head on Lara's breast. She was wearing a cotton top. Lara stroked her mother's hair softly. 'There, there,' she crooned. 'It'll be all right.' Just as Suzanne had done with Lara when she was a small child.

Suzanne was aware she was shaking. She couldn't seem to get warm. Lara tucked the duvet round her mother more tightly, like a baby.

'Percy's told you?' Suzanne asked.

'She had to,' Lara replied. 'I made her. I'm not a baby any more.'

Suzanne nodded in the darkness. It was a relief, really. She couldn't have kept it secret from Lara for long.

'I loved him so much,' Suzanne said. 'I feel like my life's over.'

Lara held her closer. Suzanne could hear her daughter's heart beating. It was strangely comforting. 'Don't worry,

Mum,' Lara whispered. 'You'll get through this, we all will. As a family. We're strong, you'll see.'

Suzanne's body shuddered with another sob. 'I don't know how I can live without him,' she said.

'Don't think about it now,' Lara murmured. 'You don't need to make any decisions straight away.'

That was true.

A thought crossed Suzanne's mind. 'Did you know about Justin and Jonty?' she asked. She had to know. It was imperative she knew. She sat up, shaking Lara off. 'You once implied something,' she said. She could hear the urgency in her own voice. 'I couldn't understand it at the time. I thought you were just being vicious. You asked, didn't I ever wonder what Justin got up to when I was at work? Lara, did you know something?'

Lara paused. Suzanne could almost hear her brain whirring. 'No, I didn't *know*,' Lara said finally. 'But I did think it was odd, the way Jonty kept phoning. The way Justin looked sort of guilty when they spoke. Miserable. I suppose I kind of suspected, but I didn't really think it could be true. It seemed too far-fetched.'

Lara started to cry. 'I'm so sorry, Mum,' she said. 'I've been such a bitch. Selfish. Thinking about my own problems when yours are so much bigger. I've been horrid to Justin, too. Ever since he came to live with us I've pushed him away. And he was always so good to me. I kind of feel it's my fault this has happened. If I'd been nicer, maybe Justin wouldn't have had an affair. Maybe none of this would have happened.'

It was Suzanne's turn, now, to comfort her daughter. She hugged her close, rocking her in her arms. 'Don't be silly,' Suzanne whispered. 'Of course it's not your fault. How could it be? I'm afraid I just have rotten taste in men.'

Lara stopped crying. She sounded fierce. 'No you don't, Mum,' she said. 'Don't ever say that. Justin's the kindest, sweetest, most lovely man I've ever met. He's done a terrible thing to you and I hate him for it, but I know for a fact that he'll be devastated by what he's done. I'm sure if he could turn the clock back, he would. I know he loves you.'

Suzanne thought for a moment. She guessed Lara was right. Justin probably would turn the clock back but, sadly, that wasn't possible. It was all over now.

Suzanne shuffled down under the covers. Lara did the same.

'I love you, Mum,' Lara said. 'I'll do anything I can to help.'

'I love you too, Lara,' Suzanne replied.

There was a pause. 'Mum?' came a small voice.

Suzanne was just starting to drift off at last. 'Yes, Lara?'

'You know on my birthday when you came home and I was behaving really oddly, really out of it?'

'Mmm,' Suzanne replied.

'Well, it wasn't just drink,' Lara admitted. 'I'd had a big fat spliff as well.'

Suzanne sighed. 'Oh well,' she said. 'I'm glad you've told me.' It would have mattered so much, just a few hours ago, but now it was nothing. Funny how she'd got so hung up on details.

'Mum, are you OK?' Ollie appeared now at the door, in a T-shirt and boxers. He looked very tall and gangly in the gloom. He sounded anxious.

'Not really,' Suzanne said truthfully.

'I can't sleep. Can I come in your bed?' he asked.

How could she say no? He hadn't done this since he was about eight.

He felt big and sort of knobbly on the other side from Lara. Suzanne felt a rush of love.

The three of them fell asleep, finally, to the sound of birds twittering in the trees outside, getting ready for the new day: Suzanne, Lara and Ollie locked in each others' arms, as if their lives depended on not letting go.

PART III

Revolution

A group cycling class that is an excellent cardiovascular workout. It is non-impact but high intensity and will take your fitness levels to a new height.

Chapter One

✦

'Lie on your back, abs in tight, arms by your sides. Now put your legs in table-top position, grip your thighs and I want you to roll back in a little ball and get your legs as far behind your heads as you can. Try to use your lower abs, not your arms or momentum.'

Percy groaned. This was a new one. She managed to get her legs right back over her head so her feet were almost touching the floor behind. But she could feel an uncomfortable wedge of flab bunching round her middle and compressing her lungs.

And how you were supposed to do it without using your arms or momentum, she had no idea.

'Now,' said the teacher, Jill, strictly 'Open your legs wide and roll down, slowly, slowly, one bone at a time. When you reach your lower back, close your legs and lower them, slowly, on to the floor.

'Try to keep them as straight as possible without arching your back, but if you have to bend a little at the knee, no worries.'

Ouch. Percy grimaced. Her knees were bent but it was still incredibly hard. Her stomach wanted to pop out. She gripped as tightly as she could.

'It gets easier,' Jill promised. 'You can practise it as homework.'

The class tittered. Homework. Thanks very much, Percy thought.

She'd felt she must go to Saturday morning Pilates. It might help save her sanity. But it seemed strange with no Suzanne or Patrice. Percy felt almost guilty for enjoying herself, if enjoy was the right word.

She glanced over at Carmen and smiled. Carmen caught her eye and smiled back. It felt as if they'd been swept up in a ferocious storm, the pair of them. They'd been phoning each other constantly, trying to agree what was best, how they could help most.

They were pretty baffled, though. Percy felt fairly useless. It's not as if there were any self-help books on the subject. All she could really do was be there.

'Now we'll add on to that,' Jill piped up. 'Lie on your backs, pull up your knees and tuck your feet in as close as you can to your bums. Roll up, bone by bone, until you're resting on your shoulders, not your necks. Really squeeze your bum and thighs.

'Now, slowly straighten one leg, without losing your balance or shifting to one side.' She paused. 'Then the other leg.

'Now roll down, slowly, slowly, curl up into a lovely little ball and put your legs over your heads again. Beautiful.'

Percy felt she'd had a really good workout by the end of the class. She and Carmen passed by the weights machines on the way out.

'Look!' Carmen squealed. 'There's a picture of you!'

Percy glanced over to the wall on the left, near the staff door. It was where they pinned up notices about events, new classes and so on.

There, on a big white sheet of paper, in technicolour, was her photo, the one they'd taken for her membership card. She had a rather silly grin. Above her face, in big letters, she read: 'Member of the Month'.

Percy was shocked. She didn't know anything about this. She looked closer. Below her photo, in smaller letters, was a paragraph of writing. It said:

Member: Persephone Redpath
Age: 44.

Percy shuddered. Seeing it there in black and white made her feel so, well, old. Did they really have to? She tended to draw a veil over her age. Now it was there for all the world to see. There was no getting away from it.

She read on:

According to our records, Persephone has been to the gym three times a week for the past month. She has been nominated by Gym and Slimline instructor, Romy, who says: 'Persephone always works hard in class and her fitness has visibly improved. Now she needs to up her cardiovascular work to continue to improve her muscle-to-fat ratio and strengthen muscle tone further.' Congratulations, Persephone. Keep it up!

Bloody cheek! Percy thought. Improve her muscle-to-fat ratio indeed. Were they calling her porky?

It was quite fun to have been picked out for good attendance, though. She felt almost like a celebrity, albeit a 44-year-old one, as she strolled into the changing room. Would anyone want her autograph?

She was surprised when she entered the café to see Carmen on the sofa with her arm round Millicent, who appeared to be sobbing into a hankie.

'What's the matter?' Percy asked.

There were quite a lot of other people about, but they were looking away politely.

Carmen looked up, her arm still round Millicent. 'Tiff with Danny,' Carmen mouthed.

Percy nodded. 'Men can be horrible, can't they?' she said, trying to be sisterly. She felt almost sorry for Millicent, even though she was a cow. She couldn't help being one, Percy supposed. She was probably just born like that.

Millicent raised her head. Her eyes were all red and her hankie looked soaking, a wet, messy blob.

'We were supposed to be going to the zoo today with the kids,' she sniffed, 'but he called to say he had to see his mum. I don't believe him. I think he's having an affair.'

Millicent virtually shouted the word 'affair'. She sounded so outraged that Percy was momentarily swept up in her indignation. Then Percy remembered it was actually because of Millicent's affair with Danny that her husband had chucked her out.

Life was complicated. It was probably best not to get involved. 'Don't worry,' Percy said soothingly. 'Danny'll probably call tonight and take you out for a really nice meal.'

Millicent narrowed her eyes. She looked really scary. 'Yeah, well, he's got some explaining to do, that's for sure,' she said. 'I'll kill him if I find out he's been cheating.'

Percy got up. 'Er, skinny latte and a choccy muffin, anyone?'

Lucian, the grumpy barman, was in a surprisingly good mood. 'Trying to fatten up Millicent, are we?' He grinned, passing Percy the muffins. 'Naughty naughty.'

Everyone knew Lucian felt he should be writing poetry rather than serving skinny lattes. He was a frustrated artist. He looked as if he could do with a good dinner, too, Percy thought. And a good woman to share it with. He was frustrated in more ways than one.

'You women, you're all the same,' Lucian went on, shaking his head. The collar of his white shirt was far too big for his neck. 'You're constantly trying to make poor Millie eat cakes. Trouble is, you end up eating them yourselves, which rather defeats the purpose, I imagine.'

Percy laughed. 'True,' she said. 'They're bloody good muffins, though.'

Millicent must be feeling bad, because she actually took a cake today. She ate it very slowly, Percy noticed, picking out the chocolate bits first, licking off the sugar, nibbling round the sides. You'd think it was from the world's top bakery.

She obviously hadn't had one in a very long time. Do her good, Percy thought. She might get a taste for them, too. Ha! Gain a few bulges.

'They're both in a terrible state,' Carmen said, shaking her head. Millicent was too busy relishing her muffin to pay much attention.

'I spoke to Patrice this morning,' Carmen went on, 'and I think she's the worst. She says she can't eat or sleep. Jonty keeps phoning, asking her to forgive him, but she's adamant she'll never have him back.'

'Good thing too,' Percy muttered. 'He's obviously been at it for years behind her back. What a bastard.'

Carmen nodded. 'But by the sounds of things, Justin's a bit different. He's not been picking up boys in Manchester, anyway.'

Percy took a sip of coffee. 'I know,' she said. 'But you couldn't forgive him, could you? I mean, it's such a betrayal. Far worse than if it had been a woman. I'll pop round and see them both this afternoon. How do they feel about each other, do you think?'

Carmen grimaced. 'Suzanne still says she couldn't possibly speak to Patrice right now. I don't know about the other way round. I haven't spoken to Patrice about it recently.'

Percy felt sad. 'But why does Suzanne feel like that? It's hardly Patrice's fault.'

'Yeah,' Carmen replied. 'But Suzanne says she can't help feeling that Patrice somehow colluded with them, by not talking about her fears. Suzanne knows it's not rational, but she feels this great aversion, as if she can't quite separate Patrice from Jonty, or Jonty from Patrice. It's complicated. I don't suppose any of us knows how we'd feel or react in that situation unless it happened to us.'

Percy realised she was biting her fingernails. There were none left now, though, so she started on the skin round her nails. All this high drama was wreaking havoc with her stress levels.

'It's tragic.' She sighed. 'Just when they need each other the most, they couldn't be further apart. I wonder if they can ever be friends again.'

Lorna, one of the girls from reception, walked by. She was wearing a regulation white shirt and black trousers. She smiled at Percy. 'Where are your mates? Aren't you normally the fab four on a Saturday?'

Percy smiled back. 'They couldn't make it today,' she said. She tried to look casual, but she felt miserable. Would they ever be the fab four again?

Carmen wiped the crumbs from her mouth and stood up. 'I have to get Ivy from the crèche,' she explained.

Percy rose, too. She'd paid for an extra half-hour for Rowan but she wasn't going to be left alone with Millicent. She couldn't face it.

'Sorry, Millicent, we have to go,' Percy said.

Millicent stayed sitting. 'That muffin was really good,' she said, licking her lips. 'I think I might have another one.'

'Good idea.' Percy beamed treacherously. 'The blueberry ones are good and so are the strawberry. Why not have one of each – you deserve it.'

'What are you up to today?' Percy asked Carmen as they picked up their sports bags.

'Simon's coming round,' Carmen said. Was there a sparkle in her eye? Percy feared so.

'Just you be careful,' Percy said severely, wagging her finger at Carmen. She couldn't deal with this as well. It was all too much. 'For goodness' sake, remember what I've told you,' she warned.

Carmen nodded. 'Yes, Mum.' She grinned. 'There'll be absolutely no naughty business whatsoever.'

When she saw Jonty's car in the drive, Percy almost turned round and drove out again. But the thought of Patrice coping with this on her own forced her to stay.

Percy parked her ancient khaki Land Rover and got out. It rattled a bit, these days, but it still went. The kids loved sitting up in the back, with the canvas flapping, the wind whistling through their hair. It was a bit different from Jonty's luxurious BMW.

Percy dreaded seeing Jonty again. She didn't know what on earth she'd say to him. It helped to remind herself he was still human and had feelings just like everybody else. He wasn't some alien, for heaven's sake. In fact, she was even a tiny bit sorry for him. After all, he didn't choose to be gay.

His big mistake was not having the courage years ago to accept it and face up to his friends and family. It was cruel of him, really, to have married Patrice, though perhaps he'd sincerely believed he could make it work. But it was incredibly cruel to have had an affair with Patrice's great friend's husband. That was the most unforgivable thing, Percy thought. The truth was, she didn't really understand any of it.

Patrice said she'd sort of suspected. But did Suzanne, as she claimed, really have no inkling that Justin might be attracted to men? It was too much to get your head round.

Patrice seemed relieved to see Percy. She looked pale and gaunt: so fragile that Percy made a mental note to cook some casseroles for her, a shepherd's pie or two. Percy was rather ashamed of her minuscule kitchen repertoire, but everyone said her shepherd's pies and casseroles were the best. Patrice could freeze them and have them when she wanted. She needed to eat, that was clear. She wasn't looking after herself properly.

The practical things Percy thought she could manage. It was the emotional support she was finding difficult. Half the time she just didn't know what to say, didn't know how best to advise.

'Jonty's packing some of his stuff upstairs,' Patrice explained, passing Percy a mug of Earl Grey. 'Then I've said he can take Seamus to the cinema.' She frowned. This was going to be difficult for her, letting Seamus go.

'How's Seamus coping?' Percy asked, sipping her tea.

They were sitting on the oak bench seats at Patrice's kitchen table. The house was spotless, as usual. Cleaner still coming twice a week by the looks of things. The white tiles on the floor were sparkling.

A thought flashed through Percy's mind: how on earth did Jonty manage to cover his tracks after he and Justin had been in bed together? Jonty must have spent ages tidying up, smoothing down the sheets and duvet, so Patrice wouldn't notice. Mark would never be able to get away with it. He never made the bed properly. But then Jonty always had been fastidious. Patrice had told her so.

'Seamus is very upset,' Patrice commented. 'He just keeps asking when Daddy's going to come back. I've told him he can see Daddy every weekend and that seems to help. It's why I've agreed, of course. I'd be relieved never to have to see Jonty again.'

Jonty appeared now at the kitchen door. Percy felt hot and prickly. He seemed smaller, less stocky. The confident, cocky air had gone and his blond hair was longer, less kempt.

He was wearing an olive-green cashmere sweater and brown corduroy trousers. His black slip-on shoes were polished to a shine. He swept his hair off his face with his hand; Percy noticed the gold signet ring, the Rolex watch. It seemed quite a girly sort of gesture. She wondered why she'd never thought so before.

She got up and kissed him on both cheeks. She couldn't

be hostile. After all, everyone has faults, and he'd spent enough time round her table, eating and laughing. Let him without sin and all that.

His face was surprisingly soft, Percy thought. He flinched, as if he thought she was going to wallop him.

'I'm so sorry about all this,' was all she could say.

He stepped back, shrugged. His eyes looked hollowed out. 'I've packed most of my remaining clothes,' he told Patrice matter-of-factly. 'I'll get the rest next weekend.'

Patrice went into the utility room and emerged with what looked like a pair of white squash shorts. 'Don't forget these,' she said. She gripped them with her finger and thumb, holding them as far from her as possible. She had a look of disgust on her face.

Jonty took them from her and walked quickly from the room without speaking.

Percy shivered. 'Is there absolutely no hope of reconciliation then?' she asked nervously.

'Absolutely none,' Patrice replied. 'He told me he's always been gay, never really enjoyed sex with women. After all these years of marriage, how do you think that makes me feel?'

She sounded bitter. Furious. Percy wondered where all that anger would go.

Once Jonty and Seamus had left the house, Percy said she'd go, too. Patrice had paperwork to do. She was seeing the solicitor on Monday and said she needed to be alone to clear her head. Percy understood.

She rang Suzanne's bell. The blue paint on the door was all chipped. You could see old red paint coming through. She could hear Ruby and Felix inside, rushing down the hall.

'No, I'm going to answer it, Felix,' Ruby said bossily.

'Me, me,' Felix shouted.

There was a bang and he started to cry.

'Stop it,' Suzanne said crossly. She opened the door with Felix in her arms, still sobbing.

'Here,' she said to him. 'Percy's come to see you.' Gratifyingly, Felix's chubby face lit up in a huge grin.

Suzanne led Percy into the sitting room. Percy had to pick her way round Felix's train set and his knights' castle. She was worried she might tread on something precious.

Suzanne looked ghastly. She was white-faced; her hair was sticking up all over in a frizzy mess. The remains of breakfast were smeared down her front. Felix's probably, Percy thought.

'Anything you need?' Percy asked.

Suzanne shook her head. 'Justin's still doing the shopping and stuff,' she explained. 'Though for how much longer, I'm not sure. We haven't made any major decisions yet.'

Her voice was trembly and Percy could see her hands were shaking. She was a shambles. This was terrible, Percy thought. Her two dearest friends were a complete mess.

'Would Ruby like to come and play with Rowan this afternoon?' Percy suggested. That might be some help, at least. 'I can have Felix, too, if you think he'll be happy.'

Felix was sitting on the carpet, playing with his Lego knights. He looked up and pulled a face. 'No go,' he said.

Suzanne looked apologetic. 'Sorry, he's very clingy at the moment.'

'It's understandable.' Percy smiled. She took Suzanne's hand. It felt small, and cold. 'Do you think you'll get a divorce?' she asked.

Suzanne shrugged. 'We've been together seven years. We have two children. There's an awful lot there. One minute I think it's over, the next I think it's too good just to throw away. We've talked a lot, but we're going round and round in circles.'

Percy frowned. She couldn't imagine how she'd react. At least they were talking, though. 'Have you thought of counselling?' she asked. Maybe there was some hope. Or maybe, if they did split up, it would help them manage things better.

Suzanne nodded. 'Justin's agreed and I think it's worth a try. We've found a marriage therapist. The first session's on Tuesday.'

'Good,' said Percy. She felt relieved. Get the professionals in, that was her view. She was scared of saying the wrong thing and making matters worse. 'Don't rush into anything,' she added. 'Give yourselves as much time as you need.'

Percy was exhausted by the time she got home. The boys were playing snakes and ladders on the sitting-room floor.

'Cup of tea?' Mark asked. She sank down gratefully on the friendly old olive sofa.

'It's all such a horrible mess,' she said sadly. 'So much unhappiness. I wish I could help more.'

Mark sat down beside her and patted her knee. 'Don't be hard on yourself. You're doing everything you can, Pers. You're a wonderful friend.'

The phone rang. Mark told the boys to ignore it. 'If it's important they'll leave a message or call back.'

Percy protested for a moment. 'It might be Pats, or Suzanne.'

Mark shook his head. 'We need an evening to ourselves for once. We deserve it.'

She knew he was right. Once the boys were in bed they sat together, his arm round her, watching a comedy repeat. It could have been almost anything: Percy didn't care. She was just grateful to do something mindless.

She thought how lovely the sitting room felt, all warm and homely. She'd replaced the broken photo frames and got copies of the photos that she hadn't been able to salvage.

She had plenty of teaching work lined up; Mark had had some lucrative jobs; the overdraft was coming down; Ben had was calmed down and both boys were doing well at school. She'd stopped spending, too. And, more importantly, she hadn't played poker. She'd discovered Sudoku instead. It didn't deliver quite the same hit, but it kept her occupied in the evenings once she'd done her marking. She'd become quite obsessed. Mark was still working incredibly hard, but he was less grumpy. She appreciated that.

'We're so lucky,' she said, snuggling into him. He was wearing his red tartan brushed-cotton shirt. She loved him in it. She thought it made him look like a big, cuddly bear. 'Our problems are nothing compared with what Pats and Suzanne are going through.'

Mark kissed the top of his wife's head. 'I know,' he said. 'We are incredibly lucky. And I do love you. Despite all your faults, of which there are many.' He chuckled.

'I love you too,' Percy replied, meaning it. 'Even though you're absolutely maddening as well.'

There was a pause, while they watched the TV. 'By the way,' Mark said, when the adverts started, 'I spoke to Zeus earlier. He told me to tell you that if you don't get your arse over to Hertfordshire or arrange to have lunch with him in London soon, he'll come here and forcibly drag you from the house.'

Percy smiled. 'I've got an awful lot to make up to him,' she said sadly.

'Just pick up the phone,' Mark urged. 'He says he'd do the same thing tomorrow if you asked – about the money, I mean.'

Percy sighed. 'I just feel so embarrassed – and ashamed . . .'

Mark shook his head. 'Think of Zeus,' he scolded gently, 'not yourself. He really misses you.'

She nodded. 'I will.'

'Promise?'

Percy opened her mouth. Closed it again.

'I promise.'

Chapter Two

Carmen hadn't dared tell Percy at Gym and Slimline earlier in the day that she'd invited Simon for dinner. Percy would have been furious.

But Simon had been behaving so well: calling regularly; taking Ivy out for walks. And now the money was going into Carmen's bank account, too. It did make a difference; it took the pressure off. And he was Ivy's father, after all. Percy didn't seem to understand that. She thought it was somehow unimportant.

'Kir?' Carmen asked, holding up a bottle of champagne. 'Or would you rather have a beer?'

'Beer,' Simon replied.

She was aware of him watching as she bent over to get a bottle from the bottom of the fridge. She was glad she'd put on her new, sexy little denim mini-skirt. She knew he'd appreciate it. The weather was so warm still, she had bare legs and feet, and a loose white shirt on top because she was still breastfeeding.

'How's Ivy?' Simon asked.

Carmen stood up and handed him the beer. 'Asleep,' she said. 'She usually goes down around seven now. It's such a relief to have my evenings back.'

Simon nodded, sat down at the kitchen table and helped himself to a handful of crisps from a bowl. He was wearing a bold pink and red striped shirt with several buttons undone. Carmen could see some of his silver-grey chest hair poking out.

He was sitting in that arrogant, male way, with his legs wide apart. Carmen was cross with herself for finding it sexy, but she did. She couldn't help it. He looked so confident, in control, as if he owned the place.

She lit some candles and dotted them round the room. 'It's only pasta, I'm afraid,' she said, putting a bowl of nuts in front of him to keep him going. 'I don't have time to cook these days. Ivy wants all my attention.'

Simon grinned. 'I know how she feels.'

He got up and put his hands on Carmen's waist, pulling her to him. He towered over her, which she liked. 'I haven't come here for the food, you know,' he whispered, his lips brushing her hair.

For a moment, Carmen allowed herself to breathe in that familiar smell, enjoy the feeling of his warm body against hers. Reluctantly, she wriggled away. 'I have to lay the table,' she said.

While she got out the knives and forks, Simon wandered into the sitting room. Dido's soft, wistful voice drifted through the flat. He'd picked out *Life for Rent*, one of Carmen's favourites.

She filled a saucepan with water, washed salad, chopped onions and peppers. This must be what it was like for married couples every night, she thought happily. You put the baby to bed and then had dinner together, all cosy.

She remembered Patrice and Suzanne and shuddered. They hadn't had normal marriages at all. She felt so sorry for them and wished she could do more to help. But some husbands and wives must get it right, surely, she thought? And Percy and Mark didn't seem to be doing too badly.

Carmen dropped the onions and peppers into a pan of sizzling oil and stirred. Thanks to Ivy, everything seemed so much simpler these days. She felt almost guilty for being so happy while Patrice and Suzanne were suffering.

For Carmen, that drifting, the sense of purposelessness,

had gone. It all seemed to make so much more sense now: marriage, babies. Somehow even the ballet seemed less important, the disappointment less acute.

She no longer even envied Hannah from ballet school all those years ago. Hannah's career was over now, anyway. Carmen had read something about her in the press. She'd given up dancing about five years ago and now she'd retired from teaching, too. Carmen, on the other hand, felt as if her career was just beginning.

But what was she doing, even thinking about marriage? It was ridiculous.

'How are your parents?' Simon called through from the sitting room. Carmen wondered if he'd noticed the postcard that had arrived this morning from Spain. She'd propped it up on the shelves by the French doors.

'Fine,' she called back. 'They're in Spain, visiting Mum's relatives.'

'It's just a thought, only a thought,' Dido sang. Carmen hummed along, boiled the kettle, poured the penne into the saucepan. The sauce was ready so she took it off the heat. It was just a question of waiting for the pasta, now.

'Well I deserve nothin' more than I get . . .' chanted Dido.

Carmen decided she could safely join Simon for a few minutes. He was sitting in her Philippe Starck perspex Louis Ghost Chair. It was a statement piece, she'd told Percy, Suzanne and Patrice, when they'd looked doubtful. It had turned out to be surprisingly practical, too, not that Carmen had practicality in mind when she'd bought it.

Ivy had got hold of some multicoloured crayons and coloured all over it. Carmen had been horrified but, happily, the crayons had washed off. She felt the company could benefit from a new marketing drive, to highlight the chair's child-friendly qualities. Ivy had discovered the chair turned into an excellent light pushable wagon when yanked down on to its side, too.

Carmen expected Simon to be browsing through her books or something. But he had a letter in his hand. The envelope was on the floor beside the chair.

'Cos nothin' I have is truly mine, nothin' I have is truly mine . . .' Dido crooned.

Simon looked up from reading and waved the letter at Carmen. 'Why didn't you tell me about this?' he said. He sounded accusing.

She caught sight of the hospital logo. It must be her appointment for laser treatment. She'd put it in its envelope on the shelf, beside the card from her parents.

She gasped and snatched the letter from his hand. 'What are you doing?' she said. 'That's private. You shouldn't have opened it.'

Simon ran his hands through his silver hair. He coughed. 'Does this mean you've got, erm, cancer?' he said quietly. 'I had no idea.' He hung his head. He seemed almost sorry for himself.

Carmen was furious. The blood rushed to her cheeks. 'No, I haven't got cancer,' she snapped. 'I've had two dodgy smear tests and a biopsy that showed moderate abnormalities. They want to do some laser treatment, that's all. It's a preventative thing. They like to play safe.'

Simon looked relieved. 'Oh, that's all right then,' he said. 'Good.' He paused and a frown appeared on his forehead. 'But why have you got, you know, abnormal cells?'

Carmen thought she detected a slight shudder. She remembered he hated anything to do with 'women's problems': tampons, thrush, period pains. He could never bear to hear her talking about anything like that.

'I don't know,' she said. A thought occurred to her. 'Sometimes it can be caused by a virus, a sexually transmitted one. Maybe YOU gave it to me, Simon,' she said with a flourish. She was rather pleased with that.

'There's nothing wrong with me,' he retorted hotly. 'Have you been sleeping around?'

Carmen flinched. 'No, but even if I had, it would be none of your business.'

Simon rose and took a step towards her. 'Look, I'm sorry. It was just a shock, that's all,' he said. He tried to give her a hug but she squirmed away. 'Just get yourself sorted out down there, and it'll all be fine,' he went on. 'How long before you're, er, back in business?'

Carmen couldn't believe what she'd just heard. Then, suddenly, she could believe it. Because it was what he'd been like all along, only she hadn't been able to see it.

She drew a deep breath and straightened her shoulders. 'No, Simon, it won't all be fine,' she said. 'I mean, I will be, I'm sure. Lots of people have laser treatment. But you shouldn't have read my letter and God forbid if I really had cancer. You obviously don't do sympathy.'

'I'm sorry,' Simon muttered again. He was staring down – at the ground, Carmen thought. Then she realised it was her legs he was looking at.

She shook her head. 'I'm sorry, Simon,' she said. 'I've made a mistake.' She had to get him out of her flat, fast. She couldn't bear him in here even for another five minutes.

He looked up. He must have noticed something different in her face because he didn't protest. She went on, rapidly. She was almost talking to herself.

'I thought we could maybe make a go of things after all, for Ivy's sake if nothing else,' she said. 'But I was wrong. It would never work. It would be a disaster. Please leave now.'

With relief, she realised she'd got through to him. He didn't speak, didn't try to talk her round. She practically pushed him into the hall, grabbed his jacket from the stand and opened the front door for him.

'I'll ring when I get back from Berlin,' she heard him say before she pulled the door shut.

She rested her back against the stained-glass door. The tears came hot and fast, now. 'Oh God,' she whispered to herself. 'Why am I such a fool? Percy was right. Why did I ever let him back in my life?'

It was comforting to sit at the kitchen table, on her own, in the dark, with just a few candles burning. Dido had long since finished.

Finally she rose and tiptoed into the bedroom she shared with Ivy. The room smelled of talcum powder and nappy cream and baby skin. The little girl was lying on her back, both hands raised above her head, breathing slowly, peacefully. Her mouth was pursed in an O shape. Was she dreaming of milk?

Carmen carefully lowered the edge of the cot, leaned over and gently kissed Ivy's forehead. 'We don't need Daddy,' Carmen whispered. 'Really we don't. We can manage on our own. Everything's going to be all right.'

Ivy stirred in her sleep and made a funny little mewing sound, like a kitten. Carmen tucked the quilt around her tiny daughter, raised the edge of the cot again and tiptoed out of the room.

She went back in the kitchen, drained the pasta that was still slightly warm in the saucepan and chucked it in the bin Then she did the same with the congealed sauce. There was no way she could eat anything now.

She opened the fridge and poured herself a glass of champagne from the bottle she'd opened earlier. She took a swig, but couldn't really taste it.

It was the end of a dream, she knew that. There would definitely be no Carmen and Simon now, no Mr and Mrs, no happy families. That was for other people. Not for her and Ivy. They were destined to be on their own.

She must have done something really bad in a previous life.

Chapter Three

'Mummy, it's you!' Ruby came tumbling towards Suzanne, hair flying. She leaped into her mother's arms, practically knocking her over, before bending down to give her brother Felix a sloppy kiss in his pushchair.

'Good day at school?' Suzanne asked, but Ruby had already forgotten about it. She was on to the next thing. 'Can we go to the swings?' she asked.

Suzanne nodded. 'Would you like a lolly from the van as a special treat?' she suggested.

'I want lolly,' Felix said, perking up immediately. 'Red one.'

Suzanne laughed. 'You can have any colour you like,' she said. 'I'm in a generous mood.'

To be honest, Suzanne was in a permanently generous mood these days, as far as the children were concerned. The little ones hadn't twigged, but she thought she'd probably say yes to anything right now. She had no will to refuse. She was exhausted. She felt defeated. It was all she could do to put one foot in front of the other, to cope with one day, one hour, at a time. She couldn't think ahead or plan anything. It was just a question of surviving, for the children's sake.

Her bosses had given her plenty of time off but she knew she couldn't stay away much longer. She'd have to go back to the office full-time soon. In a way, she wanted to. It was how she'd coped after Frank left, by burying herself in work. But this time it seemed much, much harder. Merely functioning, getting through the day, seemed difficult enough, let alone running a large team of people and making big decisions.

She bought Felix a mini strawberry lolly, especially for toddlers. It was soon all round his face. In the past, Suzanne would have worried about the mess but now it didn't seem to matter. She was just so glad to see him happy.

For a moment, as she pushed the buggy across the road towards the park with Ruby holding on to the side, Suzanne even allowed herself to imagine they were just a normal family making the most of a surprisingly sunny October afternoon. But this was pure fantasy, she knew. There was nothing normal about them really.

The playground was teeming with children, red-faced and dishevelled. Most, like Ruby, were wearing a uniform of grey skirts or trousers, and shirts which were not quite as white as they might have been earlier in the day.

They were making a huge racket, shouting and laughing, grateful to let off steam after hours cooped up in the classroom.

The mothers were standing around the corner of the playground nattering, or pushing younger children on swings and see-saws. It was a merry scene, Suzanne thought.

She wandered over to the swings and lifted Felix in. He liked nothing better than to sit for ages, going up and down, enjoying the breeze, watching the other children play. Ruby, whose lips and tongue were now stained purple from her lolly, skipped over to a multi-coloured roundabout nearby. Suzanne watched her start to push the other children sitting on it.

'Hold on tight,' Ruby shouted, mustering all her strength to make the heavy metal structure turn. 'You're going to the moon!'

It was a moment before Suzanne realised that one of the children squealing with delight on the plastic yellow bench seat was Seamus. Her stomach lurched. This meant Patrice must be here, too. Unless Seamus was with a friend.

What should she do? She scanned the playground and spotted Patrice a little way off, on her own, staring at some children playing football on the green outside the swings.

Patrice was wearing a simple white cotton dress and flip-flops, her blonde hair tied back in a ponytail. She looked very pale, in comparison with the other suntanned mothers, and very thin, as if a puff of wind would knock her over.

Suzanne felt a rush of sympathy. Patrice was going through hell and only she, Suzanne, knew exactly how it felt. Part of her wanted to race over, hug her friend, find and give comfort.

But then she thought of Jonty, and remembered some of the conversations she'd had with Patrice. She hadn't seemed happy for a long time. Maybe if she'd told Suzanne she suspected Jonty was seeing other men, all this might have been prevented. Suzanne might have been able to keep Justin away from that lying, predatory creep.

Deep down, Suzanne knew her reasoning was stupid. Justin could hardly be described as an innocent in all this. He wasn't twelve. He'd betrayed her, just as Jonty had betrayed Patrice. They were both victims. But somehow, Suzanne couldn't bring herself to reach out to her friend. What on earth would she say?

Seamus was dressed differently from the others, in prep school shorts, long grey socks, a blue shirt and smart blue cap. He'd obviously taken his tie and blazer off, though. It was too hot.

'You've got a nice hat on,' Suzanne heard Ruby say. She liked hats. Her comment made Seamus self-conscious, though. He hopped off the roundabout, ran over to Patrice and flung his cap on the ground.

Then he ran back to Ruby. 'Do you want to play chase?' he asked. They'd been such good friends before all this happened. They were almost like brother and sister, Suzanne thought sadly.

'In a minute. When I've finished pushing,' Ruby replied bossily. Suzanne watched Patrice bend down and pick up her son's cap. She turned and spotted Suzanne staring at her. Suzanne froze. Her head started to swim.

'More push!' Felix shouted. She'd forgotten about him on the swing. She sent him flying into the air. He squealed with pleasure.

'Breathe deeply,' she told herself. 'Push your knees back, keep calm.'

Ruby tugged her skirt. 'Mummy, can Seamus come to tea?' she pleaded.

Suzanne turned again to speak to her daughter. She started when she realised Patrice was standing right beside her now, just a few feet away.

'No, Ruby darling,' she heard Patrice say. There was a crack in her voice. She sounded as if she was about to burst into tears. 'Not today,' Patrice continued. 'We have to go home now. Come on, Seamus.'

Seamus took his mother's hand obediently. It wasn't how a small boy was supposed to behave, Suzanne thought. They were supposed to put up a fight, be feisty.

Seamus clearly knew his mother was upset. 'Don't worry, Mummy,' he said kindly. 'I don't mind. We can go to Ruby's another day.'

Patrice choked. The two women were only a few feet apart but there could have been a wall of ice between them. Suzanne noticed Patrice's skin looked weird. It had white patches on it, like vitiligo, and appeared paper thin. She'd aged, Suzanne thought. She looked exhausted. It was hardly surprising.

'I – how are you?' Suzanne managed to say. She couldn't look Patrice in the eye. Suzanne focused on pushing Felix, instead.

'I don't know what to say,' Patrice replied truthfully. Her voice sounded very small.

'Nor do I,' Suzanne replied.

Seamus thinking, no doubt, that the women were going to chat for hours, as they always used to, started to race off with Ruby in the direction of the big slide. 'I'll beat you there,' he shouted joyfully.

Patrice turned sharply and grabbed his arm. 'Don't run off,' she commanded. 'We have to go now.'

'Awww,' Seamus moaned, his body slumping. But he didn't argue.

'I'm sorry,' Suzanne said to Patrice, still not looking at her. 'I don't think either of us can deal with this right now. Take care of yourself – and Seamus.'

'And you,' Patrice replied quickly.

Suzanne watched for a moment as Patrice scurried off towards the gate, holding Seamus firmly by the hand. She can't get away quick enough, Suzanne thought miserably.

Suzanne felt shaken and trembly. She hadn't envisaged bumping into Patrice and it had made her realise how much she missed her friend. Not speaking felt all wrong. They should be there for each other.

She'd like to retie the threads that had bound them together but she didn't feel strong or big enough. She wanted to cry. Instead, she gave herself a mental shake, folded her feelings up and started to pack them away.

Ruby bounded up, a welcome distraction. 'I can hang upside down on the climbing frame without holding on, come and see me, Mummy,' she shouted.

'Coming,' Suzanne replied, lifting Felix out of the swing. 'Just make sure you don't fall off. You must be careful. Terrible things can happen if you're not careful.'

Justin was cooking supper for the family when they got home. Suzanne could smell bacon sizzling. She guessed he might be doing his spaghetti carbonara.

He looked up when she entered the kitchen. She caught

his eye and looked away quickly. She was shocked by what she saw. She hadn't taken it in properly before. He'd lost weight and seemed to have aged years. He was grey-faced and his cheeks were hollow. He looked almost like an old man, she thought.

His eyes seemed to have shrunk into his head, too. The sparkle had gone. They seemed full of fear and suffering. They seemed to say, 'Take me back, please take me back.'

That was why she looked away quickly. She was afraid her own eyes might betray her. They might say: 'Take me in your arms and tell me it was all a mistake.' That was the last thing she needed right now.

She'd told him he could stay for a few more weeks, while they continued their counselling and decided what to do for the best. She'd considered hiring a nanny, but he'd begged to be allowed to carry on looking after the children.

For their sakes more than anything, she'd agreed. It would be hard enough for Ruby and Felix to accept Mummy and Daddy weren't going to be living together any more, without having a new childminder as well. Ollie would take it badly, she guessed, as well. He was at such a sensitive age.

No, it was better if Justin continued to be a house-husband, though right now she wasn't going into the office. She was just doing bits and pieces of work from home.

She thought they should sort out finances and accommodation first, then decide what to do in the longer term about the children. In the evenings, when the kids were in bed, he'd head upstairs to the spare room. It was strange how, even being in the same house, two people could manage largely to avoid each other if they wanted. Suzanne saw him, but they hardly spoke, except about practicalities.

Sometimes she thought her heart might break. Sometimes she thought it would be better if he'd died. At least then she wouldn't be reminded of his betrayal every single day. But she wasn't going to crack up, not with four children to look after.

'Would you like some supper?' he asked, still stirring the bacon.

'No thanks,' Suzanne replied.

Ruby protested. 'Why not, Mummy? It's lovely supper.'

Suzanne patted Ruby's head. 'I know, sweetie, but I'm not hungry right now. I have to do some work.'

She'd wheeled Felix's pushchair into the kitchen. Justin bent down and tried to undo the straps. She noticed his hands were trembling. He smelled of cigarette smoke. He'd started smoking. He's a nervous wreck, she thought. She hated him for making her feel sorry for him.

Ruby produced a picture from her book bag. 'Look, Daddy,' she said. 'I've done a drawing for you. It's you and Mummy. There's a heart in the middle, see? That shows you're married, doesn't it?'

Justin took it. He couldn't answer, he just nodded, making a choking sound.

'What's the matter?' Ruby asked, concerned.

Justin shook his head. 'He's got a bit of a cough, that's all,' Suzanne replied for him. How long could they keep this up?

Suzanne bumped into Lara on the stairs. She'd taken out the nose ring she'd had put in a few months ago and had dyed her hair back to its normal chestnut brown. It wasn't that fake black any more. Suzanne had hated that fake black. The funny thing was, it seemed irrelevant now. Why had she been so upset about it? It was only a passing phase.

'How are you?' Lara pecked her mother on the cheek.

Suzanne sighed. 'Not too bad, thanks. Where's Ollie?'

'Doing homework,' Lara said. 'I made him finish it before he played on his PlayStation.'

Suzanne was grateful. 'Thank you.'

Later, much later, she heard a knock on the door. She'd been staring at her laptop and her eyes felt tired.

Justin poked his head in. 'There wasn't enough carbonara

left so I've made risotto. Fancy a little?' He sounded concerned, fatherly almost, as if he wanted to look after her.

Her stomach rumbled. She realised she was starving. 'OK,' she said.

They sat opposite each other at the pine table. He passed her a glass of red wine. She protested for a moment before taking a sip. She needed it.

'What are we going to do?' she asked. She realised it was a stupid question. It was her call.

'Ollie asked if I can buy him an electric razor,' Justin said, changing the subject. His voice was flat and dull.

'Whatever for?' Suzanne asked.

'Says he needs to shave his moustache,' Justin replied.

'But he hasn't got one,' Suzanne said, smiling. She couldn't help herself. That thin line of bum-fluff on her son's upper lip could hardly be described as a moustache.

'Some of his mates shave. I guess it would make him feel more manly,' Justin explained. 'He's smaller than most of the others. Maybe it would give him a bit of kudos.'

He looked up and caught Suzanne's eye. He smiled, a wary smile. She felt a fluttering in her stomach. It was one of the things she'd always loved about Justin, that he was so kind and sensitive, so in tune with people's feelings. Not like other men.

He reached his hand out to take her empty plate. She moved her fork so it wouldn't fall off and their fingers touched, momentarily. She felt a shock, like static, run through her. She had goose pimples on the back of her neck. He took his hand away, but a little more slowly than he could have done.

They both knew it had happened. She scraped her chair back and rose. 'I have to finish my work,' she said.

'Of course,' Justin replied.

Chapter Four

❦

'If you do this regularly, two or three times a week, you'll all be utterly gorgeous.' Sally grinned. 'Not that you aren't already,' she added quickly.

Sally had one of those bodies that didn't wobble anywhere. If you thumped her, you'd hurt your hand. Or that's what Percy thought.

'It's great for the lower body, and the best fat-burner around,' Sally went on. 'You'll burn four to five hundred calories an hour and your heart and lungs will be the biggest beneficiaries.'

Percy was sold. The only problem was, she had to actually do the class now and she was hung-over from the New Year's Eve party last night. Zeus had been there, too, as it was at a mutual friend's house. They were almost back to normal now, thank goodness, after she'd phoned him. She was very happy about it – it was far more than she deserved.

Gym and Slimline had made a big fuss about their new Revolution classes, starting on 1 January. They'd pinned notices up all over, urging members to come and try them. A great way to kick off the new year, they said.

They'd got rid of the old bikes and replaced them with sparkling new ones. Must have cost a fortune. There was quite a difference between these and the old machines, though. The new ones were more like mountain bikes. You could move the handlebars as well, so your upper body got a workout. And when you put the pressure gauge up, Percy had been told, they were much, much harder to push.

There was also a wide plasma screen at the front of the class, so you could watch DVDs while you pedalled, as well as a machine pumping out cold air and glittery disco lights. All very snazzy.

Percy glanced round the room. It was small and quite dark with the lights down low. Her heart gave a skip. They were all there for the first time in months: Carmen, Suzanne and Patrice.

Suzanne and Patrice had been avoiding each other, but Percy had persuaded them to come along this morning to give the new class a try. She'd convinced them it was what they needed. She was surprised and delighted when they'd agreed and hoped it would be an ice-breaker. But she knew she had to accept they might both disappear straight after the workout. Still, it was worth trying.

'I'll switch everything on,' Sally said. She walked over to the wall and the disco lights started flashing, red, green, yellow and blue. Then Sally turned on the DVD.

Percy was hoping for a cracking film. She was disappointed to see serious-looking cyclists in Lycra and helmets zooming round an extreme mountain-bike trail. It was clearly supposed to make you feel as if you were really out there doing it. But watching the bikes so close up, weaving in and out, careering round corners, made her slightly nauseous. She decided she'd better stare at the floor instead.

'Right,' said Sally. 'Just a little pressure and start to pedal steadily. That's right. Now a bit more pressure.'

Percy could feel it in her thighs already.

'And now a bit more,' said Sally.

This was getting serious. 'A bit more,' Sally repeated, 'then I want you to get up off your bikes. Push the handlebars down on the left, now the right, now the left, just as if you were going round corners.'

The handlebars were quite stiff and hard to push. Percy's arms ached. It was a most peculiar sensation. She felt exactly as if she were riding a real bike up a real hill and round steep bends, only she wasn't actually moving.

Sally switched on the air conditioner above and cold air started to pump out noisily. Now it felt to Percy as if the wind was blowing through her hair, too.

'OK,' said Sally. 'We'll do some jumps. Pressure up to maximum. Go on, higher.' She hopped off her bike and went round the class, whacking up the gauges. There was no chance of cheating. 'Up, two, down, two, up, two, down, two,' she shouted. Percy's heart was thumping. 'A minute more of this, guys. Up, two, down, two.'

Percy now fully understood the meaning of the expression weak at the knees.

She was relieved when Patrice and Suzanne followed her and Carmen into the changing rooms. She'd half expected at least one of them to shoot off without a word.

'Skinny lattes and muffins afterwards?' Percy asked Patrice tentatively, stripping off her sweaty shorts and top. She and Patrice were standing next to each other. Suzanne was on the other side of the room, nearest the showers.

Patrice looked at her watch. 'OK, just for half an hour, though. Jonty's dropping Seamus back at midday.'

Percy grabbed her towel and headed for the showers. 'Skinny latte and muffins?' she asked Suzanne nonchalantly as she walked past. Percy spoke quietly, so Patrice wouldn't hear.

'OK,' said Suzanne. 'But I mustn't be long. We're having a big family lunch.'

Percy scuttled out of the changing rooms first. She didn't bother with make-up or drying her hair. She plonked her stuff on their favourite sofa, underneath the TV screen, and went to get three skinny lattes, muffins and green tea for Carmen.

'All for you?' Lucian said sulkily, slapping the drinks and muffins in front of her. Coffee slopped on the bar. He didn't seem to take a lot of pride in his work, Percy reflected. She noticed, though, that he'd grown some designer stubble on his chin and had diamond studs in his ears. Perhaps he was marginally less grumpy these days, too.

'Got ourselves a girlfriend, have we, Lucian?' she asked, her head on one side.

Lucian raised his eyes heavenward. 'You women,' he said theatrically, 'you have such over-active imaginations. But as you ask, yes. And her name, I'm happy to say, is Dorothy.'

Percy smiled. 'Like Wordsworth's sister?'

'Precisely.'

She handed over the cash.

'Anyway,' Lucian went on, dropping the money in the till and closing it with a flourish. 'Where are the rest of the gang? I haven't seen you and your partners in crime together for yonks.'

Percy smiled. 'They're on their way.' Just like old times, she thought, crossing her fingers.

Don't be silly. This could be a disaster.

Percy, Carmen and Patrice made small talk while they waited for Suzanne to emerge from the changing room. 'Zeus invited us all for lunch next weekend, but Mark said he couldn't face Zeus's wife – or my mother,' Percy said.

'How is your mother?' Patrice enquired.

'Bossy and self-centred as ever,' Percy replied, but she could tell Patrice wasn't really listening. 'She and Zeus have had another falling out, and Philippa's barely talking to either of them. But hey, that's families for you.'

At last, Suzanne stood in front of them. Percy thought she looked tense. Her eyes were darting nervously this way and that and it appeared she was trying hard not to focus on Patrice.

'Sit down, honey,' Percy said, patting the chair next to her. 'I've got you a coffee.'

Suzanne obediently sat down. She was only there for a

couple of seconds, though, before she let out a whoop and sprang up again. Percy jumped.

'Guess what?' Suzanne squealed. 'We've got the same mutton dress.' She seemed pleased. What was she talking about?

'Patrice and I have the same dress,' Suzanne repeated. She clapped her hands. 'Fancy that! Great minds think alike!'

Percy looked. She hadn't noticed what anyone was wearing. She'd been far too busy worrying about what everyone was going to say, or not say. But now it was clear: Suzanne and Patrice were both in rather short, slightly risqué, black polo-necked jumper dresses, covered in odd purple and orange seventies swirls.

Come to think of it, Patrice never used to wear things like that. She was always rather conservatively dressed. She said Jonty usually chose her clothes for her. Well, this was a departure.

But while Patrice, ever elegant, had long black boots on and opaque tights, Suzanne had thin grey tights and ballet pumps. The ensemble didn't do much for Suzanne's ample thighs, but Percy thought she looked sort of sweet all the same. Even if the orange did clash with her red hair.

'H and M? Suzanne asked.

Patrice nodded. 'Nineteen ninety-nine. You couldn't argue with the price.' She knew Suzanne liked a bargain.

'I know,' Suzanne replied. 'I spotted it in the window and fell in love with it. It's sort of kooky, isn't it? I thought it would cheer me up. I was worried it was a bit mutton, but if you, Mrs Style Guru, chose it, it must be all right.'

'Mutton, though?' Patrice raised her eyebrows.

'Mutton dressed as lamb,' Suzanne explained.

'Oh, of course,' Patrice nodded. 'No, I don't think it is mutton.' She considered for a moment, her head on one side. 'Anyway, I think women should dress how they want, not how people think they should dress. I'm into self-expression these days.'

413

'I agree,' said Suzanne.

'Quite right,' said Percy. 'Otherwise, at our age, we'd be in twinsets, pearls and comfy beige slacks.'

'Or whatever our husbands wanted us to wear,' Patrice said ominously. 'Actually, I was more worried it made me look flat-chested,' she went on. She stuck out her chest. It's true, there wasn't much there.

'Nah,' said Suzanne. 'The swirls make you look bigger, positively voluptuous.'

'Liar,' Patrice said. She smiled and Suzanne smiled back.

Phew, Percy thought. She took a deep breath.

Suzanne stepped over to Patrice on the sofa, bent down and wrapped her arms round her. 'Oh, Pats, I've missed you so much,' she said, squeezing tight. The mutton dress rode up Suzanne's thighs, nearly displaying her knickers, but no one cared.

Patrice's arms snaked round Suzanne's back. 'I've missed you too,' she said. 'More than you'll ever know.'

It was more than Percy could take, that was for sure. She felt a lump in her throat. She glanced at Carmen, who'd got a hankie out of her bag and was blowing her nose. Soon all four of them were blubbing like babies, laughing and crying at the same time.

Percy noticed a few funny looks from the other members, but she ignored them. They squished up together on the sofa, arms round each other, heads on shoulders, half sitting on each others' laps.

There was a cough. Percy looked up through blurred eyes. 'I think this calls for a celebration, ladies!' said a voice. Lucian was standing there with four steaming mugs and a pile of muffins on a plate.

'On the house,' he said. 'Tuck in. Don't worry. It'll only take twelve hours of Revolution to burn off,' he added with a twinkle.

Suzanne was the first to rise. She sighed and settled down

on the chair opposite. She took a sip from one of her two mugs of coffee. They were lined up, waiting for her. 'How are you, Patrice?' she asked at last. She was frowning. 'I mean how are you really?'

Patrice placed her hands on her lap. Percy thought her shoulders looked bony in the dress.

Patrice sighed. 'Surviving,' she said. 'But I do miss Jonty terribly. Despite what he's done. I'll never have him back, though. How about you?'

Suzanne bit into a muffin. Percy thought she'd put on a bit of weight. She looked rounder all over, or was it just the dress? Either way, Suzanne wouldn't like it.

Funny how differently people reacted to stress, Percy reflected. Some couldn't eat; others stuffed their faces. Percy felt she probably straddled both categories: when disaster struck, she couldn't eat a morsel, but as soon as she'd sort of settled into the crisis, she couldn't stop.

'I'm bearing up,' Suzanne said. 'Justin's still living with us . . .' She looked at Patrice carefully, to check if she could cope with the news, Percy guessed. Patrice remained quite still.

'For practical reasons, mainly,' Suzanne went on. 'It's been very hard on the children.'

'Of course,' Patrice replied. 'Seamus misses Jonty badly. Jonty has him every other Saturday, and occasionally on Wednesdays after school. I couldn't deny Seamus that. But I can't bear to be in the same room with Jonty for long. He makes my flesh crawl.'

'Where's he living?' Suzanne asked.

'He's renting a flat near his office,' Patrice replied. 'I've filed for divorce. Eventually, I expect, I'll have to sell the house and buy somewhere smaller for Seamus and me. But I'll definitely stay round here,' she added quickly. 'Couldn't be parted from you lot. Can't think why.' She smiled.

'I miss Justin so much, too,' Suzanne said simply. 'I know

we're still living together, but not as man and wife, obviously. I thought I'd found the perfect man. I feel like I've lost part of my body. I can function without it, get by, but I'll never be a whole person again. I suppose that's what the expression "heartbroken" means. I really do feel as if my heart has been broken.'

Patrice leaned over and took Suzanne's left hand. There was no ring on it now. 'I really am so sorry,' Patrice said. 'We've both lost so much, but actually I think it's worse for you because you really did seem to have everything you wanted, whereas I knew things weren't right with Jonty. I just didn't realise quite how wrong they were.'

'And to think I never really suspected,' said Suzanne quietly. 'It seems so obvious now, but I didn't see it. We even had a brilliant sex life, for God's sake.'

Patrice stared down at her lap. She cleared her throat. 'We didn't,' she murmured. 'But whenever I questioned Jonty, he somehow managed to make me feel low, dirty even, for wanting sex, as if I was the one with the problem. I – I almost believed him.'

A small, blond child with a snotty nose toddled up to the group. Percy recognised him as one of Millicent's. 'Car!' He grinned, brandishing a toy.

'Yes, Dylan, car.' Percy smiled, admiring it. 'Lovely car.' Dylan toddled off again.

'I'd better get home,' Patrice said quickly. 'Jonty will be back with Seamus shortly.'

'OK, but promise me we'll meet again soon,' said Suzanne.

'I promise,' Patrice replied. 'Maybe we can go clothes shopping together sometime? Buy a few more mutton dresses?' She looked pleased with the idea. 'And I think I might try to get back to some more classes. It would do me good.'

'Pilates next Saturday?' Suzanne asked.

Patrice nodded. 'Yeah, maybe.'

'I'll hold you to that,' Suzanne smiled.

Patrice rose to leave, then paused. 'Suzanne?'

'Yes?'

Patrice hesitated. Her face was criss-crossed with lines. Percy was taken aback. Patrice looked her age, suddenly: a woman in mid-life. Percy had never thought of her like that before.

'You know,' Patrice said, 'I really wanted another baby, I desperately wanted one, but he said I was too old, made out it was a ridiculous idea.' She seemed to have forgotten the others. She was speaking straight to Suzanne. 'He even suggested I was infertile,' she went on, 'when in fact I'm pretty sure we took so long to have Seamus because we hardly ever had sex, and probably never at the right time.'

'Oh, Pats, how cruel,' Suzanne said. 'I couldn't imagine anything worse than desperately wanting a baby and not being able to have one. I feel so blessed with my four. You'll meet someone else,' she said quickly. 'I know you will. There's still time.'

Patrice shook her head. 'No, I don't want another relationship. I really don't. It's just me and Seamus now. I'm resigned to it.'

'You'll change your mind,' Suzanne insisted.

Patrice shook her head emphatically. 'I won't. But thanks anyway. I know you're trying to help.'

The two women embraced again and Suzanne stood as Patrice walked towards the exit.

'She looks so lonely,' Suzanne whispered to Percy and Carmen. 'No woman should have to go through what she's been through, and with no family to support her either.'

As if sensing what her friend was thinking, Patrice turned and blew them all a reassuring kiss. Then she gave a brave thumbs up before disappearing round the corner.

Chapter Five

Patrice felt as gloomy as the cold, wet winter weather.

She missed Seamus dreadfully now he was back at school after the Christmas break. She wandered listlessly round the house, sorting cupboards and tidying drawers that were already tidy. She seemed to have no enthusiasm for anything.

She wondered if she should move house sooner rather than later, to get right away from all the memories. Then she thought it would be unfair on Seamus. His parents had split up; he didn't need to be uprooted from his familiar surroundings and plonked somewhere else as well.

She tried to be upbeat when she picked him up from school. Occasionally she'd invite a friend for tea, but mostly they'd spend the evenings alone together, doing puzzles and watching TV. When Seamus was asleep she'd quite often go to bed herself.

She no longer had elaborate suppers to cook for Jonty, or endless shirts to iron, or cleaning to do because he'd always liked the house so spick and span.

It was weird: she'd found it burdensome and often boring, but she missed it all the same. It had been her life for so many years. Now she felt at a loss to know how to fill her time.

The evenings seemed endless. She'd read more books in the last few months than since before Seamus was born and watched masses of television, but they couldn't cure the loneliness. Nothing could help with that.

Patrice was startled when the doorbell rang around 8 a.m.

Seamus woke around six, so they were both up and dressed, but who could it be so early in the day?

She opened the door. A tall, tanned, handsome young man was standing in front of her. He grinned and thrust a bunch of wilting carnations in her hand.

'Hi, sis,' he said. It took a moment to register.

Patrice stepped back. 'Edmund?' she cried. She recognised him from the photo her mother had sent.

'Yeah, Edmund,' the man agreed. He had a strong Aussie twang, thick, dark, shaggy hair, a stubbly chin and jeans that seemed to hang down round his knees.

'What are you doing here?' said Patrice. She realised immediately how unfriendly that must sound. 'I'm sorry,' she said. 'Come in.'

He followed her into the kitchen where Seamus was eating Cheerios. 'Darling,' Patrice said. 'This is Mummy's brother – your uncle Edmund – from Australia.' That sounded so weird.

'My uncle Edmund?' Seamus repeated. 'That's funny.' He pinged a Cheerio across the table at the stranger.

'Don't do that,' Patrice scolded.

Edmund swung off his backpack and sat down on the wooden bench opposite Seamus. 'I've got something for you, little fella.' He grinned. Seamus looked interested.

Edmund produced a boomerang from his bag. 'All the way from Sydney,' he said, passing it to Seamus.

'What is it, Mummy?' Seamus asked, turning the wooden object over in his hands.

'You throw it, and it'll come right back to you,' Edmund explained. 'Not inside the house, though,' he added quickly. He glanced up at Patrice and grinned again. 'Maybe I'll show you how it works later, if that's OK with your mum?'

Patrice was pleased to see her half-brother. That surprised her a little. She sat down beside him. 'Tell me what you're doing here, your plans, everything,' she pressed.

She couldn't stop looking at him. She'd only met him once, when their mother had brought him over. He could only have been about three years old. He was blond then and very shy. Patrice had been completely confused: furiously angry but also strangely moved by this small boy she didn't know, but whom she understood to be closely related to her.

She remembered lots of rows between her mother and father, then Caroline and Edmund had left again. Patrice had been devastated a second time. She'd wept into her pillow for nights on end. To be abandoned once more seemed too much to bear.

What did she know about Edmund from their mother's letters? That as a boy he liked football and swimming, didn't work much at school, or didn't work as hard as their mother expected him to, more like. That he now worked in a surf shop and had some dubious friends, again according to Caroline. Not a lot really.

Patrice looked at him more carefully. There was something oddly familiar about him: the nose, the mouth. She realised that, despite their different colouring, they must be very alike. She felt strongly drawn to him, this stranger. It occurred to her that she'd do almost anything to make him stay. She wanted to touch his skin, his hair, his eyes and nose. Make sure he was real. She wanted him to tell her everything.

'I had a bit of a falling out with Mum,' he explained ruefully. 'She didn't like it that I chose not to go to uni and she liked it even less when I hooked up with this girl, Evonne, because she's black. You know what Mum's like?'

Patrice nodded. She knew all right: snobby, racist, you name it.

'Well,' Edmund continued, 'I was working in this surf shop, much to Mum's disgust, then Evonne and I split up and I thought I might as well see the world while I'm still young. So I thought I'd come to London first, maybe work in a bar, get some money together and go travelling round Europe. I hoped I could meet up with you guys, too,' he added.

He looked shy. What would he be? Twenty-fourish? Patrice felt suddenly strongly protective. 'It's great to see you, Edmund,' she said, touching his arm. 'I'm so glad you came. When did you arrive?'

'A couple of days ago,' he replied. 'I've been staying in a bed and breakfast place up the road. I came by a few times but I was too nervous to call, so I went away again.'

Patrice smiled. He wasn't that young, but she wanted to ruffle his shoulder-length hair and hold him to her. She managed to restrain herself. 'You'd better collect your stuff and bring it here,' she said firmly. 'I've got plenty of room. You can stay for as long as you want – if you'd like to.'

'Far out!' Edmund said, grinning. 'Are you sure? That's real good of you.'

'Sure,' Patrice replied. 'We've got a lot to catch up on. Years. In fact, I think this is cause for celebration, don't you?'

'Shampoo, shampoo!' Seamus shouted, right on cue. Patrice laughed. When Jonty had been around, there had always seemed to be plenty of reasons to celebrate: a big bonus; a promotion; just plain old Friday night; the start of the weekend.

Seamus loved listening to the pop and watching the cork fly. Only after 6 p.m. though; Jonty was very strict about that. They never had alcohol before the sun had crossed over the yardarm.

'Yes, let's have some bubbly.' Patrice grinned. 'I don't give a monkey's what time it is.'

She produced two tall thin champagne glasses and a bottle of Bollinger. Seamus had apple juice in a special, big-boy glass, too.

'A toast,' Patrice said. 'To brothers and sisters.'

'Brothers and sisters!' Edmund beamed, clinking his glass against Patrice's first, then Seamus's.

'Cheers,' Seamus said, slopping apple juice on the table.

Later, when Seamus was at school, Edmund went down the road to collect his bags and Patrice prepared his room. She felt insanely happy as she pulled out a fresh duvet cover, sheets, pillow slips. It would be lovely to have her half-brother in the house for a while, she thought. He seemed like a really nice boy – young man. It would be good for Seamus, too, to have a man around again. She realised she was ridiculously excited, like a schoolgirl.

She wondered what to make for supper. Pasta with pesto simply wouldn't do. She pulled out one of her recipe books – she hadn't done that in months – and settled on beef goulash with dumplings. Men liked beef and stodge, she thought. It would fill Edmund up. She was sure he'd have a huge appetite, being so tall. Tomorrow or the next day, she'd take him into town and help him find some sort of job. He was so polite and nice-looking, he should have no trouble getting work in a bar.

She couldn't wait to introduce him to Percy, Suzanne and Carmen. They'd love him. Patrice wondered, for a moment, what her mother must be thinking, over in Sydney. Would she be sitting bitterly by the phone, waiting for Edmund to ring? Or expecting him to walk in the door any moment and apologise? Promise to go to university and become the man she wanted him to be?

Well, that wasn't going to happen. Caroline wasn't going to get her clutches on him again. Patrice could imagine what it must have been like for Edmund, growing up in a cramped apartment with just his mother for company.

Caroline's affair with the neighbour hadn't lasted beyond his first birthday. She'd ended up short of cash and having to work for a living. Her letters to Patrice were full of self-pity. She thought the world had let her down. She seemed scarcely aware of the suffering she'd inflicted on her daughter.

Well, Patrice was going to help Edmund find his feet now,

show him there was a bigger world out there and opportunities that he could never have imagined. She had cash enough to take him to places. The theatre, perhaps? Paris one weekend? Rome, even. She'd enjoy spoiling him a little. After all, what was money for if you couldn't spend it on friends and loved ones?

And when he wanted to return to Australia, of course he could, but she'd make sure he did so with a clear idea of where he was going in life. And that wouldn't be back to his mother's.

They had supper round the kitchen table at around 6 p.m. Jonty had always insisted on dining at eight, after Seamus was in bed, but these days Patrice preferred to eat early, with her son.

'Great dinner,' Edmund said, helping himself to more. Patrice smiled. 'Hey, I'm real sorry to hear about your troubles,' he pronounced. 'Mum told me you were getting divorced.'

Patrice had written a short note, to inform Caroline of the facts, nothing more. 'Thank you,' Patrice replied. 'It has been terrible. But, you know, life goes on. I've got Seamus to think about and, well, I can't afford to fall to pieces. Caroline's advice – unsolicited, I might add – was to forget Jonty, which isn't easy after all those years of marriage.'

'Of course not,' Edmund said, taking another mouthful, 'but she never was hot on sympathy. I remember when I got dumped by my first girlfriend. I was gutted and Mum told me not to be such a wimp. It's hardly comparable, I know, but that's just how she is. Get on your bike and start pedalling again. That's her motto.'

'I wonder why,' Patrice mused. 'I mean, she can't be all bad, because she had us, and we've turned out all right, haven't we?'

'Yeah,' Edmund grinned. 'More by accident than design, in my case at least. But she does have some good points.'

423

'Like what?' Patrice was genuinely at a loss to think of a single one.

'Well, she loves us.' Edmund shrugged. 'In her own fashion.'

'She's got a funny way of showing it.' Patrice grimaced. 'She couldn't even make it over here when her daughter's marriage collapsed in shocking circumstances.'

Edmund pushed his plate away. 'You know, she really wanted to,' he said carefully. 'She talked about it with me and it wasn't the money that stopped her, really. That was just an excuse. The truth is, Mum can't fly any more, because she's got a heart condition. She didn't want to tell you because she thought it would be something else for you to worry about. She was really concerned about you.'

That silenced Patrice. She'd had no idea. She reflected how distance could create impossible chasms between people. Maybe if her mother hadn't moved so far away, maybe if they'd seen more of each other over the years, they would have understood each other better and she, Patrice, might even have been able to forgive.

But still, it had been Caroline's decision to run off with another man and leave her daughter. She must have known she risked destroying Patrice by abandoning her.

Patrice rose and started to clear the plates off the table. Edmund instinctively moved round to Seamus, helping him down from his chair. They'd bonded already, Patrice thought happily.

'Maybe we should go and visit her one day, Seamus and I,' she said vaguely as she loaded the dishwasher. 'I've had absolutely no desire to do so up to now. But I guess I might regret it if we never made the effort before she died. Besides, we wouldn't have to stay with her, we could book into a hotel and see some of the sights. Seamus would love to meet a few kangaroos and koalas.'

'Yeah, you should do that,' Edmund replied gently. 'Mum would be over the moon.'

'Would she really?' Patrice asked. 'I'm not sure she could give two hoots whether she sees me ever again.'

Seamus was holding Edmund's hand, trying to drag his new-found friend upstairs. Edmund stopped by the door. 'Look,' he said, 'she's a funny old bat, sad and bitter, and she's made a real mess of things. But one thing I do know is that she's never got over losing you.

'She once said it was her biggest regret in life that she didn't take you with her when she left England. She always intended for you to join her in Oz; it was your dad who stopped it happening. And I don't know what he told you but she believes he turned you against her.'

Patrice sat down abruptly. Was that true? She'd never believed her mother had really tried to take her to Australia. She thought Caroline just said it now, in her letters, after the event, to try to make herself look better. But hearing it from Edmund did make Patrice wonder. He had no reason to lie about it.

She didn't realise her father had stopped her going, either. Why would he have done that when he'd shown so little interest in her when she was growing up and had always seemed to dislike her so?

It was all too much to take in right now. She was still so raw from her break-up with Jonty. She couldn't cope with re-opening old wounds at this moment, but Edmund had certainly given her food for thought.

'Time for bed, young man,' Patrice said to Seamus. 'Would you like your uncle Edmund to give you a bath?'

'Yes, yes, yes!' Seamus shouted, jumping up and down. 'I've got an Action Man frogman and a shark that shoots water.'

'You have? Lucky boy!' Edmund grinned as Seamus succeeded in dragging him through the door at last. 'Come and show me.'

*   *   *

It was a week later that Patrice finally picked up the phone. She'd hardly been able to think about anything else, but she'd needed time to pluck up courage. Edmund had settled in so fast, it felt as if he'd been there always.

Already she was getting used to having his stuff around the place: the size twelve trainers, the wet towels, the extra large sweatshirts he left draped over the sofas, and the dirty washing. For some reason she didn't object to the mess at all.

'Mum? It's Patrice,' she said. There was an echo on the line. That was annoying.

'Patrice, is that you?' the voice came back. 'Oh, how are you? Is Edmund with you?' Caroline sounded much older than Patrice remembered. Quavery and anxious.

'Yes, he's here,' Patrice said. 'He's going to stay with me for a while. He's getting on really well with Seamus and we've found him a job. Don't worry, I'm taking good care of him.'

'Thank you, Patrice. I've been worried,' said her mother. 'And you?' She hesitated. 'How are you doing?'

Patrice swallowed. 'I'm feeling a bit better. And I'm enjoying getting to know Edmund. He's a fine young man.'

'I know, well, I miss him.' Caroline sighed. 'But it's good to explore the world while you're young.'

'Yes,' Patrice agreed. 'And he'll be back. And I thought . . . I thought maybe Seamus and I could come over to see you sometime, too. Stay in a hotel somewhere. Quite soon.'

There was silence at the other end. Was Caroline weeping, or was it just the echo, playing tricks with her voice?

Finally, she spoke. 'I'd like that very much, Patrice, very much indeed.' She could scarcely disguise her emotion. 'Just as soon as you can,' Caroline went on. 'I'll be waiting for you.'

Patrice replaced the phone. She put her hand to her face and was surprised to feel her cheeks were wet. Each tear seemed to her to represent years of hurt, anger, grief, despair, loneliness. Like a little girl, at that moment, all she wanted was for her mother to wipe them away, to make it all better.

She licked her lips, which had been chapped by the January wind, and pulled some lip balm from her pocket. It stung slightly, but was healing, she reckoned.

'I'm coming, Mum,' she whispered to herself. 'I'm coming.'

Patrice didn't believe in telepathy but still, she thought she could feel something like waves streaming back and forth between them through the ether.

Could you be homesick – filled with longing – for a mother you hadn't seen in years? And could that same mother reach out to you across the continents?

Patrice guessed the answer, to both questions, was yes.

Chapter Six

❧

'Hey, guys,' Percy said, her eyes shining. 'What do you say we all go to East Wittering for a few days at Easter? The weather might be OK, but even if it pours the entire time we can take wellies and raincoats and go for long walks along the beach, and climb the Trundle and have cream teas in Chichester.

'Some friends of my mother have a huge house right on the beach,' she went on. 'It's big enough for all of us and they rent it out. We might be lucky if I ring now.'

'Sounds like a great idea,' Carmen said.

'I'd love to,' Suzanne agreed.

Percy looked at Patrice. 'Look, you know, I'm not sure I'm ready,' Patrice said. 'I'm sorry, but you must all go of course.'

'Oh, come off it,' Percy said. 'Seamus would love it and it'll do you both the world of good. There won't be any pressure to do stuff. You can just laze around the house if you want. But it'll be a good break, and there's something wonderful about the seaside in spring, when there aren't too many people about.'

To Percy's relief, Patrice agreed. In truth, Percy would have liked Mark to come too, but she felt she couldn't ask him because the others weren't bringing their partners. He'd just have to stay behind and be a bachelor for a short while.

Percy got out of the car and opened the big black iron gates which led into the driveway. Catching her first glimpse of the house brought back vivid memories. She'd been there often as a child. The house had been built in the 1930s and had distinctive, curved, suntrap-style bay windows, to let in as much light as possible.

There was a large grass tennis court at the front and a small, grassy garden at the back that led straight on to the pebbly beach.

While the children raced around, exploring the grounds, Percy went inside. She was pleased to find some things weren't exactly the same as she remembered. Thankfully, the house had been extensively modernised. There was a new, airy kitchen and there were new shower rooms, as well as five big bedrooms. Plenty of space for them all.

Rowan and Seamus slept on camp beds in the same room as Ruby and Felix. Ollie and Ben shared, then there were separate rooms for Patrice, Suzanne and Lara, Carmen and Ivy and Percy.

Percy was surprised that Lara had wanted to come. She was pleased for Suzanne, though. Suzanne said her daughter had grown up a lot in the past few months and had been a real support. What's more, Lara had even dumped the awful Noah and seemed to be getting stuck into her school work. Hallelujah! It was exactly what Suzanne needed.

The younger children were in their element. They spent every day out of doors, and every evening watching movies, playing games and eating fish and chips or spaghetti bolognese. They weren't ever going to want to go home.

One night, when they'd finally crashed and Ollie, Ben and Lara were watching a film downstairs, the women lit a fire in the first-floor sitting room and settled down with a couple of bottles of Rioja.

They'd walked miles along the beach earlier in the day, collecting shells and different coloured pebbles. Then they'd wandered around the pretty fishing village of Bosham and explored the Anglo-Saxon church where King Canute's daughter was thought to be buried.

Later, they'd eaten sandwiches on the quay wall, looking out at the bobbing boats. The younger children had all had a go at trying to turn back the sea, like Canute himself, who'd proved that even the King of England, Norway and Denmark didn't have the power to hold back the tide. Predictably enough, the children had got their feet wet. Now they really knew how the old boy must have felt.

It had been a tiring but fun day, and everyone was ready for an early night. Percy was aware of the wind whistling outside and the logs crackling on the fire.

'The last two years have been extraordinary,' she mused, running her index finger round the rim of her glass. 'We've all been through so much. Obviously Patrice and Suzanne have had the worst time by far, it's been a nightmare for them both, but a hell of a lot has happened to us all.'

'It's true,' said Carmen, tucking her feet up under her on the armchair. 'And you know, I feel an awful lot better about myself than I did two years ago. For the first time in my life, or at least since I had to give up dancing, I really know what I want. Breaking up with Simon was a huge move, then nearly getting back together again. But as it turned out I was absolutely right not to give him another chance.

'I'm still furious with him,' she went on thoughtfully, 'but I know he's bad news. I had a narrow escape.' Carmen shifted in her seat, twizzled her long, black hair around her forefinger, cleared her throat. 'You know, I was so scared of having a child without a partner, but being a single mum isn't nearly as bad as I feared, thanks to all the help I've had from you lot. And Ivy's quite simply the best thing that's ever happened to me.

'I want to try to enjoy every moment of watching her grow up. I don't need a stupid, selfish man. Pushing Ivy along the towpath on a sunny day or swinging her on a swing at the park is as close to perfect happiness as I've ever got. And I bet you never thought you'd hear me say that.'

Percy grinned. 'But you'll find someone else, eventually,' she insisted. 'I know it.'

Carmen shook her head, frowning. 'Never again,' she insisted. 'I'm through with men.'

She looked so fierce that Percy didn't dare contradict her. She wrinkled her brow, remembering something different. More important. Worry snaked through her. 'What about your result, Carmen, have you had it yet?' She asked.

Carmen nodded. 'I almost forgot to tell you. The latest smear test was negative. The laser treatment worked.'

Percy clapped her hands. 'Relief!' she said.

Suzanne and Patrice beamed. 'Great news,' Suzanne said. 'Onwards and upwards, eh?'

There was a scream from downstairs. The kids must be watching something scary. Some unsuitable horror, probably. Percy had almost forgotten about them.

'You know, I feel better too,' Patrice said, after a moment. Everyone looked surprised. She'd hardly said a word all holiday. 'I do, really,' she insisted, putting her wine glass down beside the chair. 'The whole Jonty thing's been a nightmare. I'm not sure I'll ever get over it.

'But, as you know, things weren't right between us for a very long time, though I didn't understand why. I realise now I subsumed myself in him, allowed him to bully and control me. I didn't give enough thought to myself, my own needs and ambitions. I became a victim, a doormat, probably because of my peculiar childhood, I don't know.

'Now Edmund's come into my life, which is wonderful, and I'm thinking of taking Seamus to visit my mother in the summer. When I'm feeling strong enough, I've also decided I'm definitely going to go back into law. I'll need to do refresher courses, but I want to make something of myself, for my sake as well as Seamus's. I'm going to use my brain. I never want to be dependent on a man again.'

'That's great, Patrice,' Suzanne said, with feeling.

'Terrific,' Percy agreed.

Suzanne shifted uneasily in her seat, fiddling with an earring. She was wearing long, dangly blue and silver ones. Lately, she'd gone quite ethnic. She seemed to be taking more of an interest in clothes since she'd started going shopping with Patrice. Dress-wise, they were both getting wackier.

'I wasn't going to tell you this now,' Suzanne said, 'but I've done a lot of thinking, too, and it just seems the right time to share it with you: I've decided to take Justin back, to give it another go.'

'What?' Patrice gasped. Percy put her hand to her mouth. Carmen shuffled uncomfortably in her seat.

Suzanne nodded. 'I know you'll think I'm mad,' she said, 'but Justin and I have talked and talked, on our own and with a marriage therapist we've been seeing. And, well, I love him and I want us to be husband and wife again.'

'But what about the fact he's gay? How can you live with that?' Percy blurted. She knew they'd been seeing a counsellor, but still couldn't quite believe what she was hearing.

Suzanne nodded. 'We've discussed that, of course,' she said, 'and Justin says he's not gay, he's bisexual, always has been. Sexuality isn't necessarily a fixed thing, you know, it can be fluid.

'He says he fancies me, and also, occasionally, he fancies men. We're still examining why he had the affair. Hopefully, that's something the counsellor can help us find out. Some of it's to do with his past, some of it's to do with my long working hours and the stress of raising four children virtually on his own.

'I've been making a big effort to be home earlier, to spend more time with him, and Lara's helping more, too. It does seem to be making a difference. Justin's told me I'm the one he loves and wants to be with and he's promised he won't be unfaithful again. And I believe him.

'We've been on an incredible journey in the past few

months,' Suzanne continued. She cast her eyes round the room, looking earnestly at her friends, one by one. It was as if she wanted to check they fully understood. 'I'd like to think,' she finished, 'I really would like to think that in the end we'll even be able to draw some good things out of this whole bad experience.'

'But can you ever really forgive him?' Percy was incredulous. 'And won't there always be this little niggling doubt in your mind that maybe he's up to something?'

Suzanne took a gulp of wine. 'Our relationship counsellor has talked about ninety-five per cent marriages,' she replied thoughtfully. 'By that she means women who stay in marriages that are ninety-five per cent right, and put up with the five per cent that's not. Maybe the husband's occasionally even violent, but the wife reckons the good times outweigh the bad enough for her to put up with it. My marriage is definitely ninety-five per cent good. I've decided I'm prepared to live with the five per cent that's not so great. Life's a compromise,' she insisted, 'and I reckon my relationship is a whole lot better than many people's. Even if they don't have to cope with a question mark about their partner's sexuality'

The wind outside rattled against the window frames now. Patrice shivered and started to cry quietly. Percy moved over to be next to her friend on the sofa. She put an arm round Patrice's shoulder.

'I'm sorry, I can't help it,' Patrice said, wiping the tears away with her hands. 'I won't have the opportunity to give Jonty a second chance.'

Percy rested her head on Patrice's. 'What do you mean?' she asked softly.

'I haven't told you,' Patrice said. 'I couldn't quite face it. Jonty's living with another man.'

This time it was Percy's turn to gasp. She couldn't stop herself. She saw Carmen's hand shoot up to her mouth and the colour seemed to have drained from Suzanne's face.

433

Patrice pulled her long legs up on to the chair and crossed her arms around them. She was in a tight little ball.

'We've talked very honestly, recently,' Patrice carried on, 'since Jonty realised I was serious about kicking him out, that I wasn't going to let him back. He told me he's always been attracted to men. He knew from an early age, but he was terrified of his dad and his brothers. He couldn't tell his mother, either, so he created this alter ego, this macho type who bossed me around and behaved, ironically, just like his bullying old-fashioned father. His life was a total sham. He was always pretending to be someone else.

'It worked most of the time, he said. But every now and then, something would take over, some madness, and he'd have to go out and find a man to have sex with. And then he met Justin.'

Patrice shivered. Percy didn't dare look at Suzanne.

'But how could he do it to you, Pats?' Percy asked, bemused. 'How could he marry you, knowing what he knew about himself?'

Patrice shrugged. 'He says he fell for me, wanted me, and he loved the idea of being married. He just couldn't cope with the sex bit. In an odd sort of way, I can kind of understand it. I almost feel sorry for him, though I can't forgive.'

Percy thought for a moment. No one else spoke either. She imagined they were all digesting what they'd heard. You could almost hear their brains whirring.

'What about the other man?' Percy asked finally. 'Who's he?'

Patrice rubbed her eyes. 'Another lawyer, I gather. Called Robert.' She laughed humourlessly. 'I don't know much else about him. I just know he's moved in, because Jonty told me. It seems quite serious. There's no going back for us.' She gave a sad little lopsided smile.

Percy topped up everyone's glasses and took a big swig of wine. 'Does Seamus know?' she asked.

Patrice shook her head. 'He's too young. I've told Jonty there's to be no sign of the boyfriend when Seamus visits.'

Percy nodded. 'And what about Jonty's family?'

Patrice grimaced, 'Not good,' she said. 'His father's completely flipped and won't speak to him. His mother's just very, very upset. She absolutely adored Jonty, you see. They were very close. He was her baby.

'She's called me a few times, but she finds it very hard to talk about him at all. We end up discussing the weather, Seamus's school, anything except what we're both thinking about.'

'I'm sorry, Pats, it must be so hard,' Suzanne said softly. They all turned to her. 'Maybe I should have waited to tell you about me and Justin,' she went on. 'But now seemed like a good time, surrounded by my dear friends.' She swept her arm round, past each of them, to demonstrate.

'It's all right,' Patrice replied. 'I'm glad for you, Suzanne, honestly. I don't think Justin would have cheated on you if Jonty hadn't pursued him. I've always liked Justin, and I think you're good together. It's wonderful news for the children, too.'

Patrice sipped her wine, put it down again and sat back, watching the flames flickering in the fireplace. Percy thought there was something immensely comforting about an open fire, especially with such a savage wind outside.

'But what about you, Percy?' Suzanne said suddenly. 'How are you and Mark?'

Percy longed to tell them about the gambling, her fling with Danny, but she just couldn't. Funny, she thought, how she had no difficulty talking about virtually anything – from bikini waxing to optimum sexual positions – but this was just too private and painful.

Instead, she gave them this: 'Well, it hasn't been straightforward for me, marriagewise,' she said. 'Mark and I have had big problems, which I told you a little about when we went on that yoga retreat. But I'm glad to say we seem to have come through. I'd never have believed you could pull back from the brink like that, but we have.'

'Oh, Percy,' Patrice said. 'That's wonderful.'

Percy tucked her knees under her chin. 'You know, at the risk of sounding heavy,' she said, 'I've come to the conclusion that the really important thing in life is that you can honestly say you've made your own choices. Some of them may have been rubbish choices, but at least you made them, and you lived your life as you wanted to. You went for it, so to speak.'

'Well, I feel like I haven't made any of my own choices,' Patrice said sadly. 'I feel like I've spent my whole life being bossed around by other people, mostly men. Now, without Jonty dictating my every move, I'm like a ship in a storm, tossed this way and that, not knowing where to drop anchor.'

'That's understandable,' said Percy, 'given all you've been through. But you will become stronger and more in control of your destiny. It sounds as if you're already sussing out what you really want by going back to law. I reckon in a year or two you won't know yourself.'

'What about you, Pers? Have you got what you want?' Patrice queried. 'Apart from Mark and the children, I mean.'

'Me? Yeah, I think so.' Percy grinned suddenly. 'So far. But you know what? I feel like I've only just started. I want to do well at work, get a permanent job next. The supply teaching's fine, but I feel I'm ready for more responsibility now. I think I'd like to climb the ladder, become head of department maybe.

'I also want to do some travelling with Mark – and you lot, if you'll come with me. And landscape the front garden. And buy a little place in France. I'm not sure how I'm going to manage all this yet, but I'll have a go.'

'I don't doubt it, Percy Redpath.' Patrice grinned. 'And yes, I'll definitely come travelling with you.'

436

'Me too. What about India?' said Suzanne. 'Can I take a rucksack? I've always fancied backpacking. I missed out on that when I was younger'

'How about Kenya?' Carmen joined in. 'I'd like to go on a safari, and sit in a treetop hotel watching the elephants and hippos at the watering hole.'

'Can I wear desert boots and khaki trousers and a safari jacket and carry binoculars?' Suzanne squealed.

Percy smiled. 'Naturally.'

'But what about the kids?' Carmen asked. The voice of reason.

'We can bring them along with us,' said Percy. 'Ivy, Ruby, Felix and anyone else who wants to come. That'd be OK.'

'Hmmm. A dangerous age for a woman,' Carmen muttered darkly.

'What?' Percy raised her eyebrows.

'You're at that dangerous age for a woman,' Carmen went on. 'We all are – the late thirties/early forties. One minute you're all settled, feet firmly on the ground, the next, you're bobbing around like a balloon on a windy day and goodness knows where you're going to land.'

Percy nodded. 'But isn't it so much better being fortysomething now than it was for previous generations?'

'What do you mean?' Carmen asked.

'Just think,' Percy explained. 'These days, in your forties, you could be expecting your first baby. Or you could be rising to the top of your career, or becoming a granny, or both. The choice is yours.'

Everyone laughed.

Percy moved over to the CD player in the corner of the room and rummaged through a pile of old CDs. She picked one up and put it in the machine. It seemed appropriate, somehow.

'Men have always had their mid-life crises,' Percy continued, pressing the start knob. 'Maybe it's our turn to

437

behave outrageously for a bit, sort things out in our heads, reassess, change direction, or perhaps come right back to where we started.'

The music started to blare out. It was vintage Spice Girls. 'Tell me what you want, what you really, really want,' boomed the words, loud and clear.

Percy started to dance and the others joined her, laughing and singing along – not so loudly as to waken the kids, though.

'I'm Ginger,' screamed Suzanne. 'And Carmen's Scary, with all that long, black hair. Patrice, you're Posh of course.'

Patrice, realising there was no Jonty to stop her making an ass of herself, stuck her nose in the air, tossed back her long blond hair superciliously, and strutted around like a thoroughbred.

'So who am I?' Percy shouted.

'Baby, of course, *silly*,' said Suzanne, cheerily. 'That means I'll have to be Sporty, though,' she added.

'You wish,' said Percy.

Suzanne made a face. 'Watch this,' she said. Then she cartwheeled across the room in front of them all, her hair fanning out around her. They weren't the most elegant cartwheels, but they were cartwheels all the same.

'I didn't know you could do that,' Percy said. She was hugely impressed.

'I'll do it knickerless next time, if you're not careful,' Suzanne chortled.

'Euuuw, no thank you.' Percy wrinkled her nose.

'Mu-uum.' Lara appeared at the door and shook her head. 'You'll do your back in, like the last time,' she warned.

Percy smiled. 'Come and join us.' Lara hesitated.

'You can do brilliant backflips, Lol,' Suzanne called. 'Go on, give us a demonstration.'

They cleared a space in the middle of the room and Lara backflipped three or four times. 'Ta-da,' she said when she'd finished, bowing theatrically. They all clapped.

It occurred to Percy that if anyone taking a night-time stroll along the beach at that moment glanced into the upstairs window, they'd be shocked. 'Mad,' they'd say, shaking their heads, 'complete idiots. Acting like a pack of teenagers,' before passing on their way.

Chapter Seven

It was late afternoon when Percy and the boys struggled up the garden path, lugging their suitcases. They seemed to have a huge amount of stuff, given that they'd only been away for a few days.

But there were all Rowan's shells to bring back, and his special stones and bits of dried seaweed. Not to mention the buckets and spades, wellies, thick jumpers, frisbees and balls. Percy had tried to put the seaweed in the bin when Rowan wasn't looking, but he'd caught her and fished it out again.

'Shoes off, bags straight upstairs,' she commanded.

'Aww, Muuum,' the boys groaned.

But she was firm. 'I want to be able to move in the hall,' she insisted. 'Go on, up you go.'

She knew Mark wouldn't be home. He'd be working. But she was surprised there wasn't a note on the hall table, or a bunch of flowers waiting for her. The house felt different, somehow. Sort of forlorn, she thought. Oh, she was being silly. It was just that it had been empty a lot. Mark had probably hardly been there.

She took off her shoes and threw open a few windows. Filled the kettle. That made her feel better, more at home. Then she trudged upstairs with her bags.

There was a note on her pillow in an envelope with her name on. She recognised the handwriting immediately: it was big, bold, arty, just like him.

She started to read:

Percy,
I'm glad you and the boys have had a good time. I've missed you. I hope you noticed the front garden. I've cut back the bushes. I think it looks a lot better. Lighter.

Dear Mark, she thought. She'd been nagging him about the front garden for ages.
She read on:

There's no easy way to say this, Percy, but Millicent from your gym rang me. She told me you were still seeing Danny Fusco.

Percy's stomach turned over. She had to reread the words, she couldn't take them in. Millicent? She didn't even have Percy's number. And she, Percy, hadn't seen Danny for weeks, had only slept with him that once. She wanted to pick up the phone and ring Mark immediately to explain. But she had to finish the letter.

Obviously I had no idea. You're a better actor than I imagined. I didn't know if I'd be able to forgive you the first time, Percy. I was so shocked, hurt, angry. But you persuaded me it was a one-off and, fool that I am, I believed you. That time, too, I felt I was partly to blame, for being angry, tired, shutting you out. You can't accuse me of that now, though. There's no going back, Percy. I could never believe anything you said to me ever again.
Please don't try to plead or make excuses, I couldn't stand it. I've arranged to stay at Larry's and Maggie's for a while, until we get sorted. Obviously I'll want to see the boys. Tell them I've had to go away for work tonight, and I'll be round tomorrow morning. We can decide together how we're going to explain everything to them.
I'm sorry it's come to this, Percy. I really did love you.
Give the boys a kiss from me.
Mark

Tears sprang into Percy's eyes. She could hear Ben and Rowan banging around downstairs, excited, no doubt, to see their toys again. Her heart was thumping and her head felt hot, tight, as if it were caught in a press.

I've got to get hold of Mark now, put everything right. Tell him it's all a silly mistake.

She picked up the phone and dialled his mobile. It was switched off. She looked up Larry's and Maggie's number in her address book, but it was on answerphone. She didn't want to speak to an answerphone.

She felt quite desperate. Sick. Calm down, she told herself. It'll all be all right. You just need to think about this for a minute.

She sat down on the edge of her bed and took deep breaths. What time would Mark return to Larry's and Maggie's? It was hard to say. He might go to the pub after work.

She could tip up at his studio, but he might be out on a job. Anyway, she didn't want to create a scene in front of his assistant. That might make Mark really angry.

The trouble was, she had Ben and Rowan with her, otherwise she'd sit in the car and wait outside Maggie and Larry's house until Mark got home.

'Mu-um, I'm hungry.' Ben's voice interrupted her thoughts.

'Coming,' she called out.

It occurred to her the boys would need supper. Bloody hell, supper. How could she think about something so mundane at a time like this?

She opened the fridge. There was nothing in but half a carton of milk and some butter. There wasn't even any bread.

Ben had turned on the computer in his bedroom next door and was staring at the screen.

'I'm sorry, we'll have to go the shops,' Percy said. 'There's no food in the house.'

'I'm not going,' Ben said, without looking up.

'YOU'LL DO AS YOU'RE TOLD!' Percy said. She was surprised by the strength of her voice. She didn't feel strong.

Back in the car, she felt as if she were living in some sort of movie. Everything looked so familiar: the houses, shops, street signs, traffic lights. And yet she hardly recognised them at all. It was as if the whole landscape had shifted and gone crooked.

A million thoughts raced through her mind. What was Mark doing now? What was he thinking? What would he say when he saw her? What should she say? Suppose he didn't believe her?

Of course he will, don't be ridiculous.

But what exactly had Millicent told him?

Percy wasn't remotely hungry but she had this over-whelming urge to cook for the boys. She picked up a pile of recipe cards from the customer services counter and flicked through them. Fish pie. That would do. Good and nutritious. And homemade ice cream to follow. Never done it before. And muffins. Ah, homemade muffins. Comfort food. She'd make some of those, too.

She must be mad. She was mad. Not surprising, really.

She paced up and down the aisles, looking for the ingredients. Vanilla pods. Where the hell were they? And saffron. Surely they had saffron in this bloody place?

A picture of Mark's lovely, sexy, kind face swam in front of her, but then it became distorted with anger and misery, on the edge of tears. She'd only ever seen him cry twice, when his father died and when he took her back in his arms after she told him about the teaching job. She wanted to reach out and take his imaginary face in her hands. Shake it. Tell him it was all a lie.

She tried his mobile again. Still off. Damn.

She flung some flour and sugar in her trolley and trundled into the bread section. Rowan picked some biscuits stuffed with E-numbers off the shelf and put them in the trolley, too. She ignored him.

443

How could she ever have thought her marriage wasn't worth fighting for? She and Mark had been through terrible times. They'd failed to communicate; she'd got them into huge debt; he'd refused to talk, been vile; she'd cheated on him. But they'd sorted it out. It *was* possible. He'd forgiven her. They loved each other. It was all that mattered. And now this.

'Are you all right?' said a voice.

Percy jumped. Her teeth jangled.

It was Diana, the colonic-irrigation lady. Her neck seemed longer than ever, with a pin-head balanced on top. She was wearing a peculiar billowing green sweater. God, Percy thought, that's the last thing I need – a half-hour chat with mad Diana about star signs.

Diana wheeled her trolley alongside Percy's and peered at her strangely.

Percy took a step back. She hated it when people stood too close and invaded your body space. She smoothed her hair. Was she a complete mess? There must be shock written all over her face. Of course, how silly of her. You couldn't expect something like this to happen and for it not to show.

'Are you all right?' Diana asked. 'You're Pisces, aren't you?' She didn't wait for a reply. 'There's conflict between Venus and Mars today,' she went on. 'Bad news for Pisceans. You'd better be careful.' She shook her head ominously.

'I'm fine. Superb,' Percy lied. 'Never been better. Must dash. Boys starving. You know what boys are like.'

She was aware of Diana's gaze boring into her back as she trundled off as fast as possible.

Back in the car, Percy tried Mark's mobile again. No luck. She couldn't wait any longer. She'd have to go to Larry and Maggie's.

'This isn't the way to our house,' Ben shouted.

'Quick detour,' Percy said, turning on some music and chucking a tube of Pringles into the back. Anything to keep them quiet.

444

There were lights on in Maggie's front room. Percy's stomach flipped over and over, turning somersaults. She needed the loo. It would have to wait.

She rang the bell. Waiting, she stood there on the step for what felt like an age. Finally, Maggie opened the door.

Percy used to think Maggie had a kind face. They'd known each other for years. The men had met through work. Now, though, Maggie looked strange. Unfriendly. Her eyes were wary, hostile even.

'Percy,' she said, taken aback. There was no smile. 'Mark's not here.' She didn't invite Percy in.

'I can't get hold of him on his mobile,' Percy explained desperately.

'He's in a bad way,' Maggie warned. 'Don't upset him any more.'

Percy wanted to shake Maggie, the stupid woman. 'You don't understand,' she said. 'It's all a terrible mistake.'

Maggie shook her head. 'Look, you shouldn't be talking to me. Mark's on a job. He said he was planning to see you tomorrow morning. You'll have to wait till then.'

Percy felt like screaming. 'I can't,' she said. 'It's too long. I need to explain.'

Maggie started to close the door. 'He said he'd be late,' she said sternly. 'You should look after your children.'

Children? Percy had almost forgotten she had any. She wheeled round to check. Ben and Rowan had unfastened their seatbelts, climbed into the front and appeared to be trying to batter each other to death. The whole car was rocking and the windows were all steamed up.

Percy jabbed her finger in the boys' direction, narrowed her eyes and shot them a murderous look. They stopped fighting and sat bolt upright, expressions of pure innocence on their faces. She turned back to Maggie and found she'd shut the door. Percy could hear shouts and bangs coming from the car again but she ignored them. Maggie might just as well have slapped her in the face, she thought. She felt like an outcast, a monster.

As she drove home, Percy was aware of the knot in her stomach getting tighter. She unpacked the shopping and put on her stripy butcher's apron. Pans clattered and potato peelings flew. Why was she doing this? It was comforting somehow.

'What are you making?' Ben asked suspiciously.

'A surprise,' Percy said. 'A welcome-home meal.'

'I'm not hungry,' Ben said. He and Rowan had polished off the entire tube of Pringles.

Percy glared at him.

'I'll play with Rowan,' Ben said quickly.

It was nine o'clock by the time they sat down to eat. Way past Rowan's bedtime. Percy had laid the table in the dining room, with napkins and candles.

'Supper,' she called.

The boys trooped in. Percy ignored their miserable faces and plonked large dollops of fish pie and garlicky peas on their plates. She'd never used garlic in peas before. The recipe had stipulated several cloves, crushed with butter.

'What's that?' said Rowan, poking at a piece of prawn. He wrinkled his nose.

'It's got lots of different types of fish in it,' Percy said.

'Can I have less?' Ben whined. 'I'm not hungry.'

'No you can't,' Percy snapped. She knew he'd have preferred boiled eggs. For that matter, they all would. 'I've spent ages making this,' she said angrily. 'I don't know why I bother.' She slammed her elbow down on the table and accidentally caught the funny bone. It hurt a lot. Tears sprang in to her eyes. Rowan looked up, startled.

'I did tell you I wasn't hungry,' Ben said reprovingly. 'And you know I don't like fish.'

'You're so unadventurous, you and Rowan,' Percy snapped, exasperated. 'It's ridiculous. You can't just have sausage and mash every night, you know.'

446

Something in her broke. Why had she thought she could hold it all together with a stupid fish pie? Her shoulders slumped. She wasn't angry any more. 'I so wanted this to be a nice meal,' she said. Tears were rolling down her cheeks. She knew she sounded pathetic.

Ben got up and put his arm round her, all manly. 'What's the matter, Mum?' he said. He knew it wasn't the fish pie. He was cleverer than that.

Rowan jumped off his stool, climbed on her knee and joined in the cuddle, too. 'Don't cry, Mummy,' he said. 'I'll kiss it better.'

Percy kissed the top of Rowan's soft head. 'I know you will,' she sniffed. 'You both make me feel so much better. It's just that I love Daddy so much. I miss him so much. I wish he'd come back.'

Rowan patted her arm. 'It's all right, Mummy, he'll be back tomorrow. You'll soon see him.'

That set her off again. If only she could speak to someone. She'd have to speak to someone. But she needed to get the boys in bed first.

Most of the fish pie went in the bin. Percy didn't care. She couldn't stomach any herself, either. Ben and Rowan ate a bit of muffin, but the ice cream wasn't frozen enough. No one really wanted that either.

She tried Mark's mobile again and again. He must be avoiding her. She didn't dare call Maggie. She realised she'd have to wait till tomorrow.

Percy knew she wouldn't be able to sleep. What should she do with herself? She was desperate, wandering round the house, unable to sit down or find anything to take her mind off what was happening. She decided to ring Pats. She could have called any of them, but Pats's number came to mind first.

'I need to talk,' Percy said. 'There's something I haven't told you.'

She revealed everything, the whole lot: Danny, the fling, the gambling, the debts, Mark's forgiveness. It all spilled out and Patrice listened in virtual silence, just making the occasional, encouraging noise.

'Why didn't you tell me this before?' she asked finally.

'Too ashamed, guilty, scared,' Percy admitted.

'Scared?' Patrice sounded incredulous.

'It's funny,' Percy went on. 'I'm extremely tolerant of other people's shortcomings, but for some reason I find it hard to believe they'll feel the same about mine. I guess I feared you'd judge me,' she added.

Patrice's voice was very gentle now, velvety on the end of the line. It seemed to wrap round Percy like the softest pashmina. 'Dear Pers,' Patrice said. 'Always sorting out other people's problems, never sharing your own. That's a terrible burden to bear.' She paused. 'Well, thank goodness you've shared it now. At last. And see, I'm still talking to you. And I love you just as much, if not more, than before you told me.'

Percy couldn't speak. She was choked up.

'Don't worry,' Patrice went on. She sounded so comforting and in control. 'Mark adores you. It's all going to be fine.' Percy wished she felt as confident.

She couldn't understand, when Patrice made the suggestion, why she hadn't thought of it herself. Of course she still had Danny's number. She hated the idea of speaking to him but Patrice was right, this was an emergency. Desperate times call for desperate measures and all that.

Quickly, she jabbed in his number and he answered almost immediately. Thank God. There was music in the background.

'Hey, Purse-fone,' he said genially. 'Long time no hear.'

She hadn't time for pleasantries. In fact she couldn't get the words out fast enough. 'Danny, something terrible's happened,' she said. There was silence at the other end. 'You've got to help me – please.'

Chapter Eight

The bell rang. Hell, wasn't Mark even going to use his key? He was behaving like a visitor to his own home already.

Percy checked her watch. It was 9 a.m. He was usually at work by now. He must have taken the morning off. Maybe he'd told his assistant he had important business.

She felt sick. She had to admit, divorcing your wife was pretty important business.

Patrice had turned up really early in the morning and taken the boys, still rubbing their eyes, off with her. She'd said she'd have them for as long as necessary. She knew Percy needed a clear run.

Percy opened the door. Mark looked different, somehow. Unkempt. Forlorn. His eyes were dead.

'Hi,' she said stiffly. She wanted to wrap her arms round him, kiss him, but she restrained herself. She had to explain first. 'Shall we go in the sitting room?' she said formally. He nodded.

Mark started when he saw Danny sitting there. Percy saw her husband's jaw and fists clench. She feared he might thump Danny, or turn round and walk right back out.

'This isn't what you think,' she told Mark. There was steel in her voice. 'Sit down. You've got to hear me out.'

To her relief, Mark sat, as far away from Danny as possible.

Danny was in his work gear: tracksuit bottoms and trainers. He was jiggling his leg up and down nervously.

'Danny?' Percy said, trying to keep calm. 'Will you please explain to my husband what's happened.'

Danny looked embarrassed and cleared his throat. 'Listen, man,' he said. His hands were spread out, palms down, on the sofa beside him, eyes darting this way and that. He looked ready to push himself up any second and make a run for it, or turn round and hurl himself through the window behind, maybe.

He stared at the floor. 'I know I had sex with your wife . . .' he said. Mark growled like a great, grizzly bear. At least, that's what Percy thought a grizzly bear would sound like. She scarcely dared look, in case he was baring his teeth; she thought again that he might hit Danny.

She was still standing. She put a hand, gently, on Mark's arm, to restrain him. He pushed it off roughly. 'Please hear him out,' she begged.

Danny continued: 'I know it was wrong and that. But man, it only happened once, I swear to you. And now Millicent's been phoning all my clients' husbands, telling them I'm having an affair with their wives. She's dead jealous, see. She thinks I'm cheating on her. She got the numbers from my mobile. I've told her to stop but she's gone bonkers. One of these days I'm gonna get murdered.' He glanced around, as if expecting to see an assassin lurking behind the curtains or under the sofa.

Mark looked at Percy. 'Why should I believe this?' he said. Pain spread across his face. Percy hated to see it.

'Because it's true,' she replied softly. She got down on her knees in front of him and stared straight into his eyes. To her relief, this time he didn't look away. He returned her gaze. She was willing him to see the truth. 'Oh, Mark, you've got to believe me,' she pleaded. 'I love you. I couldn't bear to lose you. I desperately regret cheating on you and I'd never, ever do it again. I swear it was only the once. Millicent's mad with jealousy, that's all. It's all a huge, stupid mistake. Danny says she's been calling everyone, accusing everyone. Creating trouble all over the place.'

The April sun streamed through the bay window on to a pile of teddies, which Rowan had lined up on the carpet. In front of them was a tiny white china teapot with pink roses on, a matching jug and two weeny cups and saucers. Rowan had been having a tea party. Percy felt a rush of love. He was so sweet, so innocent. Life was still so simple for him. So long as he had his family round him, he was happy.

She glanced at Mark and realised he'd followed her gaze. His face was red and his mouth looked funny, sort of crooked. He bent down and picked up one of the smaller teddies. He straightened its blue blow tie carefully. Popped it back again in exactly the same space, in front of the cup of pretend tea.

He cleared his throat. Percy held her breath. Waited. She could see the rest of her life stretching out in front of her, like a long, dusty road that vanished into the horizon. There was a fork just ahead of her; one way went left, the other right. She knew which way she wanted to go. Right, with Mark. She was in no doubt about that. She could see them together, side by side, their backs to her as they walked away into the distance. But what about him? What if he chose the other route? She couldn't force him, couldn't drag him with her.

Slowly, tentatively, Percy put her hands on Mark's legs. Slowly, tentatively, he reached out and pulled her up from kneeling. Hugged her into him, so she was on his lap.

They were wrapped around each other, like the marble lovers entwined for eternity in Rodin's *The Kiss*.

'Oh, Percy, thank God,' he said. His face was buried in her hair now. 'Thank God,' he repeated. 'I didn't know how I could live without you.'

Percy was aware of Danny hovering. He was an intruder now. He didn't belong. What was he doing here?

'I'll leave you guys to it, then,' he said awkwardly.

She looked up for a moment. Caught his eye. Smiled. 'Thanks, Danny,' she whispered.

He shrugged. 'Don't mention it.' He picked up his bag. He was off to his next assignation. 'Glad to be of service.'

He reached the door. He was so huge, he practically had to bend his head to get through. He turned to face Percy. He had a soft, wistful expression on his face that she hadn't seen before. He looked almost sweet.

'You know what?' he said.

Percy shook her head, trying not to disturb Mark, who was still buried in her hair. She had no idea what Danny was going to say. She raised her eyebrows.

'I think you guys are real fortunate,' he murmured, 'and you just didn't know it.

'You were made for each other all along.'

Chapter Nine

❦

Carmen walked past the black railings and up the stone steps of the mansion block to the big, black front door. She scanned down the numbers, found Flat 3a and pressed the buzzer.

'Push the door and come on in,' said a voice. 'Third floor up, on the right.'

Carmen still recognised that voice, even after all these years. It sounded light, amused, friendly: just as she remembered.

She parked Ivy's pushchair at the bottom of the stairs, unfastened her straps and lifted her out. She was a year old now and getting heavy. 'Come on, baby,' she said.

Ivy's eyes were big, round pools. She was fascinated by new places, new sights, sounds, smells. Her little body was quivering with interest.

Carmen bent down to pick up Ivy's nappy bag from the bottom of the buggy. There was a sharp pain at the side of Carmen's head. She shrieked and instinctively reached up to discover what it was. Ivy had grabbed a chunk of her mother's long black hair and yanked.

'Ouch,' Carmen said, trying to extract the hair from Ivy's fingers. It wasn't going to be easy.

There was a laugh: a high, tinkling sound. Carmen hadn't heard anyone approaching. She stood up, swung round and stared at the small, pretty, pale woman in front of her. The blue-grey eyes were the same, and the brown hair, pulled back in a ponytail, and the impish, friendly smile.

But the forehead was lined; there were fine creases round

the eyes and mouth, too. Otherwise, there wasn't that much difference.

'Hannah,' Carmen managed to say before Ivy yanked again. 'Ach, will you stop it, Ivy, please. That's agony.'

Carmen followed Hannah up the three flights of steps into her flat. Hannah carried the nappy bag and Carmen's handbag and jacket, while Carmen carried Ivy. Hannah was breathing heavily by the time they reached the top. It was obviously a big effort for her.

As soon as they walked through the door, Ivy struggled. She had just learned to walk and couldn't wait to be off.

'Is it OK if I put her down?' Carmen asked.

'Of course,' Hannah replied. 'We're not particularly child-friendly here, but I don't think there's anything she can hurt herself on. I bought a few toys for her to play with. Follow me.'

The drawing room was tasteful, elegant, with high ceilings and intricate cornicing. There was a giant bay window overlooking the busy Chelsea square below. The walls and carpet were matt, neutral, and there were two big cream sofas in the middle of the room.

A chandelier hung from the ceiling. Oversized mirrors bounced light off each other. Marble consoles on either wall had vases of flowers on them and there were lots of photos in silver frames. Hannah dancing. Hannah showing off her OBE, a proud Alan beside her. Hannah meeting Prince Charles.

For a moment, Carmen imagined herself in those frames, holding the flowers, giving the dazzling smile, curtseying. She shook the image away. 'What a lovely room,' she said.

She was worried about Ivy's sticky little fingers on the cream sofas and carpets. Hannah seemed to read her mind. 'Don't worry about Ivy,' she said. 'Look, she's found the toys already. Just relax. It's so lovely to see you.'

Ivy had indeed found a box of brightly coloured toys in

one corner. She was chewing them, turning them over and over in her hands, making amazed, cooing noises.

Carmen was grateful. She hadn't packed any toys herself, not wanting to carry any more clobber on the tube than was strictly necessary. It was very thoughtful of Hannah.

Carmen sat down and Hannah joined her on the sofa. 'You look great,' Hannah said softly. 'Not a day older.'

Carmen laughed. 'I wish.'

'And Ivy,' Hannah said. 'She's the spitting image of you. Look at those brown eyes, and the black hair. I bet she's just like you when she grows up. You must be so proud.'

Ivy had found a red and yellow plastic train, which rattled when you wheeled it along. She was thrilled. She kept pushing it backwards and forwards, over and over again. Her hair was straight on top, but there were mad curls over her ears. She had rosy cheeks and creamy skin. Carmen had to admit that she was picture perfect.

'She's hard work,' she said, almost guilty to have produced something quite so exquisite. 'I never stop.'

Hannah looked at Carmen. 'Yes, but she's so gorgeous.' Her eyes were moist. 'You are lucky.'

Carmen frowned. 'I read in the paper that you were retiring from teaching,' she said. 'I thought it was odd, so I rang English National Ballet. Your former secretary told me the news. I'm so sorry.'

Hannah shrugged. 'You never know when your number's up, do you? I just felt I wanted to spend what time I have left with my husband. I enjoyed teaching, but it was a lot of stress.'

Ivy toddled over to Carmen. She'd almost reached her when she suddenly wobbled and landed on her bottom. She looked very surprised. She reached out, grasped her mother's knees and pulled herself up only to plop down again. She didn't seem to mind. She blew a raspberry. Her chin was wet with dribble. She tried to pull herself up again and failed.

Hannah laughed. 'She's pretty determined.'

Carmen smiled. 'She's going to be a nightmare teenager, I can just tell.' She looked at Hannah. 'I've always missed you,' she said. 'I've often thought about contacting you, but I didn't know if I'd be able to cope. It took me years to get over the accident, not being able to dance any more.'

Hannah was looking at Ivy, but listening intently. She held her hand out to the child. The little girl gripped on to her fingers, pulled herself up, then plopped back down again. 'I know,' Hannah said. 'I was sorry to lose you as a friend. But I understood. You've made a go of things, though, haven't you? Look at you. Interior designer, mum.'

Carmen wasn't convinced she'd made such a go of things. Relationships-wise, anyway, she'd been a disaster.

'I loved dancing, of course,' Hannah went on. 'It was something I had to do. I've met so many amazing people, been all over the world. I feel very privileged. But it was bloody hard work. And I've missed out on some things, too, like having my own little Ivy.'

'What happened?' Carmen asked. 'Why didn't you have children?'

Hannah sighed. She looked tired. 'Alan and I did try when I was in my mid-thirties, but I didn't get pregnant. They said the dancing had probably affected my fertility. I had hormone treatment, to no avail. Then I found out about the cancer. The two might not be entirely unconnected,' she said darkly.

Carmen remembered Hannah pushing, pushing in the corridor. Teasing. The laughter; excitement all around them at the end of term. The summer holidays. France. So much to look forward to. Hannah whispering in a silly voice: 'Not so fast.' Her foot in the way. The snap; the sharp pain. The cry that came from someone else.

Carmen wanted to cry, now, for what they'd both lost. But she hadn't come here to make Hannah more miserable. 'Hey,' Carmen said. She tried to sound bright. 'Let me take you out for lunch. We can talk more then. How about Bluebird Café on the King's Road? That's suitable for kids, isn't it?'

Hannah got up. 'Great idea,' she said. She was wearing jeans, a white cotton shirt and brown suede boots. Carmen could see now that her clothes were hanging off her. The shirt was supposed to be fitted, but it was much too big.

They sat outside on the terrace, under a heater, watching the passers-by. It was still cool, only May, but the sun was shining. Carmen was in a denim jacket, but Hannah had her thick winter coat on.

Ivy gnawed on a breadstick while the women ate crunchy salads and slices of warm ciabatta. Carmen was hungry and finished hers off, but Hannah only picked at the food on her plate.

'Tell me about Ivy's dad,' Hannah said. They'd covered Carmen's job, Hannah's job, her husband Alan, Hannah's family, Ivy's parents. There was a lot to get through.

Carmen shrugged. 'I just made a huge mistake,' she said. She might as well be honest. Hannah had been, about everything. 'I went out with him for four years. Then he dumped me when I got pregnant, told me he was seeing someone else.'

Hannah shook her head. 'Bastard,' she said.

Carmen nodded. 'I thought it was all over, then after Ivy was born he started coming round again. Told me the other relationship wasn't working out. For a brief moment, I even thought we might get back together – until I realised he was a selfish, self-centred prat. So I kicked him out again.'

She decided not to tell Hannah about the smear or the laser treatment. She felt it would be unkind, given that she, Carmen, was completely in the clear, while Hannah had a death sentence.

Hannah looked thoughtful, sipped her fizzy water and passed Ivy another breadstick. Ivy grabbed it and shoved it straight in her greedy little mouth.

'He sounds like a nightmare,' Hannah said. 'But I think it's important not to get too bitter.'

Carmen hadn't asked for advice, but clearly Hannah was going to give it, anyway. She'd always been like that, Carmen remembered. Keen to solve other people's problems. Slightly bossy, actually, but in a well-meaning sort of way.

'Just think of what you've got,' Hannah went on. 'You're beautiful and healthy, you have a delightful daughter and an interesting job. There are lots more guys out there. I think you have a duty to rootle them out.'

She laughed and dabbed her mouth with her napkin. But then she started coughing and couldn't seem to stop. Her eyes were watering and her face was red. Her whole body was racked with coughs.

Carmen shot up. She put her arm round Hannah and slapped her back. She didn't know what else she could do. Hannah put her hand up to stop her. 'It's OK,' she said in between the splutters. 'It'll be over in a minute.'

People on the other tables were staring. A waiter came over, but Carmen waved him away. Ivy was silent, open-mouthed. She'd never seen anything like it.

At last, the coughing stopped. Hannah looked exhausted. 'I'm so sorry,' she said. 'I'm all right now. I was going to ask, I'd love to talk to you about my bedroom sometime. It needs a makeover. Would you do it for me? I'd pay you, of course.'

They walked slowly back to Hannah's flat, Carmen pushing Ivy, Hannah holding on to Carmen's arm. They stopped at the bottom of the stone steps.

'I'm so glad I came,' Carmen said. 'I'd wanted to for years. It's so good to see you again.'

Hannah moved round to the front of the pushchair to check on Ivy. She'd dropped off to sleep at last.

'You know, I'm not religious,' Hannah said, 'but I do think, if there is a God, that He wants us to be happy.'

Carmen had never thought about it before. She supposed

He probably did. It crossed her mind: had she allowed herself to wallow in self-pity all these years? Had she concentrated too much on what she didn't or couldn't have, rather than trying to enjoy what she had? Was it possible, even, that she'd settled for Simon, who was so unworthy, because she felt, somehow, that he was no more than she deserved after her bad luck? She really should have dumped him years ago.

She was a lot better now, since having Ivy, more positive. But she was still furious with Simon, and probably with men generally. Spitting mad. She needed to move on, to look forward rather than back. Now she felt she almost owed it to Hannah, who had no future.

They kissed goodbye. 'I'll come and see you again,' Carmen promised. 'Maybe we could go to the ballet together?'

Hannah smiled. She started to walk slowly up the steps, holding on to the railings for support. She looked much frailer than she had when Carmen arrived. She was worn out from the exertion. 'I'd love that,' she replied. She put her key in the big brass lock and pushed the door open. It was almost too heavy for her.

It was dark inside. Hannah turned to Carmen once more and grimaced slightly. Was something hurting her? 'Don't leave it too long, though, will you?' she called softly. 'And don't forget about my bedroom.'

'I won't,' Carmen called back.

The next moment, Hannah had closed the door and was gone.

Ivy slept practically all the way home on the tube and train. Carmen sat, holding on to the buggy, taking everything in.

She had this weird feeling that she'd just woken from a long sleep. People's faces around her seemed so much more interesting, somehow, the colours of their clothes and their hair more vivid and intricate.

She got off at Teddington Station and found herself looking

459

more intently in the shop windows than she had in ages. The cheese in the cheese shop made her mouth water. She could almost smell the food in the delicatessen display: salamis, hams, olives.

She stopped to buy some organic chocolate, broke off a couple of pieces and popped them in her mouth. The chocolate tasted wicked, indulgent. She wished she could give some to Hannah right now. She'd buy her some, next time. She'd take her a whole box of the stuff.

Carmen's flat seemed perfect, too, when she walked in. A quarter the size of Hannah's, but perfect. The sun was streaming through the French doors. She could feel the warmth on her shoulders and face. Why had she worried about Ivy's fingerprints on the white walls? You could hardly see them. Anyway, all it needed was a lick of paint.

She lifted Ivy out of her pushchair and kissed her button nose. Then she took her over to the CD player and put on the 'Dance of the Cygnets'.

Ivy wriggled and Carmen set her down. Without thinking, Carmen arched her back, raised her head and arms, pointed her toes and began to dance. Her jeans and Converse trainers weren't ideal, but she didn't care.

Joy and relief swept through her. She was so lucky. For the first time, she really knew she was lucky. And she wasn't angry. It was so good to be free of anger. For Hannah's sake, she mustn't be angry any more.

Ivy tried to copy her mother, turning round and round clumsily on her pudgy hands and knees. She gurgled with laughter, loving it. Carmen swept her small daughter up and pirouetted with her round the room. Ivy screamed with delight.

'Come on, little baby, time for tea and bath,' Carmen said at last, smiling. She was out of breath. She danced into the kitchen and opened the fridge on tiptoes, Ivy balanced on one hip.

Carmen peered into the fridge and took out an egg, butter, milk. 'Scrambled eggy,' she told Ivy, slamming the fridge door shut gaily and twirling round. 'Your favourite.'

Ivy beamed, catching the mood, not knowing why. Carmen popped her in her highchair. 'Ma, ma,' Ivy cried, suddenly cross. Carmen knew exactly what she wanted. And it wasn't her egg. Ivy beat her little fists on the table and bounced up and down in her chair.

'Don't worry, my little cabbage,' Carmen said, passing her daughter a crust to keep her happy. 'We'll dance again soon. We can be cygnets again tomorrow.'

Later, Carmen got out her fabric samples and flicked through the pages of her interiors magazines. She began to think of themes for a client's dining room. She'd put it off for long enough. The client would find someone else if she didn't get a move on.

She got out her book on surrealism. If in doubt, you could always turn to the surrealists. She thought it was time she went to a few art exhibitions and revisited the Victoria and Albert Museum, for inspiration. She'd get the girls to come with her. Patrice, especially, adored art exhibitions.

Hannah wouldn't be able to do any of this, Carmen realised, because she was too weak. Life wasn't fair, she thought, but it also had a curious way of evening out. She didn't know if this was good or bad, it was just the way it was.

She resolved to ring Hannah tomorrow to discuss her bedroom. Plantation shutters, maybe? Wild, joyous wallpaper? Hummingbirds? Butterflies? It would be the most gorgeous room she, Carmen, had ever created. Pink and gold? Blue and silver? Whatever Hannah fancied.

She'd be spending a lot of time in there over the coming months. It had to stimulate the senses, to be just perfect. It would be a symbol of forgiveness. Carmen's magnum opus, her pièce de résistance.

Chapter Ten

❦

'Morning, ladies, or should I say pole people! Welcome to your first pole-dancing class!'

Percy felt nervous. She smiled at the teacher in front, then glanced over to her right. Patrice looked away quickly. Was she worried she'd get the giggles?

Percy glimpsed herself in the mirror and thought she looked absolutely ridiculous. No, she knew she looked absolutely ridiculous.

Suzanne had lent her a pair of Ollie's too-tight white tennis shorts. Percy hadn't wanted to buy anything new, in case she didn't like the class. She had a pink vest top and some old black stilettos. What a nightmare! Fortunately, Suzanne, in the front row, looked absurd, too. She was bulging out of a pair of unflattering apple-green shorts. She couldn't balance very well on her brown stilettos, either. Teetering was the word. Percy hoped Suzanne wouldn't fall over. She could do herself a nasty injury.

Even the gorgeous Patrice, in neat, black shorts, a white T-shirt and tasteful black kitten heels, had cellulite on the backs of her legs.

Lord, Percy thought. If Patrice has it, what hope is there for the rest of us?

Lithe Carmen, of course, looked scrumptious. Her slim legs, the colour of warm honey, were shown off to perfection in bright pink hot-pants. Don't look at Carmen any more, Percy told herself. She'll put you off.

It was annoying, Percy reflected, that she still hadn't got

to grips with her pot-belly, even after all these years of sweating it out at the gym. It had shrunk for a time, with stress. But as soon as she and Mark had sorted out their problems, the pot-belly had returned in all its glory. Now, Percy was as apple-shaped as ever.

Suzanne was comfortingly round still, too. Probably getting more so, in fact. Justin's cooking, no doubt. But, Percy thought, although she and Suzanne hadn't exactly reached their goals, they didn't look bad, really. And Carmen and Patrice were bloody amazing for their age. Positively babelicious. The classes must be doing some good, surely? They were all more flexible anyway, and you couldn't knock the skinny latte sessions afterwards.

Nah, Percy thought, on balance she'd recommend Gym and Slimline to anyone.

On Percy's left was a stout lady who informed the class she'd done pole-dancing classes in central London. 'It's thanks to me the manager agreed to lay on the class here,' she announced smugly. She was wearing nasty grey shorts, a red top and tarty red heels. And she had a dodgy perm.

From the way she was standing, hands on hips, boobs aloft, *derrière* swaying in time to the music, you'd think she was God's gift to men, though. It was marvellous how you could look like that and still think you were gorgeous, Percy thought. No self-esteem issues there.

Percy was the one who'd egged everybody on to sign up for a six-week course. It was on Tuesday evenings, from 8 to 9.30 p.m. Mark had seemed particularly keen to babysit. Funny that. He'd never been quite so enthusiastic about her doing Pilates.

The studio was filled with removable dance poles. There were about twelve women in all, most of whom Percy recognised from other classes.

'Pole dancing uses muscles that you never knew you had

and concentrates largely on the arms, abdominal area, thighs and buttocks,' said Carly, the instructor.

Thighs? Good, Percy thought. Buttocks? Marvellous. You could live in hope, anyway.

'The moves that I'll be teaching you will be a mixture of twirling, spinning, swinging and climbing moves, as well as those crucial static poses to play to your audience with,' Carly continued.

Percy sneaked a look at Suzanne, but her eyes were fixed on the teacher. Her body was rigid . . . Percy suspected she was concentrating hard on not falling flat on her face.

'You'll learn how to do the corkscrew, kneehook, fireman spin and sunwheel, among other moves,' Carly went on. 'I'll also teach you a range of floor moves, to fill in the gaps between the pole moves. You'll soon discover the power of your femininity.'

She said it in a low, sensuous voice. Percy gulped. She wasn't sure she wanted to discover the power of her femininity. She thought she might prefer to be at home in front of an old episode of *Poirot* with a box of Quality Street. But there was no chickening out now.

'Don't worry. It doesn't matter how fit or unfit you are,' Carly said, as if reading Percy's mind. 'We'll build up slowly and as the course progresses you'll notice an improvement in muscular strength and suppleness, making you stronger and more flexible. But most of all, we're going to have some fun!'

They started with a few gentle warm-up exercises. Nothing unusual there. Then Carly put on 'Do Ya Think I'm Sexy?' She stood in front of her pole and sort of writhed around to Rod Stewart, to show how it was done. Blimey, thought Percy. Here goes.

Of course Carly managed to make it look easy – tasteful, even. But when Percy tried to shimmy seductively up her pole, she didn't look tasteful at all. She glanced at herself again in the mirror in front. Her movements were all clunky. She feared anyone watching would suspect she wasn't quite right in the head. 'Poor dear,' they'd say. 'Two sandwiches short of a picnic.' At least they might chuck her some spare coins, out of sympathy. But the tennis shorts really didn't do her any favours.

Suzanne, in front, tottered, wobbled and fell flat on her back, legs akimbo. Percy was so surprised, she shrieked. She and the rest of the class gathered round and asked Suzanne if she was all right. Suzanne wouldn't let them help her up, though.

They watched her stand, mustering what dignity she could. She straightened her vest and yanked her shorts out of her bum crack with a quick tug of finger and thumb. She had a thunderous expression on her face.

Percy felt laughter bubbling up. She tried to fight it. This was too awful. Suzanne hated being laughed at. Percy glanced at Carmen. She couldn't see Carmen's mouth, because her hand was over it, but her eyes gave her away: she was having internal hysterics. Patrice had given up trying to disguise it. She was convulsed with giggles. Soon they were all doubled up, practically wetting their knickers.

Suzanne looked at her friends and glared. 'God, you're so immature,' she said imperiously, tossing her bushy hair. 'It'll take a bit of practice, that's all. I'm just not used to twirling in heels.'

Carly clapped her hands, trying to restore order. 'Come along, class, back to your poles,' she commanded. 'Now, time for the corkscrew.'

Percy decided she, Suzanne and Patrice weren't likely to wow anyone with their erotic moves just yet. Carmen, however, looked as if she were born to it.

'You've done this before, haven't you?' Percy said accusingly as they left the studio.

'Well, I did once do a bit of lap dancing, to earn some extra cash,' Carmen admitted.

'Bloody hell, you've kept that quiet,' Suzanne chipped in.
Carmen gave a wicked grin. 'It was a long time ago.'

Percy whistled. She was full of admiration. 'Imagine
anyone paying to watch you lap dance. They'd more likely
pay me not to,' she sniggered.

They wandered past the rowing machines, still in their
shorts and high heels. The gym was virtually empty now.
On the other side of the room, they spotted a hunky-looking
young man on the treadmill.

'It's Edmund,' Patrice said. 'I blagged a free pass for him.
I didn't realise he was coming down tonight.'

The women walked over. 'We must look a right sight,
waddling his way,' Percy muttered, more to herself than
anyone else. 'I hope we don't scare the poor boy.'

But Edmund's face broke into a huge grin. 'Hey, ladies,'
he said in his Aussie twang. 'Good to see you.'

He was wearing a tight white vest and navy shorts. He
was covered in sweat, but he looked really cute, Percy
thought. Although he'd addressed them all, she noticed with
amusement that he could barely take his eyes off Carmen in
her teeny hot-pink shorts. He was practically falling off the
treadmill.

'We've been doing pole dancing,' Patrice explained. 'Hence
the get-up.'

'How was it?' Edmund panted. He was running quite fast,
gazing at Carmen at the same time. He couldn't stop himself.

She did look gorgeous, Percy thought. All flushed and
bright-eyed and slightly damp from the exertion.

'It was fun,' Patrice said. 'Carmen was brilliant, of course,
because she's a dancer. The rest of us need a bit of practice.'
Something occurred to her. She clapped her hands. 'Carmen,
why don't you ask Edmund to go running with you? I'll look
after Ivy. You said you wanted to get back into it, and it's
much nicer doing it with someone else. Edmund loves
running, don't you?'

Carmen blushed. She looked at the ground. Edmund wiped the sweat from his brow with his forearm. 'Yeah, sure, I'd like to go running with you, Carmen.'

She looked up and smiled. He gave her a dazzling grin back. Percy found herself thinking what a lovely couple they'd make. OK, Carmen was older, but they didn't have to get married, did they? Carmen would look after Edmund, and it would do them both good to have a bit of fun.

'Great,' Carmen replied. 'We could run along the river maybe.'

The four women strolled together to the showers. 'How about a glass of wine?' Percy asked. 'It's not often we're here in the evening. Feels quite wicked, somehow.'

'I fancy a G and T,' said Carmen. 'Slimline, natch.'

They sat in their usual spot round a coffee table. There was just time for one drink before the gym closed.

'I love this place so much,' Percy sighed, taking a sip of Sauvignon Blanc. 'It's so important to have a third space that isn't work or home to escape to, don't you think? And imagine, if we hadn't become members when it first opened, we'd never have met each other.'

'No, I couldn't imagine that.' Suzanne shuddered. 'If we hadn't met here, we'd have found each other somewhere else – at the supermarket or somebody's party or something.'

'You think it was destiny?' Carmen asked, surprised. 'I'm not sure I believe in that.'

'Well, or magnetism,' said Suzanne. 'I do think people are drawn together like magnets sometimes. They just click. They always end up together somehow.'

'Yet we're all so different,' Percy said. 'From the outside, you wouldn't automatically assume we'd get on. I mean, look at us. A dancer – um, correction, lap dancer turned interior designer.' She smiled naughtily. 'A lawyer with a house out of *Homes & Gardens*. The Director of Communications of a huge car company with four kids, red hair – and a filthy laugh.'

Suzanne laughed filthily.

'And a secondary-school teacher and mum of two with a wild front garden,' Percy went on. 'We're an eclectic bunch.'

'A wild front garden, maybe, but a lovingly pruned bush.' Carmen sniggered. 'Well,' she said, digesting Percy's comments, 'think how boring it would be if you were only friends with people who were just like you. There'd be nothing to discuss. You'd just agree about everything.'

'Hmmmm,' said Percy, taking another slug of wine. 'No chance of that.'

'Hey, Percy,' Carmen said suddenly. 'How are you and Mark? What's happening on that score?'

Percy beamed. 'Right back on track.'

Carmen's face lit up too. 'Good,' she said. 'I'm so glad. I always thought you were soulmates.'

Percy's heart gave a little skip. Not for the first time in the last couple of rollercoaster years, she found herself marvelling at what a big, scary, tragic, unpredictable and, yes, magnificent thing life was.

'You know,' she said, sipping her wine, 'as mid-life crises go, we've just about had 'em all, haven't we?'

The other women nodded.

'But what I want to know is where we go from here?' Suzanne said. 'It's weird, but I feel like we're on the point of something, but I'm not sure what.'

Patrice grimaced. 'God, I feel like I've had enough surprises to last me for ever. I don't want any more. I just want the quiet life from now on.'

'No, I think I know what Suzanne means,' Percy said. 'Sort of. I feel the same thing. It's bizarre, but I can't help thinking there are more big changes to come. Nice ones this time, though, I reckon,' she said quickly. 'I guess we'll just have to wait and see.'

She took another sip of wine, idly picked up a glossy magazine that was lying, face down, on the coffee table and turned it over. It had *Mary-Beth* written in bold red letters across the top.

She scanned the coverlines. 'Look at this.' She tutted, then read out loud. '"Twice daily sex is great for my complexion – Britain's real-life Boardroom Babes reveal all!" What a load of bollocks.'

She glanced at Suzanne and noticed she'd gone rather pink. Suzanne jumped out of her chair and tried to snatch the magazine from Percy's hands. 'Give me that,' she squealed.

'Whoa, not so fast,' Percy replied, swinging the magazine out of Suzanne's reach. She stood up, flicking quickly through the pages. 'Hey, guess what, girls?' she cried triumphantly. 'It's Mrs Suzanne Boardroom Babe I-have-sex-twice-a-day herself! You kept this quiet, Suze.'

The others leaped up and huddled round Percy. There, on the centre spread in bold technicolour, was an enormous photograph of Suzanne giving a cat-that-got-the-cream smile to the camera. She was perched on the edge of her desk in her office in a kittenish pose, wearing a tight white blouse, a rather short navy skirt and navy platform court shoes. Her boobs looked massive and her red hair had been slicked into a curious sort of sixties beehive up-do. She had lots of blue eyeshadow on and bright pink lipstick, too. Clearly the stylists had been busy.

'You look like a porn star!' Carmen screamed excitedly. 'Suzanne's been leading a double life as a porn star!'

Suzanne knew she was beaten. She slumped back in her chair, dejected. 'How embarrassing,' she groaned, shaking her head. 'I thought the piece had been shelved. I'll never live it down. I was only trying to give the journalist something to write about. I didn't realise they'd use my picture so big – or quote me on the cover. Plus she said we were going to be called Wonderwomen, which was bad enough. Not Boardroom Babes.'

'Yeah, yeah.' Percy grinned. 'I look forward to sharing this with the neighbourhood.'

A couple of the bar staff started dropping not-so-subtle hints that it was time to go: clattering glasses and mugs, moving chairs under tables.

The women got up slowly, slinging their kit bags over their shoulders. Edmund emerged from the men's changing rooms and joined them on the way out. He looked all clean and shiny. Percy noticed he kept close to Carmen as they strolled through the reception area. You could almost feel the energy crackling between them.

Patrice sensed it, too. 'Come on,' she said strictly, taking Edmund's arm. 'I've got my eye on you.'

He grinned but said nothing. He knew what she meant.

The bar staff had nearly finished tidying up now. One was cashing up, another was going round turning out lights. Soon the whole building would be in darkness. The exercise machines would be silent, the pool still and empty until tomorrow.

'Bye,' the women called in unison to no one in particular. They pushed open the swing doors.

'Bye, you lot,' came a voice.

Percy turned. The remaining receptionist, whose job it was to lock up, had poked her head out from one of the offices. She was craning over the reception desk so they could hear her better. 'Have a good evening,' she said. 'And don't do anything I wouldn't do.'

'Wouldn't dream of it,' the women chorused. 'But, hey, how much rope does that give us?'

There was a pause. 'Ooh, quite a lot,' came the reply. 'I'd say it rules pretty much everything in, actually.'

The women giggled. They stepped out into the dark car park. 'Goodie. See you soon,' they cried.

'Yeah,' the receptionist called back. 'See ya.'

Acknowledgements

Gym and Slimline would never have reached the shelves without the inspiration and expertise of an incredible cast of women, plus a few men. Huge thanks to Heather Holden-Brown, my wonderful agent, and Rosie de Courcy, my perfect editor. And to friend and fellow author, Alison Baverstock, without whose encouragement I mightn't have started at all.

Also, love and grateful thanks to my parents, Sue and Christopher Burstall, for their boundless support and hours of 'Fred Fun', to my sister, Sarah Arikian, in whose New York basement one summer I began typing, and to my brother, James Burstall.

I must mention, too, Samantha Bates, Felicita Benedikovics, Ian Bishop, Julie Brack, Peter Cox, Celia Hayley, Kevin and Joan Healy, Elly James, Joanna Moorhead, Kate O'Connor, Natasha Owen, Paul Waugh, Roy 'The Boy' Brindley, Jackie Brindley, Richenda Todd and Liz Carter from Gamcare. Not forgetting my other, fantastic friends who have cheered and chivvied in equal measure. Thank you all.